When Stars Light the Sky

Books by Elizabeth Camden

WOMEN OF MIDTOWN

When Stars Light the Sky

ELIZABETH CAMDEN

BETHANYHOUSE

a division of Baker Publishing Group
Minneapolis, Minnesota

© 2025 by Dorothy Mays

Published by Bethany House Publishers
Minneapolis, Minnesota
BethanyHouse.com

Bethany House Publishers is a division of
Baker Publishing Group, Grand Rapids, Michigan

Printed in the United States of America

Library of Congress Cataloging-in-Publication Data
Names: Camden, Elizabeth, author.
Title: When stars light the sky / Elizabeth Camden.
Description: Minneapolis, Minnesota : Bethany House, a division of Baker
    Publishing Group, 2025. | Series: Women of Midtown
Identifiers: LCCN 2024026819 | ISBN 9780764241727 (paperback) | ISBN
    9780764244490 (casebound) | ISBN 9781493448876 (ebook)
Subjects: LCGFT: Christian fiction. | Romance fiction. | Novels.
Classification: LCC PS3553.A429 W44 2025 | DDC 813/.54—dc23/eng/20240621
LC record available at https://lccn.loc.gov/2024026819

Scripture quotations are from the King James Version of the Bible.

This is a work of historical reconstruction; the appearances of certain historical figures are therefore inevitable. All other characters, however, are products of the author's imagination, and any resemblance to actual persons, living or dead, is coincidental.

Cover design by Dan Thornberg, Design Source Creative Services
Cover image of woman by Laurence Winram / Trevillion Images

Baker Publishing Group publications use paper produced from sustainable forestry practices and postconsumer waste whenever possible.

25 26 27 28 29 30 31   7 6 5 4 3 2 1

Prologue

America was supposed to be the land of opportunity, but it seemed more like a land of hunger and confusion to Inga. Huddled on the cold floor of the empty church, she tried to calm her breathing because even the tiniest noise sounded loud in the dark, echoey chamber. It didn't feel right to sneak inside a church, but she was only ten years old and always obeyed her parents.

Papa had been robbed ten minutes after they left Ellis Island, which was why they had to sneak into the church to sleep. All three of them wore their coats, hats, and scarves, but it was still cold. Why was November in New York so much colder than November in Bavaria?

Papa lay slumped against the steamer trunk, his fist clenched around its handle even in sleep. That trunk contained the only items of value they had left: Papa's hammers, tongs, tacks, and scissors for making shoes. Mama slept with their canvas bag of clothing strapped across her shoulders like a packhorse. Inga curled around her satchel, hoping dawn would come before a scary priest or nun turned them out into the night.

5

Nobody found them. By morning she was so stiff it hurt to sit up, and yet the way the sunlight streamed through the stained-glass windows tinted the church with a rosy-gold shade so pure it gave her hope.

"What are you smiling about?" Papa groused. He always complained when she smiled for no reason because people might think she was simpleminded.

Inga scrambled for a reason to be happy. "Even though we're poor, we just got to spend a free night in the fanciest church in the world."

The comment caused a spurt of laughter from Mama. Making people laugh had always been Inga's special gift. Some people were great shoemakers like her father; others were smart or could play instruments. But Inga's gift was to cheer people up. That had been especially important over the past year when life became increasingly bleak after her sister died and then people stopped buying Papa's shoes because the factory-made shoes were so much cheaper.

"Shhh!" Mama warned, the harsh command echoing in the church. Someone was coming, and they weren't ready to leave yet.

Inga held her breath as two people entered the church. The fabulously dashing man and the lady beside him headed straight toward a bank of votive candles near the front of the church. The lady knelt, and the man tossed a coin into a metal box, the clang ringing out in the silence. He proceeded to light a few votive candles. The flickering light illuminated the couple.

They were *rich*! The man wore a silk top hat, and the lady had a diamond comb in her hair.

The man shook out the match after lighting a bunch of candles, then tossed another coin in the collection box and lit another match. He kept lighting candles until the entire rack was ablaze with light. He knelt beside the woman and whispered something in her ear that caused her to giggle. He laughed too, a hearty sound from deep in his belly, although soon the couple quieted and started praying again.

They seemed so devout . . . until the woman let out an ungainly snort and broke into helpless peals of laughter again.

Laughter was contagious, and Inga clamped a hand over her mouth. Her father shook a warning finger at her, though Inga couldn't tear her eyes away from the rich people at the front of the church. What were they laughing about?

Eventually the man rose to his feet and adjusted his coat. He then helped the lady to rise.

"Quick, hide," Papa whispered. He scooted behind a statue of a saint being tortured by an arrow, beckoning Inga to follow. Yet she couldn't leave the satchels. What if someone stole them?

The couple strode down the aisle, and the man spotted her. Anxiety took hold within Inga as he blanched in surprise, then started to close in on her, the corners of his mouth turning down beneath his clipped, dark mustache. He rambled a stream of words in a language she didn't know.

"I'm sorry," she said in German. "I don't understand."

"*Bist du Deutsch?*" the man asked.

"*Ja*," she confirmed, and before she could say anything else, Papa was beside her, assuring the stranger they would leave soon and meant no harm. Papa scooped up one of the satchels beneath his arm, then tried to hoist the trunk behind his shoulder. But it was too heavy, and it banged on the floor.

"*Keine sorge, der himmel wird nicht fallen,*" the stranger said. His accent was terrible, but a sense of well-being settled over Inga. *Don't worry, the sky won't fall,* he had said. It was the same thing her grandmother always said, and she grinned.

The man gave a hearty laugh and continued speaking in German. "Now that's the sweetest smile we've seen all day. Isn't it, Mary?"

"Yes indeed," the rich lady said. "Such pretty blond curls you have, my dear." The lady's German was heavily accented too. She had ropes of pearls around her neck, and she smelled like lilacs. "Come sit down and tell us why you had to spend the night in a church," the lady prompted.

The rich people introduced themselves as Mr. and Mrs. Gerard. They didn't look like the sort who needed to trick strangers out of all their money, so her father told them of their sad tale of how they had lost their savings as soon as they got off the ship. A stranger offered to exchange their German marks with American dollars for a better rate than offered at any bank. The stranger was German, so they trusted him. It wasn't until they tried to get a room in a hotel that they realized they'd been swindled. The paper money was fake, and they had only a few German marks left to their name.

The rich lady's eyes softened with pity when she looked at Inga's tattered hem, and she elbowed her husband, who reached for his wallet.

"Here, this should make you whole," Mr. Gerard said and casually pressed a few bills into her father's hand. Her father didn't even look at the bills, but his eyes brimmed with tears.

"Thank you, sir," he said on a shaking breath. "A million times, thank you!"

The Gerards nodded farewell and departed in a swirl of rustling silk and perfumed air.

Papa waited until the door closed behind the Gerards before counting the bills he'd been given.

A hundred dollars! It was enough to take care of them for at least a month. Inga raced to the window to watch the couple disappear onto the streets of New York, convinced she'd just caught a glimpse of two guardian angels.

For the rest of her life, she would remember to keep the Gerards in her prayers.

1

Sixteen Years Later
June 1914
The Harbor of New York City

Have you got any extra work for me?" Inga asked her supervisor at the end of her shift at the wireless office. There was usually extra work in the largest port in America. She earned a respectable salary as a wireless operator, communicating with ships coming and leaving the port, although she was always happy to earn a little more.

Mr. Guillory glanced up from his desk surrounded by file cabinets, tackboards, and cubbyholes. "Go home and get some sleep," he said, waving her away. "You don't need extra work."

True, but she was saving up to buy a tombstone to mark her parents' grave. It had been four years since they'd passed away, and now that she was earning good money, she wanted them to have a nice stone.

She scanned Mr. Guillory's cluttered desk, searching for any half-typed reports that needed finishing or shorthand documents to transcribe. Last year she completed a certificate in stenography, which opened up an entirely new category of tasks she could accomplish.

"Look," she said, pointing to the weekly tariff report. "Can I add that data into the monthly register? You know I can get it done faster than the day clerks will do it."

"The day clerks are all men, and they need the work more than you," Mr. Guillory said.

Undaunted, she glanced around for more chores, and her gaze landed on a telegram tacked to the bulletin board. Her name was printed on the outside. "What's that?" she asked with a nod toward the telegram.

"Oh, that came in for you a few hours ago," Mr. Guillory said, taking the message down. She tamped back her annoyance. Anyone sending her a telegram probably had a need for urgency, but her supervisor obviously wasn't willing to interrupt her work to give it to her.

And frankly, the job of an overnight wireless operator demanded a good deal of concentration. From ten o'clock at night until seven in the morning, she translated the electronic tapping of dots and dashes from fellow wireless operators out at sea. Who could have imagined that a shoemaker's daughter would ever become the sort of person who could communicate with mighty steamships coming into port? It wasn't a traditional choice of occupation for a woman, although it made perfect sense to Inga. She had witnessed the consequences of clinging to a dying profession. Even before her father's bad lungs made it impossible for him to keep producing his handmade shoes, Inga had enrolled in typing school. When the chance to learn Morse code presented itself, she reached out for it with both hands.

Now the only thing she wanted to grab with both hands was the telegram tacked to the board behind her supervisor.

"My shift ended five minutes ago, so may I see the message?" she asked.

Mr. Guillory hoisted himself out of the squeaky desk chair

and lumbered to unpin her message. She tore it open and read the brief note:

Inga,
> *Please meet me for lunch at the Ritz today at noon. I need to speak with you immediately.*

> *Best,*
> *James Gerard*

This *was* a surprise. As the newly appointed ambassador to Germany, Mr. Gerard was supposed to be in Berlin, not having lunch at the Ritz.

Ever since she'd met the Gerards on her horrible first day in America, Mr. Gerard had kept a watchful eye over her. He helped when her parents were threatened with eviction after Papa's bad lungs forced him to stop working. He paid for her to attend wireless school because she could never have afforded the tuition on her own. Over the years, they exchanged affectionate Christmas cards, and she eagerly watched him from afar by reading the society pages. The Gerards were famous for weekend parties at their country estate and enjoyed racing their yacht with royalty both here and abroad.

The hint of desperation in Mr. Gerard's message seemed odd. Inga normally went straight to bed after working the overnight shift, but how could she deny him? She owed Mr. Gerard everything, even if it meant her sleep schedule would be ruined.

If she couldn't go home to sleep, she intended to spend the morning earning a few extra dollars here at the port. She folded the telegram and tucked it into her pocket, then scanned her supervisor's desk.

"Mr. Guillory, our quarterly reports are due next week, and we are behind on the monthly statistics. And look." She stepped around Mr. Guillory to open the cabinet doors. "We're running out of cargo forms because nobody's restocked the inventory. Can I help you spiff things up?"

"The monthly statistics haven't been compiled because Jenkins is out with pleurisy," Mr. Guillory defended.

"Which is why you should let me do some typing for you. Or compile the statistics. At the very least you can ask me to dust and scrub this place. No wonder Jenkins has pleurisy with all this dust."

Over at the wireless station, the two male radio operators were trying not to laugh. Carson yanked off his headphones. "You tell it to him, Inga! This place is filthy."

Mr. Guillory spluttered. "Jenkins might want the extra work," he said.

"Might," Inga stressed. "I *do* want the extra work, and I'm right here for the next four hours. Tell me how I can help." A fresh load of tasks would keep her alert until her meeting with Mr. Gerard for lunch.

Mr. Guillory pawed through the mounds of paper on his desk to find several pages filled with tariff data. "Have at it, my dear."

Four hours later, Inga gaped in wonder as she entered The Ritz-Carlton Hotel. Sunlight flooded the yellow-and-white lobby from the stained-glass skylight above. Towering palm trees reached toward the vaulted ceiling, and water splashed in a central fountain. The gentlemen wore tailored suits, while the ladies looked ethereal in pastel silks with broad-brimmed hats. A smartly dressed man at the front desk cast a critical eye at Inga's plain brown frock, but his chilly demeanor vanished the instant she told him that she'd been invited to join Ambassador Gerard for lunch.

"Of course, ma'am," he said respectfully. "I'll escort you to the dining room."

She hid a grin as they wended through the palm court toward the main dining room. What a treat this was! Who cared if she looked like a crow among swans? Few people in the world could afford lunch at the Ritz, and she intended to savor every moment.

Mr. Gerard was enjoying a cigar at a corner table near the window alcove while his wife perused a menu card. He stood as she approached.

"There's my girl," he said warmly, then set his cigar down and held out a chair for her. Most women disliked the scent of cigars, but Inga loved it because it reminded her of Mr. Gerard and his boisterous good cheer. She learned years ago that the reason the Gerards were in church the morning they first met was because Mary Gerard learned she was finally expecting a child. They came to light every votive candle in the church and pray all would go well.

It didn't. The pregnancy did not last, and the Gerards were never blessed with children. Eventually, Inga became like a goddaughter to them. Perhaps the Lord had his hand in what occurred that morning, for in a strange sort of way, the Gerards got their devoted child, just not in the way they'd hoped.

Mary Gerard greeted her kindly, though her smile didn't quite reach her eyes. Something was wrong, but Mr. Gerard chatted amiably about this weekend's horse races while a waitress set up tea service and the maître d' took their order.

"I'm surprised to see you back in America so soon," Inga said. After all, he'd only been appointed to the embassy in Berlin less than a year ago. "How do you like being an ambassador?"

He stopped rotating the cup and lifted his gaze to hers. "Things could be better," he said. "You know how Germans can be difficult. Sometimes they take offense at the silliest things."

"Oh dear," Inga said, for what else could she possibly say? Yes, Germans were a prickly and proud lot, and Mr. Gerard had always been a bit blunt. "Can you give me an example?"

"Apparently I insulted their appalling displays of public art," he said in exasperation. "The grand duke of Saxe-Weimar was showing me around Berlin, and I pointed out that all the parks have statues celebrating wars or killing something. Even in their gardens! It's all about some ancient warrior wielding a club or holding up a severed head. Where's the beauty in that?"

Mary winced. "Yes, but you didn't need to point it out, dearest."

"I know that *now*," Mr. Gerard said. "Then I offended the kaiser because I was supposed to refer to him in the third person. 'Did his Excellency enjoy his tea?' Or 'Will his Excellency care to read a message from the president?' It's overbearing and ridiculous."

"Did you actually meet the kaiser?" Inga asked. She never imagined actually knowing somebody who met Kaiser Wilhelm, let alone spoke to him.

"Of course I met the kaiser," Mr. Gerard said. "I took along the embassy's chief diplomatic counselor, who is supposed to keep me in line, but it still didn't go well."

Mr. Gerard proceeded to outline his troubles. His appointment as ambassador to Germany had been controversial because he had no diplomatic experience; however, President Wilson "owed him one." Apparently, Mr. Gerard used a combination of his money and influence to deliver the state of New York to Woodrow Wilson during the 1912 presidential election, and his ambassadorship was a payback. Even the newspapers appeared shocked that a man primarily known for his prowess in hosting parties should receive such a plum appointment. Maybe it shouldn't be a surprise that things weren't going well for him.

"I had to fire my secretary for telling tales about me," Mr. Gerard said. "The staff at the American Embassy hate me, but the worst is Benedict Kincaid, the chief diplomatic counselor. Benedict is always trying to tell me what to do and how to act. I suspected my secretary, a chap named Silas, was the leak who was telling tales to Benedict, so I set a trap for him. I told Silas I was playing tennis with the staff from the Romanian Embassy, but it was really the Norwegians. Either one was likely to annoy Benedict because he's a wet blanket who disapproves whenever I do something fun.

Sure enough, when Benedict confronted me, he thought I'd been playing with the Romanians, just like I'd told my secretary. I fired Silas, and now I need a new secretary I can trust not to spy for Benedict."

"Why can't you just fire Benedict?" Inga asked, and Mr. Gerard shook his head.

"Ha! I wish I could, but that's not how the embassy works," he said. "Ambassadors like me are temporary appointments. We serve at the pleasure of the president and get swapped out with each new administration. The staff appointments are different. They can stay at an embassy for decades and carry out all the run-of-the-mill duties. None of them like me, and Benedict is their ringleader. They all look up to him like he walks on water, which makes no sense to me. Benedict Kincaid is a killjoy who casts a pall over every sunny day."

"Dreadful man," Mary confirmed. "Simply dreadful."

"I wish I could fire the entire staff," Mr. Gerard said. "They don't think I'm up to the job, and now that a war looks imminent, I think they're trying to get me fired. President Wilson summoned me home to read me the riot act about ruffling feathers at the German court. If you ask me, it's long past due for someone to shake up the kaiser and his inbred, militaristic entourage. So no, I'm afraid things in Berlin aren't going terribly well."

Inga wasn't used to seeing the Gerards so glum. "I wish there was something I could do to help."

A smile flashed across Mr. Gerard's face. "My dear, that's why we've come to you! I need a secretary I can trust. You're fluent in German. You know shorthand and typing and how to use the wireless. I'm sick of worrying that Benedict is spying on me every time I send a message to the president or the kaiser. That's where you'll come in."

Her heart started thudding, and she glanced at Mary to be sure she wasn't misunderstanding. "You want me to go to Germany with you?"

"Isn't it exciting?" Mary enthused. "You can quit that dreadful overnight shift and come to Berlin with us. It will be such fun. We go yachting and to the opera and host parties in the countryside. You'll be with us for everything!"

She rocked back into her chair, stunned. Going to Berlin would mean leaving all her friends behind . . . including Eduardo. And quite frankly, Germany didn't seem like the safest place in the world right now. It would be cowardly to point out the darkening political situation when the Gerards were heading straight back into the teeth of it, and yet she needed to know.

"What happens if a war is declared?" she asked.

Mr. Gerard was dismissive. "No fear of a war. Things don't look good for the French or the British, but America is going to stay out of it. President Wilson has repeatedly assured the whole world that he won't drag us into a foreign war, and I believe him. You'll be perfectly safe in Berlin."

She did *not* want to leave New York. She loved the city. "Surely there are other people you could hire who have the necessary secretarial skills."

"I need someone I can trust," he said. Duties as a struggling ambassador must have been terribly difficult because he suddenly looked old and tired. Even his voice sounded exhausted as he continued.

"Inga, there are people on this earth who are always cheerful and optimistic. They bob back up to the surface whenever they get clobbered. That's you. I knew it from the moment I saw you in that church, trying to smile through your fear when you were only a slip of a girl. That's the spirit the American Embassy is lacking right now. We need you. *I need you.*"

How clever he was to remind Inga of her indebtedness to him. Sixteen years ago, the Gerards swooped in to save her family and asked for nothing in return. It looked like the bill was suddenly coming due.

"Can I have some time to think about it?"

"Naturally," Mr. Gerard said. "You can call me this evening with your decision so I can arrange for passage. We sail on Friday."

Inga ran to the harbor to ask Eduardo what he thought of the Gerards' proposal. Eduardo had a fine job as an accountant at the Docks Department, but he didn't get off work until five o'clock, and her time to make a decision was running out.

She sat on a park bench, gazing at the esplanade that ran alongside the harbor. It was the best sight in the world, with ships constantly sailing in and out of this grand port. Flags snapped in the breeze, the cry of sea gulls and the clank of chains mingled with the slosh of water against the harbor wall. The thought of leaving this wonderful city triggered a pang of homesickness.

Five o'clock finally came, and Inga stood as she spotted Eduardo leaving the Docks Department. As always, his swath of dark hair was ruthlessly slicked into place for his office job, but he relaxed and turned funny whenever they were together.

Not today. A sadness overcame him as she described the job in Germany.

"But, Inga," he said, his Adam's apple bobbing, "I thought you and I could . . . well, I was hoping the two of us could make things permanent someday. Mama is already counting on it."

She sighed. "We've only been courting two months."

"I know, but you're pretty much perfect, even if you are German."

He flushed when he realized what he just said, and yet she simply laughed and planted a smooch directly on his mouth. "That's okay. If my parents were still alive, they'd probably think the same thing about an Italian."

Eduardo held her hands tighter. "Berlin is a good opportunity, but do you truly want to go?"

She couldn't bring herself to answer as she watched a tugboat guiding a mighty steamship into port. Her love for New York went all the way to the marrow of her bones, and yet she owed the Gerards everything. Eduardo escorted her to the subway stop, expressing his disapproval the entire way.

Back at her apartment, the women who lived on her floor were equally skeptical. Inga moved into this all-female apartment building six years ago. The Martha Washington was created to provide safe housing for the growing class of professional single women. Over five hundred teachers, nurses, secretaries, and other professional women who could afford the monthly rent made their home in this apartment building. Each floor had a communal room, which was where Inga told the other women from the eighth floor about her dilemma. So far, all six women gathered here were doubtful about the wisdom of taking the job. All of them had valid observations for which Inga had no answers.

"What if you don't like the work?" Margaret asked. "You'll be stuck in Germany with no way to get home."

"What if the war breaks out?" another asked. "Maybe the ships will stop sailing, and you'll be trapped there for years and years."

"What about William?" Blanche asked.

Finally, an easy question. "William and I split up a few months back," Inga said. "I'm with Eduardo Cipriani now."

"*Again?*" Blanche asked incredulously. Inga was used to being teased for her merry-go-round with boyfriends, but she liked men, and they liked her back. Whenever they got too possessive, like William did, it was time to move on. The fact that Eduardo and his mother were already hoping for a long-term commitment meant Inga would probably need to move on soon anyway.

Across the room, Delia Byrne watched with skeptical eyes. Delia was not only Inga's best friend, but she was probably the smartest person here. And so far she'd been silent.

"Dee, what do you think?"

"I think you'd be insane to say no," Delia replied. "Why are you hesitating? What are you afraid of, Inga?"

That she didn't belong in Germany anymore. That she wouldn't know how to act in an embassy where she'd meet kings and princes and diplomats. That she would fail and disappoint the Gerards. She drew a sobering breath and met Delia's gaze. "I'm not smart like you, Dee. I only have an eighth-grade education and can be so dumb sometimes."

"Inga, stop!" Delia ordered. "You speak two languages, plus Morse code. You can take shorthand, type, and organize an office better than anyone I know, all of it while wrapping every man in the vicinity around your soft little finger, so shut up about being stupid, okay?"

Inga choked back a laugh. "I wish you weren't so nasty."

"And I wish you weren't so good-natured!"

Some people didn't understand the way she and Delia bickered, but they'd become instant friends the moment Inga arrived at the Martha Washington six years earlier. Yes, they were opposites. Inga was cheerful and blond compared to Delia's dark and serious, but they'd always been closer than sisters.

"When would you have to leave?" Blanche asked.

"The Gerards sail on Friday," she said.

Blanche folded her arms across her chest. "If everyone at the American Embassy hates Mr. Gerard the way you described, what happens if President Wilson fires him? You will have lost a good job at the harbor and be out of a job in Germany."

"You'd lose your apartment at the Martha Washington," another woman pointed out. "There's a two-year waiting list to get a place here, and you'd be out on the streets."

"Not if Eduardo had his way," Margaret teased. "He'd take her in a heartbeat."

There were so many excellent reasons to stay she hadn't even considered. She loved living at the Martha Washington. It was a sisterhood here, and if she left, she'd have to get at the end of that two-year waiting list for an apartment. Inga turned her attention to a rail-thin, elderly woman perched on the couch who hadn't said a word as her knitting needles clicked with practiced rhythm.

"Midge, what do you think?"

At seventy-four, Midge Lightner was the oldest person at the Martha Washington. She'd been a nurse during the Civil War and still worked the overnight shift at a nearby hospital.

"I think the best opportunities in life are usually the scariest."

Inga sagged. She didn't want a scary opportunity; her life was already perfect. She loved the bright lights of Manhattan and letting handsome men court her. New York had parties and theaters and fresh-baked pretzels. There was ice skating in the winter and baseball in summer.

The only thing she remembered about Germany was living in a tiny town with dirt roads surrounded by a forest, the trees so tall that they blotted out the sun. Berlin would be different, yet the prospect of abandoning everything for it . . . no.

"I think you should stay here," Blanche said. "A new theater season is about to open. You don't want to go be on the front lines in Germany. Stay back in New York where it's safe."

"Safe?" Delia said, a hard edge in her voice. "I can't become an attorney even though I'm smarter than ninety percent of the lawyers I clerk for. I've had doors slammed in my face all my life. I would give my eyeteeth to have an opportunity like this. Inga, you need to go! Maybe it will be hard in Berlin, but don't quit before the game even begins. If things get hard, you buckle down, burn your candle at both ends, and rise to the occasion."

Delia in her Valkyrie mood was always so intimidating, and Inga stood to pace in the crowded room. She needed time to think without all these people chiming in. She ignored the ongoing chatter as she wandered to the window overlooking the city she loved so well. Even from here it was possible to see the spire of the church where she and her parents huddled overnight all those years ago. How afraid they'd been that terrible night. She'd often wondered what would have become of them without the openhanded generosity of the Gerards on that long-ago day. Over the years they had intervened on her behalf time and again, never once asking for anything in return.

She didn't want to leave New York. She didn't want to head into the unknown. And yet, a few hours later as the sun sank low in the evening sky, she called the hotel where the Gerards were staying and agreed to accompany them to Berlin.

2

The morning after Inga accepted Mr. Gerard's offer, his wife arrived at the Martha Washington to take Inga shopping.

"No offense, darling, but you'll need to look a little sharper than the sad dress you're wearing. That fabric could double as a horse blanket."

Inga grinned. Mary had a way of delivering a blunt message in a delightful tone that made it impossible to disagree with her. They headed to the Ladies' Mile, a collection of streets where a woman could buy anything from shoelaces to a diamond tiara. They started with the ready-made clothing stores, and Mary assured Inga there would be a seamstress aboard the ship who could tailor the clothing to a perfect fit.

By the end of the afternoon, Inga was the proud owner of five complete suits, eight coordinating blouses, two walking gowns, and an evening gown. Mary insisted on all the accoutrements and bought gloves, handbags, shoes, stockings, and a parasol. Most fun was picking out a variety of hats to go with each suit. Some had wide brims with lavish trim, while others were tiny and sleek to be pinned to the side of her head at a saucy angle.

What a heady experience it was to walk into a store and not

even glance at the prices. When Inga offered to help pay the bill, Mary instantly waved it away. "You're doing us a tremendous favor, and a new wardrobe is the least we can provide."

Inga didn't own any suitable luggage, so Mary shelled out for a new trunk with leather straps and a paisley fabric that lined the interior. A clerk wrapped the gowns between layers of tissue paper and folded them into the trunk while Inga changed into a new gown to wear out of the shop. The powder-blue skirt was so sleek she could only take tiny steps, but Mary assured her this was the latest fashion in Europe. The suit had a nip-waisted jacket of matching fabric and a darling white blouse with a lacy neckline.

With all her other new clothing packed, Inga wore the blue suit to board the ship on Friday morning. Eduardo came to see her off. The gangway was lowered, and the Gerards boarded the steamer ahead of her. She had to anchor her new straw boater to her head lest the breeze carry it away.

"You won't forget me, will you?" Eduardo's dark, gentle eyes implored her with such kindness, and yet it wouldn't be right to leave without telling him the truth.

"Please don't wait for me," she said. "I don't know when I'll be back, and I'm not the right girl for you."

"Oh, but Inga, *you are!*"

She wasn't. Eduardo deserved someone eager to settle down and start a family, not a flighty girl whose roving eye was still irresistibly drawn to any charming man who could make her laugh. She gave Eduardo a quick farewell kiss, disengaged her hands, then turned to board the steamer.

A handsome ship's officer stood at the top of the gangway to welcome passengers aboard. The gleam of male appreciation in his gaze was unmistakable, and she instinctively sent him a dazzling smile in return. See? A whole new world was about to open before her if she could just forget about New York. Even so, she feared if she turned around to see Eduardo's mournful face or the beloved skyline of Manhattan, she wouldn't have the strength to go.

She smiled at the handsome ship's officer and let him lead her aboard.

Crossing the Atlantic with the Gerards was a shockingly different experience from when Inga traveled as a child. Instead of huddling in steerage, she had a room adjoining the Gerards' first-class suite because rich people always traveled with staff they wanted nearby. They even wanted her to dine with them during the lavish, multicourse meals.

On her first night aboard, Inga glided alongside the Gerards into the grand dining room covered with royal-blue carpeting and lit by crystal chandeliers. For the first time in her life, she wore a silk gown. The lilac organza made a whispery rustle with each step as they walked through the dining room to their table. Heads turned, and it seemed everyone was watching her.

Did they know she was a fraud? She didn't belong among all these fancy people. The menu card was in French, but Mr. Gerard translated for her. Who could imagine four different choices for beef? She hadn't heard of most of them and simply asked Mr. Gerard to order for her.

A waiter dressed in a formal coat and white gloves delivered bowls of fragrant lobster bisque. It was the first course of six, and while it was tempting to indulge in the luxury, she mustn't forget the reason she was here. The embassy staff in Berlin despised Mr. Gerard and wanted him to fail. She could use the six days of the transatlantic voyage to glean insight into her new post.

"What exactly will my duties as your secretary be?" she asked, then took a delicate sip of bisque.

"Mostly taking dictation and typing letters," Mr. Gerard said. "Larry Milton will show you the ropes. Larry is Benedict Kincaid's private secretary, and you'll be sharing an office with him. Nice enough chap if a bit of a drip."

"Larry is all right, but watch out for Benedict," Mary warned. "Benedict is the chief of staff and casts a shadow wherever he goes. He is the fly at every picnic, the storm cloud on every sunny day. Benedict Kincaid is the living, breathing embodiment of the four horsemen of doom."

Inga stifled a laugh. "Surely he can't be that bad."

Mary cocked a brow. "According to the cook at Alton House, Benedict begins every day with a cold shower and has a bowl of ice-cold oats for breakfast. Yes, he *is* that bad."

"No wonder his wife left him," Mr. Gerard snickered.

"Shhh!" Mary said, then turned to Inga. "Pretend you didn't hear that, my dear."

"Mr. Kincaid is married?" she asked.

"Was. Not anymore," Mrs. Gerard said. "We mustn't discuss such things, but look, here comes the gentleman in charge of the dining room."

The ship's maître d' approached, an elegant man in a tuxedo with a voice that sounded like it came from Buckingham Palace. "It is a pleasure to welcome you aboard, Ambassador," the maître d' murmured. "The pastry chef would be delighted to prepare whatever special desserts you would like for the duration of your voyage."

"Oh, what fun," Mary said, taking a card he offered with a long list of selections. "Inga, what would you like? Pick something!"

Once again, the card was in French, but Inga didn't need to consult a card to know what she wanted. "Can he make a Black Forest cake?" she asked. It had always been her favorite, and it seemed fitting for her return to Germany.

"I shall consult with the chef and return with an answer," the maître d' said with a bow before slipping away. Was she supposed to bow in return? This was all so new and foreign and wonderful.

"When we lived in Germany, my mother always celebrated every

Christmas with a Black Forest cake," Inga explained to the Gerards. "She scrimped to buy a jar of brandied cherries and real dark chocolate, and those cakes made Christmas magical. She always insisted on a Black Forest cake at Christmas, even the year . . ."

A sudden lump formed in her throat. All the people she once celebrated Christmas with were now gone. She rarely thought of her little sister anymore, but it was Marie's death that taught Inga so much about the importance of smiling through the pain.

Both Gerards looked at her with concern, and she decided to finish the story.

"My little sister caught a terrible fever when she was only six, and she died right before Christmas. My parents couldn't stop crying for two days, and I remember thinking we were going to have to forgo Christmas that year, and yet, on Christmas Eve my mother dried her tears and proceeded to make a Black Forest cake like always. Marie had died, but the rest of us were still alive. God was good even if our hearts were breaking. The earth was still full of blessings, though sometimes we need to look for them." Inga drew a fortifying breath to shake away the shadow of old pain. "Anyway, I still love Black Forest cake," she said with an apologetic smile.

Mary's face was gentle. "Then we shall have a Black Forest cake to celebrate your return to Germany, my dear."

It turned out there were no brandied cherries aboard the ship, but Mary insisted they could buy some at the Port of Hamburg and have the cook at the embassy bake a fine Black Forest cake.

Excitement warred with anxiety as Inga nodded in agreement. Soon she would be back in Germany, and a new adventure would begin.

3

Benedict Kincaid spent the morning cleaning up a series of gaffes made by Ambassador Gerard.

When James Gerard arrived in Berlin late last year, he freely shared his poor opinion of the squat, ugly building that housed the U.S. Embassy and wanted something grander. His loud-mouthed criticisms insulted the German architect of the original embassy, and his behavior reflected badly on the United States. Thus Benedict spent the morning signing a flurry of legal forms to break their lease on the building, paid the early termination fee, and soothed offended sensibilities. It was all part of his job at the embassy, working behind the scenes to ensure the ambassador's success.

Tension began to unwind as Benedict walked home toward the Alton House, where most of the embassy staff lived. This tree-lined street was his favorite in all of Berlin. It was fittingly named Linden Avenue, for the long street was shaded by hundred-year-old linden trees planted at regular intervals, creating a tunnel of greenery arching over the cobblestone lane. Dignified houses nestled on large plots of land well back from the street. Some were owned by wealthy merchants, but most were leased by various foreign embassies for their staff. The residential neighborhood had a timeless atmosphere of peace and stability. They were in the heart of urban Berlin, and yet the air was still alive with birdsong and the scent of lilac and sweet autumn clematis.

He walked up the graveled path to Alton House. Ivy climbed the walls, covering most of the stonework on the first floor, cleared only around the mullioned windows. The steeply pitched roof had a number of dormer windows, each one denoting a bedroom tucked within. Nine people, all embassy employees, had made their home here for the six years that Benedict had been stationed in Berlin. During that time, they'd grown to feel like a family. Mercifully, Ambassador Gerard and his wife chose to live in the residential apartments on the top floor of the new American Embassy, meaning the staff could relax here at Alton House.

A cluster of employees gathered around the dining table positioned at the far end of the kitchen. Most were dressed casually, but one man was in uniform. Colonel Reyes was their military attaché whose job it was to monitor Germany's military prowess and advise how it might affect the United States. He clenched a telegram in his hands, and the rest of the staff looked grim.

"What's happening?" Benedict asked.

Colonel Reyes held the telegram aloft. "Ambassador Gerard is due back in Berlin tomorrow."

That explained the glum faces. None of them liked the fickle leadership of James Gerard, and his absence over the past few weeks had been delightful.

He wandered forward to join the group. All were men except Mrs. Barnes the cook and her assistant Nellie Chapman. Nellie scooted aside to make room for him at the kitchen table, but he remained standing. It wouldn't do to appear close to a young woman because he had to be on guard against rumors, even inside Alton House.

Benedict studied the telegram, reporting the imminent arrival of the ambassador along with Inga Klein, a new secretary who would be joining their household. He hoped Miss Klein was a woman of strong fortitude who could stand up to the ambassador.

"We will make Miss Klein welcome," he said reluctantly, then glanced at Nellie. "Keep an eye on her. Befriend her and gain her trust. We cannot assume Ambassador Gerard will have chosen wisely." Secretaries could get their hands on almost anything inside an embassy, and he doubted Gerard went through the proper channels to verify the woman's suitability.

"We can't even trust Ambassador Gerard to walk across the street without embarrassing himself," Larry Milton whined. "He is a complete and total dilettante."

Larry was Benedict's secretary and had been here for years. His fretful hypochondria seemed to get worse with age, but Larry was loyal, and that counted for a lot.

Nevertheless, the contempt for Ambassador Gerard among the staff was getting out of hand. As the ranking career diplomat, Benedict needed to set the tone among the embassy staff. He spoke kindly, but firmly.

"Ambassador Gerard has the faith of our president and enjoys friendships with many of the kaiser's sons. I expect each person here to treat him with respect. Europe is tottering on the edge of war, and our only concern should be to support President Wilson's desire to keep the United States neutral. Our embassy will be a haven of peace, a beacon of hope in an otherwise dark world. Understood?"

Colonel Reyes lifted a cynical brow. "*We* understand that. Does Ambassador Gerard?"

It was a good question, and one which Benedict still could not answer.

"At least Mrs. Gerard can sometimes rein him in," Colonel Reyes said. "I once saw the ambassador tell the wife of a rich industrialist that she'd be better served buying her gowns in London or New York instead of Berlin. The lady took it as a personal insult, and Mrs. Gerard rushed to compliment Mrs. Schmitt's gown. Apparently, Mrs. Schmitt's husband owns the largest clothing factory in Munich. Mrs. Gerard made a point of visiting the factory and arranged for Macy's to place a large order for their department stores in New York."

It was a clever move. Benedict had to admit that Mrs. Gerard was helping smooth over some of her husband's more egregious blunders. Navigating different cultures and forming ties with the wives of local dignitaries could quietly work magic behind the scenes. Life as an ambassador's wife could be a lonely job. Many ambassadors left their wives back in America, so he had to give Mary Gerard credit for accepting the heavy responsibilities that came along with accompanying her husband to Berlin.

"Mrs. Gerard is a credit to the embassy," he said. "Whatever our feelings for her husband, or the new secretary he is bringing, we must grin and make the best of it."

But Benedict would be watching them both like a hawk.

4

The first thing Inga did after arriving at the Port of Hamburg was to indulge in a leisurely lunch with the Gerards at a café overlooking the Planten un Blomen, a famed park tucked inside Hamburg's old city walls. How wonderful to be on solid ground again! They found a table with a view of the lake, where a fountain sprayed arcs of water into the air. Mr. Gerard insisted on schnitzel and stuffed cabbage for lunch because this was the same place he and Mary shared a meal on their honeymoon, and he wanted to recapture the memory. Inga gladly listened to them wax poetic about their honeymoon and wondered if she would ever get married. The Gerards made it seem so wonderful, but she had yet to meet a man who could hold her interest more than a few months.

For dessert, Mr. Gerard ordered a large platter of vanilla-drenched *spritzkuchen*, which were a little like American doughnuts. "These are even better than I remembered," Inga said as she broke off another sweet, perfectly golden wedge of dough.

"Let's have another round," Mr. Gerard boomed.

It didn't take long for a second platter to arrive, along with another pot of tea. They lingered so long over dessert that they missed their train to Berlin.

They didn't mind. It was easy to book another train that would leave three hours later, which gave them time to browse in delightful gourmet shops, where the aromas and flavors seemed wonderfully familiar. Mary insisted on buying a jar of brandied cherries so that Inga could have a Black Forest cake. She also bought Inga a new hat with a floppy brim and a spray of silk sunflowers on the side. They ended up trying on so many hats that they almost missed their second train, then ended up laughing about their adventures during the entire ride to Berlin.

It was late by the time they pulled into their train station, and past midnight when their carriage rolled up the drive to Alton House.

It was hard to see much of the darkened house. While it would be nicer to live with the Gerards at the embassy, she mustn't forget that her primary job was to lower the tension between the ambassador and his staff. That was best done here at the Alton House.

It was too late to wake the staff, so Mr. Gerard unlocked the door to let them inside. He lugged her trunk up the stairs while she and Mary quietly tiptoed up the darkened staircase and into her very own bedroom.

How darling it was! The single brass bed was tucked beneath a slanted roofline. The other side of the room had a wardrobe and a quaint little vanity table with an oval mirror. An electric lamp cast an amber glow that looked even warmer because of the pale wallpaper covered with tiny mauve flowers.

"It's humble, but comfortable, yes?" Mary asked.

"Oh yes," Inga breathed, still amazed she actually had such a cozy room all to herself. The oak wardrobe had little trailing vines hand-carved along the top cornice. The cabinet doors opened and closed without a single squeak, and her new clothes fit perfectly inside it.

Excitement made it hard to sleep that night. She hugged a pillow to herself, hoping she had made the right choice by coming back to Germany. She would learn tomorrow if the embassy staff were as terrible as the Gerards believed.

Inga awoke to sunlight streaming through white, filmy curtains. She hadn't been able to see much of the neighborhood last night and so eagerly hopped out of bed and drew the curtains aside.

Her room overlooked the backyard garden. Greenery and shrubs surrounded a flagstone patio, a green haven in the middle of the residential neighborhood.

Old paint on the window sash scraped as she lifted it a few inches to hear a bird chirping nearby. The twittery birdsong was familiar, something she hadn't heard in ages. It felt like a greeting from long ago, calling out to welcome her home.

A scrape and a bump sounded from the side yard.

Inga slid behind the drapes because she wore nothing but a flimsy nightgown. A man dressed in a riding jacket and tall boots wrestled with the door of a carriage house. He rolled the sliding wooden door to the side, then disappeared into the interior. He emerged a few moments later, leading a horse from the stables.

Something deep inside tugged, an instinctive feminine appreciation for an attractive man. He had the lanky, lean build of a European aristocrat, though if he lived at Alton House, surely he was American. He saddled the horse with competence. At one point the horse shifted and nickered, and the stranger ran a soothing hand over its flank until the horse was calm again. A moment later, he swung his tall frame into the saddle with impressive ease. He flicked the reins, and the horse trotted off, its iron horseshoes striking the cobblestones in that familiar clatter as they headed toward the street.

Inga never learned to ride. Riding was a rich person's sport, not something for a shoemaker's daughter who lived in a city with a perfectly fine subway system. How far away New York suddenly seemed.

No more wallowing in memories! It was time to get dressed and head downstairs to meet the embassy staff. She was prepared to give them all the benefit of the doubt despite their callous treatment of the Gerards.

She chose one of her new outfits, a bottle-green skirt paired with an ivory blouse. It had a portrait collar and looked professional yet still feminine and pretty. On impulse, she grabbed the large jar of brandied cherries to share with the others. The Black Forest cake could wait. What better way to liven up boring oatmeal or waffles than with a splash of syrupy cherries?

The hall outside her door showed plenty of closed bedroom doors. A staircase divided the middle of the hall, and she trailed a hand along the carved banister on the way downstairs. The same dark, carved woodwork was everywhere, from the crown moldings all the way down to the baseboards. She headed toward the sound of clattering dishes and female voices down a hallway and into a brightly lit kitchen. Two women turned to look at her, surprise on their faces.

"Good morning," she greeted. "I'm Inga Klein, Mr. Gerard's new secretary."

A doughy-faced woman mixing batter set down her spoon. She was middle-aged with frown lines along the sides of her mouth.

"Welcome," the older lady said. "I'm Mrs. Barnes, the cook here at Alton House. This is Nellie Chapman, who helps me out. Nellie, set the kettle on for tea."

"Coffee, if you don't mind," Inga said, which caused a glower from the cook. Had she said something wrong? Didn't everyone have coffee in the mornings?

"Here," Inga said, setting the jar of cherries on the scarred wooden counter, a peace offering to the scowling cook. "I brought brandied cherries. If that batter you're mixing is for pancakes or waffles, the cherries will make it an extra-special treat."

"I should say so," the cook said, making no move to touch the cherries as she continued mixing batter. "Why does the ambassador need another secretary? I thought Larry Milton was going to take that role."

According to Mr. Gerard, Larry was a whiny man who idolized Benedict Kincaid, the chief troublemaker at the embassy. Neither Gerard wanted anything to do with Larry, so she chose her words delicately.

"My understanding is that Larry's duties supporting Benedict Kincaid are very demanding, and sometimes the ambassador is called away on business. I'll be able to help with secretarial duties while he's traveling."

The cook's frown deepened. "That doesn't exactly seem proper."

"Ambassador Gerard always travels with his wife, so everything will be *very* proper," Inga replied. "And he needs his own secretary. I'm looking forward to meeting Larry so we can work things out however will best serve the needs of the embassy."

Mrs. Barnes grunted in reply, then proceeded to outline the house rules. Staff were to help themselves to breakfast each morning and eat at the table in the kitchen nook. The cozy table had stacks of crockery and a basket of silverware in the center, along with a pitcher of cream, a bowl of sugar cubes, and a dish of butter.

Following instructions, Inga helped herself to toast while Mrs. Barnes continued thrashing out more rules, mostly emphasizing that Inga shouldn't ask for special requests or expect maid service. The house had a formal dining room, but Mrs. Barnes refused to use it because it was too much trouble.

"Are you frightening the new secretary, Mrs. Barnes?" A masculine voice sounded from the doorway, where a stocky young man with light brown hair entered the kitchen and introduced himself as Andrew Dolan, the second deputy assistant at the embassy.

He seemed friendlier than the kitchen staff, and Inga stood to greet him. "It's nice to meet you, Mr. Dolan."

"Andrew," he corrected. "We're on a first-name basis here at Alton House. None of that German formality here." His teasing expression shifted into wonder as he stepped farther into the kitchen and sniffed.

"Coffee?" Andrew asked. "What fairy godmother worked her magic to conjure up a pot of coffee?"

"I asked for coffee," she admitted. "Was that overstepping?"

Andrew reached for a cup. "Ma'am, you worked a miracle. We've been wanting to switch to coffee for ages, but Mrs. Barnes says it's too expensive for every day."

"Don't expect favors in the future," Mrs. Barnes said, then went back to pouring batter into a waffle griddle. Inga intended to pass the comment about coffee to Mr. Gerard, who'd gladly spring for coffee if it bought him goodwill.

Soon others began gathering for breakfast. A growly man whose flushed face matched his ginger hair and simply went by McFee was the embassy chauffeur. Colonel Reyes, with neatly clipped blond hair, was the military attaché. Inga could spot Larry Milton even without an introduction. He was exactly as Mary described: thin, sickly, and whiny.

To Inga's delight, plenty of the staff helped themselves to coffee, and the cherries were disappearing fast. "Should we save some of the cherries for Mr. Kincaid?" she suggested.

"He's already had breakfast," Nellie chimed in. "Cold oats. It's what he has every day before his morning ride. It has something to do with the scary boarding school he attended."

Anyone would be grim on a diet of nothing but cold oats. "Maybe he rode off to indulge in something scandalous," Inga teased. "Like eggs with bacon and a huge cheese Danish I'll bet he eats all by himself."

"Not likely," Nellie said. "Benedict lives like a monk. He never goes to any of the street fairs with us. He'd rather stay home and read the *Encyclopedia Britannica*."

The cook shot Nellie a glare. "That's enough," Mrs. Barnes cautioned, then turned to Inga. "Now listen up, Miss Klein. We all like Benedict, but he's got his quirks, and whatever you do, don't touch his *Encyclopedia Britannica*. He's got all those volumes dog-eared and marked with notes in the margins. He underlines and circles things, and I think he loves those books more than his firstborn child. Not that he has a child, mind you, but if he did, the poor mite would be a distant second in his affections to that set of books."

"He's reading them from cover to cover," Andrew said. "I think he's somewhere in the P's by now."

The slamming of a door from down the hall signaled a new arrival. A moment later, the tall man she'd seen down at the carriage house strode into the kitchen, still wearing his riding clothes. Up close he was even more imposing, with fine features and an air of brooding vitality. His dark hair was windblown, and he immediately honed his gaze on her. The intensity of his stare was disconcerting as he tugged off his riding gloves.

"Benedict!" Andrew said, pushing back his chair. "Come meet the ambassador's new secretary. Inga brought us drunken cherries."

"Drunken cherries?" Benedict asked. The two words were laden with disdain, and his appalled expression made her instinctively defensive. She cleared her throat and stood.

"Brandied cherries," she clarified. "I bought them in Hamburg, and they're delightful on waffles or porridge. I'm Inga Klein. I'll be working for Mr. Gerard as his new secretary."

She offered her hand, but he made no move to accept it. His gaze sharpened as he scrutinized her, and he tilted his head a little closer as though listening for something. "Do you have an *accent*?"

She smiled. She'd been told she spoke English so well that she barely had an accent at all anymore, but he obviously spotted it. "Yes," she said brightly. "I'm originally from right here in Germany. A little village in Bavaria that's famous for its shoes."

Benedict's face went very still, and yet she sensed a cyclone of disapproval whirling behind his cold, stone mask.

"Hmph" was all he said. It was amazing how he packed so much censure into a single syllable. No wonder Mr. Gerard didn't like him. She'd been prepared to grant him the benefit of the doubt, but how could she warm up to a man who brought an arctic blast into their cozy little breakfast? It wasn't her imagination. Everyone else in the room sensed his disapproval, and the air crackled with tension.

Benedict gave a brief nod of acknowledgment to the others in the kitchen, then turned and strode down the hallway, disappearing into a side room. The door slammed behind him.

"Don't let it worry you," Andrew said. "He doesn't like anybody."

"That was still rude," Mrs. Barnes said. "Inga is new here, and there was no cause for that."

It seemed Inga had managed to soften up the surly Mrs. Barnes. Perhaps she could make progress with Benedict Kincaid as well. She wanted to be on decent terms with the second-most powerful man at the embassy, but her sour feelings were already snowballing, and she needed to nip this in the bud.

"Excuse me," she said to the others around the table, then hurried down the hall to follow Benedict. What a relief it smelled only of lemon polish and not brimstone.

She needed to quit thinking of Benedict as the enemy and somehow mend fences with him. Winning him over would be her first step toward helping soothe tensions at the embassy. She rapped quietly on the door.

"Come in," Benedict said from the other side.

She entered the room, which was obviously a library. Floor-to-ceiling bookshelves covered one wall, while the rest of the room was furnished like a sitting room. Benedict sat at a desk, a hefty tome opened before him.

She drew closer to peek at the book, and it was exactly as Andrew said. He was reading the *Encyclopedia Britannica*, and a bubble of laughter escaped.

"I heard a rumor that you're reading those books from cover to cover but didn't believe it."

"It's true," Benedict said dryly.

"Do you read the boring parts too?"

"There are no boring parts."

Oh, good heavens, he really was allergic to fun, and he still hadn't looked at her since she entered. Maybe bringing the brandied cherries on her first day had been a mistake. If it was a faux pas, she would apologize.

"Is there a rule against serving alcohol in this house? You seemed upset about the cherries."

"Fruit steeped in liquor is not exactly a healthy start to the morning."

"Not like cold oats."

"Precisely."

Still no thaw. "It won't happen again. I believe Andrew has helped himself to a second round of waffles, so that will finish off the brandied cherries. Unless you want to supply the next round, Cold Oats."

He swiveled to look at her. "Did you just call me Cold Oats?"

Cold Oats seemed the perfect nickname for this chilly, joyless man. She summoned a smile. "You haven't introduced yourself," she pointed out. "Shall we try again? I'm Inga Klein, and you are?"

"I'm reading," he said. "Saturday mornings are one of the few times I have for recreational reading, which I look forward to all week, and which you are currently interrupting."

She couldn't imagine anything more tedious than reading an entire encyclopedia cover to cover. "Aren't you ever tempted to skip ahead to the good parts?"

"And what would those be?"

She shrugged with a helpless grin. "Oh, you know, juicy scandals like Lucrezia Borgia or the Salem Witch Trials. But no, it seems you'd rather read about . . ." She leaned in to look at his current article. "Pollination behavior of insects."

She said it in a deliberately teasing tone, and yet his voice was utterly serious when he replied, "One-third of the world's food supply depends on insect pollination, but Miss Klein finds it beneath her. Interesting."

She sighed. "It seems we've gotten off on the wrong foot, and I'd like to change that. I promise not to call you Cold Oats anymore if you'll call me Inga."

With great deliberation, Benedict placed a bookmark and closed the heavy volume with slow, deliberate motions. Then he stood to face her, and for the first time a hint of softening eased the sharp planes of his face. "Miss Klein, although it is no fault of yours, I don't like the fact that you are German."

It felt like a slap in the face, and she took a step back. "That sounds rather small-minded."

"No, it's called diplomacy. Right now, the whole of Europe is balancing on a knife's edge. War between Germany and the Allied Powers is almost inevitable, and don't believe the newspapers. The war won't be a cakewalk that will be over before Christmas. My goal is to keep the United States out of this pointless, bloody war. To do that, our embassy needs to maintain a reputation for strict neutrality. Your presence endangers that."

"I'm only a *secretary*," she pointed out.

"You're someone who has the trust of the ambassador, and that puts the reputation of our embassy in jeopardy with the French and English, who will be suspicious of your influence at the embassy. Please don't be offended, but I'm going to ask the ambassador to send you back to America. I don't want you here."

She exhaled sharply. No one had ever come after her so aggressively, and it rattled her. "Mr. Gerard won't send me away. He needs me, and he obviously has no concerns with my being German."

"That's because he is still a novice in diplomacy. Mr. Gerard is the public face of the American Embassy, and his behavior needs to be flawless. If he stumbles, it's my job to clean it up."

"You answer to Mr. Gerard, not the other way around," she pointed out, but it made no dent in the ironhard expression on Benedict's face.

"Ambassadors come and go with each new administration," Benedict said. "The diplomatic corps stays, and we'll be here long after Gerard is gone. We know how to get things done, how to swim beneath the surface and leave no ripples in our wake. If you are to be part of that team, you need to understand the rules."

"Fair enough. What are the rules?"

Benedict walked around the desk to stand before her. "Every person who lives at Alton House is part of the diplomatic corps. That means you must be patient, respectful, and resist taking sides. Right now most nations are forming their alliances, and they'll attempt to persuade the United States to join their team. Don't let them."

"Of course not! Just because I was born in Germany doesn't make me disloyal. I'm an American now."

He looked at her for so long, a frisson of tension began gathering along her spine, and it was hard to resist shrinking beneath his scrutiny.

"None of this is going to be easy," he cautioned, and for the first time his voice actually had a note of compassion. The unexpected dose of kindness sent a tiny shiver down her arms. "My goal is to have this embassy serve as a peace broker," he continued. "Both sides will need to trust in America's neutrality. If someone punches you in the jaw, you can't lose your temper and retaliate or it endangers our neutrality. We won't be able to fight with anything but our intellect, and one wrong foot can topple that. Miss Klein, you are a wrong foot."

She took a moment to digest that statement before responding with equal resolve. "I am a wrong foot who is going to remain firmly planted at this post."

"If I fail in convincing Mr. Gerard to send you home, you need to be aware that Berlin is filled with spies, and you must be on guard against that."

"I repeat, I'm just a secretary—"

"Who has no idea what she's stepping into, or you wouldn't sound so baffled. Exactly one month ago today a crazed Serbian nationalist assassinated the Archduke of Austria. Most people can't even find Serbia on a map, and yet that tiny country has triggered a worldwide catastrophe. Germany doesn't want a war. Neither do the Russians or the French or the British, but ironclad agreements for mutual support are dragging all of them toward the precipice. As Americans, we're lucky to be standing outside the quagmire. The neutral nations are trying to be a voice of sanity before time runs out."

He walked to the window and beckoned her to join him. The view was partially obscured by green viburnum leaves as he pointed to a brick house next door.

"That's where the staff of the Bulgarian Embassy lives," he said. "We are next-door neighbors but cannot interact with them because Bulgaria has already lined up behind the kaiser. The French staff live across the street, and they're off-limits to us as well because they're on the Allied side. Colonel Reyes is good friends with a number of the French staff, but that's over now because if he socializes with them, it opens the American Embassy up to charges of either favoritism, or worse, spying. Do you understand why you are the worst possible secretary for the American ambassador?"

She understood why the Gerards disliked Benedict.

The coffee in her stomach began to sour. She didn't yet understand the diplomatic landscape but was smart enough not to wade into an argument she couldn't hope to win with a seasoned diplomat like Benedict Kincaid. She glanced at his encyclopedia.

"Forgive me for interrupting your Saturday morning," she said. "I'll let you get back to the fascinating world of insect pollination."

She couldn't escape the room and Benedict's disturbing presence fast enough.

5

Benedict would never admit it, but Ambassador Gerard's idea to move the American Embassy to a better location had been correct. The old embassy building was small, shabby, and on the outskirts of town.

The new embassy was located on Wilhelm Platz, in the heart of Berlin and a stone's throw from the German chancellery. Ambassador Gerard had expensive taste, and he selected a palace that once belonged to a German princess for his new embassy. The ground floor featured rococo architecture with plenty of gilt mirrors and chandeliers. The dining room accommodated sixty guests, while the ballroom could host twice that number. It was far more grandiose than any other embassy building paid for by the U.S. government, and Gerard was paying the shortfall from his own pocket.

The new embassy had enough electrical power to triple the number of telephone and telegraph lines into the building. A team of soldiers from the American Corps of Engineers had finally arrived to wire the building and install the new equipment.

Benedict, Ambassador Gerard, and the lead engineer toured the first floor of the palace to determine which rooms were to be wired for telephone service. The first stop was Ambassador Gerard's private office. Unlike the gilded splendor in most of the embassy, Gerard's office was lined with rich wooden paneling, bookcases, and maps. A single telephone already sat atop the ambassador's imposing walnut desk, but naturally, Gerard tried to tell the engineer how to do his job the moment the three of them entered his office.

"I want to keep this telephone for my own use, plus an additional line in my upstairs apartment."

"Why do you need two lines?" Benedict asked.

"My wife ought to have access to a telephone while I'm using the office line."

Benedict turned his attention to Lieutenant Carter, the engineer responsible for wiring the embassy. "Lieutenant? How many telephone lines can the building support?"

"No more than eight," the young man answered.

The ambassador smiled. "See? There shouldn't be a problem letting my wife have her own line."

Benedict had to be smart about this. Too many important battles loomed on the horizon to argue over a telephone line.

"I have no objection to a line for Mrs. Gerard, but please be sure her line will support a second telephone for her use in the ground floor reception hall." Having that second telephone downstairs meant that in the event of war, they could take it over for official business. The ambassador seemed pleased as punch that Benedict didn't object to his wife getting a dedicated telephone, which was good because the discussion about kicking Inga Klein out of the embassy was still ahead.

They moved into the small room off the ambassador's office designated for secretarial staff. It currently belonged to Larry Milton, Benedict's own secretary, and it would be a tight fit to add the ambassador's secretary.

Gerard frowned as he surveyed the space. "I'm not sure we can fit two telephones and two telegraph machines in here."

The technician agreed. "Probably not, sir. Could we move one of the secretaries to a different room?"

Benedict cleared his throat. "This is something I'd like to discuss with the ambassador in private," he said. "Lieutenant, do you mind checking the utility box outside the building to be sure it can be protected from tampering?"

"Of course, sir." The engineer collected his blueprints and toolbox and left the room.

"What now?" the ambassador asked in annoyance as soon as they were alone.

"The selection of Miss Klein as your secretary is problematic."

Ambassador Gerard crossed his arms and shook his head. "Miss Klein is nonnegotiable."

"She's German."

"So? I need her."

Benedict had to remember that James Gerard was still a newcomer and ill-equipped to understand the diplomatic implications of such a choice. He kept his tone carefully neutral as he replied, "I'm not calling her character or qualifications into question, but her nationality gives the appearance of favoritism. We cannot afford it. I would be happy to help select a more appropriate secretary."

"Like the one I just fired?" the ambassador scoffed. "I need someone I can trust, not someone who gossips behind my back."

Benedict owed it to the diplomatic corps to defend their integrity. "No one in the embassy spreads gossip." The ambassador's previous secretary relayed information whenever Gerard was about to shoot himself in the foot, but that wasn't gossip—that was common sense.

The ambassador didn't want to hear it. He turned around to leave the office and wandered into the front hall. The huge space was intended to host formal balls and receptions, although at the moment it was where workers from the corps of engineers stored oversized coils of wire, ladders, drills, and construction equipment.

It was an odd contrast to the tall windows draped with gold silk panels and a crystal chandelier twinkling in the morning sun.

Ambassador Gerard strolled to a table crowded with freshly delivered bouquets of flowers for his upstairs apartment. He twisted off the head of a pink carnation and pinned it to his lapel. "If I need to let one of the secretaries go, it's going to be Larry, not Inga. You are dismissed. I'm taking my wife to luncheon with the Duchess of Mecklenburg."

Benedict seethed in frustration as the ambassador carried the bouquet upstairs to his apartment. If the Gerards didn't have such a blatantly loving and affectionate marriage, he'd think the ambassador had an unseemly interest toward Inga. The young woman practically oozed feminine appeal with her delightful figure and bubbly good cheer. Any man with blood in his veins would be attracted to her, which was yet another annoying distraction.

He joined Lieutenant Carter outside to inspect the telephone equipment mounted to the exterior of the embassy.

"Can we ensure the wires can never be spliced by someone tapping the telephone?" Benedict asked the engineer. It might seem paranoid, but a telephone wire anchored outside the building seemed to be begging a spy to eavesdrop on it.

"Not to worry," the engineer said. "We'll be covering the entire line with iron cladding anchored to the building all the way up to the ambassador's apartment upstairs."

Good. There were spies everywhere in Berlin, and tapping into the ambassador's telephone line would be tempting.

"Can I ask something?" Lieutenant Carter said as he hunkered down to put his tools away.

"Of course."

"There's been a lot of chatter over at the Soldat Barracks." The Soldat was where the American engineers and Marine Corps who guarded the embassy lived. "When President Wilson summoned Gerard home last month, everyone thought he was going to get the boot."

So did Benedict. It was a disappointment when Ambassador Gerard returned to his post, but Benedict reverted to a smoothly professional answer. "Given the delicate political situation, I believe President Wilson wished a face-to-face meeting to reiterate the American position on neutrality."

Lieutenant Carter closed his toolbox and stood. "Everyone was hoping *you* might get the appointment. You should have had it in the first place. If not for your wife—"

Benedict held up his hand. The less said about Claudia, the better. "That's all water under the bridge. My job is to make sure the new ambassador carries out the will of the president."

It didn't matter that Benedict wanted the ambassadorship so badly he could taste it. He'd spent the last fifteen years serving in diplomatic posts all over the world. Gerard was a novice, which was annoying in the best of times, and could be deadly if a war broke out.

Mention of Claudia haunted Benedict as he set off for Alton House. The damage to his reputation from their disastrous marriage was finally starting to fade, but diplomatic circles were small, and plenty of people still remembered Claudia and those dreadful final years.

And yet he had once loved her. At first, Claudia had been the answer to a prayer. His nomadic childhood following his father to embassies all over the world had been lonely. His mother died when he was a toddler, so Benedict accompanied his father to diplomatic posts in Tokyo, Cairo, and Buenos Aires. There were no English-speaking schools, so Benedict always had a tutor. Maybe he wouldn't be so lousy at making friends if he'd gone to school instead of mingling only with adults. He'd never had friends his own age and certainly no girlfriends.

At fourteen he was sent to England to finish his education, where British boarding schools weren't the warmest place for an American boy.

Actually, they were absolutely awful, which was why he yet

again failed to make friends. He studied hard to be accepted to college early, and it worked. His first day at Oxford was quite possibly the best day of his life because that was when he met Claudia.

She was captivating, with long red hair that fell in waves down to her waist. Better still, Claudia's father was a professor of ancient languages, and she enjoyed arcane academic subjects as much as Benedict. She grew up living on a college campus and was the smartest girl he'd ever met. She was beautiful and friendly and smart. Maybe a little spoiled. Her father never paid her much attention, so she sought it out from the young men on campus. By the time Benedict met Claudia, her reputation had been ruined by her penchant for being overly familiar with the men who flocked around her.

He didn't hold it against her. He knew what it was like to be lonely, but Claudia's parents were desperate to see her safely married. She was bound to get into real trouble soon, and Benedict was willing.

More than willing. He was enchanted and dazzled and grateful. He and Claudia were both only eighteen, but her parents encouraged the match, and he was eager for it too. After they married, he moved into their home, and all felt right with the world. For a blissful few years, he'd found a family.

What a disaster it turned out to be. His marriage to Claudia nearly destroyed his reputation in the diplomatic community. It was probably why he'd been passed over for the promotion here in Berlin. But one thing was certain: He would never again give a woman the power to trample his heart or destroy his career.

6

Inga's first week working at the American Embassy passed in a blur. She unpacked endless crates of paperwork from the old building and helped set up the new office she would share with Larry. It took Larry forever to make decisions about how best to proceed, wringing his hands and sweating bullets over everything.

Inga soon tired of watching Larry agonize over how to organize the records and took charge of helping him arrange the files in the same manner she used at the Port of New York.

"It's quite simple," she explained to Larry. "We'll organize the files in alphabetical order, then each morning we can retrieve whatever is on the embassy agenda."

Little did she know that Benedict lurked behind her like the Grim Reaper, waiting for the chance to pounce.

"International diplomacy is not arranged in alphabetical order, Miss Klein," he snapped out. "I want my office files arranged by diplomatic alliances, with separate files for short-term problems and long-term strategic objectives. Don't encourage my secretary to emulate your slipshod behavior."

That was typical of her interactions with Benedict, who was the living embodiment of a prophet of doom. After failing to get her sent back to America, he seemed determined to look down his stern nose at everything she did. He made her first week feel like a month, triggering a round of homesickness for New York so acute she had to fight the temptation to take the earnings from her first paycheck and flee home. Only her loyalty to the Gerards kept her in Berlin.

On Friday evening she retreated to her bedroom in exhaustion, even though it was only seven o'clock. If she had been back home, she'd be going out with Eduardo to Coney Island or sharing a banana split with him in an ice cream parlor. Instead, she curled up alone in her bedroom to write a letter to Delia:

Hello Delia,

I have just completed my first week at the American Embassy in Berlin! Dee, I work in an actual palace that was once owned by a German princess. The first floor has a ballroom, three reception halls, and a kitchen that can cook for hundreds of people. Such a change from the sloppy Port of New York!

I share an office with a peculiar man named Larry, who never stops complaining about this or that, but he's nice enough. Our desks face each other in a compact room that had once been a storage closet back when the princess owned the palace. Thankfully, I get to be with Mr. Gerard most of the day, taking dictation or handling his calendar.

Mr. and Mrs. Gerard live in a private apartment on the top floor of the palace, while the rest of the staff live at the Alton House and a chauffeur drives us to work each day. We have breakfast and dinner at a cozy table in the kitchen. I've made friends with almost all of them, except the grumpy cook and a wet blanket named Benedict, who is the chief of staff.

People claim that Benedict is smart and good at his job, but he rarely says anything. While the rest of us gossip and have fun at meals, Benedict sits at the end of the table and does nothing but listen. Behind his sneaky eyes, he's constantly finding fault or calculating how to suck all the joy from the world.

The Gerards are famous for entertaining, and one of my jobs is to help arrange parties for high-society people. Can you imagine? Almost every weekend they either have a fancy dinner, a garden party, or a sporting tournament.

Berlin is wonderful, but I'm a little lonesome for New York. Please don't tell anyone! I even miss baseball. After years of suffering through baseball games with every man I've ever courted, I actually long for a lazy Saturday afternoon in the bleachers. I miss the smell of popcorn and the crack of the bat against the ball and cheering my head off with the rest of the crowd. Berlin is far too formal for such frivolity.

The possibility of a war has everyone gloomy and on edge. The ambassador and Benedict think there might be a chance to keep it to a small, isolated conflict between Serbia and Austria-Hungary. The embassy is hosting a garden party tomorrow because Mr. Gerard is determined to keep people's spirits up. The guest list is filled with artists and aristocrats and "very important people," as Benedict would say. He warns that I shouldn't talk to anyone because he thinks I'm stupid and might somehow trigger a war all on my own.

Wish me well. And if I accidentally start a war at Mr. Gerard's garden party, please remember me fondly.

Inga

Despite her good cheer in the letter to Delia, Inga was mildly terrified of facilitating her first garden party at the embassy. There was no such thing as a "modest garden party" for seventy-five aristocrats, diplomats, and high-profile guests from all over Europe.

Larry was on hand to help, but his anxious nerves made things worse. Nevertheless, Mr. Gerard brought Inga to Germany to spread good cheer at the embassy, and it was time to deliver.

Mrs. Gerard would be busy with hostess duties, so Inga's job was to ensure things ran like clockwork behind the scenes. She and Larry would monitor the party and orchestrate the serving staff. It was the grandest event she'd ever witnessed as an army of caterers took over the kitchen to prepare tiny sandwiches, miniature quiches, and darling teacakes. Towering floral arrangements decorated the patio and an ice sculpture of a swan with outstretched wings had been wheeled into the garden. A string quartet played Mozart while uniformed waiters circulated with flutes of champagne and hors d'oeuvres on silver trays.

Inga and Larry retreated to the salon once the guests had all arrived and been led into the garden. Now their job was to monitor the party through the open French doors and be on hand to facilitate anything Mrs. Gerard needed. A vase filled with gladiolas, gardenias, and daffodils provided a partial screen as they secretly ogled the elegant people swanning about on the terrace, sipping champagne, and talking in low voices. The men wore ordinary suits, but the ladies had on long gowns in silky shades of peach and lilac and aquamarine.

The garden party was as lovely as a painting, and yet something seemed off. She couldn't put her finger on it, but people weren't at ease. Nobody was laughing or terribly engaged in conversation. Nobody seemed happy.

Larry agreed. "Everyone is worried about the political situation." He sneezed, then nodded to a cluster of men huddled near the ice sculpture, and she spotted her nemesis, Benedict Kincaid, looking typically cheerless. "Those men are diplomats from other embassies," Larry said. "You'll meet them eventually. Most of them are from the nations doing their best not to choose sides. Look! There's Claude Debussy."

Inga brightened at the sight of the famous composer. Who

could have imagined that such a giant in the world of music was so short in real life? He looked bored, or perhaps those heavily lidded eyes always made him look sleepy.

Would she ever get used to being around such distinguished people?

Larry sneezed again and apologized for his hay fever. "These gardenias are pure torture," he said with a nod to the towering floral arrangement they hid behind. "I'll be lucky to survive the next few hours without fainting."

"You poor dear," Inga said. "I had no idea you were suffering from the flowers. Let me move them for you."

"No, no," Larry rushed to say. "Mrs. Gerard placed them there herself."

Inga brushed his concerns aside. "She didn't know about your hay fever or she wouldn't have set them here." It would be easy to move the vase a few yards onto the terrace and spare Larry such misery.

The stoneware vase was heavy as she lifted it, her face plunged into the fragrant petals. Yet she could see well enough through the profusion of blooms as she carried it a few yards outside. There! She found a spot for it on a table where it could be appreciated by everyone.

Benedict sent her a poisonous glance before she scurried back to hiding in the salon. Maybe she'd been in America too long, but she didn't think appearing at the party for thirty seconds to reposition some flowers had tainted the air with her low-class presence. She felt his glare drilling into her back as she returned to the salon.

"Why does Benedict have to be so grim all the time?" she groused.

"Don't mind him," Larry said. "Nobody is happy today. The deadline on the war ultimatum is getting near, so the sword of Damocles is hanging over everyone's head. We're all afraid it is about to drop."

Inga couldn't do anything about the war, but she could help

make this party a success. A grand piano sat unused in the corner of the salon, and it had wheels.

"Why don't we ask Mr. Debussy to play something for us?" she asked. "We could wheel the piano onto the terrace and listen to something more appealing than the dirge coming from the dreary string quartet."

Larry twisted his hands. "I imagine Mr. Debussy would prefer to enjoy the reception instead of performing for a crowd."

"Let's go see, shall we?" She didn't wait for him to respond. Mr. Debussy looked as glum as the others at the party, and he could always decline if he didn't want to play.

She cautiously approached the group surrounding Mr. Debussy, where a Spanish diplomat droned on about the amount of rainfall this summer. That settled it. Anytime the conversation resorted to a discussion about the weather, emergency remedies were needed. When the Spanish diplomat paused for a sip of champagne, Inga inserted herself into the group to speak with Mr. Debussy.

"Sir, we have a piano just inside the salon. If we wheeled it into the garden, would you be willing to play something for us?"

"Ha!" Mr. Debussy said. "I've been silently praying that someone would ask. I'd be delighted."

She flashed a grin to Larry, hovering in the doorway of the salon, then hurried inside to help him wheel the piano onto the terrace. Benedict must have noticed because he blocked the cumbersome advance of the piano before they could get it through the open doors.

"What are you doing?" he hissed.

"Mr. Debussy wants to play for us," she said. Moving the piano required considerable strength to wheel it through the opening of the salon and onto the flagstone patio, and Mr. Debussy soon joined in to help push it through.

Mary Gerard noticed the commotion and hurried to the salon. Inga silently cringed. She didn't mind overstepping with Benedict, but perhaps she should have asked Mrs. Gerard's permission.

"It's not too late to wheel it back if you object," Inga hurried to say.

Mary leaned in close to whisper, "My dear, I only wish I'd thought of this myself."

People began gathering around, some of the ladies even calling out requests. Rather than play one of his own compositions, Mr. Debussy broke into a fantasia by Rachmaninoff, and it was spectacular. A newfound vitality brightened the atmosphere. Even the leaves stirring in the summer breeze seemed to be part of the magnificent crescendo as the melody enveloped the garden.

"Bravo!" a Russian duke called out from the far side of the terrace.

Inga watched the performance from the open salon doors and couldn't stop smiling. Guests abandoned their dreary conversations and gathered around the piano. Some of the serving staff began hovering in the salon too. It was a once-in-a-lifetime opportunity to hear a master at his craft.

Laughter and applause greeted the end of the Rachmaninoff performance, and then Mr. Debussy launched into one of his own compositions. The delicate melody of "Clair de lune" filled the air, the dreamy longing in the music casting an enchanted spell through the garden. Everyone paused to listen. Even Mr. Gerard and his group of diplomats at the far end of the garden turned to listen.

This was the right thing to have done. Anyone who heard Claude Debussy play "Clair de lune" on a warm summer afternoon would never forget it.

Inga was so entranced she didn't notice the darkening weather until a fat raindrop landed on the flagstone patio in front of her. Then another.

Larry groaned. "Oh boy, here it comes."

A cool wind gusted through the shrubbery lining the yard, bringing a spatter of heavy droplets pelting the ground. Ladies squealed and dashed for cover.

The piano!

"Oh, Larry, please help me get the piano inside," she begged, but he'd already fled, both hands shielding his head from the sudden downpour unleashing from the sky. The crush of people came running toward the salon doors, making it hard to fight through them to get to the piano. Somebody knocked over the towering floral arrangement, which smashed against the flagstones.

She ran to save the piano. It was heavy and barely moved an inch as she shoved it toward the open doorway. Benedict appeared, looking furious as he joined her. Rolling it inside was much easier once Benedict's forceful push got it going, but they were both sopping wet by the time they got the piano through the salon doors.

Inga couldn't tell if people were happy or horrified. Everyone was talking at once as the rain hissed against the slate terrace. Mary dispatched the servants to fetch every dry towel in the embassy while Inga blotted the piano's ivory keys with her handkerchief, but it was hopeless. This piano probably cost more than she would earn in her entire life. Could a piano survive getting drenched?

To her delight, Mr. Debussy sat down before the keyboard and commenced playing a lively tune that immediately set the crowd at ease. Some of them laughed, some applauded, while others went directly back to their conversations that had been interrupted by the downpour.

Inga grabbed a stack of towels from a maid and helped distribute them. Nobody was sopping wet except her, Benedict, and the grand piano. She found a spot in the corner to discreetly dry off as the music continued, which sounded different now from what it had been like before the drenching. Some notes sounded clear as a bell, but others had a muffled, discordant quality to them.

"I shall take requests!" Mr. Debussy called out at the completion of the song. Had there ever been a more memorable afternoon? It was a tight fit in the salon, but the rain had injected a bolt of energy and excitement into the group.

Inga twisted her hands as another sour note rose from the soaked piano. Would the instrument sound better once it was completely dry?

Suddenly, Mr. Debussy stopped playing. Chatter among the crowd settled, and Inga looked up, searching for whatever had cast a pall on the gathering.

A man in uniform stood in the entrance to the salon. Tall, grim, and dressed in the uniform from the German Imperial Court. He walked straight to Ambassador Gerard, clicked his heels, and handed him a message.

Mr. Gerard popped the seal and read. Even from across the room, Inga saw the color drain from his face.

"My friends, Germany has just declared war against Russia. Declarations of war with France and Britain are expected imminently."

A wave of dizziness descended on her. It was happening. Rain and garden parties and ruined pianos no longer mattered because half the world was about to be at war. Benedict had warned them to expect this, but somehow she didn't really believe it would happen.

The Russian duke strode from the room, his wife trailing behind him. The Germans left too. Mr. Debussy was French, and he joined a cluster of Frenchmen near the far windows to confer.

Already people were retreating to their sides, and the earlier joyful mood of the party vanished. The sunlight was gone, the music over, and she feared it would be a long time before any of them would know such a carefree afternoon again.

7

Pounding on her bedroom door awakened Inga the following morning. She bolted upright, baffled because it was still dark.

"Wake up, Miss Klein. We've got work to do and must leave for the embassy in ten minutes."

She pulled on a robe and hurried to answer her door. Benedict had already moved on and pounded on Andrew's door, delivering the same message.

"I hoped to go to church," she called out to Benedict.

There was no change in Benedict's expression. "There's already a line forming outside the embassy, filled with anxious Americans who want to get home. No time for church. It's going to be a long day, so hurry up. We leave in nine minutes."

There was no point in arguing when he was this stern. She splashed cold water on her face, then pulled on a blouse and her honeysuckle yellow suit. She wouldn't put it past Benedict to leave her behind if she wasn't ready when McFee arrived with the automobile. She scooped up her boots, stockings, a hair ribbon, and hurried downstairs in bare feet.

Everyone else was bleary-eyed too, but at least Mrs. Barnes

packed some sandwiches from yesterday's garden party for them to eat on the short drive over. Inga sat on the bottom step while hooking up her boots.

"Why are people coming to the embassy?" she asked Andrew.

"They all need passports to get out of Germany."

"What's a passport?"

Andrew's mouth dropped open in astonishment. She must have just said something terribly stupid, but Andrew explained that passports were official documents well-traveled people used to expedite crossing national borders. Normally they weren't necessary, but Germany announced that they were about to start requiring them from everyone leaving the country.

"The Germans are afraid men of military age might try to flee the country," Andrew explained. "Anyone who wants to leave will need to prove they aren't German. That's what a passport does."

A queasy feeling lurched as Inga absorbed the information. "Do I need a passport?"

Andrew shook his head. "Probably not, since the ambassador can vouch you've lived in America for most of your life."

Relief flooded her as they boarded the Pierce-Arrow limousine to set off for the embassy. McFee drove, and he hadn't even had a chance to put on his chauffeur's uniform. Eight people crammed into a car built for seven meant they were shoulder to shoulder. She was mashed against Benedict's side, which probably annoyed him to no end. Everything she did seemed to annoy him, especially when she started finger-combing her hair.

"Get your hair out of my face," he groused.

She gathered the long fall of her hair over her other shoulder to weave it into a loose braid. Without a mirror, a braid was the best she could manage to control her wild mane of hair. Corkscrew curls didn't obey orders, and she tied a ribbon around the end.

To her amazement, the line of people snaked all the way down the front path of the embassy and around the block. Hundreds of them!

"Everybody out," Benedict said the instant the automobile stopped rolling. She was closest to the door and hopped out first.

A man carrying a suitcase and wearing a bowler hat approached. "Are you the embassy staff?"

"We are," Benedict confirmed.

"When are you opening up?"

"In about five minutes. Hang on."

People in the crowd looked anxious and uneasy. Everything suddenly felt terribly real. Inga scurried to catch up to Larry, grabbing his elbow. "I don't know what I'm supposed to do," she whispered.

"I don't either," he whispered back.

Benedict overheard and scowled. "We are going to process twenty thousand passports for every American in Berlin who wants to leave," he said. "Brace yourself. This crowd is desperate to get out of the country before the shooting starts, and we are their only hope of getting that piece of paper."

Inga gulped, wishing she could be on her way to New York as well.

Benedict concentrated on getting a production line set up inside the embassy ballroom. Worktables were placed at intervals, each staffed with an embassy clerk and a stack of passport applications. He arranged for the Marines living at the Soldat Barracks to come help with the processing. He sent a clerk to a printer to run off five thousand copies of passport applications as soon as possible. In the meantime, the staff interviewed each applicant, asking a handful of questions to verify they were eligible for an American passport.

They were from all walks of life, but most were students, businessmen, and tourists. Others were people who had been born in Germany but immigrated to America decades earlier. They had been in the country visiting relatives or on business, and so getting them a passport was going to be a challenge.

The case of Dr. Werner Haas was typical. Dr. Haas was a physician, making him a valuable asset for a nation heading into war. He was fifty-nine and too old to join the army, but not too old to serve in a hospital.

"Sir, I appeal to your sense of justice," Dr. Haas implored in a heavy German accent. "I have lived in Philadelphia for thirty-five years. I am an American citizen. My children and grandchildren were born in Philadelphia. I own a home in Philadelphia. I came to Berlin for my mother's funeral, and now I am not permitted to leave?"

"I'm going to help you, but it will take time," Benedict assured the older man. "We'll need to wire to Philadelphia to confirm your residency, then we'll expedite your passport as soon as possible."

He led the man to the room where Larry and Inga were busy sending wires. Inga concluded her message first, and Benedict introduced her to Dr. Haas.

"Inga, this is Dr. Haas. I need you to wire his name and address to the mayor's office in Philadelphia to confirm his residency. Send a similar message to his church to document how long he's been a member there."

It was a more rigorous procedure than most applicants, but the Germans might try to block Dr. Haas from leaving unless his paperwork was flawless. Even as he spoke, Benedict sensed tension rising from the older man, who gritted his teeth and choked back a curse.

Inga's smile was gentle as she guided the older man to a chair. "Have a seat," she said, her soft voice filled with reassuring cheer. "And don't worry. We're going to get you home, okay?"

The man visibly relaxed, even though he still looked ready to weep. "Thank you," he stammered.

Benedict returned to the reception hall, now overheated with hundreds of people lined up before the ten tables. Ambassador Gerard hadn't stopped jabbering on the reception hall telephone ever since they started processing applications. Benedict had overheard a few snatches of his conversation about tickets and box seats and dinner arrangements. For pity's sake, it sounded like Gerard was worried over his opera tickets being canceled. Mrs. Gerard kept running to-and-fro like an eager puppy, even tilting the telephone receiver to listen in on her husband's call, giggling and grinning and annoying Benedict to no end.

A panicked man from Milwaukee reported that his son, a young man of eighteen, wanted to volunteer to fight for the Germans. The man's English was so bad that Benedict switched to German to ask if his son was an American citizen.

"*Ist Ihr Sohn amerikanischer Staatsbürger?*"

"*Ja!*" the man replied forcefully. He went on to report that the boy was born and raised in Milwaukee, but always loved Germany and was fluent in the language. This was his first trip abroad; the boy made fast friends with his German cousins, and all of them were on fire to join the military.

"Please," he begged. "Jacob is my only child. He doesn't even know what this war is about, and now he will become cannon fodder. Please help get him out."

There wasn't much Benedict could do. He could get the young man a passport but couldn't force him to board a ship to go home. Benedict sagged in his chair as he watched the man depart. The lines of people at the tables for American citizens moved much faster. The clicking of typewriter keys and thumping of papers being stamped and stapled were the sounds of progress.

Meanwhile, Benedict's line moved at a snail's pace since he handled the troublesome cases of people who'd been born in Germany. The next two people approaching his table were elderly German nuns, swathed in black habits.

"Someone tried to block you from leaving?" he asked.

"*Ja,*" the younger nun replied. "They think we are spies for the Vatican. I told him we are nuns from Brooklyn who only came to celebrate the anniversary of our holy order."

Benedict frowned as he began the paperwork. Paranoia was to

be expected in the early days of any conflict, and these two old ladies were going to be forced to prove their innocence before the German Foreign Office would let them leave. He wrote out instructions for Larry to contact the nuns' convent in Brooklyn to begin the process of verifying their identities.

He'd just begun taking the information from his next case, a father with a wife and twin toddlers, when Ambassador Gerard inserted himself at the front of the line, pushing aside a haggard mother holding a squirming toddler.

"Success!" Ambassador Gerard chortled, oblivious to the poisonous look from the mother he had just elbowed. Benedict could use some good news, but if this involved opera tickets, he'd be tempted to strangle the ambassador.

"I have chartered a steamship to carry Americans back home. The Holland American Steamship line shall have slots reserved for eight hundred American citizens to sail for New York on Friday."

Benedict rocked back in his chair, stunned at the extraordinary news. He stood and offered a handshake. "Well done, sir."

Ambassador Gerard pumped his hand. "Thank you! It gets better. I had to pay the fees myself in order to secure the berths, but I'll spring for the first shipload of passengers from my own pocket. Going forward, the weekly sailings will have a hundred berths reserved for Americans wishing to get home. My wife shall set up a table in the dining room, and anyone who wants a berth can come pick up tickets as soon as we have them."

It was beyond generous. The Gerards were among the wealthiest people in America, but leasing a steamship was still a major expense. It was especially valuable because word had been sent that Germany had frozen all foreign bank accounts to stave off a run on their currency.

By two o'clock in the afternoon, hunger began to claw. They'd brought cheese and crackers from Alton House, but the cheese was gone because Inga started doling it out to hungry people waiting in line. It was Sunday, so the markets and restaurants were all closed.

Inga looked affronted when he told her to quit giving away their food, but at least they still had plenty of crackers left.

He was about to return to his desk when he spotted a familiar figure wandering into the processing room.

"Fräulein Zinnia?" he asked in surprise. The aristocratic young German woman was not someone he expected to see at the embassy. It looked as if she was on the verge of tears.

"Mr. Kincaid!" she said, grasping his arm. "My father's butler reports he was arrested in London. The British won't let him leave."

"Why have they arrested him?" Benedict asked.

"Because he's German, and they think he might be a spy. It's ridiculous! My father was in England to teach a class at Oxford. Please, is there anything you can do?"

What a disaster. Baron Werner von Eschenbach was an Anglophile whose moderating influence on easing relations between Germany and the British could have been helpful. Arresting him was the height of stupidity, but tempers were running hot.

"Do you know where he was taken?"

"I have no idea, and I don't know what to do."

Zinnia couldn't go to the British Embassy for help since a state of war made it impossible. Only the neutral nations still had open diplomatic channels to find Baron von Eschenbach and arrange for his release.

Negotiating between the warring nations was going to become one of his new duties. As more nations descended into the abyss of war, Benedict prayed the United States could remain a voice of sanity in a world spiraling out of control.

Closing the embassy that night was a challenge, as the line of Americans desperate to obtain a passport still stretched around the block. Benedict instructed the Marine Guard to spread the word that the embassy would close at nine o'clock and would reopen at eight the following morning. He hoped people would heed the message and disperse, but dozens of people still lingered outside at closing time. Benedict ordered the Marines to stand by as they boarded the waiting automobile to get back to Alton House. Even so, a few in the waiting crowd castigated them for leaving when people still needed passports.

Those people were probably in no mood to hear that the staff had been on duty for twelve hours, and that they had more work ahead of them at home tonight. Benedict put a sheltering arm around Inga as she hurried toward the car. He eyed the crowd and held the car door as the others scrambled aboard. He was the last to squeeze inside, pulling the door shut behind them with a resounding thud.

"Thank goodness that's over!" Inga said once the wheels started rolling.

"It's not over," Benedict said dryly. "Today was merely the opening salvo. Brace yourself for the ensuing barrage tomorrow morning. There are an estimated thirty thousand Americans stranded behind German lines, so we have an avalanche of work ahead of us. As soon as we get home, we will meet in the kitchen for a quick meal and do a postmortem of our performance today."

Everyone in the car looked aghast, except Inga, who chimed in with her typically bright, curious tone. "What's a postmortem?"

"It's an examination of a dead body to account for why the patient died," Andrew said. "Thank you for that lovely assessment of our work today."

Andrew sounded annoyed, but Inga burst out laughing. "You're so funny," she said and nudged Benedict's arm, prompting a pleasant, tingling sensation to flare from where she'd touched him. It must be the exhaustion because Inga Klein was the last woman on the planet who ought to appeal to him.

"I'm not funny, I'm serious. In the coming days our work is going to get harder as the reality of war sinks in and more people decide to evacuate. Today was a trial by fire, but now we have a better understanding of the problems and which areas to improve. I'll ask Mrs. Barnes to make us some sandwiches, and then we'll discuss our plan for tomorrow."

"We've had nothing but crackers all day," Larry grumbled. "I have a weak constitution and could use something more substantial. Can't we have a proper dinner?"

Everyone was famished, and Benedict was in no mood for whining. "Sandwiches are perfectly adequate. We have got important work to do, so choke them down and quit complaining."

"Cheer up," Inga told Larry. "Maybe there are some cold oats left."

Dead silence reigned for approximately two seconds before everyone else burst out laughing. It wasn't even funny, but Larry chortled so loudly it hurt Benedict's ears. The laughter went on and on. Andrew had to wipe tears from his eyes. Why was everyone following Inga's lead instead of his own? They were heading into a crisis, yet Inga never missed an opportunity to poke fun.

He was still annoyed as they arrived at Alton House, dark and closed up for the night. Inga ran ahead into the kitchen, and her voice was as bright and cheerful as though she hadn't just worked twelve straight hours.

"Oh, look," she chimed from the dark recesses of the kitchen. "Mrs. Barnes made us a huge pot of chicken and dumplings. And an apple pie!"

Benedict strode toward the kitchen, which smelled amazing. Sure enough, a large pot of stew was in the warming oven, and Inga was already cutting the apple pie into slices. Plates and silverware clattered as people began lining up, and everything smelled so good he was tempted to scoop up a spoonful directly from the pot. Instead, he waited until everyone else had filled their bowls before he helped himself to a serving of meaty chicken and dumplings, his mouth watering at the prospect.

Chatter abounded as he joined the others around the kitchen table. Everyone had a story to tell about interesting people who'd flooded the embassy today. A group of traveling acrobats from San Francisco, a student from Chicago training to become a church organist, a traveling salesman from Cincinnati selling coonskin hats. The embassy staff had been hunkered down at their posts all day, and it felt good to touch base and simply share for a while.

In a few hours it would begin again, and they needed to do a postmortem on their operations today. Maybe he could think of a better term for it that wouldn't leave him wide open to Inga's teasing. An assessment of their operations? An audit? None of it sounded any friendlier than "postmortem," but perhaps there was a way to phrase things in a more positive manner.

Their biggest problem was the lack of preprinted forms. They ran out of passport applications before lunch. It was anyone's guess as to whether a printer would be able to supply more.

"Maybe we should buy our own duplicating machine," Inga suggested. "That way we won't be at the mercy of the printer." She went on to describe a mimeograph machine, which she used at her former job in New York. Benedict once considered buying one of the hand-cranked duplicating machines for the embassy but rejected it in the interest of staying on good terms with the local printers. Germans weren't overly friendly to foreigners in the best of times, and patronizing the local tradesmen seemed a politically astute decision.

"Aren't those copying machines terribly difficult to use?" Larry asked, casting a worried look over the top of his spectacles.

"Not at all," Inga said. "So long as you've got the right carbon-backed paper, any typewriter can make a master copy of a form, then run off copies on a rotating drum. I've done it a million times. Can I get anyone seconds on chicken? There's plenty left."

She thoughtfully refilled bowls for Andrew and Colonel Reyes, but Benedict kept his arms folded. He'd get his own refill before he'd accept help from Inga.

Why he wouldn't let her do a favor for him didn't warrant too much scrutiny. It would be best to keep her at arm's length. Inga's riot of blond curls spilling over her shoulders was continually distracting. Her soft smile that was never far beneath the surface was appealing and warm and well . . . sexy.

He dragged his mind back to the business at hand. "Miss Klein, please look into the viability of purchasing a mimeograph machine for the embassy. Larry, contact the Corps of Engineers and see if they can spare us another wireless operator. I propose we ask the Marine Guard to establish order among the crowds that will be forming outside the embassy. Can I entrust that to you, Colonel Reyes?"

"Certainly," he replied.

Benedict nodded. Exhaustion tugged, but it was a good sort of exhaustion. It came from a job well done. Although they'd made mistakes today, they succeeded in helping hundreds of people on their journey home. While darkness began engulfing the world, the people in this room had worked in tandem to stave it back while creating an avenue of escape for countless people. They would keep the beacon of hope lit at the embassy until everyone who wished to escape back to America could get there.

8

Over the coming days, the crush of Americans desperate to leave Germany intensified, challenging Inga's ability to swiftly send and receive telegrams. There wasn't a line outside the embassy each morning; it was a mob. They weren't violent, but thousands of desperate Americans packed the front of the embassy every day.

In the first week of the war, she sent out over two hundred telegrams to cities all over the United States, seeking verification of people's citizenship. Soon the replies started coming in, and she was now fielding as many incoming telegrams as outgoing ones. Almost all the incoming messages were positive, affirming citizenship and allowing Benedict to grant a passport.

Sending and receiving Morse code demanded complete concentration, but a niggling worry tugged at the back of her mind. Could her lack of citizenship be a problem? She had lived in America for sixteen years but never bothered to apply for it. Why should she? It cost four dollars to take the test, and there wasn't any need for it. It wasn't as if women could vote or serve on a jury, so why waste the four dollars to become a citizen?

Andrew assured her that a lack of a passport wasn't a problem for her, although he might not know she wasn't an American citizen, and Mr. Gerard was too busy for her to ask. He was completely distracted by meetings as one nation after another got sucked into the war. It felt like the whole world was going to war, and Inga gave thanks to God and President Wilson for keeping America out of it.

Two weeks after the outbreak of war, the chaos at the embassy began to ease, and Inga hoped to find time during her lunch break to ask Mr. Gerard about her citizenship problem, but he was busy posing for a formal portrait in the ballroom. It was an odd portrait because the ballroom had been transformed into a workaday office to handle passport duties. Mr. Gerard posed before a huge gilt mirror and pretended to survey the ongoing operations like a general reviewing the troops. The photographer posed him at several different angles, some close up and others back far enough to capture the entire room.

"Why such a strange portrait?" she asked Mr. Gerard after the photographer completed his work.

"We are living through a momentous time," Mr. Gerard said. "Someday it shall be pleasing to remember these things."

It was already pleasing for Inga because she'd never felt so needed in her entire life, but it was hard to smile when she was so nervous about her legal status.

"When you have a moment, can I ask you a question in your office?"

"You can have a moment right now, my dear."

She followed him through the gilded halls into the less imposing privacy of his walnut-lined office. It was blessedly quiet after the echoey ballroom with its harried voices and the incessant clatter of typewriters. Now all she could hear was the thudding of her own heart.

"I'm sorry to disturb you with my piddly, insignificant problems," she began.

"Ha! Inga, you've been bothering me with your problems

since I found you in that church, and have I ever minded? Out with it!"

She clenched her fists and stared at a spot on the wall as she confessed her lack of American citizenship, but mercifully, Mr. Gerard waved her concerns away.

"You are under my protection," he assured her. "I can easily vouch for your long-term residency in the United States."

Her heart warmed with fondness. If she lived to be a hundred, she would always be grateful for this man's openhearted generosity and good humor. And yet she'd feel better if she could get her citizenship. Mr. Gerard could be recalled by the president at any moment, and then what?

"Could you help me become a citizen while we're here in Berlin?"

The humor faded from his face. "Confidentially, I can't do anything that will rock the boat. I'm already on thin ice at the German chancellery. They've been in a bad mood ever since the war broke out and have been demanding concessions I have no authority to grant."

"Such as?"

His shoulders sagged. "They want the United States to stop trading with the British and cut off food supplies to the French. We're a neutral nation, but they view our trading as siding with the enemy, even though we still trade with Germany too. The ice is getting thinner and thinner beneath us. But enough about that! What's this I hear about some mechanical copying machine about to arrive? Larry said it was your idea."

She nodded with a smile. "The mimeograph is arriving later today. We're constantly running out of blank forms because the printer says he's been deluged with war work, and our business has become a low priority for him."

With luck, the mimeograph machine might even force Benedict to finally admit that Inga had good ideas and was a worthy secretary for the American Embassy.

Benedict wished there was anyone else in the universe he could ask for help setting up the new mimeograph machine, but Inga was the only person at the embassy who'd ever used one. The machine had already been set on a table in the butler's pantry, which had been converted to a storage closet since the outbreak of the war. The walk-in closet had a large table that was formerly used for polishing silver, but now held the bulky new machine. The floor-to-ceiling shelves intended for bottles of wine and crystal goblets now held office supplies. The butler's pantry had plenty of space for one person, yet it was cramped with him and Inga. She was so close, he couldn't escape the lemony scent of her hair.

The mimeograph machine was about the size of a horse saddle, with a paper tray, a hand-turned crank, and a rotating metal drum.

"The ink goes into this chamber, where it will soak a pad," Inga began, looking impossibly lovely in a sage-green suit with a spray of lilies of the valley pinned to her lapel. When she had the time to clip flowers from the garden was a mystery, although hardly relevant at this point.

Larry haunted the open doorway. "The smell of that ink is giving me a sinus headache. I don't think I'm going to be able to use that thing."

"The ink is odorless," Inga said. "What you're smelling comes from the waxed-paper stencils we'll use to make the master copy for printing. See?"

She held up a blank page backed with carbon paper, then explained how she'd use a typewriter to turn the carbon page into a stencil. Once made, the waxy master copy would be wrapped around the rotating drum. A clerk would crank the drum, and rubber wheels would roll blank pages against the master stencil. Inga boasted she could make two hundred freshly inked copies of any document they needed in five minutes.

"I've already typed up a test stencil, and as soon as I've got the machine filled with ink, I can give everyone a lesson on how to make copies." She smiled at him in that relentlessly cheerful way, as though she expected him to return her sunny enthusiasm.

"I'll let you and Larry finish setting it up," he said, anxious to get away from her. Being trapped in this confined space stirred too many uncomfortable thoughts, and he needed to send another batch of messages to the foreign office.

He hadn't gotten very far when Inga's panicked voice stopped him.

"Help!" she cried out, and he dropped the paperwork to run back to the butler's pantry. Inga stood aghast beside the new machine, her hands held out and dripping with ink that splattered on the hardwood floor. A tin funnel rolled in the puddle of ink on the floor, creating a half-moon ink stain.

"It wasn't my fault!" Larry said. "You should have let me use the funnel."

"I didn't need the funnel," Inga retorted. "You shouldn't have shoved it at me once I started pouring the ink!" Inga looked at Benedict in desperation, her hands stretched out and still dribbling ink. "Please help. This suit cost more than I earn in a month."

"Don't move," Benedict said, hurrying into the kitchen for a rag.

"Stop, come back!" Inga called out after him. "I need you *here*."

He ignored her while soaking a rag beneath the kitchen tap. What sane woman would handle a gallon of ink while wearing such fine clothing? He squeezed the rag out and grabbed a stack of dry ones before heading back to the pantry.

"Where did you go?" she demanded. "The solvent for cleaning this is right here in the box of carbon stencils."

How was he supposed to know that? "Let me have your hands," he said, enveloping them in the damp towel. Inga kept complaining he wasn't doing it right, that the machine came with a whole gallon of cleaning solvent and water wouldn't work, and if he hadn't disappeared so quickly, she would have explained that.

He peeled the towel back to inspect her hands. The inky stain remained, but at least her suit was no longer in danger.

"Your suit is fine," he said bluntly, which was better than his own shirt. Somehow his left cuff got a smear of ink against the snowy white linen, and it would probably never come out. He tossed the ruined towel into the wastebasket, then reached for the jug of solvent. It released a pungent stink after he twisted the cap off.

Larry recoiled. "That stench is making me dizzy. I need to get out of here."

"Wait, check your feet first," Benedict ordered because he had stupidly stepped into the puddle of ink on the floor and tracked it into the kitchen. Now he had a ruined pair of shoes too.

"My feet are fine," Larry said. "My sinuses are not."

"Then go," Benedict ordered. The more people near that puddle of ink, the bigger problem they'd make. He glared at Inga as he held the jug of solvent in one hand, a rag in the other. "How am I supposed to use this stuff?"

"I have no idea."

"You just howled at me that I was wrong to get the rags, and you don't even know what you're doing?" He squinted to read the tiny print of instructions on the jug of solvent. It didn't need to be diluted, and it was perfectly fine to use on skin, just dab and swipe.

"Hurry up," Inga ordered. "If you hadn't abandoned me with Larry, this never would have happened." Friendly, kind Inga was gone, replaced by angry, snippy Inga. *He* was the one with the ruined shirt and shoes. He ought to be working on salvaging his expensive Italian leather shoes instead of rushing to her rescue. He tipped a little cleaning solvent onto a new rag, then reached for her hand. Getting the ink off wasn't as easy as the instructions implied. Some of the ink smeared onto the rag, but her hands were still stained.

"We're standing on a handmade parquet floor," he grumbled. "Do you know how much work goes into the creation of a parquet floor? It's been here since the palace was built in 1790. It's survived fires and civil wars and Napoleon's march through Berlin, but it couldn't last two months with you living here."

"It wasn't my fault," Inga defended. "Larry shoved the funnel at me while I was already pouring."

"Why didn't you take sixty seconds to outline your procedure instead of barging ahead without warning? Getting this machine was a stupid idea."

"Ha!" Inga retorted. "You were using a nineteenth century printing press to make your essential office documents. Think about *that*!"

"Shut up, Claudia." He instantly caught his mistake and corrected it. "Miss Klein."

Inga sucked in a quick breath. "Who is Claudia?"

"She's nobody," he bit out, working the cloth a little faster and praying Inga would let his gaffe pass. The only time in his entire life he'd ever been reduced to shouting matches with a woman had been with Claudia, and it was mortifying that her name had slipped from his lips. She and Inga couldn't be more different, except that Claudia was dead and Inga was very much alive and there to torment him every hour of each day.

He forced his breathing to remain calm, marveling at how tiny Inga's hands felt inside his palms, and wishing this solution would work faster so he could get away from her. He soaked another rag with more solution and kept working.

"Tell me how those stencils are going to be made," he said, desperate for something to latch on to other than Claudia, or the way Inga's head nestled right below his jaw and how perfectly she would fit against him.

"You're not going to talk about Claudia?"

"Very perceptive, Miss Klein. Who's going to type the stencils?"

"I am." He only half listened as she explained that carbon paper was expensive and mistakes were difficult to correct, so only a skilled typist should be charged with the task.

The ink finally began dissolving from her fingers. It required rubbing the rag slowly. Too fast and it wasn't effective, but a slow wipe with just the right amount of pressure seemed to work as he pulled the rag down each finger. A little more ink vanished with each pass. Such long fingers she had. Maybe that's why she was such a fast typist.

Footsteps sounded down the hall, and Larry appeared. "We're out of passport applications," he announced.

Benedict released Inga's hand and gave her the rag. It wouldn't do to be seen helping Inga with something she could manage on her own.

"Inga, type up a passport application stencil," he ordered.

Benedict returned to his office, trying to forget about how perfectly her slim hand fit within his own.

9

SEPTEMBER 1914

Whenever Benedict needed to read the ambassador the riot act, they took a walk along the Bellevuestrasse. The tree-lined street took them to the Tiergarten, the largest park in Berlin, with six hundred acres of trees, ponds, and meandering walkways. Once it had been a hunting preserve for royalty. Now it was the only place Benedict could be certain there weren't spies listening in on his conversation with the ambassador, and today's topic was a doozy. Ambassador Gerard had been personally affronted when his request to meet with Kaiser Wilhelm was rejected, and he wanted to retaliate.

"I have an important message from the president of the United States," Ambassador Gerard groused. "I want to personally deliver it into the kaiser's hands, along with a piece of my mind."

That was exactly what Benedict feared. It had been a month since the outbreak of the war, and this sort of diplomacy required the skill of a surgeon, not a bludgeon from James Gerard. The kaiser was as hot-tempered and unpredictable as Ambassador

Gerard, and cooler heads were needed to handle the first crisis between the U.S. and Germany.

The kaiser put a naval blockade around the United Kingdom and threatened to blow up any American ship attempting to trade with the British. President Wilson wanted them to reverse their decision, but Gerard lacked the diplomatic skills to accomplish the delicate negotiation.

"The president's message *will* be delivered to the kaiser, but it must go through the German Undersecretary of State," Benedict said. Undersecretary Arthur Zimmermann was a coolheaded and crafty diplomat who understood the gravity of the situation and would work with Benedict to come up with a solution to appease both the kaiser and President Wilson.

"An undersecretary is beneath my status," Mr. Gerard complained as they continued striding along the path leading into the park.

"I thought you were friendly with him," Benedict said. The two men certainly seemed friendly when they spent a weekend grouse hunting last month.

"I thought we were too! Then I read in the gossip columns that Zimmermann was offended when I said German cuisine would be better if they didn't use so much disgusting organ meat—which is completely true, by the way. Zimmermann also said he is compelled to maintain friendly terms with me on account of my position. The nerve!"

That was bound to smart, but the job of a diplomat was to rise above personal affronts in the interest of their nation.

"I understand your concern," Benedict said. "I would be perfectly happy to represent you in a private discussion with Undersecretary Zimmermann." Let the kaiser and Ambassador Gerard bluster in public, but the fate of millions of Americans depended on diplomats to quietly work their magic behind the scenes.

They continued walking along the sun-dappled path while chattering sparrows flitted in the trees above. The park could not be more idyllic. Mothers pushed baby carriages, and children rode bicycles. Only the occasional man in uniform gave any hint that the nation was at war. Ambassador Gerard paused his tirade to watch a pair of young boys lean over the rim of a splashing fountain to launch a toy sailboat.

"Why can't we all just get along?" the ambassador asked, his voice suddenly sad and tired. "I didn't come to Berlin to fight a war. We've always been friends with Germany. And the Germans are friends with England and France. None of us should have gotten into this mess."

Benedict propped a foot on the rim of the fountain, watching the toy sailboat bob in the water as it drifted closer to the cascade spilling from the tiered fountain. It was the picture of innocence, but all over the Atlantic Ocean, real warships and submarines were setting off, armed with munitions and torpedoes. Britain was surrounded by a naval blockade, and thousands of their sailors had already been killed by German U-boats. It was going to get worse in the months to come.

The toy sailboat drifted beneath a splashing cascade of water and flipped over. The two boys howled in delight as the boat floundered for a moment, then righted itself to continue bobbing in the choppy water. Would that real ships could survive so easily.

"Yesterday I saw a British man dragged off his horse by a mob and beaten within an inch of his life," the ambassador said. "The police intervened and wanted to take him to a prisoner camp. I persuaded them to take the poor chap to the hospital first, but almost got a beating myself when the crowd mistook me for an Englishman."

All across Germany the authorities were rounding up men from hostile nations and confining them in detention centers. The British and the French were doing the same thing to German civilians trapped in Allied nations. His friend Baron von Eschenbach had been arrested in London on the first day of the war. Despite the baron's wealth and connections, his family had yet to learn where he'd been imprisoned.

The baron was among the thousands of prisoners Benedict needed to help. The initial rush of Americans seeking passports had eased, and now he could address the complicated task of negotiating for prisoner release on behalf of the warring nations.

Provided the United States could maintain its neutrality, Benedict intended to ease the suffering on both sides of this senseless war.

Inga nearly levitated with excitement after finally tracking down the missing German aristocrat Benedict had been trying to find since the first day of the war. It had taken a dozen telegram exchanges, cutting through mountains of red tape and chasing countless leads, before she found Baron von Eschenbach at a civilian detention center on the outskirts of London. It felt like she'd just discovered the holy grail, and she couldn't wait to boast about her triumph to Benedict. Perhaps it would make him finally admit she was a good secretary and an asset to the embassy.

"I found your baron," she announced the moment Benedict walked through her office after a meeting at the chancellery. She savored his fleeting look of relief as he took the telegram from her.

"Good," Benedict said after reading the telegram, his expression once again reverted back to its normal moodiness. "Please set up a time when I can have a wireless exchange with the administrator of the detention center. Do so quickly."

Inga tried not to roll her eyes as he walked away. Would it have killed him to offer a word of thanks or maybe even congratulate her on a task well done? No matter what secretarial miracle she accomplished, Benedict never praised her for anything. Did he acknowledge that her mimeograph machine was infinitely better than being at the mercy of a printer? No. Did he praise her ability to keep Larry cheerful and productive during his latest bout of hay fever? No. Could he bring himself to thank her for finding Baron von Eschenbach? Of course not.

She was a good secretary. Scratch that, she was a *great* secretary, even though Benedict would never admit it. And if she sometimes made a mistake, like when the embassy's grand piano got soaked in a summer rainstorm, well, Benedict never let her forget it.

"It cost a small fortune to replace the soundboard, the hammers, and the dampers on that piano," he'd mention whenever he wanted to score a point against her.

"The piano is now in perfect working order, isn't it?" she'd reply.

"It never would have been damaged if you hadn't foolishly pushed it outdoors."

Honestly, their bickering could go in circles for ages if Inga didn't leave to escape his critical scrutiny. Everything Benedict did annoyed her. When mail arrived at his office, he took persnickety care opening each envelope. Why couldn't he just tear them open like normal people? No. Benedict used a letter opener to surgically slice along the top edge, extract the folded piece of paper, and then actually *returned the letter opener to its drawer* before unfolding the letter to read. It drove her batty.

Whenever Benedict was critical of something, which was often, he had the strange ability to narrow an eye while simultaneously lifting the same eyebrow. How was that even possible?

That skeptical eyebrow was never more on display than when Inga's friends from New York sent her a bulky care package. It arrived at Alton House as everyone was lingering over after-dinner coffee. She opened the big box at the table so she could share it with everyone. She lifted out bars of Hershey chocolate, a goofy snow globe from Coney Island, and two bags of butterscotch candy. There were postcards of New York landmarks, sticks of licorice, and a tin of expensive loose-leaf tea from Bloomingdale's.

Then came five issues of *The Perils of Pauline*, a long-running cheap serial with lurid covers and scandalously fun story lines.

Nellie squealed when she recognized the garish covers. "Can I read them after you?"

"Of course!" Inga said. "I adore *The Perils of Pauline*. I buy each issue on the day of release."

"Somehow this does not surprise me," Benedict said, his voice as dry as the Sahara.

Inga lifted her chin. "Have you actually read any of them?"

"I wouldn't pollute my eyes," he replied.

She ignored the comment and went back to unpacking the box. Next came five cakes of her favorite bath soap infused with the aromatic fragrance of apples. She gave both Nellie and Mrs. Barnes a bar of the divine soap.

"Oh, this does smell heavenly," Mrs. Barnes agreed.

Inga savored a deep breath of the paper-wrapped bar of soap. Nothing triggered memories of New York so much as this apple blossom soap. She beat back the homesickness to lift her chin in pride. "New York grows the finest apples anywhere in America. It has something to do with the climate that gives the apples that crisp, heady scent."

She sent a look of superiority at Benedict, who was typically curt. "Miss Klein, the only good thing to come out of New York is candy corn." He stood and peeked into the bottom of her empty box. "And since there isn't any, I shall take my leave."

He left without touching a single item from the box of goodies.

Miss Klein. That was another reason she didn't like Benedict. He called everyone else at Alton House by their first names, but he never called her anything but Miss Klein. Whenever she entered a room, he stopped talking and folded his arms across his chest. He never made eye contact with her. Sometimes she wished for a crowbar to pry away the iron mask he wore whenever she was near to see if there was an actual human being behind it.

As autumn deepened, a troubling new type of problem arose. An American salesman in Munich had been mistaken for a Brit and been brutally beaten by the crowd. Larry was confronted at the drugstore by a pharmacist who wouldn't sell him anything unless he could prove he wasn't British. So many Americans were being mistaken for Brits that Benedict wanted to order embassy staff to carry their paperwork identifying them as Americans, but Inga had a better suggestion.

A little American flag lapel pin was all it took to quickly announce their nationality, and Mr. Gerard gladly commissioned the pins. Benedict never once acknowledged her solution was superior to his or even thanked her for the suggestion. He clearly didn't like her, and yet the only time he lost his temper was when she spilled ink at the mimeograph machine, and he called her "Claudia."

She suspected Claudia was his missing wife, the woman Mr. Gerard said had left Benedict because he was so stuffy.

Curiosity about the mysterious Claudia nagged at Inga. One rainy afternoon while Benedict had gone to Leipzig on business, she asked Larry about the woman during a lull in their duties.

"Claudia was his wife," he whispered. "She was the smartest woman I've ever met. Her father is an Oxford professor, and she grew up on a college campus. She spoke six languages. She used to charm the Greek ambassador with arguments about the Peloponnesian War."

Everything Larry just said was in the past tense. "What happened to her?"

"Oh, she died," Larry said. "It was a dreadful scandal and nearly destroyed Benedict."

She wanted to know more, but Larry seemed so ill at ease with the topic that she felt sorry for him and backed off.

And yet her curiosity about the enigmatic Claudia escalated by the day. Benedict was so reserved, so staid. What sort of woman had managed to crack through his iron reserve to stir his passion?

Stop! The last thing she needed to worry about was Benedict's manly passion. She shouldn't care what Benedict thought of her since she disliked him intensely. He didn't like her either, and Inga wasn't used to people not liking her.

It made her wonder about the brilliant Claudia all the more.

10

Inga's torture being forced to work with Benedict intensified in October when Larry contracted a case of pinkeye and had to be isolated in his bedroom at Alton House to stop it from spreading to the others. It meant that for the next two weeks, Inga would handle secretarial duties for Benedict in addition to her work for Mr. Gerard.

Their first assignment was to visit the Ruhleben internment camp holding detained British civilians. The exchange of civilian prisoners was a major priority because tens of thousands of men were now trapped behind warring lines. It fell to the neutral nations like the United States to negotiate the exchanges.

The task was difficult because the Germans refused to exchange a prisoner unless a German prisoner of similar rank or skill set could be found. An aristocrat for an aristocrat, or a blacksmith for a blacksmith.

Inga rode beside Benedict in the enclosed carriage, listening to Benedict's instructions as they neared the Ruhleben internment camp. It was housed in a converted racetrack with horse stables, viewing stands, and a large open field. It contained three thousand

British men who'd been refused permission to leave the country. Those men were packed into the stables, six men per horse stall.

"So far, spirits among the men are good because they all expect to be released within a few more weeks, but never underestimate prickly German obsession for details to throw a wrench into the works."

She smiled at him. "Maybe you'd like me more if I eased up on my prickly obsession with details. Perhaps I shouldn't have noticed that the pharmaceutical supplies sent by the Red Cross needed to be refrigerated and arranged for proper storage. It would have been faster if I just let them go to the warehouse."

Naturally, Benedict couldn't spare her a compliment. "Collect your belongings, Miss Klein. We're here."

She hopped down from the carriage and gazed at the entrance leading into the racetrack. A few uniformed soldiers loitered near the front, and Benedict flashed his diplomatic credentials to get them inside. Both soldiers immediately complied. *See?* Germans weren't so bad. One of the soldiers even smiled and held the gate for her. She returned the smile before scurrying after Benedict, eager to point out how polite both soldiers had been. But now didn't seem the right time in the dim, narrow tunnel beneath the stadium stands.

"Oh, my word," she whispered as she emerged into the sunlight. The racetrack grounds lay before her, crowded with men walking on the tracks, sprawled out on the lawn, and loitering in the stands. *Three thousand men.* She'd never seen so many people crammed into such a tight space.

"At least they are allowed plenty of sunlight," she managed to say. "Exercise too."

"Yes, it is a veritable amusement park," Benedict said, his tone wry. "Come along. We're meeting with Dr. Keel to work on getting these men home."

Inga craned her neck to take it all in. A few dozen men played a round of cricket in the center field. One man had a sketch pad balanced on his knee as he drew the bleachers filled with men reading, reclining, and playing cards. Beside her a group of shirt-less men dunked rags into a water trough to bathe. One man was completely naked!

She averted her gaze and hurried after Benedict, who was al-ready introducing himself to a couple of gentlemen standing near the grandstand. It took a few moments to realize these men weren't fellow diplomats but were actually prisoners. Dr. Keel was a profes-sor of chemistry who'd been teaching in Berlin and now assumed a leadership position among the internees.

They sat at a table beneath a large sail strung between two poles to provide shade, and Inga began taking shorthand notes of the discussion.

"I need a list of everyone's name and age," Benedict said. "Any man older than fifty will surely be considered too old to fight and perhaps will be an easy candidate for release."

The professor nodded. "Already done. We've also got a handful of boys under the age of fifteen who might qualify for the same reason. I want those boys out first. If negotiations drag on for years, those boys will eventually come into fighting age, and the Germans won't let them go."

Inga had to bite her tongue. This couldn't drag on for years, could it?

"Are there any men here with an aristocratic title?" Benedict asked.

"No, sir." It was bad news. That meant an easy exchange for Baron von Eschenbach wouldn't be happening anytime soon.

The professor showed them crates with notecards denoting each man's age, profession, medical concerns, and home address in En-gland. Inga's first job upon returning to the embassy would be to organize the cards and start typing lists of men to be considered for a prisoner exchange, starting with the young boys first.

After an hour, it was all over and they were heading back to their carriage. She paused by the man with the sketch pad. Everything about the lanky, brown-haired man was ordinary except that he had a patch covering one eye.

"Is there anything you need to be more comfortable?" she asked him.

The man looked up and smiled. "Just seeing a pretty lady is doing the trick, ma'am."

She laughed, then repeated her question because she was serious. The man sobered and had a list of requests.

"We could use some lightbulbs," he suggested. "There's only one lightbulb per stable block, and ours has already burned out. Most of us don't have any pillows, and fresh fruit would be manna from heaven. And maybe some good books or magazines, anything that can—"

"Come along, Miss Klein," Benedict said. "Our carriage is waiting."

"Please wait a moment. This man has been telling me—"

"Now, Miss Klein."

This time Benedict's voice wasn't as polite, and she closed her notepad. Benedict was many annoying things, but he wasn't cruel. Something must be wrong, and she nodded a quick farewell to the artist before following Benedict out of the stadium.

Benedict didn't say a single word until they were safely behind the closed door of the carriage. "Don't ever initiate a conversation with a British prisoner," he said. "It could be misconstrued as an attempt to spy."

"All I wanted was to see if I could—"

"I know what you wanted, and it doesn't matter. You are a representative of the American Embassy. If a German officer saw you consorting with a prisoner, it could be misconstrued."

"All right, fine," she conceded. She was ignorant of the rules for this terrible game, and she would follow Benedict's lead, even as she planned to somehow get that man the supplies he'd requested.

The next two days were a flurry of messages between Benedict and his counterparts in London and Berlin. All of them wanted the prisoner exchanges to go through, and yet with the exception of a few elderly or critically ill men, nothing happened.

As Inga prepared lists of the men for the Ruhleben prisoner exchange, she figured out the artist she'd spoken to was named Percy Dutton. He was the only one-eyed man in the camp, and his profession was listed as a Presbyterian minister. Benedict allowed her to start corresponding with Percy so that he could compile requests from the prisoners for relief supplies. She sent the lists on to London, where British citizens began sending relief packages.

"Miss Klein!" Benedict rapped out one morning when she was running off more copies of blank forms on the mimeograph machine. "I need you to find lodging for twenty-five volunteers from the American Red Cross. They will arrive this weekend."

It was a typical request. Hundreds of American volunteers from the YMCA, the Salvation Army, and medical volunteers were flooding into Europe. Inga helped find them lodging and taught them how to distribute emergency services to hospitals and families who'd lost their breadwinners.

October turned into November, and there was still no exchange of prisoners. The men at Ruhleben had set up a printing press and were producing their own camp newspaper. The Red Cross supplied them with sporting equipment, and leagues took shape. Many of the interned men were professional athletes who'd been stranded in Germany when the war was declared, and they went into high gear getting the sporting leagues established.

Yet despite the stiff upper lip displayed in Percy's letters to her, she sensed a growing fear and frustration as the days stretched into months without any hope of release. His letters showed the corroding effects of helplessness on a man's soul.

One morning she brought the issue up at the breakfast table. "Thanksgiving is coming up," she said. "Perhaps we could arrange a Thanksgiving meal for the prisoners at Ruhleben."

Benedict looked up from his bowl of cold oats. "They're British, Miss Klein. They don't celebrate Thanksgiving."

Embarrassment clobbered her, but at least Colonel Reyes complimented her for being thoughtful. Mrs. Barnes said they never celebrated Thanksgiving at Alton House because it was on a Thursday, which was a normal working day in Germany.

"But we're Americans, and we should be able to celebrate," she said as another platter of breakfast rolls circulated around the table. "The Gerards are going to Keil for the holiday. I think we ought to at least have a Thanksgiving meal to relax and give thanks for our good fortune."

Benedict remained inflexible. "Thursday is a normal working day throughout Europe, so we shall not be caught lollygagging. Besides, you'll find that turkeys are scarce in Europe. Turkeys are native to America and are hard to come by here."

Hard, but not impossible. Turkeys had been imported to Europe because they made for such fine hunting, and many of the aristocratic hunting reserves had them. Mr. Gerard went hunting almost every weekend, and when she mentioned Benedict's comment about the scarcity of turkey, he promised to solve their problem. The Monday before Thanksgiving, Ambassador Gerard arrived at Alton House with a dead turkey in each hand.

"Compliments of the weekend hunt with the Grand Duke of Hesse," he said. "The duke has a fabulous hunting lodge just south of here. Happy Thanksgiving, everyone!"

Inga was delighted they would have a real Thanksgiving dinner, but not thrilled when she learned she would be the one to pluck the turkeys. Mrs. Barnes had sprained her wrist, and Nellie flat-out refused to pluck.

It was left to Inga, then, who was huddling in the Alton House garden, apologizing to the two dead turkeys lying on the cold slate patio. Why hadn't she realized how difficult it was to actually yank each of these tough quills off the bird? She never once set foot inside the kitchen back home at the Martha Washington, so plucking a turkey was a new and horrible experience.

Mrs. Barnes instructed that Inga must not yank too many feathers at once or the skin would tear, so it had to be done one by one, and each pluck made a disturbing noise. Maybe it wouldn't be so awful if she didn't have to hear that popping sound with each pluck, but after ten minutes she'd only cleared a few square inches of the first bird.

Inga yelped when the chilly November wind scattered a handful of feathers across the garden. With a moan she ran after them. Benedict would have a fit if she made a mess of his precious garden.

"Need some help?"

The friendly voice came from the other side of the fence. A young man with neatly groomed blond hair and an impish grin peered over the garden wall.

"I've never plucked a turkey, and I'm making a mess of it," she said as she raced after another cluster of feathers tumbling toward the barren rose garden.

The man behind the fence rattled the hardware of the gate. "Let me in and I'll help," he said. "I used to pluck chickens all the time when I was stationed in Canada."

Inga flung open the gate in gratitude. The man introduced himself as Magnus Haugen, junior secretary at the Norwegian Embassy. He lived two houses down at a place called Little Bergen, along with most of the staff from the Norwegian Embassy. Inga wasn't allowed to socialize with the Bulgarians right next door, but Norway was a neutral nation and so befriending Magnus wasn't a problem. He joined her on the bench and showed her the right way to quickly pluck and dispose of the feathers.

Inga, not knowing the first thing about Norway, asked, "Do you eat turkey in Norway?"

Magnus shook his head. "Mostly fish. Sometimes we have lutefisk, which is cod soaked in lye. Or sometimes we have *pinnekjøtt*, which is dried sheep."

Inga tried to keep a pleasant expression as Magnus explained the foods that seemed simply awful, but good heavens, he was a pleasant man! He finished plucking the first turkey in short order and seamlessly took the second bird from her and continued working.

"Will you join us for dinner on Thursday?" she impulsively asked. It didn't seem fair to send him home to a meal of lutefisk when he did all the work preparing the turkeys. Magnus accepted the invitation with a grin, and suddenly Inga's dormant interest in a handsome man came roaring back to life for the first time since leaving New York.

Normally, Benedict would have been at the embassy until seven o'clock, but Inga's resolve to host a Thanksgiving meal required him to be home three hours earlier. Inga wanted to use the formal dining room, which annoyed Mrs. Barnes, and yet Andrew and Larry both asked for it too. Eating in the dining room required ironing a tablecloth, getting out the good china, and lots of extra trips to the kitchen to carry food to the table.

Mrs. Barnes did heroic work preparing this feast with a bad wrist, and Benedict ordered the cook to take a seat while he carried the platters of roasted turkey, sweet potatoes, and green beans almondine. There were bowls of gravy, butter dishes, and a basket of rolls, all because Inga was homesick and wanted a real Thanksgiving meal.

Although she wasn't so homesick she couldn't make a new friend from the Norwegian Embassy. The junior diplomat had fine manners and an oversupply of charm. Most annoying, he shared Inga's groundless good cheer for just about everything.

"Thank heavens, you Americans aren't stingy with the heat," Magnus said as he polished off another roll. "Our commanding officer is tightfisted with the coal, so we are only allowed to heat the house when the temperature drops below twenty degrees. Inga, will you pass the rolls?"

"Don't get used to it," Benedict said. "Coal is likely to be rationed soon. War shortages haven't reached Berlin yet, but the western part of Germany is suffering. We should all become accustomed to doing without."

"Didn't I warn you?" Inga said with a teasing glance at Magnus. "We're all grateful that Benedict is here to remind us that the world is a very serious place."

The jollity continued until Benedict stood to begin clearing the table. He didn't want Mrs. Barnes doing it, and the others seemed determined to polish off another bottle of wine. If he moved quickly, he could complete another batch of letters to London.

He closed the door on the study to blot out singing from the dining room, then got to work. It had been almost four months and there'd been no real progress on getting the British prisoners trapped at Ruhleben traded or released. Their ranks had grown to four thousand men, and it took almost an hour to draft letters to the appropriate officials in London. He would have Larry type them up tomorrow.

A movement outside of the window caught his eye. It was Inga, escorting the young Norwegian to the back garden gate. Why weren't they leaving through the front? It wasn't any of his business, but he stood off to the side of the window so they wouldn't spot him and watched.

Inga leaned against the gate as Magnus stood far too close to her. She tilted her face up, and even from here, Benedict could see their joyous faces shining in the moonlight.

Magnus leaned down and kissed her. Inga made no move to stop him or step away.

Benedict clenched his pencil, and the kiss went on for several heartbeats before Magnus gave her a little salute, then crossed through the gate and headed for home.

Inga watched him leave. She wasn't wearing a coat and would catch her death from the cold if she kept loitering much longer. Benedict lowered his head to glower. It wasn't any of his business who Inga kissed or if she wanted to catch pneumonia.

He wasn't jealous. *He wasn't.* There were no rules against fraternization between employees of a fellow neutral embassy . . . but he still didn't like it.

DECEMBER 1914

Benedict always enjoyed the Christmas season at Alton House—except for this year, of course. Inga couldn't resist butting in and telling everyone how to properly celebrate. She wanted to attend a midnight Mass on Christmas Eve just like she did in New York. After her rapturous descriptions, Nellie wanted to go too. He couldn't let them venture out at midnight without protection, and since nobody else wanted to go, that left only Benedict to accompany the two women.

So he'd dragged himself to midnight Mass and was now bleary-eyed and in a bad mood the following morning as everyone gathered around the Christmas tree in the main room to exchange gifts. Mrs. Barnes made spiced cider, and Inga put a Christmas record on the gramophone as they prepared to open the presents.

As the senior officer and only independently wealthy man living at Alton House, Benedict was usually the only person to buy everyone a gift. Normally he enjoyed shopping for the perfect gift for each staff member. This year he bought an embossed set of Charles Dickens's works for Andrew, and tickets to the opera for Larry, Colonel Reyes, and the other men living in Alton House. He bought a silver comb for Nellie and a cashmere scarf for Mrs. Barnes. And for Inga? He didn't know her that well, but she always waxed poetic about the village where she'd been born in Bavaria. When he saw a music box shaped like a chalet from the Bavarian Alps, he instantly thought of her and bought it.

He didn't want anything in return. That wasn't the way giftgiving worked at Alton House. He was a senior staff member and could afford a nice gift for everyone, but it would have been awkward to expect them to return the sentiment. In the past, the staff had always honored that.

Inga didn't. First thing in the morning, there they were. A bunch of presents Inga had bought for everyone in the house, including him. It was easy to guess what it was because everyone had identical flat squares wrapped in brightly colored paper.

Gramophone records.

Would it be possible to return the records to the store? "Inga, you shouldn't have," he said as she held the record toward him. He'd taken his traditional seat in the wing-back chair by the fireplace while Inga floated around the room, handing out gifts.

"I wanted to," she said. "Please take it. I miss home, and giving presents makes it feel like a real Christmas morning." The hollow look in her eyes took him aback. Inga wasn't ever hollow. She was supposed to ooze with annoying good cheer.

Andrew noticed. "Have you thought about going home for a visit? You could be there in a week."

Benedict stiffened, praying she'd say no. Transatlantic crossings were getting more dangerous by the week. The Germans agreed not to torpedo passenger ships carrying citizens from neutral nations, but mistakes could happen. Even more dangerous were the underwater mines planted all over the Baltic and North Seas. Too many ships had already been blown to pieces by such mines, and the thought of Inga thrashing in the water, trying to stay afloat . . .

Luckily, it didn't take her long to reject the idea. "I can't go home," she said. "I don't have a passport."

"Benedict could get you one by the end of the day," Nellie said.

Benedict could, but he won't, he thought. Why he instinctively recoiled at the prospect of letting Inga go didn't bear too much scrutiny, but her next words stopped him cold.

"I'm still a German citizen, and that may cause problems," she said.

"You're still a *what*?" he lashed out.

Inga jumped a little. "No need to sound so huffy. I never got around to taking the American citizenship test. It didn't seem necessary, and it cost four dollars."

Anger simmered, making it difficult to keep his tone calm and professional. "Four dollars? I don't understand. You just spent a fortune buying everyone gramophone records we don't need, but you won't spring *four dollars* to become a citizen of the country you call home?"

Inga looked heavenward. "Why do you have to be such a killjoy?"

"Hey, it's Christmas," Andrew said, always the voice of reason. "Nothing bad is going to happen to Inga. She's a woman."

"The chancellery accused two old lady nuns of being spies and held them in detention for a month. I spent six hours in court arguing their cause. You think they'll be any kinder to a woman working in our embassy?"

"Inga," Andrew said in a conciliatory tone, "why don't you promise Benedict you'll take the citizenship test at your first opportunity? Then he can pipe down and not have a heart attack."

Inga shrugged. "If that will make things better, of course I'll take one right away."

"You can't," he snapped. "It has to be done in the United States, and then you're required to pass an interview with a judge."

Inga gave Benedict the wrapped record she bought him. "That

settles it then. I can't take the test, so why don't we all enjoy Christmas and unwrap our presents?"

"Yes, let's do," Mrs. Barnes said, unusually siding with Inga.

Although Inga bought records for everyone, they all had different musical selections. A mournful piece by Chopin for Larry, ragtime music for Andrew.

Benedict pulled the wrapping back from his own record and blinked. It was *Moonlight Sonata* by Beethoven, his favorite. "How did you know?" he asked, and she flashed him a grin.

"I peeked at your *Encyclopedia Britannica*. The notes you scribbled all over the Beethoven entry made it clear you have pretty strong feelings for him."

It was true. When had she poked through his encyclopedia? He'd never told her she couldn't, but the notes he made in those volumes were deeply personal, almost like a diary. Still, it was enormously thoughtful, and he hadn't expected it of her. "Thank you, Miss Klein."

He watched as she unwrapped his own gift to her. She squealed, actually *squealed* when she recognized the Bavarian chalet with its wooden logs and steep roof, complete with flower boxes and shutters that could open and close.

"Oh, how I longed to go inside one of these fancy lodges when I was little," she enthused, her eyes sparkling as she lifted the lid. Inside were two miniature figurines, the lady in a traditional dirndl and the man in full-length lederhosen. The figurines twirled to the music, making a loop around the balcony as the music played. Despite himself, a hint of a smile tugged at the ridiculous delight Inga took in admiring the twirling couple.

"Oh, thank you, Benedict!" Inga rarely bestowed one of her heart-stopping, dazzling smiles on him, but her fresh, wholesome smile was unabashed, and it got to him.

"Who is this for?" Nellie asked, holding up a final unwrapped gramophone record.

"Oh, that's for Magnus," Inga said, a blush staining her cheeks.

"It's a traditional Norwegian Christmas carol. I'll give it to him this afternoon because he has invited me over to have Christmas dinner at Little Bergen House."

"My, my," Andrew said. "Can we expect to hear wedding bells soon?"

Benedict froze. Everyone knew Inga had been spending time with the young officer, but this was something he hadn't considered.

"Heavens, no," Inga said. "I'm too homesick as it is to think of marrying someone from so far away. I must admit, though, it's been flattering."

The muscles Benedict hadn't realized he'd been clenching eased, and he settled back in his chair to watch as the others continued celebrating the day.

Benedict took one day off for Christmas, then went back to work trying to facilitate an exchange of civilian prisoners. January brought a new and unwelcome development, and this time it was triggered by the British.

A young man named Winston Churchill had been appointed First Lord of the Admiralty, and he took an unusually harsh stance toward German submarine warfare. Rather than treat captured German submariners with the respect owed men in uniform, Churchill ordered them to be isolated and treated the same as pirates and murderers.

Naturally, the Germans retaliated by singling out an equal number of British officers and subjecting them to similar conditions. The British officers were to be held in solitary confinement until the German submarine crews were granted better treatment.

Benedict headed to Magdeburg, where the British officers had been relocated to substandard German prison cells. His diplomatic credentials from a neutral nation ought to afford him private visits with the interned men, but the commandant of the jail refused.

"You may pass by their cells but will not be permitted to speak with the prisoners," the commandant insisted.

Benedict kept his tone cool but firm. "That would be a violation of the international agreements regarding prisoners of war. Many of your own superiors signed those documents in Geneva and at the Hague. I hope I don't need to return to Berlin to get authorization to override your order."

The commandant glared, but then gave a brusque nod to a subordinate to escort Benedict to the basement cells where the British officers were being held. He silently cringed at the stink down here. The light was dim, and each cell was four feet by eleven, barely enough for a man to stand since the cot took up most of the room.

The first officer, Lieutenant Goschen, lay on the cot and was unable to stand or speak. He was awake, his eyes fixed and staring at the dank brick wall a few feet away.

Benedict knelt beside the cot and spoke in a soothing voice so as not to alarm the young man. "Sir, my name is Benedict Kincaid. I've come from the American Embassy to help."

The man kept staring straight at the wall, not moving, not blinking.

Benedict tried again. "Sir? Can you hear me?"

"That one doesn't talk," the German sergeant said from the doorway of the cell. "I think he's deaf, dumb, and blind."

Benedict reached for the man's hand. "Lieutenant Goschen, can you hear me?"

The young officer was startled, as if aware of Benedict's presence for the first time. The lieutenant met his gaze. Oh yes, Lieutenant Goschen could see. No blind man could lock gazes like Goschen was doing. There was a desperate, pleading quality in his expression. He didn't say anything, but it looked like he wanted to.

"You can hear me?" Benedict asked again.

A squeeze of his hand was the only answer. Again, the man seemed desperate to talk, but simply couldn't. It seemed cruel to keep pressing.

Benedict covered the man's hand with both of his own. "I'll be back in a little while. I'm going to speak with some of your fellow officers. If you think of something to tell me, or some way of communicating, you'll have your chance."

A sheen of tears clouded Lieutenant Goschen's eyes, and he squeezed Benedict's hand again. The wall of sympathy nearly clobbered Benedict flat, but he forced it back and rose to his feet.

The next cell contained a man in much better health, if a little emaciated. The prisoners weren't allowed to communicate with each other, although the narrow slits in the doors let them hear what was going on in neighboring cells, and Colonel Blaydon was eager to talk.

"The krauts took Goschen out of a hospital bed to send him here," Colonel Blaydon explained. "He was shot in the head at Ypres and hasn't been right since. His father is an earl, and they want to mistreat an aristocrat."

Benedict tamped down the anger swirling inside. He had a lot of men to interview today and couldn't afford to let emotion get in the way.

"Tell me how they've been treating you," he asked, and was relieved to hear the prisoners were being fed. But they had no water to bathe, nor were they permitted exercise outside their tiny cells. Over the next hour he heard the same story from all the prisoners. A few weeks ago, they'd all been in well-run camps where they had freedom of movement, the ability to socialize, and almost anything a prisoner could hope for except freedom. Now they were locked in solitary confinement and trapped underground like animals in a burrow. It was retaliation for the way the British had changed the rules regarding submarine crews.

As requested, Benedict headed straight to Ambassador Gerard's office upon his return to Berlin. Hopefully, the ambassador could persuade the British to stop their punitive treatment of the submarine crews, as it would be the fastest way to get Lieutenant Goschen and the others returned to a normal detention camp.

Inga was in the ambassador's office, taking dictation about relief supplies. After a day of sitting with grimy men in dank cells, Inga's fresh, wholesome radiance was a welcome sight. The sage-green suit fit her to a tee. Her blond hair was coiled atop her head artfully, as if a Renaissance painter had arranged it that way. On her collar was a *solje* brooch, a traditional Norwegian pin of delicate filigree and tiny shining disks that shimmered in the sunlight. It was probably a gift from Magnus, but he didn't ask. It wasn't any of his business.

He turned his attention to Ambassador Gerard to begin his report. "The rumors about conditions of the British officers are as bad as we were led to believe. One of the officers is being denied medical care. All of them are confined in solitary cells where they can barely move."

Inga stood, her expression troubled. "Is there anything we can do?"

Just when he was convinced Inga was a completely vain and frivolous creature, she always surprised him with flashes of genuine compassion.

He wished she wouldn't. It was easier to keep her at arm's length when she flirted with Larry or spent too much time fiddling with her hair.

"I'll let you know," he said, his gaze sliding away from her cornflower blue eyes and retreating back to the safety of his office.

12

FEBRUARY 1915

Inga stirred a touch of nutmeg into the fragrant hot cider simmering on the stovetop. Nutmeg wasn't her favorite, but Magnus liked it, so she always added it to the cider when they snuck out for a moonlit evening in the garden. It was almost ten o'clock, the time they'd been meeting, because most people in Alton House had gone to bed, and they could be alone. Germany was such a conservative society that it would raise eyebrows for an unmarried woman to waltz about town with a young man, so they snuck out at night whenever it wasn't too frigid, and Inga always brought the hot cider.

A movement outside caught her attention. It was too early for Magnus to come, but someone was in the garden. She peeked out the window, surprised to see Magnus had already arrived. He sent her a guilty smile when he caught her looking at him.

She grinned back, holding up three fingers to let him know it would be a few more minutes. The cider was warm enough, and she poured it through a funnel and into a thermos bottle. The steel thermos had a leather carrying case and would keep the cider warm for at least an hour.

She screwed on the cap, hurried into her coat, then tiptoed to the back door leading outside. "You're early," she greeted him.

"And freezing!" He gave her a quick kiss, and yes, his nose was like an icicle. She pushed the thermos into his hands, and he cupped it gratefully.

"Why don't you ever wear gloves?" she asked.

"Because real Norwegians aren't supposed to be such weaklings."

They huddled next to each other on the garden bench and shared a few sips of cider from the thermos. Larry would have the vapors at the prospect of drinking from the same thermos, but she and Magnus shared kisses, so it seemed harmless.

"Tomorrow is Valentine's Day," he said. "Tell me how Americans celebrate it, so I don't do it wrong."

There was no wrong way to celebrate Valentine's. A girl ought to consider herself lucky if a man simply remembered the date. "Tell me how to say it in Norwegian," she prompted.

"*Valentinesdagen*," he said, then made her repeat it until she got it right. It was always like this when they met. Laughing and teasing. Magnus was the complete opposite of Benedict, who wouldn't know how to laugh if she gave him an instruction booklet.

Magnus tipped the thermos back and drained the last of it. "Is there any more inside?"

"A little," she said. She always made extra because she liked nursing a cup after he left, but he held the bottle out to her with such an eager expression she couldn't resist.

"I'll be back," she said and hurried inside. Mrs. Barnes kept the stove warm all night, so it only took a few minutes to heat up the last of the cider and fill the thermos. By the time she returned, the garden was empty.

"Magnus?"

Some shuffling of leaves sounded from the side yard, and he quickly returned, a guilty look swamping his face as he tugged at his trousers.

"Sorry," he said. "Too much cider, and it can run straight through a man."

"Magnus! If you needed the washroom, I could have let you inside."

"And risk running into Mr. Doom and Gloom? I wouldn't want to get you in trouble."

Maybe she shouldn't have shared her private nickname for Benedict because it would be hurtful if he ever got wind of it. She joined Magnus on the bench and glanced toward the side of the house. Could he have hidden something back there? Valentine's Day was tomorrow, and he'd already said he wanted to do something nice for her.

He cradled the thermos between his hands, all red and chapped in the cold night air. It made her shiver just looking at them.

"Dear, you're miserable. Go home and get warm. And wear gloves next time!"

Again, he gave her that lopsided, abashed grin that made him such fun. "You're probably right," he said. He gave her a quick good-night kiss, then let himself out through the gate, blowing in his hands as he scurried back to Little Bergen.

She daydreamed while cleaning up the kitchen. What sort of Valentine's Day surprise was Magnus planning? He'd seemed embarrassed when he returned from the side of the house. Maybe he had truly been relieving himself like he claimed. It seemed a little tacky to use someone else's yard for that, but he probably wasn't the first to have done it. In the future, maybe she shouldn't bring so much hot cider.

And yet . . . something didn't seem quite right. She would have to check it out in the morning.

––––––––––

Inga slipped out of the house early, just as the sun was rising and Mrs. Barnes opened the kitchen to begin breakfast. Benedict had already left on his morning ride, giving her the privacy to slip on a jacket and head to the side of the house to see if Magnus had been up to something.

If he had hidden some sort of Valentine's Day treat, she would simply pretend she hadn't seen it so as not to spoil his surprise.

She followed the slate footpath to the side of the house, where the scraggly vines were barren and bleak. Only the laurel shrubs along the side of the house stayed green all year. They'd grown so bushy they would make a good hiding place. She scanned the ground, covered in a light film of frost, but didn't see anything out of place. She even pulled a few fronds back to see if anything had been hidden in the brambles.

Then she saw it. The metal sheath that covered the telephone wire leading into Alton House had been tampered with. The paint was chipped, and a joint was crooked, as though it had been pried open and pressed shut.

A chill racked her body, and she covered her mouth. Magnus had done this. It was why he came early to meet her, and it was why he never wore gloves.

How stupid she had been.

Stupid, *stupid* girl. Just like her father always said. The dented metal sheath blurred before her eyes, but when she reached out to trace the casing, her icy fingers felt every ridge and scrape in the paint.

Maybe Magnus hadn't done it. Maybe a gardener or construction worker accidentally bumped into the sheath years ago. But even as she scrambled for an excuse, she knew it was a lie. Magnus almost certainly tampered with their telephone wire, and she'd have to tell Benedict so an expert could examine it.

It had to be done immediately. Even now somebody could be eavesdropping on their telephone calls. She moved like a sleepwalker back inside the house, listening to distant voices in the kitchen. Larry was annoyed because Mrs. Barnes had run out of cheese, and nobody liked omelets without cheese. He complained that the cook should have made waffles or oatmeal if there was no cheese.

Didn't he know there was a war going on? Shortages were beginning to happen all over Berlin, and Larry had the nerve to complain. She ran up the stairs, desperate to hide until she could quit shaking in fear and embarrassment and dreading her coming confession to Benedict.

Benedict helped himself to a bowl of cold oatmeal and took a seat at the kitchen table, trying to ignore Larry and Silas complaining about the lack of cheese. Didn't they know there was a war going on? The British POWs in Magdeburg would be thrilled with a platter of hot eggs.

Inga hovered in the doorway, looking unusually timid.

"Don't be shy," McFee said. "Come have some plain scrambled eggs. It's all the rest of us are getting. Except for Cold Oats, of course."

The nickname Inga slung around his neck was now so common that even the embassy chauffeur felt comfortable using it. He slanted an accusatory glance at Inga, but she didn't notice his ire.

"I need a moment to speak with Benedict," she said. "Alone."

He set his spoon down. Inga rarely initiated any contact with him, and she looked strangely petrified. He stood. "The study," he simply said, abandoning the kitchen table and walking down the hall. Inga followed.

He closed the door but didn't bother sitting. He was due at the embassy in a few minutes. "What do you need, Miss Klein?"

She still hadn't met his eyes. "I'm afraid I've made a terrible mistake," she said, staring out the window. "I'm afraid that Mag . . . that Magnus may have been flattering me to get close to Alton House so he could do something underhanded. I met him in the garden last night after everyone had gone to bed."

Benedict fought to keep his expression neutral. She already looked mortified, and he wouldn't make a fuss until he understood what had her so upset. "Go on," he coaxed.

"At some point he asked me to go inside to get more cider, and when I got back, he was around the side of the house. He made an excuse about needing to relieve himself, but when I checked this morning . . . well, it looked like someone had tampered with the telephone wires leading into the house." For the first time she met his gaze, and her lip trembled. "I'm so sorry," she whispered.

He drew a steadying breath as anger began uncurling deep inside. If someone was spying on them . . . if *Norway* was spying on them, this was a breach of diplomatic etiquette demanding immediate reprisals.

"Show me," he said, carefully keeping the anger from his voice.

Inga nodded and headed for the back door leading to the garden. Larry tried to get his attention to talk about the cheese issue, but Benedict waved him away, following Inga into the cold morning air. The frost had melted, leaving glittering drops scattered across the grass. He pulled his collar up as they rounded the side of the house where the electrical and telephone lines were secured beneath a slim metal conduit that ran up to the roof.

He spotted the intrusion immediately. Unfolding his pocket-knife, he wiggled it beneath the dented seam and pried it wider. It wasn't easy, and he pushed farther into the damp shrubbery, ignoring the cold flecks of dew as he opened the seam wide enough to look inside.

A splice had been added to their telephone wire.

He pushed the metal flat to protect the split wire from moisture should the weather turn bad, then stepped away from the shrub, shaking the droplets off his coat.

"Well?" Inga asked.

"Yes, the wire has been spliced," he confirmed. "Thank you for telling me this."

"What are we going to do?" Her voice sounded pale and brittle in the cold morning air, but he liked that she'd used the word *we*.

This was an offense against all of them, but especially Inga. Magnus had been hanging around this house for months, gradually sweet-talking Inga and gaining her trust.

He knew what it felt like to be betrayed and softened his voice. "You needn't do anything. I will discuss this immediately with the Norwegian ambassador."

"Are you going to tell everyone what happened?"

He had to inform Ambassador Gerard and Colonel Reyes. Someone from the Corps of Engineers would need to see it, but no one else needed to know.

"I'll keep it as private as possible," he assured her. "The only thing the rest of the staff needs to know is that Magnus is no longer welcome on Alton House grounds. There's no need for additional details."

Her lip started wiggling again, and she mouthed the words *thank you*, even though no sound came out.

Later that day, he summoned Lieutenant Carter from the U.S. Corps of Engineers to inspect the splice and confirm his suspicions.

It wasn't hard. Their metal conduit had been tampered with in two places: the spot Inga identified, and then a few inches below the soil where a buried line went all the way through their backyard. They couldn't investigate now, but Benedict would bet his bottom dollar that the wire ran directly to the house used by the Norwegians.

Lieutenant Carter eyed the gardens of the neighboring yards. "It would have been easy enough to bury this line in the dead of night, but he probably didn't want to risk fooling around on the side of the house without an excuse. I gather that is where the young secretary came into play."

Benedict nodded, still silently fuming.

"What I don't get is why the Norwegians would be spying on us," Lieutenant Carter said.

Benedict huffed. "It's not like we aren't spying on them," he admitted. Norway was a brand-new country, finally throwing off the yoke of foreign rule less than ten years ago. Control of the sparsely populated country had been tossed between Denmark and Sweden for the past five centuries, so it was anyone's guess how Norway would form alliances in the years to come.

One thing was sure. Benedict wouldn't let this insult be ignored.

13

Benedict made an appointment with the Norwegian ambassador for the morning after Valentine's Day. Their embassy was located in one of the less prestigious diplomatic neighborhoods, but the ambassador's office was impressively furnished with a mix of European grandeur and a few decorations reflecting Norway's naval heritage. Nautical maps and paintings of ships from the age of sail covered the wall. Brass and copper accents were everywhere, and a standing telescope was angled to point out the window.

Ambassador Salvesen stood as Benedict entered. They'd often met at social gatherings and had a cordial relationship, although that was about to change.

"Mr. Kincaid," Ambassador Salvesen greeted. "Fine weather we are having for the middle of February, aren't we?"

Benedict said nothing as he approached. He merely set the cluster of spliced wires in the center of the ambassador's desk.

The pleasant expression on Salvesen's face evaporated.

"Would you care to explain this?" Benedict said, still standing.

The ambassador chose his words carefully. "We were given to understand the Americans wanted to stifle our ongoing trade partnerships with Germany. It is in our interest to keep abreast of such discussions."

True enough. Norway wanted nothing to do with this war, and loss of their fishing exports to Germany would cripple them. Nevertheless, Benedict's job was to protect American interests, not sympathize with the Norwegians.

He kept his voice carefully controlled. "You are a new nation, only free from Danish rule for ten years. This is not how you make friends. I want the transcript of every telephone call you intercepted."

The Norwegian ambassador lifted his chin a notch. "The line only became functional two days ago. We heard your cook telephone an order for sugar beets, and your call with Ambassador Gerard concerning submarine warfare."

It sounded accurate. Thanks to Inga's quick confession, the wiretap had yet to do any real damage, but he still had a right to ask for amends. "I am willing to keep quiet about this gross violation of our privacy on the condition you transfer Magnus Haugen out of Germany."

"Done," Ambassador Salvesen quickly agreed.

Benedict watched over Inga from afar.

In the week since she'd been knocked off-balance by the incident with Magnus, the breezy good cheer she brought to Alton House and everyone else at the embassy had vanished. She functioned with silent professionalism. Although most of the others at Alton House assumed it was due to a romantic breakup, Benedict knew she was withering beneath a tidal wave of shame. He wanted that to end. He needed her heart and head and intelligence back in the game. As annoying as she could be, he wanted the old Inga back.

After a fine roast beef dinner at Alton House, he asked her to accompany him on a walk, even though it was freezing. She dully nodded and grabbed her coat before following him outside. She probably expected a reprimand for what happened, but that would be like kicking a wounded puppy.

Frigid air pinched his cheeks as he stepped outside. The cold prompted a brisk pace as they set off beneath the avenue of barren trees, their scraggly limbs creating an arcade as he headed to the fountain at the end of the street.

"I wanted to let you know that Magnus has been sent back to Norway," he said, trying to sound as gentle as possible. "You need not fear encountering him again."

Her breath left her in a rush, a little white puff that vanished in the wind. Her shoulders sagged, but she looked relieved as she plopped down onto the rim of the empty fountain.

"I feel so stupid," she said. "I think I should resign."

"Don't."

Why did Inga continually refer to herself as stupid? It bothered him, and the only thing that could make this situation even worse was if she quit. He took the seat beside her on the rim of the fountain. "Inga, I need you to quit berating yourself. Mistakes happen. When they do, you need to get back on your feet, dust yourself off, and stay the course. All right?"

She still wouldn't look at him, and he touched her chin to lift it up a notch. "It's okay, Inga," he said gently. "It's over. There's been no damage, and we won't ever speak of this again."

She nodded, her gaze darting around as she struggled to find words. "I expected you to gloat a little more."

He knew what it felt like to have his feelings stomped. "Sorry," he said with a hint of a smile. "I'm fresh out of gloats today."

For the first time in days, he caught a hint of a smile from her. She averted her eyes and bit her lip. Then she took a fortifying breath. "I haven't always treated you very kindly," Inga said. "I know we won't ever be best friends, but could we have some sort of truce?"

"A professional détente?"

She laughed a little. "That sounds much more diplomatic. Yes, a professional détente."

The momentary lilt of her laughter sent a wave of longing through him. He missed the sound of Inga being happy.

"Good," he said. A professional détente would be wise, even though he liked Inga far too much as it was. Détente aside, he rather enjoyed sparring with her and secretly hoped it wouldn't end.

14

Inga's professional détente with Benedict held for only a few weeks. As the weather warmed up, so did their bickering. It seemed he couldn't help nitpicking the way she handled her duties. He went back to calling her Miss Klein in that prickly manner of his. She remained aggressively cheerful whenever he entered a room, which seemed to irritate him because Benedict couldn't help being a wet blanket.

Still, he had been true to his word and kept news of the Magnus scandal limited to only a handful of people in the American Embassy. Nobody at the other neutral embassies had been informed, which let Inga join in the periodic social gatherings without the mortifying incident tainting her reputation.

She loved the chance to unwind with staff from other neutral nations, like today's lawn party at the Danish Embassy. It was a chance to quit worrying about the war and enjoy the comradery of people who lived in the same diplomatic limbo as she. The fine early May weather was perfect for tea in the garden overlooking the tiered lawn that gradually sloped down to the Spree River.

A game of croquet was set up on the upper tier, where Inga paired with Andrew to represent the Americans. They were competing with the team from Spain, while teams from Denmark and Argentina would play the next round.

Inga positioned her mallet carefully, then gently smacked the ball through the final wicket.

"Well done!" Andrew enthused, for they'd just run all seven hoops and won the round.

Inga let out a squeal and glanced over at the tea tables, where Benedict sat hidden behind an open newspaper. Everyone else at the tea table politely clapped, but soon went back to chatting and sampling the splendid array of tiny cakes and pastries.

"Mrs. Torres, you're up!" Andrew called out to the wife of the Argentinian ambassador.

"Good luck!" Inga said as she handed her mallet to Mrs. Torres.

"I shall need it," the older woman said. "It's been years since I've played croquet."

Felix Jeppesen, the chief of staff at the Danish Embassy, chimed in. "Not to worry, just be thankful the Swiss aren't here today. They play hard, fast, and mean. There's no beating the Swiss whenever they're on the court."

"Why is that?" Inga asked.

"They have a frustrated sense of competition because they've been forced to stay neutral in every war dating back to the Treaty of Paris in 1815," Benedict said from behind his newspaper. Ah yes, reader of the *Encyclopedia Britannica* strikes again.

"Lucky Switzerland," Mrs. Torres said. "I fear that Argentina may be forced to choose sides before much longer."

That cast a pall over the gathering. At the moment, everyone there had the luxury of sitting on the sidelines while helping the Red Cross and other charitable organizations provide relief. They needn't worry about draft riots back home or arrange to have the bodies of fallen soldiers transported back to America for burial.

"None of us have a prayer of beating the Swiss at croquet," Felix said in an obvious attempt to recapture the mood. "They take it all so seriously. There's too much German in them to be lighthearted. Sorry, Inga," he said and flashed her an apologetic wink.

"Not to worry," she replied. "You should brace yourself to be trounced in the final round. After all, we beat Spain straight up."

Benedict finally lowered his newspaper to peer down at her from the upper terrace. "Inga, you don't have the necessary gravitas to beat the Danish."

"What does 'gravitas' mean?" she asked. "Something boring, I'll bet." If gravitas was a quality Benedict valued, it was almost certainly boring.

The Spanish ambassador supplied the answer. "It means heft. Solemnity of manner."

"Austerity," Felix added. "Heavy and ponderous and serious."

Inga smiled up at Benedict. "You are correct, sir. I have no gravitas, nor do I want any." She wandered to the upper terrace for a glass of lemonade. The Gerards made space for her at the tea table, and she scanned the delightful assortment of pastries displayed on the dessert stand. How charming everything looked! She helped herself to a raspberry pastry and went back to hectoring Benedict.

"Would you like something to eat?" she asked. "They have pear tartlets, raspberry streusel, and delightful little coconut sponge cakes."

"No, thank you," Benedict said.

"I'm sure they can produce a wedge of lemon to suck on if you prefer." She kept her tone bright and airy, prompting another round of laughter from the group. Even Benedict's lip quivered, and she almost succeeded in making him smile, though he managed to kill it before it could break free.

It was a triumph. Cracking Benedict's ridiculous austerity had become something of a challenge she almost always lost but would never quit trying.

Soon waiters rolled out another tea cart, this one filled with elegant sandwiches and finger-sized quiches. The British blockade obviously wasn't working very well if the lovely assortment of gourmet delicacies was any evidence. The Germans howled about the blockade and had been trying to paint the British as savages, denying milk to starving German babies, but Germany had never been dependent on imported food to feed itself. The markets still brimmed with produce, bread, and milk. Although the price of meat had risen sharply, few in Germany went hungry.

She helped herself to a watercress sandwich, dimly aware that a servant had interrupted the croquet game to carry a message to the Danish dignitary, who studied the slip of paper with a frown. It looked like a telegram.

Soon all four people playing croquet had gathered around the message, their faces grim. Mr. Gerard hurried down the terrace steps to read the message.

Benedict stood. "Something is happening," he said darkly, his point underscored as Mr. Gerard came striding up the stairs with the news.

"The Germans have torpedoed a passenger ship off the coast of Ireland. The *Lusitania*. It sank in less than twenty minutes. The loss of life is going to be considerable."

Inga crossed herself. "Poor souls."

"The ship was sailing from New York to Liverpool, so there are bound to be Americans on board," Mr. Gerard said.

"How could a ship of that size sink in twenty minutes?" Benedict asked. "It took the *Titanic* almost three hours to go under."

"The *Titanic* wasn't torpedoed," Mr. Gerard bit out. "Early reports claim a huge explosion took out the *Lusitania*. The Germans will be made to pay for this."

Inga turned away as a wave of guilt settled over her. Maybe the reports of how fast the ship sank were inaccurate. Maybe there weren't any Americans on the ship. It was too early to start panicking.

"Do we know how many people were aboard?" Mrs. Torres asked.

"Almost two thousand," Mr. Gerard answered. "Since it was sailing from New York, I'd estimate that as many as half of them were American. We need to return to the embassy to await news."

The moment Benedict feared for over a year had finally happened, and the United States was about to be dragged into a pointless war they had no business fighting. At this very moment, millions of American farmers, factory workers, students, and young men were going about their ordinary lives. Unless Benedict could navigate this diplomatic minefield, those young men might be scooped up by the thousands and sent into the trenches.

He'd been locked in Ambassador Gerard's office all morning, negotiating with German Undersecretary Zimmermann as they tried to find a way out of this quagmire. Inga sat in the corner, her fingers moving across the keys of a steno machine to record every word spoken. Zimmermann insisted that the *Lusitania* was a legitimate target because he believed it was carrying munitions, a charge that directly contradicted the American position.

Benedict tried to take the lead in negotiations, but Gerard was angry and belligerent, leaning far across his desk to be nose to nose with Zimmermann. "The United States demands a personal apology from the kaiser, monetary compensation for the families of every American victim, and a pledge to cease all unannounced submarine attacks."

Zimmermann bristled. "That will never happen. Not one of them! The *Lusitania* was carrying munitions. It would not have blown up like it did if it hadn't been stuffed to the gills with bombs. The violation of the treaty is on *you*, sir! Your nation was the one to break our agreement of neutrality by supplying munitions to the British."

Gerard was speechless. The only sound in the room was the

clattering of a stenograph machine as Inga typed every word. Her face looked white and tense, but her fingers kept firing.

"At this point, suggesting the *Lusitania* carried weapons is pure speculation," Benedict said. "There will be time to assign blame in the future. Our mission today must be to find a path toward peace. We *do not* want war between our two nations."

"Who doesn't want war?" Gerard barked. "The moment the president gives me instructions, I shall deliver his declaration with great delight. We are this close to declaring war," he said as he leaned across the desk, fingers pinched together.

Zimmermann scoffed. "President Wilson won't declare war. He knows your country has half a million German immigrants living in America who will rise up in arms against your government if you declare war on us."

Ambassador Gerard pounded his fist on his desk. "That may be, but we have half a million *lampposts* in America, and that is where those German citizens will find themselves swinging from if they rise up against us."

Inga gasped. Even Zimmermann looked stunned, but Gerard didn't back down. Anger crackled in the air, and Zimmermann reached for his walking stick and prepared to leave.

"I shall carry your tender sentiments to the kaiser," Zimmermann said stiffly. Then he looked at Inga, who remained frozen in the corner, fingers suspended above the steno. "I am sorry you had to hear that, Fräulein," he added. "How terrible that Ambassador Gerard should say such a foul thing before a citizen of Germany." He turned and left the room, closing the door quietly behind him.

"H-how did he know I'm a German citizen?" Inga stammered.

Benedict sagged. "Because there are spies everywhere in Berlin."

"He only said that to threaten me," Ambassador Gerard said. "He knows of my friendship with Inga, and he said it to throw me off-balance."

For the first time all morning, Benedict agreed.

Gerard stood and began pacing. "War is almost a certainty.

President Wilson has already instructed that if our demands are not met, he is ready to declare war. We leave Germany tomorrow morning. I will not loiter and risk being arrested like they did to the British diplomats after they broke relations."

Benedict met Inga's gaze. The Germans wouldn't let her leave. They knew she was a German citizen, that she didn't have a passport, and they were in no mood to be conciliatory. They might even accuse her of being a spy.

Inga's face remained white with fear. She clearly understood the danger she was in. It hurt to see, but Benedict couldn't help her. If America declared war, within days a million young men would be called up and drafted to serve in muddy trenches. *A million men.* There wasn't time to intervene on Inga's behalf. The clock was ticking, and he needed to begin strategizing with his counterparts at the other neutral embassies about how to avert this disaster. He refused to concede war was inevitable.

"I'm going to the Swiss Embassy," he told Gerard. "Marc Siegrist has decades of experience walking a tightrope of neutrality with the Germans. If anyone can help us stay the course, it's Marc. It's not too late for us. I'll figure a way out of this short of war."

"You won't do anything without my authorization."

The pugnacious expression on Ambassador Gerard's face was terrifying. It looked as if he *wanted* to go to war. President Wilson didn't, and ultimately Benedict worked for the president, not the ambassador. It seemed as if Benedict was the only American diplomat in Berlin desperate to preserve peace.

He met Gerard's gaze squarely. "We both work for the president," he said. "Of course I can't negotiate behind your back, but I owe it to President Wilson to investigate all our options. I believe we can convince the Germans to agree to the president's demands. I'll take any help I can get with that. We *must* get there; this is too important."

"Very well," Gerard conceded. "Go and do your best, but in the meantime, we're packing up both the embassy and Alton House."

Benedict swept papers and telegrams into his attaché case. Inga remained frozen in the corner, looking petrified as she watched his every move. He paused before her. "Don't let what Zimmermann said frighten you, Inga. We'll find a way to get you out of Germany should the need arise."

She gave the barest nod of her head, but it was obvious she didn't believe him, and her instincts were absolutely correct. As he left the embassy, for the life of him, Benedict could see no logical way for Inga to escape from Germany.

15

Benedict met with his counterparts from the other neutral nations at the Swiss Embassy. They gathered in the library, twelve men who all understood the gravity of the situation. The bookshelves were filled with brown-and-gold leather volumes that looked as though they'd never been opened, yet they were a soothing sight in contrast to the acid filling Benedict's gut.

He sat in an upholstered armchair while he outlined the situation as concisely as possible. "President Wilson is desperate to keep America out of the war, but tempers back home are hot. Germany's refusal to grovel in remorse over sinking the *Lusitania* is throwing gasoline on the fires of pro-war sentiment."

"Germans aren't good at groveling, my friend," Felix Jeppesen of Denmark said.

Everyone there had good cause to want to stay out of the war— the United States, Greece, Argentina, Spain, Mexico. All of them teetered on the brink, and each time another neutral nation was dragged into the war, it sent a tidal wave into their fragile alliances.

"I toured the trenches along the Marne last month," Felix said. "I had expected the filth and the despair. I expected the endless miles of bombed-out craters in the mud, but I hadn't expected the smell. There were open latrines and unwashed bodies, and the air tasted like sulfur and gunpowder. There were corpses everywhere, and they covered them in chloride of lime, which creates its own horrible smell. It's been six weeks since I was there, and I still smell it. I'm not even sure it's my imagination because I think perhaps it soaked into my skin. It's the only explanation I can think of."

Everyone in the room remained motionless. Felix sat two feet away, and Benedict could smell nothing but the dusty scent of old books, but he didn't doubt Felix's words. He could only pray to God he would be able to spare the millions of American men and boys from becoming the next round of cannon fodder to fill those trenches.

"I wish every warmonger back home could experience an hour of what you just described," Benedict said.

Marc from the Swiss Embassy was matter-of-fact. "Delay. Stall. Suggest you are waiting for more advisers to arrive from the United States or more instructions. Anything to slow the drumbeat for war."

It was good advice, and he prayed the ambassador would agree. It was past dusk when the gathering began winding down. Felix stood, and the men from South America began lighting cigars. Benedict had one last favor to ask.

"We have a German American woman who works at our embassy," he said. "Inga is an excellent secretary and a skilled wireless operator. Could any of you find a place for her on your embassy staff?"

The Argentinian ambassador paused so long that he burned his fingers on his lit match. He shook the match out and sent him a reluctant shake of his head. "I'm sorry, my friend."

Marc from the Swiss Embassy concurred. "It's too hard to remain neutral without rocking the boat over a single individual."

"What about safe passage into Switzerland? Surely you could accommodate that?"

"I could," Marc said reluctantly. "And yet this isn't something I am willing to do. I am sorry."

A scan of the other men in the room was no more helpful. A few men looked away as they fiddled with their cigars.

Felix walked Benedict to the door of the embassy. He was about to leave when Felix stopped him with a hand on his arm. "I'm sorry about the German woman," he said. "You're speaking of Inga, correct?"

Benedict nodded.

"And she has nobody in Germany? No husband or family?"

Only some distant relatives she hadn't seen in decades. "None," he said.

"No husband at all?"

What was Felix driving at? "Correct. Inga is completely on her own."

Felix took another glance down the hall as if to confirm there were no loitering servants or diplomats who might overhear. "Perhaps you would like to know that I am married to a German woman."

"Astrid is German?" It was a surprise because Astrid seemed completely Danish to Benedict's eyes. She had no accent or other trace of German heritage.

"She was born in Munich," Felix said. "She moved to Copenhagen as a child and never bothered with legal issues like citizenship. When we married, she came under my protection. We have been able to travel all over the world together, and she is the beneficiary of the same diplomatic immunity that I carry. If there is a diplomat at your embassy who is willing to offer marriage, it might be a solution to Inga's dilemma."

Benedict gave a nod of his head, even though he was the only single man at the embassy, and marrying Inga would be out of the question. He'd already endured one catastrophic marriage; he wouldn't knowingly enter another.

He would simply have to find another solution to save Inga.

It was almost midnight before Benedict arrived back at Alton House, where most of the house was dark except for a faint glow from behind the drapes of the front room. He wondered who was still awake. His horse's hooves clattered on the pebbled drive as he rode up and exhaustion tugged, but he needed to unsaddle Sterling before he could find the comfort of his bed.

He'd gone to the Swiss Embassy hoping for a miracle but came away with little but ominous warnings. The nightmarish images of Felix's visit to the trenches haunted him as he led Sterling into the stables. Last August a dozen nations got pulled into the vortex of war because of a catastrophic failure of diplomacy. Now he stood on that same precipice, fearing failure as each passing hour brought them closer to the brink.

Benedict took the extra time to brush the horse down, using short, brisk strokes along Sterling's neck, spine, and legs, murmuring a constant stream of soothing words. He checked her hooves for stones, hoping whoever was still awake in the Alton House front room would be gone by the time he finished, for he didn't care to talk to anyone. Sometimes it was easier to pretend confidence and calm, but tonight wasn't one of those times. The smothering fear of failure enveloped him, and panic raced through his blood. There had to be more he could do, a new door to knock on, a new strategy to try.

He finished with Sterling, but the dim light still burned in the front room, and he sighed. There was no avoiding it. He headed through the rear entrance into the darkened house, where the crackling of a fire in the front room beckoned him. He made plenty of noise walking down the hall so as not to alarm whoever was still up; he just prayed they weren't in the mood to talk.

It was Inga, kneeling before a roaring fire. Books and papers were scattered all around as she carefully sliced pages from a book. Colonel Reyes, the embassy's military attaché, stood a few feet away, flipping through a thick codebook.

"What are you doing?" Benedict asked.

"We're burning the codebooks," Colonel Reyes replied. "There are too many to take with us, and we can't let the Germans get their hands on them in case they seize this place before we can leave."

Benedict sagged and plopped onto the couch opposite Inga. "Thank you for staying up to do this," he told her. The firelight on Inga's profile made her appear enchanting. Her blond hair had mostly come loose from its pins and spilled over her shoulders in a glorious cascade.

"Of course," she said, her hand dragging a cutting blade to remove more pages from the codebook. She still hadn't looked at him. This afternoon Inga had been white with fear, but now she seemed resigned. Inga could be annoying, bossy, naive, and she sometimes got on his last nerve, but she didn't deserve to be left behind.

"Have you decided what you're going to do?" he asked.

She shook her head. "For now, I'll keep helping out as long as I'm needed. Perhaps the war will not come."

Colonel Reyes frowned as he set another book onto Inga's burn stack. "Anti-German protests have erupted all over the United States," he said. "President Wilson won't renounce them, and William Jennings Bryan has resigned in protest."

The news hit Benedict like a fist to the gut. Bryan was the secretary of state and the only committed pacifist in the president's cabinet. His resignation moved them even closer to the brink. "Any word on who will be appointed in his place?"

"Robert Lansing," Colonel Reyes said flatly, and Benedict cursed under his breath. Lansing made no secret of his partiality to Britain. As secretary of state, he would lean on the president to demand a break in diplomatic relations.

Benedict scrubbed a hand over his face and sighed. "Tomorrow I'll release an announcement recommending that all Americans still in Germany evacuate." It would be a dereliction of his duty not to warn them of the danger in remaining.

A danger Inga now shared. He began cracking his knuckles,

thinking. Overall, Inga Klein was a good woman. Felix's suggestion of marrying her was beyond the pale, but she didn't deserve the fate looming before her. Impulsively, he stood and said, "Colonel Reyes, a word if you don't mind."

The attaché followed Benedict down the hall to the darkened library, lit only by the moonlight streaming through the tall window. Benedict closed the door but didn't bother to light a lamp because this wasn't going to take long. It was a mortifying conversation, and he wanted it over with as quickly as possible.

"I know your wife is back in Charleston, but are there any of the other American officers stationed with the Marine Guard who are unmarried?"

Colonel Reyes was only momentarily taken aback as he processed the question. "No, I think we're all married," he said. "Captain Jemison's wife is here in Berlin, but the other men all have family back home. Oh! Lieutenant Givens. He was engaged until his fiancée threw him over last year, so I think he's still a bachelor, sir."

"Is he a man of good character?" Benedict asked.

Colonel Reyes blinked. "Of course. He's been promoted up the ranks ahead of schedule, if that's what you mean."

Benedict crossed his arms. It wasn't at all what he meant. "If you had a daughter of marriageable age, would you have any concerns if she was to marry Lieutenant Givens?"

Instead of answering, Colonel Reyes gave him a hard look of scrutiny. "What's this all about?"

"Inga," he said simply. "She's in a tight spot, and someone pointed out that marriage to an American citizen would make it possible for her to leave Germany with the rest of the embassy staff."

Understanding dawned. "Well, that's a solution that hadn't occurred to me. There aren't many of us who aren't married. Doesn't being a widower count as unmarried?"

Benedict straightened his spine. "Obviously, but she and I are a terrible mismatch. Do you suppose there is any possibility Lieutenant Givens would be interested?"

"Is *Inga* interested? I think that should be the starting point of this rather unconventional proposal."

No doubt Colonel Reyes was correct. He ought to consult Inga before taking this any further, but he was too exhausted to handle it tonight. In the light of day, his mind would be fully functioning again and perhaps a miracle would have happened by then or a better solution would present itself.

He couldn't marry Inga. She would pickle his brain, and he would drive her insane. There was simply no way he could ever marry Inga. Could he?

16

Inga braced herself for a busy day at the embassy, yet she was still taken aback by the crush of Americans anxious to get a passport. Why had they waited so long? She would have given her eyeteeth to get a passport back in August if it had been possible, but these people obviously felt confident in President Wilson's assurances that he would keep them out of the war. They were mostly artists and musicians and performers, the carefree sort who always believed the worst would never happen.

Once upon a time, Inga had been carefree too. How long ago that all seemed now.

An early spring downpour darkened the day even further. Rain spattered against the windows, adding to the claustrophobic sensation of being trapped. At least there was plenty of work to keep busy. She sent telegrams, filed paperwork, and cranked the mimeograph machine so much her arm began to ache. She took shorthand at meetings between Mr. Gerard and low-level German diplomats sent to negotiate with him.

With each meeting Inga saw the transformation in Mr. Gerard. The man she always believed to be the soul of good cheer now scowled, demanded, and shouted. The Germans returned fire, and the room crackled with antagonism. After almost a year of enjoying being his stenographer, Inga tried not to cringe as she recorded the angry negotiations. It was a relief when Mr. Gerard stood and ordered the German undersecretary of the foreign office out of his office.

Inga left to type up the notes, but Mary Gerard intercepted her before she could reach her office.

"Inga, come quickly, there's something we need to discuss."

She eagerly abandoned notes of the hostile meeting to follow Mary through the reception room jammed with passport seekers, down the hall, and into the kitchen. Mrs. Barnes and Nellie were making sandwiches to hand out to people waiting for passports. Mary asked them to step outside for a few minutes, and Inga braced herself. This surely wasn't going to be good, even though Mary tried to compose herself before turning to face her.

"Inga, my dear, you know we all hate the thought of leaving you behind."

Her stomach churned as a rumble of thunder sounded from outside. "You mustn't worry about me. I'll figure something out."

"But that's just it! Some of the gentlemen at the embassy have thought of a solution. I've heard through the grapevine that Benedict is trying to find someone willing to marry you so that you can be granted diplomatic protection and sail home with us. I gather he was thinking someone from the Navy might be willing. Personally, I don't see any reason why he can't marry you."

Inga rocked back. Marry Benedict? It would be funny if she wasn't so horrified. "I-I'm not ready to marry anyone," she stammered.

Mr. Gerard wandered into the kitchen and helped himself to a sandwich. He obviously overheard the tail end of the conversation and already knew about the subject because he joined in with ease. "Marriage would be an easy solution, and since I'm still technically a judge in the state of New York, I could perform the ceremony. Tonight if you wish."

Mary frowned. "She wouldn't want to get married tonight, my dear. She needs more time to become accustomed to the idea. Sharing a bed and all . . ."

Inga sagged, appalled they should be discussing this so openly. She didn't want to marry Benedict at all, let alone share a bedroom with him. The prospect would give her nightmares for weeks. "Please, this is foolish," she said, eager to change the subject, but it was too late.

Mr. Gerard beckoned someone forward. "Benedict! Just the man we were discussing."

Benedict strode into the kitchen, obviously having been caught in the downpour because he was soaked. He held his fedora hat over the sink to drain rainwater from its brim. Then he used a towel to blot the damp from his shoulders. "What can I do for you, sir?"

"Nothing," Inga rushed to say, but Mr. Gerard cut her off.

"My wife reports that you've been sniffing around in search of someone to marry poor Inga. Why don't *you* do it? She's a fine woman, and we think you'd be a better match for her than anyone from the Marines."

Could a person die from mortification? She battled the compulsion to flee as dread settled over Benedict's face.

"Never," he choked out, then turned his appalled gaze on her. "Inga, please don't misunderstand. I think you are a fine young lady, but I would never marry you even if the stars fell from the sky."

"Marry?" another voice shrieked out from the hallway. Oh, good heavens, Nellie and Mrs. Barnes were on their way back, followed by Andrew and Larry. All of them hurried inside when the rain kicked up, and all of them had overheard their conversation.

Nellie thought it hysterical. "Inga and Benedict? Can you imagine!" She clamped her hand over her mouth to smother a giggle. Andrew and Larry looked like they were struggling not to laugh too.

This was beyond enough. Inga scrambled for the fraying ends

of her dignity and finally found her tongue. "Thank you all for joining in the hilarity. Benedict, I don't want to marry you. I have no idea how this even became a topic of conversation."

"It's not a bad idea," Mr. Gerard said. "If the two of you could manage to choke out the vows, I can declare you married, and we can all leave the country together. I've already booked a train for Switzerland in the likelihood we'll need to make a speedy exit. The two of you can get along for a few weeks, can't you? You can apply for an annulment once we get to New York."

"On what grounds?" Andrew asked.

"Non-consummation," Inga blurted out. The thought of lying down next to Benedict, pretending to like him? No, just no.

Benedict looked annoyed. "Inga, I'm not going to marry you at all."

"Who asked you?" She bristled. "Apparently you've been running around offering me up on a platter."

"I was trying to do you *a favor*," he bit out.

"Well, please stop!" It was excruciatingly hot in the crowded, cramped kitchen as everyone looked at her in varying stages of pity. "I am going to be perfectly fine and don't need anyone sacrificing themselves on the altar of matrimony on my behalf."

Panic began to escalate. She needed to get out of here before things got any worse. She angled sideways to escape down the hallway, but the reception room was loud and crowded. Where to go?

A hand suddenly clamped around her elbow, propelling her toward the line of private offices.

"To my office," Benedict said. There was no point in resisting because this ridiculous idea needed to be dismissed in short order. It needed to be silenced, with a stake driven through it.

Keys rattled as Benedict unlocked the door to his private office. The room was uncharacteristically sloppy, with half-filled boxes and open file cabinet drawers he had been packing, another sign that war was imminent.

He closed the door, but she still kept her voice low. "Benedict," she whispered furiously, "I did *not* ask to marry you."

He shoved the keys in his pocket and began pacing before the window, not meeting her gaze. "I know, I know. This whole thing is my fault, and I apologize. I mentioned your troubles at the Swiss Embassy last night and, well, here we are."

She sagged. Could this get any worse? "Does everyone from the neutral embassies know about this?"

"No! I asked if any of them could give you a job after we leave."

Hope took root, and she met his gaze. "And?"

He shook his head. "I'm sorry. All of them are balancing on a knife's edge at the moment, and they don't want to rock the boat by employing a German."

That meant she was going to be trapped in Berlin. She leaned against the cool wood paneling of the wall, willing her heartbeat to calm. All around her, evidence of Benedict's half-packed office underscored the fact that he was leaving along with everyone else, and she'd be left here alone.

"Don't worry. We won't simply abandon you," Benedict said. "We'll make arrangements to send you somewhere safe after we leave."

"Can't I stay at Alton House? I can look after the building and keep it safe. I can feed Larry's goldfish because I'm afraid he's spoiled it terribly."

Benedict's face softened in pained compassion, and she had to look away. She hated it when he was nice to her.

"Inga, it would be best for you to leave Berlin. Too many people know you're here, and you'll be open to the charge of treason because of your work at the embassy. Where would you like to go?"

With you! To America! Anywhere so long as I won't be alone. She couldn't say any of that. Instead, she answered with the best cheer she could dredge up. "I'm sure anywhere will be fine."

She had never been a good liar, and all she saw now was pity in Benedict's eyes.

There was little change in the diplomatic stalemate over the next two days. Benedict pinned all his hopes on a Friday morning meeting with the German Foreign Office. There was still hope of negotiating an apology from the Germans and a promise to end unrestricted submarine warfare.

The problem was that Gerard's temper had ratcheted ever higher in the past two days. The American ambassador arrived at the chancellery itching for a fight, and Benedict feared the Germans intended to give him one.

Benedict did his best to calm Gerard as they walked down the imposing hallways of the Reich Chancellery. Everything about this building was designed with magisterial intimidation in mind. High ceilings and endless marble corridors made their footsteps echo as they were escorted to the council chamber. They were to meet with Foreign Minister Von Jagow himself. Until now, the kaiser had sent underlings to negotiate, so an audience with the top minister gave Benedict hope.

"Keep your voice calm," he advised Gerard as they approached the council chamber. "They already know our demands, so don't needlessly antagonize them by restating the obvious. This must be handled delicately."

"Thank you, but I'll follow my own counsel," Gerard said.

They were led into the stately room, where a long wooden table was flanked by German officers in full military dress uniform with epaulets, sashes, and gleaming medals. The men stood as Benedict and Gerard entered, but their faces remained carved in stone. The only two Germans not in uniform were Foreign Minister Von Jagow and Undersecretary Arthur Zimmermann.

Benedict and Gerard took two seats at the end of a long table.

"Thank you for agreeing to see us," Benedict began. "I believe you already have a copy of President Wilson's note outlining the American position regarding—"

"The American *demands*, you mean," Gerard corrected.

Benedict curled his hands into fists beneath the table. There was no call for needless antagonism, but Benedict couldn't directly contradict his superior. The best he could do was fall back on the wording of President Wilson's note. He kept his tone calm, placating.

"As a neutral nation, President Wilson insists that Americans have the right to travel on ships of their choosing without fear of torpedo attacks. He denies the *Lusitania* was carrying munitions, and as such, the families of Americans killed on the ship deserve an apology and compensation."

"They deserve nothing," Foreign Minister Von Jagow asserted from the other end of the long table. "The *Lusitania* was loaded with munitions intended to kill German soldiers. The deaths of the civilians, while regrettable, was more humane than what the ordinary German citizen is enduring. The English blockade is condemning our people to a slow and painful death by starvation. We won't apologize for our navy's defense of our homeland."

Gerard's expression hardened. "The average German is the plumpest, best-fed example of starving citizenry anywhere in the known world," he retorted, which had the ring of truth since

Germany didn't lack for food as of yet. Their farms still operated, although their diversion of nitrogen from making fertilizer for crops to produce munitions would start having an effect if the war dragged on much longer.

"There is no call for insults," Von Jagow said. He was a sharp-featured man of surprisingly small stature, yet his militaristic demeanor made him seem taller. "I reiterate: The American civilian deaths are regrettable. That is the extent of our official comments on the matter."

Gerard's chair slid out with a scrape as he stood. "Is it?" he barked, feeling around in his pocket. He took out a gold coin and threw it across the table, striking Von Jagow in the chest. "Explain that coin," Gerard said, his voice vibrating.

Benedict silently cringed, wishing he could rewind the last five seconds and snatch that inflammatory coin back, for he knew exactly what it was. Someone in Germany had cast a commemorative medal to celebrate the sinking of the *Lusitania*.

Von Jagow didn't look at it but instead slid the coin back down the table with a hearty push toward Gerard. Benedict trapped it with his hand before it could reach its destination. Gerard might conceivably throw it a second time.

"That coin was struck by a private party," Von Jagow said. "Our government had nothing to do with it."

"Newspapers are reporting that the crew of the U-boat were awarded medals for sinking the *Lusitania*," Gerard said, which incensed Von Jagow even more.

"*British* newspapers are making that claim, and it's a lie. A deliberate attempt to besmirch German character when we did nothing wrong by targeting a ship carrying bombs to hurl at our soldiers."

The insults went back and forth. Never in Benedict's years serving in the diplomatic corps had he witnessed such unbridled verbal attacks without any attempt to address the issue at hand. President Wilson's demands lay ignored on the table as Gerard batted down every defense offered by the Germans. Both sides were digging deeper into their entrenched positions, both sides allowing anger to get the better of them. Someone needed to lower the temperature here.

Benedict met Von Jagow's gaze. "Sir, give us something," he implored. "At the very least, renounce that coin on behalf of your government. Give me something to soothe tempers back home. We *do not* want to go to war with you."

The plea caused a silence. Von Jagow shifted in his chair and looked out the window, his fist clenched. Benedict held his breath.

"Our people are angry too," Von Jagow finally said. "You scoff at our food situation, but famine is coming. We lost a quarter of a million men at the Marne, and here you speak to me of a hundred and twenty-eight dead Americans. We have a right to defend ourselves."

Benedict remained implacable. "Please. We do not want to go to war with you. Give us something. Renounce the coin."

Von Jagow gave a single nod of his head. "We can do that."

Benedict had to kick Gerard beneath the table to warn him against speaking. Plenty of the Germans around the table weren't happy either, but at least it was something.

President Wilson's demands were ignored. Benedict had failed to gain a single real concession, and war looked more likely than ever.

Benedict spent an excruciating two hours in Gerard's company at the embassy, arguing about the outcome from the disastrous meeting. Gerard was itching for a declaration of war, but Colonel Reyes threw cold water on the prospect.

"America isn't ready to go to war," Colonel Reyes insisted in the quiet of Gerard's office. "We have no tanks and only a few modern battleships. We don't have enough rifles for new recruits; they're being trained with wooden rifles. War may be inevitable, but we need to stall. Our military isn't ready."

The arguments dragged on long into the night, and with each passing hour the weight on Benedict's chest grew heavier. He was failing. Today had been a disaster, and the best he could do was stall for time. But war was coming.

A gentle tap sounded on the door. "A telephone call from Alton House, sir," a clerk said. "Andrew reports that someone threw a can of red paint against the front door and hurled rocks through the windows."

Gerard let out a string of curses. "Was anyone injured?" he asked.

The clerk shook his head. "No, sir. The Marine Guard you stationed scared the troublemakers off, and they've been working to clean up the paint mess. The staff is upset. Most of them started packing their bags and are ready to leave at a moment's notice. We thought you should know."

Benedict stood. "I should get home. If I sense any lingering trouble, I will collect the staff and bring them here to the embassy for their safety."

It was almost ten o'clock by the time Benedict returned to Alton House. Shadows of red paint still marred the front door despite attempts to wash it away, and the broken windows had been boarded up. A sergeant in uniform sat on the front porch, shuffling a deck of cards.

"Is everything calm now?" he asked the soldier, who pocketed the deck and stood.

"Yes, sir. It was probably just some drunken rabble-rousers. It shook everybody up, but they've all gone to bed. Inga might still be up. She was in the library earlier."

Inga. She was yet another worry on his growing list of failures. He and Inga had been butting heads since the hour they met. She was frivolous and flighty, but she was also smart and hardworking. Honorable. No matter how things played out in the coming days, he would not leave Berlin until Inga was safe. Although he'd never go so far as to marry her, he would think of something to protect her.

He thanked the sergeant, then headed into the darkened interior of the house. A beam of amber light slanted into the hallway from the library. He paused to gather his thoughts before approaching the open door.

She sat on the floor of the library. Dozens of volumes lay scattered on the floor and stacked on the tables, and an open trunk sat beside her. They were his volumes, the *Encyclopedia Britannica*.

"What are you doing?" he asked in confusion. Inga looked like a sloppy mess. Her blouse was untucked, sleeves rolled up, and her hair had spilled free of its pins.

Her face was grief-stricken as she looked up at him. "I'm helping pack your books," she explained, "but I can't fit them all in the trunk."

The encyclopedia was twenty-nine volumes, and it looked like she'd tried packing the trunk a dozen different ways to fit all the oversized books into the trunk. Benedict's heart squeezed. He hadn't given a thought to taking the encyclopedia with him, even though leaving the set behind would pain him.

"Don't feel bad," he murmured. "There are copies of the *Britannica* in America. It's okay."

"It's *not* okay," she insisted, and it sounded like she was on the verge of tears. "These books have all the notes you've written in the margins. So many underlined paragraphs and turned-down corners. I found ticket stubs marking entries for each opera you attended. Postcards and newspaper clippings and book reviews, all tucked into the right spots. Benedict, you can't leave them behind. No other encyclopedia in the world will be the same."

A surge of affection welled inside because she understood. He looked away as another weight landed on his shoulders.

"The meeting at the chancellery did not go well," he said, changing the subject. It was perhaps the understatement of the decade. Inga's fingers curled around the edges of the volume she held, the only sign of emotion.

He couldn't abandon her. She could be bothersome and frustrating, but she was burning the midnight oil to save his set of the

Encyclopedia Britannica. She was a good woman who deserved his help.

"Come with us," he said. "We can be married tomorrow morning."

He couldn't believe he'd just said that, and from the look of astonishment on Inga's face, she was stunned too.

"I couldn't ask that of you," she said on a shaky breath, although she didn't look repelled. She looked . . . hopeful.

"It would only be for a few weeks. As soon as we get to New York, we'll get an annulment."

Inga didn't move but stared at him from her position on the floor. He waited, hoping she'd turn him down. Maybe she'd succeeded in tracking down a family relation in Bavaria and had a safe place to go.

"Okay," she whispered. "Yes. Thank you. *Thank you.*"

He let out a heavy breath. There wasn't any going back now. "I will send a message to the ambassador tonight, asking for him to make it happen. It is best done quickly and quietly."

"I agree."

He didn't want any flowers or parties or pretense. Everyone at the embassy knew this was nothing more than a legal arrangement that would be terminated as soon as possible.

"Wear your sage-green suit," he said.

She looked momentarily surprised, then quickly nodded. "All right."

He liked the green suit. It looked fresh and pretty and uniquely Inga. It shouldn't matter what she wore, but he was a normal man with blood in his veins, and he liked the look of her in sage green. Not that it mattered. He would keep her at arm's length for however long this sham of a marriage lasted.

"It will only be for a few weeks," he reiterated.

"We shall both grin and bear it," Inga concurred. "Smile even."

He snorted. "Let's not get *too* carried away," he said before retreating upstairs, bothered by the gratitude shining from Inga's eyes. He didn't want Inga's gratitude. He wanted something else from her, though he couldn't quite put a name to it. Respect? Admiration? He closed his bedroom door with a gentle snick, then braced his hands on top of the bureau.

He shouldn't have done it. He should have found another way to save Inga short of marriage, but there was no going back now.

He opened the top drawer of his bureau, where he kept a few personal possessions. At least he already had a wedding ring. He slipped the thin gold band on his pinky finger, remembering the last time he'd offered it to a woman.

Claudia had scoffed when he offered his mother's wedding band to her.

"Benedict," she scolded, "you're a rich man. I think I'm entitled to a diamond, don't you?"

At that point, Benedict was so grateful that Claudia was willing to marry him that he would have bought her an entire diamond mine if she wanted.

The fact that their marriage had been a catastrophe wasn't entirely Claudia's fault. Some men simply weren't cut out for marriage, but Inga already knew that and would have no expectations of him.

There was nothing worse than a one-sided marriage, and despite all of his efforts, he'd begun to care for Inga and feared she could never return the sentiment.

18

Inga wore her sage-green suit the following morning and tried to quell the jittery feeling as she fastened the tiny mother-of-pearl buttons on the jacket.

This is my wedding day, she silently thought. It wasn't a real wedding, of course, and not at all like she'd always imagined, but Benedict's unexpected act of kindness would make her forever grateful.

Word of the impending marriage spread like wildfire through the staff at Alton House, though Benedict did his best to throw a bucket of ice over everyone's excitement. He made it clear there wasn't a flicker of romance on either side, nor should the occasion be treated as some celebratory rite of passage.

"It is nothing more than legal paperwork conducted in the privacy of the ambassador's office," he said. "Mrs. Gerard will serve as matron of honor, and Andrew will be my witness. Then I have an eleven o'clock appointment with my counterpart at the Argentinian Embassy to discuss the neutrality of shipping lanes."

Inga still couldn't resist pinning a little spray of white flowers on the lapel of her suit. Lily of the valley had always been her favorite, not only for their heavenly scent, but there was something about the tiny bell-shaped blossoms that made them look both pretty and tragic at the same time.

Benedict skewered her with a glare as she arrived at the carriage house to drive to the embassy. "I thought we agreed there would be no flowers," he said with a fleeting glance at her lapel.

"Lilies of the valley are too lovely for me to resist."

"They're poisonous," he said. "Ingesting them can cause irregular heartbeat, vomiting, and diarrhea."

Such a lovely thought. Normally she'd order Benedict to stop showing off by reciting facts from the *Encyclopedia Britannica*. Then she remembered the immense favor he was doing for her and kept her voice sunny.

"Goodness! Thank you for letting me know because I might have accidentally devoured them the next time I get hungry. You shall probably tire of being my hero before too much longer."

He opened the door for her. "I'm already tired of it, Miss Klein. After you."

She wouldn't let his flat tone darken her mood. She hadn't stopped smiling since agreeing to this marriage because she'd be safely on her way to New York soon, and this thrilling, difficult, and wonderful interlude in Berlin would be nothing more than a memory. She would never regret coming to Germany, but she was ready to go home.

The Gerards must not have gotten Benedict's dour command to stifle all hint of celebratory cheer because a bottle of champagne rested in a bucket of ice on Mr. Gerard's desk.

"My dear!" he said warmly, wrapping her in a welcoming hug.

"Isn't this exciting?" Mary enthused after kissing both her cheeks.

With a little smile, Inga said, "Benedict says it's nothing more than a tedious business transaction. You're quite sure it can be annulled once we get to America?"

"Just don't sleep with him," Mr. Gerard said in a matter-of-fact tone. "Failure to consummate the marriage is the only grounds you'll have. Can I trust you two lovebirds to keep your hands off each other?"

"Absolutely," Benedict said.

Mr. Gerard chortled. "Ha! Don't answer so quickly next time. Poor Inga might take it personally."

She grimaced. "I'm well aware that Benedict finds me as desirable as a case of shingles."

"This is a marriage of convenience," Benedict asserted. "Just think, you won't even need to change your monogrammed handkerchiefs, Mrs. Kincaid."

"Do I really need to change my name?" she asked, and Benedict gave a stiff nod.

"As long as we are in Germany, it is essential that we appear truly wedded. After today, you will be known as Mrs. Kincaid."

She'd always liked the way Benedict called her Miss Klein. At first it seemed aloof and unfriendly, but over the months it felt almost . . . affectionate. Like a special code between them that symbolized their "professional détente."

Andrew soon joined them, and Mr. Gerard motioned for her to stand side by side with Benedict in front of his desk. Inga clasped her hands, wishing she'd had a bouquet after all. It was awkward without anything for her hands to do.

"As a former judge and current ambassador, a man who has known both parties for many years, I see no reason why these two individuals, both of sound mind and body, may not enter into a legal marriage recognized by the state of New York. Inga, my dear, take Benedict's hands and repeat after me."

Her mouth went dry as she turned to look up at Benedict, who frowned at her. How steady his hands felt, while hers were icy and shook like a leaf. Mercifully, the phrases Mr. Gerard asked her to repeat were easy:

"I do solemnly swear that I, Inga Lissette Klein, have no lawful impediment to be joined in marriage to Benedict Michael Kincaid, who I take to be my lawfully wedded husband."

She couldn't look him in the eyes as he repeated the same vow back to her.

"And the ring?" Mr. Gerard asked.

To Inga's surprise, Benedict produced a simple gold band so thin it looked like it could snap. It got stuck on her knuckle, and she had to wiggle it down.

"I want it back when this is all over," Benedict murmured.

"Of course," she agreed. She would agree to anything so long as she could get on that ship with everybody else.

"Excellent," Mr. Gerard said once the ring was securely on her hand. Benedict didn't let her go. They both stood awkwardly as the final words were said. "I call upon these persons present to witness the joining of Inga and Benedict Kincaid into the bonds of legal matrimony. Benedict, you may kiss the bride."

Inga squeezed her eyes shut as Benedict pressed the world's lightest kiss on her cheekbone. Once Mr. Gerard pronounced them man and wife, Benedict let go of her hands and stepped away from her.

"I'm due at the Argentinian Embassy," he said.

"Not without a glass of champagne first," Mr. Gerard insisted. The bottle had already been uncorked, and he poured a few inches into each glass.

Benedict swallowed his in a single gulp, then set the glass down. "Thank you, sir. And now . . . off to business. Andrew? We're going to be late."

At least Andrew appeared a little apologetic as he congratulated Inga before following Benedict out the door.

"Benedict can't help being Benedict," Mary said as she topped off Inga's glass. To her surprise, Mr. Gerard ordered her to sit so he could give her a new assignment.

"I'm afraid there's no time for a proper celebration," he said. "I have been remarkably unsuccessful impressing the hostility of American popular opinion on Kaiser Wilhelm. It's time he understands the gravity of the situation."

"How can I help?" she asked.

He pointed to a stack of newspapers on the table beside the standing floor globe. "Those are American newspapers. They are filled with incendiary press and vicious political cartoons attacking the kaiser. I want you to cull through them and clip out the worst, most inflammatory articles and cartoons. He doesn't believe me, but perhaps he will believe the *New York Times* or the *San Francisco Chronicle*. All across America, the tide is turning against Germany. The nation is ready to take up arms, and he needs to see it in black-and-white. Find the most insulting stories, then paste them into a scrapbook. I shall present it to him at our next meeting."

It was possibly the strangest request Mr. Gerard had ever asked of her, but she nodded and collected the newspapers to carry to her tiny office.

She was married. *She was married!* How odd that she didn't feel any different. The trembly, jumpy fear that Benedict might back down before seeing it through had faded, but now she was Mrs. Inga Kincaid.

She rotated the thin gold band on her finger. This marriage wasn't going to affect her whatsoever after she arrived safely back to New York. The legal ties would be dissolved as if they'd never taken place. She'd take her old name back, and then she and Benedict would go their separate ways and probably never see each other again.

All she had to do was survive the next few weeks. After that they could mercifully escape each other.

Benedict wasn't able to draw a deep breath until he escaped Gerard's office and Inga's disconcerting presence. She was his wife now, and that carried certain obligations. He had respected his vows to Claudia until her dying day, even though she went out of her way to communicate her contempt for their marriage and all it entailed.

This marriage would be entirely different, with clear expectations from the outset. This evening at dinner he would announce the terms of their marital agreement to the Alton House staff. He thought they were clear this morning when he made an announcement at breakfast, and yet he had to stop Mrs. Barnes from making a wedding cake for dessert. He caught her assembling the tiered cake after returning from the Argentinian Embassy this afternoon.

"I said there was to be no celebration," he reminded her.

"Oh, it's no trouble at all," Mrs. Barnes said brightly. "I was making a cake anyway because of Larry's birthday, but he told me it was fine to turn it into a wedding cake instead."

"Please change it back to a birthday cake," Benedict instructed. "There are to be no gifts, toasts, or any other rituals associated with a wedding. This marriage is nothing more than a scrap of paper."

Mrs. Barnes looked properly chastened, which made him feel a little bad, and yet it was best to set expectations from the outset. Doing so might have saved him and Claudia immense suffering over the last few ill-fated years of their marriage.

Inga was still wearing the green suit when she arrived for dinner. He wished she'd changed into something different, but asking her to do so would be too intimate a request, well beyond anything a man would request of a colleague. Worse, Inga might wonder why, and he could hardly confess that the green suit made her look like the epitome of an ideal woman in his eyes. Fresh and willowy and alluring.

As usual, he was asked to say a blessing once everyone was seated at the kitchen dining table. The words came easily, for they were straight from his heart: "Dear Lord, we thank you for the blessing of this food. We are humbly aware of the millions across Europe who have fallen under the cloud of war and do not share this bounty. We pray for peace and thank you for our many blessings. Amen."

There was a resounding echo of "amens" around the table,

followed by the clattering of silverware as they began eating. Inga started filling bowls from the pot of beef stew in the middle of the table. He waited until everyone had been served before making his announcement.

"I'd like to say a few words about what happened this morning," he said, and immediately the room fell silent. "As you are aware, Miss Klein and I have entered into a legal arrangement so that she can leave the country with us when the time arrives."

Larry cleared his throat. "Are we supposed to call her Miss Klein or Mrs. Kincaid?"

Heat crept up from beneath Benedict's collar at the mistake. "Thank you, it is essential that we all refer to her as Mrs. Kincaid whenever we are in public. To the rest of the world, this is a legitimate marriage. Inga's safety depends on the marriage being recognized as real and lasting, and yet I do not intend to carry on the charade beneath this roof. We will not be sharing a bedroom, nor shall we pretend any sort of affection for each other, physical or otherwise."

Someone dropped a fork. Andrew's mouth twisted, and he covered it with a napkin. How nice that Benedict's awkward situation caused such hilarity among his co-workers. At least Mrs. Barnes and Nellie appeared attentive. Inga looked as mortified as Benedict felt.

He continued. "There is no way we could fool the people in this house about the state of affairs between Inga and myself." He couldn't yet call her Mrs. Kincaid with ease. All he needed was to get to the end of this embarrassing announcement and finish dinner. "In order for Germany to honor the marriage as legally binding, I am imploring you to refrain from gossiping about the marriage with anyone. Inga's safety depends on it. Is that understood?

He scanned everyone sitting around the table. "Larry. Is that clear?"

"Yes, sir."

"Mr. McFee?"

"Of course," the chauffeur said with a nod.

He scanned the faces of all those at the table until he had verbal confirmation from everyone that they understood the importance of maintaining the public appearance of a real marriage.

The only person he didn't question was Inga herself. The green suit must be warmer than it appeared because she fanned herself with her hand. She had cause to be embarrassed, and it was about to get a lot worse.

"I regret that I must be explicit, but there is no avoiding this detail. Inga and I will not be sharing a room. We will not consummate the marriage. Upon arrival in New York, we intend to seek an immediate annulment of the marriage, and our only grounds are non-consummation. You may be asked to testify in court that we used separate bedrooms. I can assure you that at no time will we give you cause to believe that we . . . that I have . . . that there has been any untoward behavior that would prevent the annulment."

Not so much as a muscle moved from anyone in the room. Even Inga had stopped fanning herself, and it was so quiet the sound of the clock ticking down the hall kept pace with his thudding heart.

"That's all then," he finished, sitting back down and spearing a chunk of beef with his fork.

Inga shook off her awkwardness first. "Happy birthday, Larry."

Mrs. Barnes followed suit. "Yes! Happy birthday. My goodness, it seems like only last year it was your birthday, doesn't it? Funny how these things keep coming around."

Everyone else joined in the birthday wishes while Benedict counted down the minutes for the dreadful dinner to end.

19

The next two weeks were no honeymoon. Ever since the sinking of the *Lusitania*, Inga was fully engaged in taking dictation and wiring a flurry of cables as they attempted to keep America out of the war. Sometimes the meetings were between Mr. Gerard and other neutral nations who tried to negotiate a compromise between the U.S. and Germany; other times it was tense negotiations with President Wilson's staff in Washington. Nothing appeared to be working. Both nations were digging themselves deeper into their entrenched positions in a grim stalemate.

Mr. Gerard's demands for an audience with the kaiser were repeatedly denied. He was beginning to take it as a personal insult, as was President Wilson. With two powerful nations on the brink of war, why couldn't Kaiser Wilhelm spare an hour to meet with the ambassador?

Benedict tried to explain it to her one night at the dinner table. "The Germans surround themselves with layers of hierarchy. Permitting a lowly American, one without a drop of royal blood, into the exalted kaiser's presence would be tantamount to admitting the need to make amends."

"But Mr. Gerard and the kaiser have often socialized," she said.

Andrew helped himself to another serving of potato salad. "But not when the two nations were on the brink of war. If the kaiser accepts the meeting, it will be considered a sign of weakness."

Maybe this was why Mr. Gerard was so adamant that she compile the horrible scrapbook of anti-German stories from the American press. She hated reading such vile content and was surprised to see how the American press celebrated the taunt Mr. Gerard threw at the German minister about using America's lampposts for hanging disloyal German Americans. Inga had been in the room when the taunt occurred, and it was shocking how popular it made Mr. Gerard back home. He was celebrated as a bold new force in diplomacy, a man who took charge, having put the kaiser back on his heels. New York City announced that their iron lampposts that had recently been replaced would be melted down and made into bullets.

The cartoons were blatantly disrespectful. One portrayed the kaiser in diapers, crying like a spoiled baby; another showed him as a turkey with his feathers being plucked by gleeful soldiers from France and England. Plenty showed him personally drowning women and children of the *Lusitania*. The cartoons seemed needlessly inflammatory to Inga, but when she tried to protest to Mr. Gerard, he demanded she include them in the scrapbook.

"This is exactly what I want him to see," Mr. Gerard insisted. "The kaiser is surrounded by underlings who tell him only what he wants to hear. He has no idea what the rest of the world thinks of him."

So Inga collected the revolting cartoons and pasted them into the book. One of the cartoons even made fun of the kaiser's withered left arm, caused by a difficult delivery at birth. How could people be so cruel? And what good could shoving this beneath the kaiser's nose do?

Thankfully, compiling the scrapbook was only a small portion of her job. Most of the time she was in the ambassador's office, taking dictation during his meetings. One day she typed sixty-five letters. She became accustomed to the strange language of diplomacy. In letters, Mr. Gerard displayed immaculate formality, with lavish use of official titles and effusive praise before getting to the point.

Then one morning, exactly three weeks after the sinking of the *Lusitania*, Mr. Gerard dictated a startling change of style in a letter addressed to the Chancellor of the German Empire, Herr Theobald von Bethmann Hollweg:

> *Your Excellency,*
> *Three weeks ago, I asked for an audience with His Majesty the Kaiser. Last week I repeated the request. Please do not trouble yourself further.*
>
> > *Respectfully,*
> > *James W. Gerard*

Inga stared at the words she'd just typed. The implications were shocking, for this letter was a declaration that negotiations were at an end.

"Are you sure this is what you want to send?" she asked Mr. Gerard.

"I'm through with niceties, Inga. I've tried to follow the recommended protocol, and it has not succeeded. Please prepare the document on embassy letterhead so that I may put my signature to it."

She did so, watching in trepidation as Mr. Gerard signed the document with a flourish. Thank heavens, she was safely married and could leave the country if this letter resulted in an immediate break in diplomatic relations. It was hard to even draw a full breath as she watched Mr. Gerard dribble a blob of scarlet sealing wax over the flap of the envelope, then press his ambassadorial stamp into the damp wax.

She said a silent prayer as he passed the letter to an army officer, who would then deliver it to the chancellery.

Mr. Gerard summoned Benedict and the rest of the diplomatic corps to inform them of the letter. "Be prepared to leave the city tonight," he said. "If I don't have an appointment with the kaiser before dinner, we'll leave on the midnight train."

The ploy worked. Two hours after the blunt note, Ambassador Gerard received an invitation to meet with Kaiser Wilhelm II at his castle in Upper Silesia.

Castle Pless was on the kaiser's favorite hunting grounds. It was located in a hilly Polish region that had been annexed by Germany in the eighteenth century. Although the castle dated all the way back to the Middle Ages, it had been completely rebuilt in the nineteenth century, giving it a baroque style that made it look more like a palace than a castle.

"The meeting is in two days' time, so we must leave by train tomorrow morning," Mr. Gerard told Inga. "Pack your bags with a week's worth of clothing. You're coming with us."

She gasped. "Me?"

"Yes, you. I need a translator I trust. The kaiser speaks very quickly, and your German is better than mine or Benedict's. I want you in the room with us, transcribing what's being said *exactly* as you hear it."

A weight landed in her gut. "I'll be in the same room as the kaiser?" It wasn't right, not for the daughter of a shoemaker. The kaiser's image was pressed onto all the coins. Each Sunday his name was spoken in churches, and the congregants prayed for him.

Mr. Gerard must have sensed her dismay because he clapped her on the shoulder and said, "He's an intimidating person, but he bleeds red just like the rest of us. Bring the scrapbook you've been compiling. I intend to present it to him on our first day at Castle Pless." He had a spring in his step as he left her office.

Giving the kaiser the incendiary scrapbook seemed like a

terrible blunder, and she needed Benedict's advice. Maybe he could talk Mr. Gerard out of it.

It was eight o'clock in the evening before Benedict returned to Alton House. He must have dined at the embassy, for he went straight to his bedroom to pack.

Inga didn't want to be caught in his bedroom, but she was going behind Mr. Gerard's back by showing Benedict this scrapbook, and it was best done privately. She tucked the book beneath her arm, squared her shoulders, and knocked on his bedroom door.

"Come in," he called out.

She cracked open the door but averted her eyes, praying he was fully clothed. "Are you sure? It's me."

Benedict blocked the entrance. Mercifully, he was still wearing the same three-piece suit he'd worn to the embassy. "What do you want?" he asked—not in the warmest of tones, but not hostile either.

"I need to show you something in confidence," she replied in a low voice. "I fear the ambassador is about to make a terrible mistake."

Benedict nodded. "I'll meet you in the library in two minutes."

She hurried downstairs to switch on the lamps in the darkened library. The *Encyclopedia Britannica* remained safely boxed up in the corner, as were all the important papers and correspondence from Alton House. They would be ready to leave within minutes if diplomatic relations were severed.

She put the scrapbook on the desk just as Benedict arrived. "What do you have to show me?" he asked, closing the door behind him.

She explained how she'd been charged with collecting the articles from American newspapers to show the kaiser and opened the leather cover of the scrapbook for Benedict to see. The articles were full of anger and hate and made Americans look like awful people.

Benedict remained standing, his gaze darting across the first set of clippings on the opening page. A muscle in his jaw worked as he turned to the next page while she silently cringed, ashamed that she had anything to do with this scrapbook. Benedict remained expressionless as he turned the pages. Vile cartoons lampooned the kaiser and portrayed German soldiers as barbarians as they raped and pillaged the countryside.

"Well?" she asked as he came to the last page. "I thought perhaps you should discourage Mr. Gerard from giving this to the kaiser."

Benedict closed the book and pushed it toward her. "No, we should show it to him. Kaiser Wilhelm is surrounded by men who tell him only what he wants to hear. He needs to see this."

She blanched. "You're sure?"

Benedict nodded. "The kaiser knows President Wilson doesn't want to get dragged into this war, but he doesn't understand that Wilson is at the mercy of the voters. They don't have elections in Germany, and Wilson is facing one next year. The scrapbook will show the kaiser that he can't take President Wilson for granted."

It was the last thing she expected Benedict to say, yet it lifted a weight from her shoulders. She trusted his judgment more than anyone else in the embassy. The wisdom of his reasoning made the world seem a little less chaotic, a little more certain. Amber light from the electric lamp cast shadows on the planes of his face, making him unusually handsome as he regarded her. He seemed almost kind.

"Thank you," she said and gathered the scrapbook back in her arms. It was time to get out of here and put behind her these uncomfortable feelings. She turned away and opened the door when his voice stopped her.

"There's something else you need to know," Benedict said, and suddenly he didn't sound so confident anymore.

She closed the door. "Yes?"

"We won't actually be staying in Castle Pless," he said, his eyes averted. "There is a hunting lodge a few miles from the castle, which is large enough to hold the American delegation. It's where we will be staying for the duration of our visit."

A hint of disappointment tugged. She'd never been inside a castle before and had been looking forward to staying there. A hunting lodge seemed a bit of a letdown. "I'm sure it will be fine."

Benedict cleared his throat. "There are only five bedrooms. You and I will be required to share one."

That would be awful for them both. "If we're in a private hunting lodge, why can't we have separate rooms?"

"Because there are spies everywhere in Germany. There will be servants at the hunting lodge who will be fluent in English, even if they pretend ignorance of it. They will be spying on everything we do, say, or write, so be mindful of that, even if it appears we have complete privacy."

She braced herself. She owed Benedict a great deal and would not embarrass him by letting anyone in Germany know their marriage was less than genuine. It would be exquisitely awful, but she would do as he asked.

20

Benedict expected the kaiser's hunting lodge to be impressive, yet he was still surprised when the carriage rounded the bend to reveal the Gothic masterpiece nestled amid towering pine and oak trees. The lodge was like something from a Tudor fairy tale, with timbered beams, a steeply pitched roof, gables, and turrets.

All five of their delegation were exhausted after the twelve-hour train ride. Benedict, Inga, Colonel Reyes, and both Gerards had been jostling in a carriage for an additional two-hour ride through dense forestland to get here, but at last they had arrived.

He'd kept a careful watch on Inga, gauging her reaction as the carriage rolled to a stop. She looked radiant as she marveled at the view through the window. Sunlight dappled the secluded glade, and butterflies flitted above wildflowers scattered in the grass. Summer had definitely arrived, and the nearby stream gurgled as snowmelt from the Tatra Mountains flowed through the meadow. Though it looked enchanting, it was a dangerous enchantment.

He leaned forward to speak to the group quietly. "Remember, trust no one. Not the maids, the gardeners, not even any little children you see. Understood?"

For once, Ambassador Gerard took him seriously. "Understood," he said.

Benedict exited the carriage first, his feet sinking a bit in the damp soil. He extended a hand to help Inga down.

"It smells so fresh," she said of the green, peaty scent. It smelled cold and damp to Benedict, and despite the grandeur of the hunting lodge, he wasn't looking forward to their stay.

A pair of stable hands walked out to greet them. The older man had ruddy cheeks and a long, drooping mustache. "*Willkommen*," he said. "*Hatten sie eine sichere reise?*"

Benedict answered in English, "Yes, thank you. We had a safe journey."

The ruddy-faced man looked at him blankly. Benedict repeated the phrase in German, even though he'd wager his last dollar that the stable hands were completely fluent in English. They assisted in unstrapping the trunks secured to the roof of the carriage. For a three-day visit, they had brought enough clothing any normal family would need for a month because this was no relaxed weekend in the country. It was a court visit, with all the necessary diplomatic dress, evening wear, and hunting clothes. No article of clothing would be worn twice.

"My dear?" he said, offering his arm to Inga, then escorted her into the lodge as though they were genuinely man and wife. The cobblestone walkway seemed almost quaint as they approached the front entrance protected by a timber alcove. Inga murmured something about the darling mullioned windows, but Benedict eyed the series of stag antlers mounted atop the gables and suspected it didn't bode well for the decor inside the lodge.

"Can this be real?" Inga said as she stepped inside. It sounded as if she couldn't decide whether to be charmed or appalled. The entrance was decorated with mounted stag heads, a snarling boar with pointy tusks, a mountain ram with curling horns, and geese with outstretched wings. Smaller animals were stuffed and perched on windowsills in realistic poses. Hunting trophies graced every wall and mantelpiece inside the vaulted interior of the lodge. A stunning chandelier built entirely of antlers hung above the great hall.

A plump housekeeper named Frau Huber welcomed them inside, her rustic German accent charming. "Will you show us the bedrooms?" he asked Frau Huber, praying there might be one with two beds. While it might seem odd for newlyweds to take a room with separate beds, he could always make an excuse that he was a light sleeper.

Carpet covered the wooden stairs as they headed to the second floor. There was a generous selection of bedrooms, all with slanted roofs, mullioned windows, and massive wooden headboards.

None with two beds. He chose one that had an upholstered chair in the corner. "This will do," he said to Frau Huber. The housekeeper motioned for a servant to bring their luggage into the room. Inga instinctively reached out for her hatbox, but he took her hand to stop her. No wife of a ranking diplomat would carry her own baggage, no matter how light.

He was spared the need to make conversation with Inga over the next few minutes as servants lugged suitcases, trunks, and hatboxes into each of the bedrooms. Benedict pretended to be at ease while unpacking his trunk to hang his diplomatic suit. Inga followed his lead, hanging her navy walking suit beside his in the wardrobe. Seeing their clothes snug together in the same wardrobe seemed uncomfortably intimate.

"I wonder what this means?" Inga asked as she studied the carving along the top of the large headboard.

Benedict leaned forward to study the carved lettering. *Bóg, Honor, Ojczyzna.* "It is the national motto of Poland," he said. "It translates to something like 'God, Honor, and Homeland.'"

"You speak Polish?" she asked in amazement.

Hardly, but he'd read the lengthy sections on Poland in the *Encylopedia Britannica*, which was a good thing because this part of Europe had been Polish before it was swallowed up by Germany.

"The servants working at the lodge will certainly be German. Should you travel into the village, the people will all be Polish. I would prefer you stay on the hunting lodge grounds if I'm not with you."

He insisted on it actually. It wasn't safe to wander about.

A collection of owls arranged on perches rimmed the top of the room, seeming to stare down at them.

"I don't know how I'm going to sleep with those owls watching me," Inga said.

I don't know how I'm going to sleep with Inga two feet away, he thought.

Before he could worry about the situation, Ambassador Gerard appeared in their doorway. "We've been summoned to the castle," he said. "We leave in ten minutes."

Benedict opened his pocket watch: four o'clock in the afternoon. It was too late for hunting, too early for dinner. That meant it was most likely to discuss the political situation and required the appropriate diplomatic uniform.

He closed the door. "Please change into your maroon suit, and I'll be wearing my diplomatic attire."

Her eyes widened. "That seems so formal."

It did, but he couldn't be sure of the intention of this meeting. "It's better to be overdressed than underdressed. I'll leave for a few minutes while you change, then we can trade places."

Inga's fingers trembled as she fastened the buttons on her crisply tailored maroon jacket. This was the richest of all her suits, but she looked like a ragpicker compared to the men. Diplomatic attire consisted of a single-breasted black tailcoat with high-stand collars. Because it was daytime, Benedict advised against the scarlet sash in favor of a small dress sword with an embellished hilt and scabbard. Gold buttons with tiny American eagles were the only hint of color on the shockingly impressive attire.

Colonel Reyes wore his formal Army uniform with gold braiding on the epaulets, collar, and gauntlet cuffs. The only other color was a thin red stripe down the side of his trousers.

Only four of them were attending the gathering, as Mary was exhausted from traveling and opted to stay at the hunting lodge. Benedict and Mr. Gerard sat in the carriage opposite her and Colonel Reyes.

Inga clutched the bag carrying the scrapbook on her lap as the carriage rolled ever closer to the castle. Never in her wildest dreams did she imagine that she would see the kaiser in person, but instead of dropping into a curtsy like she ought to do, she carried a book filled with vile cartoons and insulting press. Thank goodness she wasn't going to be the one to put it into his hands, yet even being in the background while someone else did the deed would be unnerving.

Benedict continued to give her last-minute instructions as the carriage approached the castle. "Don't look the kaiser in the eye, and don't initiate a conversation. You are attending the meeting as a secretary, not as a guest or my wife."

All to the good. Kaiser Wilhelm had a fearsome reputation, and she'd be too tongue-tied to speak. Benedict took the scrapbook from her arms and set it on the bench beside him.

"We shall leave it in the carriage until the appropriate time," he said. "If the meeting goes well, there may be no need to hand it over. In the likelihood our relationship with Germany continues to sour, I'll find the best time to show the kaiser the precarious situation in America."

She breathed easier once the awful book was off her lap. Now all she carried was a slim leather case that Mary loaned her, with a notepad and pen for taking shorthand notes of the meetings with the kaiser.

Her mouth went dry. The men in the carriage were trying to keep America out of the war, and she would do everything possible to support them. *Dear Lord, please bless them with strength and wisdom and courage.*

Castle Pless loomed before them, a baroque building of white granite topped with a mansard roof and the flag of the German Empire flying from the spire, the unmistakable sign that the kaiser was in the residence. Manicured hedges and topiaries filled the gardens beneath a shockingly blue sky.

The carriage rounded the large expanse of lawn and then crossed a stone bridge spanning a stream. The stream fed into a picturesque lake beside the castle, where swans glided among lily pads and fronds of grass. Surely this was what heaven must look like.

The carriage soon arrived at the stables. Half a dozen men dressed in scarlet livery with white stockings and white wigs came out to greet them. Benedict got out first, then helped her down. She tried not to look at the fancy servants with their gold braid and gleaming shoe buckles. If she met their gaze, they might spot her for a fraud.

A handsome young man wearing a tweed jacket and jodhpurs strolled over to meet them. "Welcome," he said with a nod to the ambassador. "I hope you are game for a round of shooting. We're hosting the Turkish delegation around back and have been shooting clay pigeons. Care to join us?"

As if on cue, the report of a gunshot blasted through the air. Inga flinched as the boom echoed and rolled across the countryside. She glanced uneasily at the others. Everyone wore their finest diplomatic attire and certainly weren't here for backyard shooting contests. Rather than be insulted, Mr. Gerard seemed amused.

"Sorry, Your Highness," Mr. Gerard said. "I'm due to meet with your father or I'd have brought my gear. Nothing beats a good round of trapshooting."

Inga sucked in a quick breath. She'd never seen an actual prince before, but this laughing young man must be one of the kaiser's six sons. All of them were high-ranking military officers, although none had been sent to the front. She tried to be invisible as Ambassador Gerard introduced Prince Adalbert to Benedict and Colonel

Reyes. The prince looked around thirty and spoke with an upper-crust accent with lovely, precise diction and vocabulary.

Mr. Gerard did not introduce Inga, nor did Prince Adalbert acknowledge her presence, which was fine. Servants were used to being in the background.

Another crack of a gunshot rang out, and the prince gestured for the delegation to follow him toward the sound of the shooting. This wasn't going as expected. Nobody was dressed for trapshooting or a garden party. The repetitive gun blasts ratcheted her tension even higher. How ironic that the first time she heard a gun fired during this war should be at Kaiser Wilhelm's castle.

The prince led them around to the back of the castle, where a line of men stood in a grassy field. Most of them casually held rifles while one aimed at a clay disk launched into the air from a trap machine. *Boom!*

Other men sat beneath a cluster of shade trees, watching the sport from garden chairs. Her breath caught when she spotted the kaiser, who was wearing tweedy garb like all the others. He sat in an ordinary garden chair, but still held himself as though it were a throne. Someone leaned down to whisper in the kaiser's ear, and he casually glanced at them as they approached.

Her mouth went dry, and her heart thudded as Kaiser Wilhelm stood. The ends of his mustache were ruthlessly waxed to turn up in little tufts pointing toward his eyes. Ambassador Gerard led the delegation forward, Benedict and Colonel Reyes a step behind. Inga walked an additional three steps behind but wished she could be invisible.

Everyone in the American delegation was painfully overdressed in formal black and ceremonial swords. Ambassador Gerard halted a few yards away from the kaiser, who looked mildly amused.

"Ha!" the kaiser said. "The three of you look like a flock of blackbirds."

From behind, Inga spotted a slight stiffening of Benedict's spine, but Mr. Gerard affected jovial good cheer. "Had I known we were shooting, I'd have worn my hunting garb. I have fond memories of our weekend shooting grouse at Blutenburg. Come! I can't resist a quick go at those targets. Somebody hand me a rifle."

Mr. Gerard shrugged out of his formal coat, handing it to Benedict. A stout, tweedy man agreeably handed over his rifle, and Inga glanced among the Germans. How smoothly Mr. Gerard just turned the tables on them all. It looked like the kaiser deliberately lured them here under the pretense of a diplomatic meeting so they would arrive overdressed and off-balance.

Mr. Gerard wasn't off-balance. He seemed delighted as he shouldered the rifle and nodded to the servant at the trap machine. Inga held her breath as a clay disk soared into the air, then shattered into pieces after Mr. Gerard shot the gun. Six more disks were launched into the air in rapid succession, and Mr. Gerard shot four of them, pieces of clay pigeon falling into the grass.

Mr. Gerard asked for another round while Inga eavesdropped on Prince Adalbert, who introduced Benedict and Colonel Reyes to the other five men. Two were from the Ottoman Empire, two from Austria, and a gentleman from Bulgaria. There were *three* German princes! Prince Adalbert was the one who had met them at the carriage. The stout man was Prince Eitel, and Prince August was the knee-weakening handsome man with a slim pencil mustache. Imagine . . . she was breathing the same air as three real princes and the kaiser.

An assortment of other men in ordinary business attire stood well back from the diplomats. They were secretaries like Inga. It was extremely uncomfortable to stand there doing nothing while the introductions among the envoys and ambassadors unfolded in a well-oiled sequence. Inga mirrored the stance of the other secretaries, keeping her expression neutral and hands at her sides.

A small army of servants soon appeared with additional wicker chairs for the Americans. A few more chairs were set out in a line several yards behind the diplomats for the secretaries, and Inga finally sat. She was on the end of the row, beside a dapper young man with dark hair and eyes. He held a notepad on his lap, prompting Inga to hold her pad exactly like the other secretaries.

The man next to her leaned close to whisper, "Vasil Petrov, aide to the ambassador from Bulgaria. And you are?"

"Inga Klein. *Kincaid*," she hastily amended. "Secretary to the American ambassador."

"Welcome, Miss Klein-Kincaid," he said, and she didn't correct him. Hopefully her blunder would never matter.

They were close enough to hear the chatter among the diplomats. Mr. Gerard was jovial, praising the quality of shooting to be had in the region and reminiscing about yachting with the princes at Kiel.

The kaiser turned to the Bulgarian ambassador. Bulgaria was a small nation, but it was strategically located between Germany and their Ottoman allies, and a new railway was under discussion. The Bulgarian secretary began jotting down notes in a style of shorthand unfamiliar to Inga and prompting her to begin taking notes as well, even though the discussion didn't directly relate to America. All the other secretaries took notes, so she would too.

Ambassador Gerard interjected himself to ask if the kaiser had the chance to read President Wilson's latest missive regarding the *Lusitania*, the one that reiterated the need for an apology.

"Why should we apologize for the *Lusitania*?" the kaiser barked. "Every American who set foot on that ship had been warned not to do so."

"Nonsense," Mr. Gerard retorted. "If you warned me not to ride my own horse, the fact that you gave me a warning would not give you permission to shoot me in the head for doing so."

Apparently the kaiser wasn't used to being spoken to in such a manner. The princes shifted uneasily, and the other diplomats looked away. Benedict didn't. He kept his eyes trained on the kaiser, who refused to answer.

Finally, Prince Adalbert broke the tension. "Say, how about we find you some appropriate clothes, and we can all go for a round of tennis? We have an indoor court. Where is Silas? He was always good for keeping track of the score."

Silas was Inga's predecessor, the secretary Mr. Gerard fired, and Inga was surprised the prince remembered him.

"Silas has been reassigned," Mr. Gerard replied. "Inga is now my personal secretary."

Several heads swiveled to look at her, including the kaiser, who snapped his fingers. "Stand up, then," he ordered in the same tone he might use to bring his dogs to heel, but Inga instinctively obeyed. How could she not?

"A secretary, is she?" an Ottoman diplomat said. "How convenient. I wish I had such a pretty secretary to accompany me while my wife was safe at home."

Mr. Gerard shot to his feet. "Sir, my wife is two miles away at the hunting lodge. You insult both my wife and my secretary by suggesting anything improper."

Inga felt the blood drain from her face as she remained standing, frozen and uncertain what to do. Everyone was still looking at her, and one of the other diplomats gave a good-natured chuckle. "Please give her my salutations. It is an understandable mistake, is it not? Anyone would be forgiven for thinking so."

Benedict stood. "Inga is my wife," he bit out. "There is nothing improper about her, and she deserves an apology."

The world tilted. This wasn't the apology they came here for, but mercifully the Ottoman diplomat stepped forward and offered her the slightest of bows.

"My apologies, Mrs. Kincaid."

The kaiser waved a dismissive hand. "Yes, yes. Mrs. Kincaid, sit down before you fall down."

"No need," Ambassador Gerard said, motioning for Colonel Reyes to stand. "Tempers are too hot for any productive discussion today. Hopefully we can reconvene tomorrow to discuss the president's note. Neither one of us wishes to go to war, but we are fully prepared to do so." He turned and strode toward the carriage house, Benedict and Colonel Reyes close behind him. Inga scooped up her notepad, an avalanche of heat engulfing her as she followed the group.

The carriage ride back to the lodge was awful, though Mr. Gerard did not seem all that distressed. "We shall wear our traveling clothes tomorrow," he said. "It will send a message more powerful than any words can deliver."

Sharing a bedroom was nothing new to Inga. She grew up sharing with her baby sister, and then after moving to New York, she shared a bedroom with Delia for two years before she could afford her own room.

She was *not* going to share a bedroom with Benedict. Her sole objective tonight was to convince him it would be okay for her to sleep downstairs in the billiard room, which had a padded bench big enough to sleep on if she curled up tight. That bench was the answer to their problems. It was going to be impossible to sleep if Benedict was in the room, and all those stuffed owls mounted on the wall gave her the willies.

Benedict changed in the washroom while she quickly donned a nightgown. She wished the cotton wasn't so thin and that it didn't dip so low in the front, but at least she had a robe. It was a ratty old yellow robe that once belonged to her mother. She perched on the corner chair and grabbed fistfuls of fabric to gather up beneath her chin and waited for Benedict to return.

Even so, she was still startled by the brisk knock on the bedroom door. "Come in," she said, clutching her robe tighter.

Benedict entered, a thick green robe covering a white shirt. It looked like he still wore slacks beneath his robe. He frowned at her.

"That is likely the ugliest robe in this world or the next," he said dryly, then flipped the bedsheets down. "Hop in. I'll take the chair; you get the bed."

She cleared her throat, ready for battle. "You take the bed. I'm heading down to the billiard room to read for a while. I might end up falling asleep down there, so please don't wait up for me."

His expression looked as enthused as a man facing an execution. He leaned in closer and spoke in a low voice, "Get in the bed, Inga. This place is swarming with servants, and they all work for the kaiser."

"So?" she said in a harsh whisper. "Maybe they understand that people sometimes read at night and fall asleep on a cozy bench."

Benedict folded his arms. "Get in bed, Inga."

She lifted her chin. "You might say 'please.'"

"Please."

She scooted deeper into the upholstered chair. Benedict did her a huge favor by marrying her, and if they were forced to share this room, the least she could do was take the chair. She curled her feet beneath her. "I'll stay here—you take the bed."

He snapped his fingers. "In the bed. Now."

Oh, for pity's sake. She kept her eyes averted as she sprang off the chair and jumped into the bed, horrid yellow robe and all. Her nightgown bunched up beneath the covers, and she struggled to yank it down even though Benedict surely couldn't see a thing. Still, it bothered her. There would be no exposed legs while he was in the room.

She kept her eyes closed but sensed him moving around the room, removing his shoes and settling into the chair. He must have turned down the wick of the kerosene lamp because the light behind her lids faded, and she tentatively opened her eyes.

She sensed him in the chair beside her. It couldn't be comfortable. In fact, it was probably awful.

"Thank you," she whispered into the darkness.

He grunted in reply.

It was an oppressively long night.

21

Benedict woke early to escape the bedroom, tiptoeing to the wardrobe to remove a clean shirt before heading to the washroom down the hall. The change in Inga's breathing made it obvious she was awake, only pretending to sleep.

Fine. The less interaction the better. Every muscle in his back ached from being slumped in the upright chair for the last seven hours. He awoke every few minutes throughout the night to shift to a better position, but he had no cause for complaint. The stiff-backed chair was the lap of luxury compared to what the soldiers in muddy trenches had to endure.

Icy water in the bathroom taps helped jolt him awake. He washed and changed into a set of fresh clothes, bracing himself for the day ahead.

Yesterday couldn't have gone worse. The kaiser showed no interest in granting any of President Wilson's demands, and it hadn't been wise to call attention to his marriage to Inga. The publicity would make it harder to unravel. He'd already been through one bad marriage all the way to its bitter end and so didn't want a repeat of that.

Everything felt different this morning as they arrived at Castle

Pless. There was nobody to greet them at the stables with a taunting invitation for trapshooting. No servants in gold-and-scarlet livery, but only a single groom to look after their horses. Benedict helped Inga down from the carriage, glad to see she didn't look so intimidated this morning.

The stakes couldn't be higher. President Wilson had issued his final demand, and if the Germans didn't concede, the ambassador was to sever diplomatic relations. Once that happened, war wasn't far behind. Young men from all over America would be required to leave their jobs, bid farewell to their families, and pick up a rifle.

The groom directed them toward the rear entrance of the castle, but there was no way they would use the back door.

Benedict retrieved the scrapbook from the carriage before hurrying to catch up to the others as they walked around the side of the palace and up to the front entrance. The main door was a masterpiece of carved wood and elegantly forged ironwork. There was nowhere to knock or ring a bell. Guests arriving at the castle were expected or not received at all.

The scrapbook grew heavy in Benedict's arm as the four of them waited. Mr. Gerard wore a pugnacious expression that did not bode well, but they'd already gone through the mannerly steps of diplomatic etiquette yesterday. The kaiser didn't believe they would call his bluff, and it was time to make him believe.

The clicking of metal sounded from behind the castle doors, and a butler slowly pulled the door open. "His Excellency is not available today."

Mr. Gerard lifted his chin. "Then we will meet with von Jagow, and he most certainly is available to the American delegation."

Gottlieb von Jagow was the Foreign Minister of Germany and more astute than the kaiser. Kaiser Wilhelm might risk a war over a matter of pride; von Jagow wouldn't.

The butler gestured for them to come inside. They silently crossed into the light-filled foyer. Beside him, Inga made a tiny squeak as she caught sight of the grand staircase spiraling up the side of the great hall. Priceless tapestries and marble statuary added to the grandeur.

"I guess they couldn't help themselves," Inga whispered with a nod to the chandelier above, and he had to smother a laugh. Yes, in a world of gilded splendor, Inga immediately spotted the cluster of deer antlers fashioned into a light fixture.

They declined the butler's offer of refreshment and were shown into the castle library to await von Jagow. It wasn't any kind of library that Benedict recognized. There were only a dozen antique books with gilt lettering stored behind a glass display case. The delicate table in the center of the room was small enough to be easily carried away. The room was probably used as a ballroom more than a place to study, but he'd be willing to meet in an out-house if it made progress toward peace.

He set the red leather scrapbook on the table before him and waited. Inga sat to his left, Ambassador Gerard and Colonel Reyes to his right. Six empty chairs faced them. Would the Germans even meet with them?

The door opened, and two men arrived. Benedict immediately rose to his feet. The slim man wearing a business suit was Foreign Minister von Jagow, while the older man in the army uniform was a stranger.

"Ambassador Gerard, we weren't expecting you," von Jagow said.

"You should have," Gerard said. "We came all the way from Berlin to offer the kaiser a chance to salvage the situation we find ourselves in."

Von Jagow gestured toward his companion. "Allow me to intro-duce General Erich Ludendorff, just back from the Eastern Front."

This was a surprise. General Ludendorff was the military strat-egist already famous for trouncing the Russians at Tannenberg. He'd just been ordered to the Western Front, where the war had ground to a standstill. If America went to war, it was Ludendorff their soldiers would face.

"I'll get straight to it so I don't waste any of your valuable time," Ambassador Gerard said. "I come bearing a final demand from President Wilson, insisting that the German Navy honor America's freedom of the seas. We will view any additional German attacks on vessels carrying American citizens as an act of war."

General Ludendorff smiled. "Consider the message delivered," he said. "Forgive us if we do not tremble in fear. Our army consists of eight million soldiers, all of whom are equipped and mobilized. You have an army of two hundred thousand and a paltry sixteen battleships. We have the largest, strongest, and fastest fleet of submarines in the world. We have more U-boats than the rest of the world's nations combined."

Colonel Reyes lifted his chin. "Much of what you say is accurate, though the world is changing quickly. In the past year we have ramped up production of tanks, battleships, and weaponry. We have bottomless reserves of coal, iron, and oil, while you're cutting down your forests for heat. Our population is clamoring for war, while yours is growing weary of it."

It looked like General Ludendorff wanted to respond, but von Jagow cut him off. "Our quarrel isn't with America," he said earnestly. "All we ask is that you stop exporting munitions to our enemies. Keep to your side of the Atlantic, and we can remain friends."

"We are no longer friends," Benedict said as he slid the scrapbook Inga compiled across the table to von Jagow. Proof of decaying relations was emblazoned on every page of the book. "*That* is what America thinks of the kaiser and his refusal to back down from firing torpedoes at civilian ships. President Wilson doesn't want war, but he is up for reelection and is answerable to the people. President Wilson needs an unequivocal statement from you, backing off from submarine warfare, or he will lose the next election. And may heaven help us all if a warmonger is elected to the presidency instead of Wilson."

Von Jagow opened the scrapbook. The foreign minister's

expression remained inscrutable as he paged through the clippings. General Ludendorff looked insulted. It didn't matter. They needed to smash Germany's belief that America was content to sit on the sidelines of this war.

"Show that book to Kaiser Wilhelm," the ambassador said. "Our president will settle for nothing less than a reversal of the current submarine policy, or he will begin mobilizing for war."

They stood. The meeting was at an end.

JULY 1915

Inga arrived back in Berlin tired, dispirited, and afraid. She didn't bother to unpack her suitcase, nor did anyone else. A final break in diplomatic relations was expected shortly, and they would need to leave within twenty-four hours of that happening. Everyone was packed and ready to leave at a moment's notice.

She saw little of Benedict, who spent the next two days making the rounds at other neutral embassies. Just as the Americans served as intermediaries for the British and the French after their embassies closed, now the Americans needed to line up friendly neutral nations willing to facilitate American relations after their departure.

With all her other clothing packed, Inga wore her best traveling suit, a two-piece tailored skirt and jacket of gabardine twill in deep plum. She'd been wearing it for the past two days, and for the past two days it came to nothing. Each night she slipped out of her suit and wondered if tomorrow would be the day that America got dragged into a war nobody wanted.

On their third day back in Berlin, she once again pulled on the plum traveling suit, but she was tired of living in limbo. The kitchen was fully stocked, including two large jars of brandied cherries Mrs. Gerard gave her for Christmas.

"Let's bake a cake," she impulsively said to Mrs. Barnes. "If this is to be our last night at Alton House, let's make it a glorious one."

"That's the spirit!" Mrs. Barnes said. "I've been saving a fine smoked ham for Colonel Reyes's birthday, but who knows if we'll still be here. Nellie, fetch the cake pans."

And with that, Inga went into high gear alongside Nellie and Mrs. Barnes to whip up a fine meal. Everyone in the house had endured a miserable few days, worrying about something over which they had no control. Inga couldn't make the kaiser see reason, but she *could* decide her own attitude, and for tonight she intended to be joyful.

She covered her suit with one of Nellie's white aprons, then went about measuring, mixing, and baking. According to Benedict's encyclopedia, Black Forest cake was a hallmark of Bavarian baking that made heavy use of regional produce. Lots of sour cherries, rich cream, brandy, and plenty of cocoa. Nellie whipped the cream while Inga strained the cherries, then simmered the liquid to reduce it to a heavy syrup.

Soon the kitchen smelled divine. Once the cakes were out of the oven and cooled, Inga began frosting them with swirls of whipped cream while Nellie shaved big curls of chocolate.

The front door slammed, startling her so much she dropped the knife. Somebody was shouting in the entrance hall, and thudding feet made the whole house vibrate.

Were the Germans coming to throw them out? Ransack their house like they'd done at the British Embassy? Footsteps came running down the hall toward them. Inga snatched up the frosting knife, holding it before her. What good would a knife with a rounded tip do?

Benedict strode into the kitchen, disheveled and out of breath.

"Inga!" he shouted. "Unpack your bags. The Germans have caved. We're staying."

"What?" She gasped in disbelief, and Benedict grinned.

"The kaiser has accepted President Wilson's demands. We're not going to war."

She dropped the knife and flung herself into his arms. He laughed and lifted her into the air, twirling her in a circle as the amazing news sank in. She'd never heard Benedict laugh before. The sound was rich, warm, and wonderful, for they were safe. *They were safe!*

Benedict set her down but didn't release her, and before she knew it, he planted a long kiss directly on her mouth. And he didn't draw back! His kiss lingered as he clasped her to himself, and . . . well, it was all rather wonderful.

Wonderful, but he was *Benedict*! She drew back to stare at him in astonishment. He seemed as stunned as she was, though hardly remorseful.

"Pardon me," he said with a dazed smile. "I'm so relieved, and the sight of you . . . I mean, it's natural to kiss someone when you're this happy, right?"

His humor was contagious, but the kiss still had her rattled. "I'll bet you didn't kiss Larry that way."

Benedict swallowed back a laugh and struggled to regain a hint of his old formality. "You are correct, Miss Klein." He glanced at both Mrs. Barnes and Nellie. "Please disregard the momentary lapse of judgment. I'm just . . . I'm just so relieved."

Inga couldn't resist beaming at him. She didn't mind the kiss. In fact, she rather liked it. Being able to puncture Benedict's self-restraint and provoke him into a kiss like that was rather thrilling. Embarrassingly so.

"You keep your hands off our girl," Mrs. Barnes cautioned, but she was smiling too.

That night they dined in the formal dining room. It was a rare opportunity for an unabashed celebration. Candlelight illuminated the table, and they used the best crystal and china. They toasted Colonel Reyes and Benedict in praise of their fortitude while waiting for the Germans to blink. Benedict even led them in a toast to Ambassador Gerard, who was off being wined and dined at the Swiss Embassy.

"I confess to having been skeptical of Ambassador Gerard's confrontational tone in dealing with the Germans," he admitted. "I'm not sure we could have won this concession without his blunt and pointed delivery. Miss Klein, I know you had legitimate worries about the scrapbook; however, it may have helped dispel the fairy tales the Germans have been telling themselves." Benedict raised his glass. "To Miss Klein. We are in your debt."

Her cheeks heated in stunned pleasure as everyone toasted her. Then Colonel Reyes stood with a toast for Benedict. And the giddy toasting went on and on. McFee the chauffeur praised Mrs. Barnes for managing to keep the kitchen running and stocked as food shortages began pinching the grocers in Berlin.

Larry chimed in, reaching across the table to pat Inga's hand. "And now you can get your annulment. You can go back to legally being Miss Klein again."

Oh, yes! The ticking time bomb had been defused, and it felt marvelous, but she needed to properly acknowledge Benedict's heroism. She tapped a fork against her glass until she had everyone's attention.

"Benedict, I know you didn't want to marry me, but I will be forever grateful. Soon we will have the world's friendliest annulment, and I wish you nothing but the best."

"Hear, hear," Colonel Reyes said, and everyone else joined in.

And yet . . . Benedict didn't look as pleased as she would have thought. He gave a brief nod of acknowledgment, though he didn't raise his glass, and he didn't smile.

Well, Benedict probably couldn't help it. It must have been exhausting for him to smile all evening, so she sent him a radiant grin to compensate. She *was* grateful to Benedict, and he *had* been valiant in stepping up to rescue her. She put her worries about

Benedict's strange reaction to the side when Mrs. Barnes wheeled the Black Forest cake out to delighted murmurs. Somebody popped another cork.

Typically, the people in Alton House refrained from imbibing, but they'd all been teetering on a knife's edge since the day the *Lusitania* sank, and relief had made them giddy. Millions of men had just been spared. All across America, there were farmers at their plows, young men studying in college, fathers tucking their children into bed. Those men would be allowed to carry on their normal lives because of what happened today, and that was worth celebrating.

It was almost midnight before dinner broke up, but Benedict had important business to settle before he could head upstairs.

"Inga, a word, please."

Her foot paused on the bottom step of the staircase. "Can it wait until tomorrow? I'm exhausted."

"I'm afraid not." The conversation was going to be dreadful. He'd gone out on a limb for Inga, and now she needed to return the favor. He hated asking this of her, yet it had to be done.

She assumed a pleasant expression and joined him at the base of the stairs. In the kitchen, pans clattered as Mrs. Barnes cleaned up the last of the evening's feast.

"Let's step outside," he suggested. The only thing that could make this conversation even more embarrassing was if Mrs. Barnes overheard it.

Outside, the heat of the evening had begun to cool. He'd hoped to sit on the front porch to talk with Inga, but next door the Bulgarians were having a lively outdoor party. Mandolin music and male laughter floated on the evening air. If he could hear them, they could hear him.

"Let's keep walking," he said, offering his arm. They probably looked like an ordinary husband and wife on a nice evening stroll.

Their marriage was a sham, yet he still liked the feel of her beside him. Streetlamps illuminated the lush greenery of the tree-lined avenue. A fountain at the end of the street had plenty of seating around the wide rim of its circular wall.

"Benedict, I want you to know that I meant what I said this evening," Inga began. "You didn't have to help me out, and I'll be forever grateful."

Lord above this was awful. "You may want to hold off on the gratitude," he said. "We're not going to be able to get an annulment yet."

"Of course we can," she said, her voice as light as if debating whether to go to the theater or the opera. "I know I still need to become an American citizen, but the emergency is over, and I'll have plenty of time."

They arrived at the public fountain, babbling at the end of the street. He braced his foot on the rim and focused on the water dribbling from the tall spout.

"Inga, you and I have held ourselves out to be a married couple in front of the German court and several embassies. That was fine provided we left Germany and returned to America, but we can't easily annul the marriage now that we are intending to stay. Not without significant damage to my standing in the diplomatic community."

"Oh," she said.

"A diplomat's reputation for honesty is an essential element of his work. I must be seen as one hundred percent trustworthy. Participating in a fraudulent marriage would undermine that."

"What if I . . . simply returned to New York?"

He was afraid she was going to ask that. Now he had to get into an even thornier topic. "It would cause people to talk," he said. "If you simply disappear after we just got married, it will reflect poorly on me." He cleared his throat and parsed his words with care. "My first marriage was less than a shining success."

That was perhaps the understatement of the century. "What

happened between me and my first wife caused something of a scandal back in 1906 when I was posted in Rome. Memories are long. A second failed marriage would doom my career. If you disappear now, it will bring back talk of her."

"Claudia?" Inga asked.

"Yes, Claudia." The girl he had fallen in love with when he was eighteen. The girl he'd hoped to be the answer to his lonely, rootless life. Everyone warned him that eighteen was too young to marry, and he should have listened to them.

Inga lowered herself onto the rim of the fountain, looking pale and worried. He sat beside her, staring at the paving stones beneath his feet. "I met Claudia my first week at Oxford, and we married six months later." He then told her how he believed they were in love and that the early few years of marriage were easy, joyful even.

The trouble had started after they left England for Benedict's first diplomatic post as a deputy assistant in Istanbul. Claudia hated it. There weren't many other wives for her to socialize with, and she pressured Benedict to get a better posting somewhere in Europe or America.

"I managed to get a posting to the American Embassy in Rome. Claudia started a . . . well, a relationship with an Italian baron. Baron Agosti." It was difficult to hide his contempt for the penniless noble who had never done an honest day's labor in his life, but the baron was a charming man, and he had a title after all. He was also infatuated with Claudia. The baron's adoration was heady stuff, and Claudia fell under his spell. She'd asked for a divorce, which Benedict refused. Baron Agosti wasn't the first man she'd strayed with, and yet she always came back.

Not this time, however. After Benedict refused to grant Claudia a divorce, the lovers ran off together, traveling all over Switzerland and not even bothering to hide their affair. They accepted invitations at country estates owned by the baron's extended family. They dined in public and shared a room in cozy Alpine resorts.

And all the while Benedict carried out his duties at the embassy, negotiating trade deals and trying to ignore the whispers. The American ambassador suggested Benedict take a leave of absence until he could get his house in order. It was mortifying, but he'd already been in the process of tracking Claudia down in hopes of salvaging both his marriage and his career.

It ended up not being necessary. A fierce, late-spring storm swept down from the north, blanketing half the continent beneath snow and ice. Claudia and her lover had been on a train snaking around a dangerous pass in the Alps when the train derailed. The train plunged over the side, killing thirty-two people, including Claudia and Baron Agosti.

Benedict went to Switzerland to retrieve her body and accompanied it back home to Oxford. The blizzard that killed his wife still held the continent in its grip, and the chill penetrated straight into his soul as the train chugged onward. Never had he felt like a bigger failure than when he met Claudia's parents at the railway platform, waiting for porters to bring her casket out. If he'd have been a better husband, their daughter would still be alive.

"Danger to my career died with Claudia," he said. "People from the diplomatic community offered genuine condolences when she died, even though they knew it was hardly a match made in heaven. To this day I overhear whispers and catch curious glances. I probably would have been promoted to an ambassadorship by now if it hadn't been for Claudia."

And he desperately wanted to be an ambassador. He had the temperament for it and was ready for the challenge. He could be a peacemaker. It felt as though his entire life had led to this point where the world was on the brink, giving him the chance to use his wisdom, intellect, and tenacity to save it.

He met her eyes for the first time. "Inga, my career cannot survive the scandal of another runaway wife."

She swallowed hard, her face pale in the moonlight. "How long do we have to pretend?"

"Until we're no longer posted to Germany."

Inga drew a big, watery gulp. Then another. She covered her mouth with a hand, but the despair in her eyes was heartrending. Was being married to him *that* horrible?

"Inga, are you all right? You don't look good."

She squeezed her eyes shut and shook her head, turning her entire body away from him. Great, shuddery breaths racked her frame. Never had he felt so helpless as he waited for the avalanche of grief to subside. It appeared every woman he'd been attracted to in his entire life found marriage to him revolting.

"I'm sorry," she finally choked out. "I thought we could be through with all this."

Another jab from a stiletto. She didn't mean to hurt him, yet she had. "It won't be so bad," he said. "We don't have to pretend inside Alton House."

She sniffled and nodded. "You're right, of course. I'm sorry for being such a baby. It's just been a challenging time. I'm happy for the peace, but I'm ready to go back home. I miss New York." She swiped her nose with a handkerchief, then laughed lightly. "Look at me, worrying about being homesick when the rest of the world has it so much harder than me. I'll be okay."

She stood and started back home without him. He had never felt lonelier in his life than now as he watched her walk away.

23

It was still dark when Inga awoke in a bad mood, which was ridiculous. She ought to be on her knees and giving thanks for the miracle of diplomacy that had just spared millions of Americans from being flung into the muddy trenches of France, but no. All she could think about was the marriage chaining her to Benedict that neither one of them wanted.

She lay in bed, staring at the darkened ceiling and worrying about how miserable Benedict looked last night as he spoke of Claudia. All this time Inga assumed the breakdown of his first marriage had been Benedict's fault because . . . well, because he was Benedict.

And yet he was actually a fine man. Beneath his old-school manners and withdrawn demeanor, maybe he was a smidge shy.

She rolled over in bed and punched her pillow. Benedict couldn't be shy. She'd seen the way he confronted von Jagow and took command at the embassy during the crisis. It seemed his shyness was mostly around women. Or maybe it was just *her*.

His kiss hadn't been shy. Yesterday he had swooped into the kitchen and made a beeline for her, sweeping her into a magnificent kiss. Maybe it was so wonderful because they'd both been happy.

It could happen. That was surely the only reason she could have shared that fleeting, amazing moment of joyous intimacy with him.

She wouldn't let herself think about that kiss again.

Ever.

A whirlwind of activity greeted her when she arrived at the embassy. A backlog of normal business had been accumulating ever since the *Lusitania* went down, and she rolled up her sleeves to tackle it.

At one o'clock, Benedict rapped on her door. "Snap to it, Miss Klein. You're needed to accompany me on a trip to Ruhleben. We leave in five minutes."

The kind, regretful man from last evening was gone, replaced by the Benedict of old. A bit of laughter bubbled up inside because, despite herself, she rather liked the Benedict of old.

Normally, Benedict would take Larry to help with clerical duties, but Larry's persnickety fear of dirt made him terrified of prisoner camps. Inga had no such qualms, and he quickly outlined the problem for her.

"The Germans are starting to be difficult about the relief supplies shipped into the camps by the YMCA. I need to step in and put an end to it."

"Why are they being difficult?"

"Because the YMCA hasn't gone through the customary channels, and Germans are linear thinkers who can't tolerate that."

"I'm not a linear thinker," Inga defended.

True, there was nothing linear about Inga. She was all soft curves with wavy hair and a kissable mouth. He should be ashamed of himself for thinking such things, though any man with a pulse would be drawn to her.

"We're here," he said as they pulled up outside the racetrack that had been home to four thousand men for the past year.

Inga strode beside him, notebook at the ready as they stormed the fortress of Teutonic bureaucracy. It took two hours to cut through the necessary red tape and authorize the YMCA to ship books for the camp library and writing supplies for classes many of the prisoners agreed to teach. Throughout it all, Inga quietly sat beside him, her pencil flying across the page as she recorded every word of the conversation in shorthand. Upon returning to the embassy, she would type two copies of the conversation, sending one to the administrators at Ruhleben and keeping the other in their file at the embassy so there could be no confusion about relief supplies in the future.

On their way out, Inga paused beside a one-eyed man perched on a haystack, making a sketch.

"Percy?" she asked. "Do you remember me?"

The man tossed down his sketchpad and stood. "How could I forget the prettiest lass in all of Germany?"

Inga laughed, and the two began chatting, but not before Inga sent a questioning glance at a nearby guard to be sure he'd allow the conversation. Inga had learned techniques for navigating inside the prisoner camp, and the guard nodded his permission.

Benedict still had to tamp down the initial spurt of jealousy, but it subsided when Inga asked after the man's wife and children back in Edinburgh. It turned out that Percy was a Presbyterian minister who had a lot to say about conditions in the camp.

"Our biggest challenge is barbed-wire disease," Percy said. "Boredom can kill a man. Take away his purpose and lock him up with nothing to do, and he will languish and die."

Benedict gestured toward an outbuilding the prisoners had converted into a chapel. "Surely you've been able to help with religious instruction?"

Percy gave a halfhearted nod. "I'm a Presbyterian, which isn't much good to a Catholic or a Jew. Last month we had two hundred prisoners from India transferred to the camp. What do I know about Hinduism? The men want pastors and priests and rabbis of their own faiths, only they are scarce."

Benedict mulled over the problem on the drive home. It was becoming increasingly likely these men would remain confined for the duration of the war. The ability to lean on spiritual comfort might become a lifeline for them.

"What about prisoner swaps?" Inga suggested. "You said there were two rabbis among the prisoners at the POW camp in Magdeburg. Maybe one of them could be transferred to Ruhleben."

Benedict was embarrassed he hadn't thought of the idea himself, but Inga was good at clever solutions. "Excellent suggestion, Miss Klein."

They were still married, and although he referred to her as Mrs. Kincaid in public, she remained Miss Klein to him otherwise. It helped keep a professional distance between them because there were times when he wanted to haul her into his arms and run his hands through the glorious mass of her blond hair. It was unbelievably tempting to unfasten the hair clip that held the heavy coil in place. Over time the impulse to yank that clip free and watch her hair go spiraling down her back was getting stronger instead of fading.

As September turned into October, he and Inga traveled throughout the region, visiting detention camps and interviewing the various religious leaders trapped behind barbed wire. They found men who'd be willing to move to a different camp, where a Catholic priest or a Baptist minister would be eagerly welcomed.

At Christmastime, instead of buying gifts for everyone at Alton House, Inga used her money to buy something for the prisoners at Ruhleben. Better still, she leaned on the Gerards for a substantial donation, so there was plenty of money to make care packages. He and Inga lined up a hundred crates down the center hallway of Alton House. Everyone in the house grabbed a sack of the items Inga bought to distribute them across each crate.

Benedict added jars of candy while Colonel Reyes added bars of soap. Other items included cigarettes, new socks and underwear, tinned beef, and dried apples.

Larry opened the next box of supplies and looked aghast. "Inga, you didn't," he said, his voice a combination of surprise and horror.

"Indeed, I did," she replied with a grin.

Benedict strode over to examine what had Larry so bewildered. It took only a fleeting look into the box to understand. Honestly, sometimes this woman was beyond belief. A full run of *The Perils of Pauline* filled the box.

"Miss Klein, really?"

"Yes, really," she said. "I saw what the YMCA has supplied for the library, and it's nothing but educational books and classics and training manuals."

"Do you think *The Perils of Pauline* will hold a man's attention for more than five minutes?"

She shrugged. "I have no idea, but I know one thing for sure. At the end of each issue, the men will ask that wonderful, immortal question: *What happens next?* And that's worth a lot."

Benedict tossed an issue into a crate because she was right. For men trapped with nothing to do, these frivolous stories packed with adventure and lurid story lines might have a place. Luckily, she had selected a number of westerns and detective stories in addition to her trashy *Perils of Pauline*. By the end of Christmas Eve, they had filled one hundred care packages.

Everyone at Alton House wanted to help deliver the crates. Even Larry volunteered, having gotten over his squeamishness by asserting that the freezing temperatures kept germs at bay.

Christmas Day afternoon was spent walking alongside Inga as they delivered a hundred care packages to the Ruhleben Interment Camp. It was unlike any Christmas celebration Benedict had ever experienced, but it was perhaps the holiest. They were doing God's work, bringing compassion and kindness to a place in desperate need of such blessings, and it was the finest Christmas in his memory.

24

SUMMER, 1916

Inga battled an escalating case of homesickness as Berlin shook off the depths of winter. The weather was unusually balmy, coaxing the tulips and cherry blossoms in the Tiergarten to bloom early. A joyous riot of color filled the city with a flowery display, as though nature were determined to ignore the war raging to the east and west of Berlin.

She had now been in Berlin for two years and been married to Benedict for half that time. They were rubbing along quite well, despite their smashing differences. He continued to roll his eyes whenever she reached for the gossip pages, and she teased him for his relentless slog through the *Encyclopedia Britannica*. Lately she'd been catching him looking at her when he thought she wouldn't notice. She might be helping in the kitchen or arranging a bouquet of flowers, and if she turned quickly, he was always watching her. She'd flash him a grin and told herself the little tug in her heart didn't mean anything.

He was forbidden fruit, that was all. Every young man she'd

ever courted, and there had been *a lot*, were Benedict's complete opposite. They liked to have fun. They were rowdy and roguish and couldn't keep their hands off of her.

Benedict could. Aside from that single time he kissed her after Germany caved to the president's demands, Benedict seemed completely immune to her. Was that why she was starting to have feelings for him? Ever since coming to Germany, she'd been surrounded by handsome men in uniform, and yet she'd never seen anything sexier than the way Benedict Kincaid filled out a passport application. He was always so polished, his suit and tie pressed, his collar starched. He never had a hair out of place as he handled embassy affairs with flawless professionalism.

Who could have imagined she'd find such a thing attractive? Work at the embassy grew more challenging as the war dragged on, but Benedict remained smoothly confident. By the summer of 1916, he had succeeded in the redistribution of religious leaders among the internment camps. Percy wrote Inga a letter of thanks, saying that Ruhleben now had a priest, a rabbi, and a Methodist minister.

Her proudest accomplishment was the improved relations between Benedict and Ambassador Gerard. Even so, the ambassador was becoming weary beneath the weight of his duties. One morning she arrived at his office to find him exhausted and disheveled. Papers cluttered his desk, and the room stank of cigar smoke. He hadn't shaved and wore the same dress shirt from the evening before. She opened the window to let in a little fresh air, then reached for the ashtray overflowing with cigar butts to carry outside.

"Inga, I need you to make arrangements to get me to Washington," Mr. Gerard announced.

She froze, the crystal dish balanced in her hands. "How long will you be gone?"

"A month? Six weeks? I have no idea, but I want to be on a train to Hamburg tomorrow morning. The president wants a meeting, so we need to put Benedict in charge of the embassy in my absence."

"I'll get the tickets, but what's going on?"

Mr. Gerard sagged. "The Germans are saber-rattling again, threatening to go back to unrestricted submarine warfare. The president wants me to confer with his team because he doesn't trust the krauts any more than I do."

The ambassador's growing hostility to Germany was worrisome. Maybe he saw how upset she was because he immediately apologized for his tone.

"Sorry, Inga. *You're* not a kraut. You're as much an American as anyone at the embassy. Say, why don't you come with us back to the States and get that citizenship business squared away? Pay the fee, pass the test, and then you can be an official American."

She could see New York again? A surge of longing filled her. "I can go home?"

Mr. Gerard clapped her on the back. "Of course! Now that you're married, you can come and go without worrying about it. Still, it would be good to get your citizenship on your own behalf, right?"

A sheen of tears filled her eyes. He knew how homesick she'd been and what a kindness this was.

"Thank you," she said, a grin breaking out across her face. "Thank you! I'll make the arrangements right away."

Benedict greeted the news that he was to be in charge of the embassy with mixed feelings. It meant for six weeks he needn't fear Gerard's antagonism toward the Germans. But why was Inga going?

Ambassador Gerard didn't need a secretary back home, nor did Inga have family to visit. She'd been battling homesickness for a long time, and once she returned to the comforts of New York, the odds of her returning to Berlin were almost nil. He couldn't force her to return, but if she didn't . . .

He raced back to the Alton House, where she had already gone to pack her bags. What was he going to say to her? He didn't want her to leave. She mattered to him. Once home, he bounded up the steps two at a time. Her bedroom door was open, as was the trunk on Inga's bed. She carefully laid the green walking dress inside it, the dress she'd worn for their wedding.

"You're leaving?"

She startled, then grinned. "Yes. Mr. Gerard suggested I should go home to take the citizenship test. I think that's past due, don't you?"

Except he still needed her to return if he was to ward off rumors of another runaway wife. He said nothing as she continued packing.

"I'm worried I might not be able to pass the test," she added. "I've never been all that smart, you know?"

"Nonsense."

She held up a copy of *The Perils of Pauline*. "This is what I read. Not the *Encyclopedia Britannica*." She tossed the flimsy issue toward the bed, but it splatted to the floor, and she didn't bother to pick it up. Did Inga truly believe she was slow?

He turned away for a quick glance up and down the hallway outside her room. They were alone in the house except for Nellie and Mrs. Barnes in the kitchen. He closed the door anyway.

"You're not stupid, Inga."

"Mr. Gerard told me what kind of questions will be on the test. Something about the Bill of Rights and the *Mayflower*, and I have no idea what those things are. I always got bad grades in school. At first because I couldn't speak English, and then because I'm not very bright. I only finished the eighth grade."

Benedict quirked a brow. "You didn't graduate from school?"

She shook her head and kept folding the green suit, refusing to look at him as though ashamed. "I needed to work," she said. "My father said it was pointless to keep going to school because I was dumb and old enough to start earning money. He was the one who asked Mr. Gerard to sponsor me for a class on shorthand."

Anger gathered inside because Inga was one of the brightest people he knew. Even if she wasn't, no parent should tell a child they were dumb.

He moved to her side to stop her from abusing the green skirt. He liked the suit too much to see it ruined. He shook the wrinkles out and folded it in half lengthwise, then set it on the mattress.

"Roll it from the bottom like this," he said. "It won't get so wrinkled that way."

"You see?" Inga said. "I can't even pack a skirt. Women are supposed to know housekeeping tricks like that, but I need you, a man, to show me."

He hid a smile. "One of the benefits of a nomadic childhood," he said as he tucked the skirt gently into the trunk. She smelled good. Was it the apple soap she used? It was tempting to bury his nose along the smooth column of her neck to find out.

He took a step back to avoid the temptation. "Follow me down to the study," he said. "I'm going to make sure you pass that citizenship test."

The twenty-nine volumes of his encyclopedia had been returned to their proper place on their bookshelves. Only the volume for Q lay open on the desk.

"How far along are you now?" she asked with a nod to the open book.

"Quicksand," he said. It felt like he'd been standing on quicksand ever since war was declared last year.

Inga turned a single page of the open book. "Quicksilver," she said, landing her finger on the next entry. "I don't even know what that is."

"Read it," he prompted.

"A liquid form of the chemical element mercury," she read, then met his gaze. "Is that what's in a thermometer?"

"Yes." He found the volume that covered the U.S. Constitution and the one for American history. He put a bookmark in each to mark the right entries. "Here. Take these and study them on the trip home."

She took a step back. "What if I lose them?"

"They're only books, Inga." He cared about her more than any book, and she'd be devastated if she failed the test. If it were possible, he'd scrub away every hurtful comment her father ever made that damaged Inga's belief in her abilities. Inga was a woman whose optimism brightened every room she entered.

She took the volumes and hugged them to her chest. "Thank you. I promise to take great care of them."

The following morning, he accompanied Inga and the Gerards to the train station. Once they reached Hamburg, they would board a ship for New York, where Inga would remain on her own to pass her citizenship test, while the Gerards traveled on to Washington.

Inga seemed overjoyed to be leaving. She'd been homesick for New York ever since she arrived, and her excitement was worrisome. Maybe she was planning to escape their marriage. If she didn't come back, he'd think of a way to explain things at the German court. It wouldn't be the end of the world, but still . . . he would miss her. Her cheerful smile gave him the jolt of electricity he needed to face the trials of each new day.

He held Inga's elbow as they funneled along with a crush of people waiting to board the train. "You have the encyclopedias?" he asked, and she nodded.

"I shall start studying immediately."

They reached the wrought-iron fence separating the crowd from the train platform. Only ticketed passengers would be allowed through the gate, and the line was moving quickly.

He shouldn't touch her. They didn't have that sort of marriage, but he couldn't help himself. He placed a hand on her shoulder, then pressed a brief kiss to her forehead.

"Good luck, Inga. Please come back . . . we need you."

I need you. He ought to say it but couldn't make his tongue utter the words. She gazed up at him with something that looked like genuine affection. Her eyes held a wistful look, almost as if she'd welcome a real goodbye kiss. Almost as if they were a real husband and wife. It was an intoxicating feeling, and he wished things had been different between them.

"Come along, Inga!" Mr. Gerard called, his voice cutting through the din at the station. "We're ready to board."

She glanced at the Gerards, where they awaited her on the other side of the fence. Most passengers had already boarded, and they only had a few moments left. Inga lifted the satchel containing his books.

"Thank you for the encyclopedias," she said, smiling up at him. "I shall study them diligently."

She turned to hand her ticket to the gate agent, then hurried through the opening. She sent him a final goodbye wave before rushing to catch up with the Gerards.

It did not escape his notice that Inga said nothing about agreeing to return.

25

Inga hadn't realized just how desperately homesick she was until she saw the Statue of Liberty standing over New York Harbor. She burst into tears at the familiar sight, laughing and crying at the same time.

The achingly familiar sights and smells of home enveloped her like welcoming arms. She disembarked on her own, waving farewell to the Gerards as they prepared to sail toward Washington.

Inga couldn't stop smiling as she lugged her suitcase down 29th Street. It took two subway connections to get there, and her heart raced faster with every step, knowing she was only a few blocks from home and from everyone at the Martha Washington. Delia had promised Inga could stay in her apartment for however long it took to pass the citizenship test.

Hopefully, she could slip upstairs without attracting attention because, for whatever strange reason, she was about to burst into tears again. Was it joy from being back home? Relief from escaping all the rules and stress of Germany? She couldn't think of the words to describe this mix of joy and nostalgia. Her lips started wobbling as she spotted the Martha Washington two blocks ahead.

After two long years, she was finally home.

She quickened her pace, breathless from lugging the bag but starting to laugh as she hurried to the front of her wonderful old apartment building.

Jared Ingersoll, her favorite doorman, was on duty. "Heavens above, it's Miss Inga Klein!" he bellowed. "I thought you'd left us for good."

"Shhh!" she said. "I'm trying to slip in without anyone noticing."

Mr. Ingersoll grinned and held the door for her. "It's sure nice to see you again. Nobody else has your smile."

Tears threatened again, and she dropped her bag to give Jared a hug and a kiss on the cheek. Such familiarity would give people a heart attack in Berlin, but she was home now.

The comforting scent of vanilla from the ice cream parlor filled the lobby. Her eyes drank in the sight of the warm walnut paneling, the cozy library, and straight ahead the main dining room stuffed to the gills.

Oh dear, she'd been spotted. Blanche at the front desk squealed, and she just glimpsed a bunch of her old friends through the plate-glass window of the dining room. Delia had her back to the window, so her apartment upstairs was probably locked.

"Shhh!" she said to Blanche. "Can I stow my suitcase behind the counter for a moment?"

Once that was done, she tiptoed into the restaurant. With five hundred residents, she knew only a fraction of them, but the ladies from the eighth floor were seated near the front. A few recognized her, and she put a finger to her lips, urging them to be silent as she crept up behind Delia.

She did her best to imitate a stern, Germanic tone. "What are you doing home from the office so early, young lady?"

Delia nearly leapt out of her seat, then let out a shriek as she dragged Inga into a hug. Suddenly it felt like half the women in the dining room crowded around, hugging and talking over each other.

They fired a million questions at her all at once. When did she get home? Did she see any fighting at the front? What were the men in Berlin like? They admired her spiffy coral suit and wanted to know if she'd met the kaiser. Once the flurry died down, someone dragged another seat over, and she happily joined them.

"Please don't make me talk about Berlin," she said. "I'm just so happy to be home."

Inga was too excited to sleep. She lay on a cot in Delia's darkened apartment, continuing to talk with her friend long into the night. She could tell Delia anything, no matter how embarrassing, and she confessed her fear about failing the citizenship test.

As a legal assistant, Delia had excellent insight into the process. "The written part isn't hard, but then you have to be interviewed by a judge. That's where it can get sticky."

Inga propped up on an elbow. Light from the streetlamps leaked through the thin sheers covering the window, illuminating the dark shape of Delia's outline. "How so?"

"It depends on what judge you get. Most of them are honorable men and only want to confirm you're not likely to become a public charge, but some of them hate immigrants and will use trick questions to fail an applicant. Judge Keating is the worst for that. Don't worry. I have a lot of connections down at the courthouse and can make sure you get funneled to one of the good judges. Say, how are things with Cold Oats? Is he still horrible?"

Inga flopped onto her back to stare into the darkness. She hadn't told anyone about her marriage to Benedict because it would be too hard to explain the annulment that was inevitably going to happen.

"It turns out he's not so bad," she whispered. Benedict had saved her time and again, like when he patched up the mess she'd made with Magnus from the Norwegian Embassy, or when he married her to help with her citizenship problem. He was actually quite kind beneath his intimidating, starchy exterior.

No, Benedict wasn't bad at all. Someday he would probably

find a woman as smart and sophisticated as he to love, and Inga would be happy for him.

Even if in her heart she'd be a little jealous.

Inga didn't spend a single hour studying during the next few days because she was too busy savoring the joy of being back home. She splurged at her favorite delicatessens and the wonderful Italian bistros. She and Delia went to Coney Island, where they took a gondola ride along a series of canals and lagoons meant to look like Venice. Inga constantly had to tilt the brim of her hat to block out the sunlight, and she couldn't stop smiling. People in Europe might think these attractions tacky because they had the real thing, but every second of the gaudy, glamorous fun was a balm to her spirit after two years of stress at the embassy in Germany.

The days passed in a whirl of activity, although the date for her citizenship test loomed, and finally there was no more delaying her need to study. Delia had already gone over the three branches of government, the main points in the Declaration of Independence, and all ten amendments that made up the Bill of Rights. While aboard the ship, Inga tried to read Benedict's encyclopedias, but they were so dry she couldn't keep her eyes open. Delia had proven to be a much better teacher.

But alas, Delia had a job, and Inga couldn't afford to fail this test. After Delia went to work on Monday, it was time to get serious about studying Benedict's encyclopedias. She carried them down to the library on the first floor of the apartment building, determined to make sense of the wordy articles now that Delia had explained the basics.

She had the library to herself. Surrounded by shoulder-high bookshelves on three sides, the room had plenty of natural light through the front windows overlooking 29th Street. She cracked open an encyclopedia and tried to read the pages covering American

ELIZABETH CAMDEN

history. Sadly, it was no more scintillating now than it had been aboard the ship.

It was far more interesting to flip through the pages and read Benedict's notes. "Marginalia," he had once called them. Some pages had no notes at all, while others were so dense that his penmanship grew tiny as he wrapped the sentences around every bit of blank space. He put an exclamation mark next to passages that had captured his attention, and on rare occasions, two exclamation marks. One section had so many dog-eared pages, the book naturally flipped open to it.

The entry was about Abelard and Heloise, and she was curious about the topic that meant so much to him. Soon she was transported back to medieval France and the tragic story of a famous philosopher named Peter Abelard and his passion for Heloise. At first, Heloise was his pupil, then his mistress, then his secret wife. Her uncle disapproved and did everything possible to separate the lovers, but their passion had no limits. Even after Heloise's disapproving uncle sent her to a convent, the dashing Abelard continued to secretly visit her.

The pages were littered with Benedict's notes and exclamation marks. Inga spotted one paragraph with an unprecedented *three* exclamation marks, and she eagerly read. Her jaw dropped upon reading that one night after dark, Abelard snuck into the convent, where he and Heloise had carnal relations in her abbey's dining hall.

No wonder this passage warranted three exclamation marks!

"You naughty man, Mr. Kincaid," she whispered, her eyes continuing to devour the text. Abelard was a member of the lower clergy, which was why he'd hidden the illicit marriage to Heloise. She eventually became pregnant, which outraged her uncle, who ordered his henchman to castrate Abelard. Amazingly, he survived the brutal attack. It put an end to his wild romance with Heloise, though not their enduring friendship.

Over the decades, Heloise rose to become an abbess, while

Abelard withdrew to a monastery and became a monk. They carried on a correspondence that reminisced about the passionate fires of their youth, which was how so much was known of their intimate lives. Heloise outlived Abelard by twenty years. They were ultimately buried side by side at the Père Lachaise Cemetery in Paris.

Benedict circled the name of the cemetery where the lovers were buried and made a note of the day he visited their tomb. A postcard from the cemetery was among the scraps of paper he had slipped into the book. It showed a lithograph of the two effigies, lying side by side, their stone faces expressionless and their hands in prayer. Such a formal, stiff pose for the two lovers.

She flipped the postcard over to read Benedict's notes. *Too formal. Too stiff for these two lovers.*

She stifled a laugh, for who could have imagined that Benedict was a secret romantic?

"Hello, Inga."

She dropped the postcard and looked up. "Eduardo! What a surprise."

He pulled the chair out and sat opposite her. "I might say the same. I heard you were back in the city, but you didn't let me know."

He looked both hopeful and hurt. How to handle this? She carefully returned the postcard, along with all the other scraps of paper marking the entry, then closed the book. "I remember saying I hoped you would find someone else," she said carefully. "That the perfect girl was out there. Did you look?"

"Yeah, I met a few girls, but they don't mean anything to me. Not like you."

She clenched her hands beneath the table. She wasn't wearing her wedding ring, yet even having this discussion felt wrong.

"Eduardo, I'm sorry. I only came back to New York to get my citizenship papers."

"And then you're going back?"

Was she? It would be so easy to stay here in New York. There were plenty of jobs for a skilled secretary, and all of them would be easier than working at the embassy in Berlin. She already dreaded leaving the comfort of home for the stress and uncertainty of Europe.

"I'm not sure what's going to happen," she said, "but I know you and I aren't destined for anything more."

He shoved the encyclopedia aside, and it fell to the floor, scattering Benedict's papers and mementoes. She jumped up to collect them, flipping through the pages to put the bits of paper back where they belonged. Eduardo reached for a clipping from a lecture Benedict once attended.

"Aquatic science," he scoffed. "Why are you wasting time on boring stuff like this? Let me take you out to lunch. I'll buy you a root beer float."

She snatched the clipping back. Eduardo had no business saying something was boring if he didn't know the first thing about it. It would probably take hours to figure out where each slip of paper belonged in Benedict's dog-eared volume. "I'm sorry if I sound short, but you need to leave now."

"Come on, Inga. Give me a chance."

She glanced through the windows toward the lobby. The doorman was there. She didn't want to make a scene, and yet Eduardo had ignored everything she said. Benedict always listened to her. Benedict could be curt, maddening, and inflexible, yet he respected her enough to listen.

"I don't want to summon the doorman to throw you out," she said gently. "I'm grateful for the good times we once had, but that's over now. I wish you well."

Eduardo crossed his arms and refused to budge.

She stood. "Mr. Ingersoll?" she called out. "Could you come help me with something?"

Eduardo got up and glared. "Don't worry, I'm leaving," he grumbled. "I always liked you, Inga, but you're not the same girl anymore."

He slammed the door on his way out, the bang echoing in her ears. One thing Eduardo said was undoubtedly true. She *wasn't* the same girl he once knew.

Inga retreated to Delia's apartment to organize the mess Eduardo had made of Benedict's encyclopedia. She laid each of his postcards, photos, and clippings on her cot, trying to figure out where they belonged in the fat volume. Most of the clippings were lofty intellectual book reviews or philosophical treatises, but one nearly stopped her heart:

It was a recipe for Black Forest cake. It had been snipped out of a newspaper and dated from six months ago. Why would Benedict keep this recipe? He never cooked or baked, nor was there an entry for Black Forest cake in the encyclopedia. What had prompted him to save the recipe?

A hunch led her to check the entry for Bavaria. She flipped through the volume until she found it, and sure enough, the margins had plenty of Benedict's compact, neatly written notes. She leaned in close to read them.

The notes were all about *her*.

They weren't terribly personal or even particularly flattering, but he certainly had a lot to say. He circled a passage about Bavarian love of folk music and added the note, *This accounts for Inga's propensity to hum at all hours.* Under the passage about Bavarian dialects, he listed several observations such as, *Inga consistently rolls her "r" sounds more than standard German speakers.*

How interesting that he referred to her as Inga and not Miss Klein.

The next subheading was for Traditional Bavarian Cuisine, and Black Forest cake was listed among a dozen other dishes. Instead of commentary beside the entry, Benedict simply wrote down a date: July 21, 1915.

Her heart began to thud. That was the date the kaiser accepted

President Wilson's demands. It was the day she'd made a Black Forest cake, the day Benedict barged into the kitchen and kissed her in a wild surge of impulsive joy.

She drew a ragged breath as she placed the recipe back into the book. Well, the mystery was solved. This was clearly where the Black Forest cake recipe belonged, but why had he made a note of that date? Or cared enough to save a recipe? There were probably lots of reasons, although only one stood out. The incident in the kitchen meant a lot to him, and he wanted to remember it.

She had been battling an unwelcome attraction to Benedict ever since that day, but never imagined that he might actually return her sentiment.

Feeling overheated, she used the Abelard and Heloise postcard to fan herself and calm her galloping heart. She mustn't jump to conclusions, even though it seemed Benedict had been paying an extraordinary amount of attention to her. It was flattering. Immensely so, actually. And contrary to external appearances, he was a deeply romantic man. His fascination with Abelard and Heloise proved it.

She turned her attention back to the encyclopedia. The entry for Bavaria contained a half-page map of the region, and Benedict had marked the mountainous Black Forest area. The margin note was in his small, meticulous handwriting:

This is where she grew up—poor and isolated, mostly among shoemakers and woodworkers. It's impressive she became so worldly and accomplished.

Benedict thought she was worldly and accomplished? She always felt inadequate and overshadowed by him. She even felt overshadowed by Claudia, his dead wife who spoke six languages and could play hostess to diplomats and aristocrats.

She closed the encyclopedia and held it close to her chest as she paced the small confines of Delia's room. She and Benedict were a terrible mismatch, but the world had turned upside down in the past two years. Anything was possible. If Benedict returned the secret attraction she felt for him, maybe there was a way forward for them after all. She used to be drawn to boys like Eduardo, but not anymore. Benedict was a mature man, one who had repeatedly protected her. He was brave and resolute, and yes, so smart that he sometimes scared the dickens out of her.

He also thrilled her. Watching him in action, wielding his intellect to carry out the embassy duties made her proud to know him. She loved cracking his formal reserve to make him laugh or throw caution to the wind and kiss her as if there were no tomorrow.

Benedict cared for her. The way he looked that last day at the train station was burned in her memory. His heart was in his eyes, if only she hadn't been too blind to recognize it. *"Please come back . . . we need you,"* he had said.

And yet she didn't want to go back to Berlin. Did Benedict really want her? The random notes he wrote about her could simply be intended to help him understand Bavaria. Maybe he had similar notes written about Claudia all over the entry for her hometown. It was unlikely somebody like Benedict could genuinely care for a peasant girl from a tiny speck of a mountain village. He might be horrified if he knew how his notes about her had stirred a whirlwind of hidden longings.

She'd almost convinced herself to stay in New York. Her old job at the harbor would be so much easier than the one in Berlin. Was it even still available? Perhaps a visit to her comfortable office at the harbor would be the perfect remedy to get her mind off Benedict.

26

At eight o'clock on Thursday evening, Inga headed to the wireless office where she once worked the overnight shift in a tower overlooking New York Harbor.

It had been two years since she left, but the old crew was still here. Mr. Guillory leaned back in his swivel chair, casually reading a report at his sloppy desk. Carson and Jenkins were both at their stations, seated before a wide counter overlooking the harbor. Both wore headphones, although neither was currently handling a message. That was the thing about the overnight shift: There was rarely any traffic unless an emergency arose.

"Anybody home?" she called.

"Inga!" Carson shouted, tearing off his headphones to greet her. "Are you coming back to work with us?"

She shook her head. "I'm back in New York on business but couldn't resist a visit to the best wireless crew in the city."

"The most fruitful, that's for sure," Carson said. "Jenkins's wife just had another baby."

"Boy or girl?"

"Boy, of course," Jenkins laughed. "That makes five boys, and my wife says she is cursed."

Oh, it was good to be back! She grabbed a vacant seat at the counter to get caught up on all the gossip, although Jenkins wanted to know why she returned to New York.

"I need to take the citizenship test," she replied. "It seems everyone in the world is choosing sides right now, and I'd rather be an American citizen if the worst happens. I've been studying the Constitution and the Bill of Rights. Go ahead, ask me anything."

"What's the Eighth Amendment?" Jenkins asked.

"It prohibits cruel and unusual punishment."

"And the Tenth Amendment?"

Prickles of heat broke out across her skin. The Tenth Amendment was one of those confusing ones, something about the power of the federal government. How embarrassing to have Carson and Jenkins both watch her struggle to conjure up the answer.

Finally, she had to give up. "I'm exercising my Fifth Amendment right to remain silent," she said, causing both men to laugh . . . and yet it wasn't funny. The test was coming up in a few days and she still got so flustered. She summoned a smile and glanced over at her former supervisor.

"Mr. Guillory, you'd still rehire me even if I don't know the Tenth Amendment, wouldn't you?"

"Are you willing to work nights?" Mr. Guillory said.

"If I must."

"Then I suppose I must find room for you."

She lingered a little longer, but then had to get back to her apartment. They locked the doors of the building at eleven o'clock each night. It was ten-thirty when she arrived back home, yet she was still too wound up to sleep.

Thankfully, she found company in the cozy communal room on the eighth floor. Midge Lightner was like everybody's grandmother, and the residents naturally flocked to her to tell the woman their problems. Midge probably knew more secrets than most priests working a confession booth.

"I've read the section on the amendments to the Constitution a hundred times, and I still get it wrong," she said as she flopped onto a sofa in the communal room. "Nothing sticks, and I feel so stupid."

Midge's knitting needles clicked as she worked. "You're not stupid, Inga. You're one of the hardest-working people I've ever known."

She snorted. Plow horses worked hard, but they weren't the brightest creatures on earth. Besides, she was tired of working hard. Her test was on Monday, and the Gerards had wired to say they were booked to sail back to Germany on Wednesday. The prospect of getting on that ship landed like a weight in her gut.

"Everything would be easier if I stayed in New York," she confessed to Midge. "Berlin is becoming a scary place. It wasn't when I arrived, but things are getting darker now."

Midge gave her a sad smile. "I was scared every day throughout the four years of the Civil War," she said. "I couldn't wait for it to be over so that I could scrub it from my mind and never think of it again. And yet I wouldn't trade those years for anything. Despite all the horror, all the tragedy, it became the most important few years of my life. It's how I define myself. For as long as I live, I know that when duty called, I had the strength to answer."

Inga drew a sobering breath. She went to Germany to repay Mr. Gerard by supporting him until he could find his footing at the embassy. That debt had been repaid, and he didn't need her anymore. And Benedict? He was the most self-sufficient man she'd ever met. He surely didn't need her either. He could never return her affection . . . could he?

The temptation to stay in New York or gamble everything and return to Benedict clawed at her all through the sleepless night.

Inga clenched the freshly inked document as she approached the suite of judges' chambers in the courthouse. The document proved she'd passed the citizenship test! It hadn't even been all that difficult, and now the only thing she needed was to complete the interview with the friendly Judge Bancroft, who would sign off on her paperwork and make her an American citizen.

This seemed too good to be true, too easy. Feeling nervous, she approached the clerk behind a tall counter. "I have an appointment with Judge Bancroft."

The clerk didn't bother to look up from the stack of papers he was sorting. "Sorry, he's out sick today. Judge Keating is taking his appointments. You can take a seat, and we'll call you when it's your turn."

Inga felt the blood drain from her face. Judge Keating was the one Delia claimed hated immigrants and used trick questions. Her heart began pounding, and her mouth went dry. This was a disaster. Delia had warned her to avoid Judge Keating at all costs.

"Is there a different judge I can see?"

"Nope," the clerk said, now stamping a bunch of papers before him. "Keating is the only one in the building today, and Bancroft is going to be out for the rest of the week."

"Sir," she whispered, and something in her tone finally caught the clerk's attention. He set the stamp down and met her gaze. "Please, can you tell me . . . what happens if I fail the interview?"

"You can try again in thirty days," he said and gave her a sympathetic nod. "Keating fails a lot of people. Don't worry. When you come back, maybe you'll be assigned to a different judge."

Every muscle in her body tensed as she dropped into a chair in the waiting room, wondering what to do. Only a coward would run away without even trying, but it was tempting.

The door to the judge's chambers opened, and an elderly woman came out, her face despondent. The old man beside her stood. Speaking in German, he asked how it went.

The woman replied in the same language, "What a horrible man." She shook her head and walked away.

"It's your turn," the desk clerk instructed Inga.

She stood and approached Judge Keating's closed door, her fingers icy as she knocked.

"Come in!" the judge barked, and she quickly entered the chambers.

Sunlight gleamed atop the bald crown of Judge Keating's head. He didn't look at her as he perused her paperwork through the half-moon spectacles balanced on the end of his nose.

"Another German," he said sourly. "Very well, young lady. Have a seat and let's get on with it."

She sat, and he fired his first question before she could even arrange her skirts. "How tall is the Statue of Liberty?"

She blinked. This wasn't the sort of question she expected, and her tongue felt stuck to the roof of her mouth.

"Come now," the judge prompted. "Your paperwork says you've lived in New York since childhood, and you don't know the answer to such a simple question?"

A knot tightened in her stomach as she scrambled for the answer. She couldn't afford to get it wrong, but the longer she sat there, frozen and mute, the happier the judge looked.

"I'm not sure," she finally said in a thin voice. "It's very tall."

"You can't do better than that?"

What would Benedict do in this situation? He'd think of some clever response, even if he didn't know the answer. "The Statue of Liberty is tall enough that my father could see its light all the way from Germany."

The judge gave a dismissive snort and marked an X on his form. "So you don't know the answer. Next question: Why doesn't Germany have a Bill of Rights?"

The interview was supposed to be about the United States, wasn't it? Her palms began to sweat, her heart racing. The smirk on Judge Keating's face made her even more nervous. He looked like a hovering vulture, waiting for a chance to pounce.

"I don't think the kaiser would permit a Bill of Rights," she ventured. "I think that—"

"Wrong," Judge Keating interrupted. "It was a trick question. The German Imperial Constitution of 1871 granted limited civil rights through parliamentary representation. But it's a pale, puny document compared to the majesty of the U.S. Bill of Rights. Let us proceed."

The judge's verbal test got even worse after that, and Inga sensed her dream of American citizenship slipping further away with each awful question.

OCTOBER 1916

B enedict arrived at the Anhalter Bahnhof well ahead of the appointed time to meet the Gerards' train. The ambassador had sent a telegram instructing him to bring the largest carriage to take them home. Apparently, Mrs. Gerard had spent so much time shopping in New York that they bought an additional trunk just to accommodate her purchases.

No mention had been made of Inga.

It had been six weeks, and Benedict hadn't received a single telegram or letter from Inga. Had she passed her citizenship test? According to the ambassador, unsympathetic judges were notorious for springing trick questions on immigrants they didn't want to pass the test. With the hostility toward Germans these days, Inga might have faced an uphill battle attaining her certificate. Foreign-born or not, Inga understood what it meant to be an American citizen more than most.

If Inga failed the test, or a small-minded judge blocked her out of spite, Benedict would personally figure out a way to call that judge on the carpet.

If she came back.

He continued pacing in the waiting area outside the steel-girded terminal that stretched across four city blocks. It was always loud in here, with steam engines barreling into the central concourse, the noise echoing off the iron-and-glass vaulted canopies.

One end of the terminal was reserved entirely for departing troop trains, but even here in the civilian section, signs of the war were everywhere. A one-legged soldier hobbled with the aid of crutches, and another had bandages covering half his face. Countless women were swathed in black, and the men wore black armbands. Though the nearest front was five hundred miles away, the shadow of war was growing darker over Berlin.

The one o'clock train from Hamburg arrived precisely on time, triggering a mild rush of anxiety. If Inga wasn't aboard . . . well, he couldn't really blame her. She'd been homesick for New York and a normal life ever since arriving in Berlin. Why should she come back and endure their awkward marriage? He'd figure out how to explain her absence to the Germans, but he would miss her.

Quite badly.

When the passenger gates finally opened, businessmen and soldiers on leave came rushing through, heads down, faces serious. Benedict scanned the crush of people on the other side of the gate. It was hard to make anyone out amid the dense crowd, and Inga was short.

Far back on the platform, Ambassador Gerard helped his wife pin her wide-brimmed hat atop her head. Benedict frowned. There was no sign of Inga, only Ambassador Gerard helping his wife fuss with her hat.

"Benedict!"

He jerked his attention to the passenger gate. The voice sounded like Inga, yet he couldn't see her anywhere. But that cheerful voice *had* to be Inga. Then a dainty hand reached above the crowd, dancing and waving at him.

He grinned as the top of her head popped above the crowd. Just a fleeting glimpse of blond curls and a radiant smile as she hopped up and down to make eye contact with him. Tension unknotted from his shoulders. There was no cause for this sudden rush of joy because they still had nothing more than a marriage of convenience, and yet . . . everything was a little brighter with Inga around. *Today* was a little brighter knowing she was there.

He shoved both hands in his pockets so he wouldn't do something stupid like sweep her into an embrace she probably wouldn't welcome. It took a few more moments before she finally cleared the throng of passengers and made it through the gate. She paused about ten feet away, facing him but standing stock-still.

What was she waiting for?

He was about to head toward her when she lifted a piece of paper, holding it proudly before her with both hands.

It was her citizenship certificate.

His chest filled with pride. He *knew* she could do it! Suddenly she was in his arms. He buried his face in her neck and lifted her high. "Congratulations," he said.

She returned his embrace, hugging him tightly. Maybe it was wrong to cling to each other in the middle of the Anhalter Bahnhof, but if there was anywhere on earth two people ought to be able to embrace each other, it was at a train station.

"Well, well, well," a blustery voice said, and he reluctantly untangled himself from Inga as the Gerards approached. The ambassador was the man who would someday sign off on their annulment, so groping Inga in front of him was a bad idea.

"You had a safe journey?" he asked the ambassador, trying to get his breath under control. Inga leaned over to slip her certificate safely back into a leather binder. Citizenship records were filed at multiple government offices so there was no worry if it got misplaced, yet he predicted Inga would pass that slip of paper down to her children and grandchildren.

"Yes, yes," Ambassador Gerard replied. "Mary did her best to spend me into bankruptcy, but that's what I get for leaving my wife unattended in New York City."

Benedict noticed Inga's delightful new traveling suit for the first time. The wool was a robin's-egg blue with ornate trim along the lapel that looked like it came from a medieval tapestry.

"You've been shopping as well," he said to Inga, who flushed in pleasure.

"Mrs. Gerard was very generous," she replied.

Benedict arranged for a porter to wheel their luggage out to the street, where the trunks were strapped to the roof of the carriage. He slipped inside the carriage with Inga. "Congratulations again. Was the test difficult?"

"Not the written part, no. The spoken part, however, was dreadful. The judge asked me the most unfair questions, but in the end he decided I managed well enough to pass. Thank you for the encyclopedias! They were a great help, and I'll return them as soon as we get home."

He'd never heard Inga refer to Alton House as home before, and he liked it.

"Oh, I bought you something in New York," she said, rummaging through her canvas satchel. Hopefully, whatever she'd bought wasn't too expensive. He hadn't thought to buy anything for her, and she didn't earn enough to splash money around on gifts.

Inga held the sack before her like a prize. "A pound of candy corn," she said. "My friend Katherine is a dentist, and she says candy corn is nothing but pure sugar. You should be *ashamed*, Benedict."

"I'm not," he said as he took the sack from her, amazed she'd remembered his long-ago comment about his guilty fondness for candy corn. "Are you sure there's a pound in here? It feels a little light."

She shrugged. "I had to sample it to see what all the fuss was about. It's sinfully good, isn't it?"

"It's awful," Mrs. Gerard interjected. "I told Inga she needs to upgrade her standards."

Inga laughed. "Never! I'm a lowbrow girl and won't ever change."

Benedict didn't want her to change either. He once considered her to be shallow and silly; now he understood the value of Inga's lighthearted optimism.

After delivering the Gerards to the embassy, they had a rare opportunity of complete privacy on the short ride to Alton House, and Benedict intended to take advantage of it.

"I like that shade of blue on you," he said with a nod to her suit. "The color matches your eyes." He'd never had a favorite color before, but he did now, and this was it. The cornflower blue flecked with hints of silver and gray was the exact color of Inga's eyes.

She flashed him an alluring smile. "Did you miss me?"

"Ridiculously so." The answer was instinctual, even though he was surprised by it. Inga flirted all the time, but this felt . . . different. Her gaze seemed warmer and uniquely focused on him. He picked up her hand, thrilled that she made no move to pull it back. He stroked a thumb along the soft kidskin leather. "New gloves?"

"They're too tight," she said.

"Then let us dispose of them." He pinched the tip of her index finger and tugged. She made no objection, and he moved to her middle finger to give it a pull, then the ring finger, and finally her pinky. He wiggled the glove from her hand and tossed it onto the bench.

Amazingly, she extended her other hand for the same treatment. Now he *knew* she was flirting with him. This was playing with fire, but he couldn't help himself. He locked gazes with her, enjoying the way she smiled into his eyes as he divested her of the second glove. This time she was the one to toss the glove aside.

"Much better," she said. It might be his imagination, but the blue of her eyes seemed to have deepened a shade.

He lifted one of her liberated hands and kissed the back of it. When was she going to stop him? He breathed in the scent of her skin. Apples. Yes, it was her favorite apple soap from New York. It was his new favorite scent in the world.

He lowered her hand but couldn't bear to release it. "I'm glad you're back home," he said, holding his breath and awaiting her response.

"I'm glad too."

A quiet sense of elation filled him, and she let him hold her hand the entire ride back to Alton House.

28

A rush of affection surged as Inga returned to Alton House. For as long as she lived, she'd probably associate the scents of woodsmoke and lemon oil with Alton House and the challenging years of her life there.

Mrs. Barnes insisted on a celebratory dinner in honor of Inga's brand-new citizenship papers and even opened the formal dining room for the occasion. She made Inga's favorite chicken pie recipe, along with bowls of ice cream swimming in brandied cherries for dessert. Inga had the place of honor at the head of the table, and Benedict sat at the opposite end.

She liked sitting across from him. Ever since resolving to return to Berlin, she looked forward to the prospect of advancing her relationship with Benedict. Sitting opposite him at the table made it feel as though they were a real married couple. It gave her a perfect view of him as he cradled the goblet of wine when he drank, then slowly rotated the stem with his long, slim hand. He looked stern and sexy at the same time. She especially liked the way he watched her when he thought she wasn't looking.

Benedict had gone back to his taciturn ways during dinner, but everybody else chatted with abandon. Larry couldn't stop complaining about a new carpet at the embassy that gave him a headache, and Nellie recounted every guest they'd hosted in the six weeks since Inga had been gone.

One name came up over and over: Fräulein Zinnia von Eschenbach. Inga vaguely remembered the pretty young woman who came to the embassy for help after her father had been arrested in London.

Apparently, the baron's daughter visited the embassy several times over the past few weeks, and Benedict escorted her all over the city. Last weekend the two of them went rowing on Lake Tegel. Baron von Eschenbach had been released last month, so there was no reason for Benedict to keep meeting with his daughter.

Was she allowed to feel jealous? She and Benedict didn't yet have *that* sort of marriage. She tried to sound nonchalant as she prodded for more information. "I've heard that the rowing on Lake Tegel is lovely," Inga said to Benedict. "What was it like?"

"Tedious," he replied. "It rained."

He must be very enraptured with Zinnia if he would go boating during such poor weather. "Why did you go rowing on a rainy day?"

Instead of answering her, Benedict glanced at his watch and pushed away from the table. "Forgive me, I have more letters to complete." He stacked his silverware atop his plate and carried it toward the kitchen, but then paused when he came to her chair.

He touched her shoulder. "It's nice to have you home, Inga."

Well, *that* was unexpected. Benedict almost never touched her when they were in Alton House. The light brush of his hand sent a shiver down her entire body.

Did he care for her or not? She couldn't let Benedict go on thinking she was happy with a completely platonic marriage, especially if he'd started squiring other women around town.

It was time for her to act.

Benedict needed to keep his distance from Inga. Although the flirtation in the carriage this afternoon had been delightful, he needed to quit playing with forbidden fruit if they were to maintain their marriage of convenience. He'd managed to tamp down his feelings for her when she'd been four thousand miles away, but now she was back. Everything about her was alluring, from her sense of humor to her curvaceous figure and kissable mouth and flirtatious gaze. The troublesome attraction came roaring back the moment he saw her at the train station, and it had grown every hour since.

He turned his attention back to the list of British prisoners still held at Ruhleben. They'd been penned up for two years, and only a few had been successfully exchanged. He'd finally managed to get Baron von Eschenbach traded for a British viscount held in Austria, but thousands of others had little hope for release from the bleak, muddy racetrack.

A tap on the library door broke his concentration. "Come in."

Inga stepped inside, holding two volumes of his set of *Encyclopedia Britannica*. "I hope I'm not disturbing you?"

She'd been disturbing him since the hour they met. "Not at all."

"Thank you for these," she said, setting the two oversized volumes on the desk.

"Did they help?"

"Oh yes! Although, I must confess, I spent far more time reading your notes than studying American history."

Heat gathered beneath his collar. He hadn't said she couldn't read his notations, but it struck him as an intrusion, like someone peeking at one's diary. He pulled the two volumes a little closer to himself.

"Thank you for returning them," he said, hoping she would leave now. Instead, she propped a hip on the edge of his desk and toyed with the edge of an encyclopedia. Inga clearly wanted something.

"Yes, Miss Klein. What else can I do for you?"

She flushed a little. "About that time you went rowing on Lake Tegel . . ."

What a miserable day it had been. He needed to be alone with Zinnia to discuss what she'd learned on her trip to London regarding the German civilians still imprisoned in England, and rowing in the middle of a lake ensured they couldn't be overheard. He and Zinnia both got soaked that dismal afternoon, but that couldn't account for why Inga should look so uneasy.

"Just say it," he prompted. "Whatever is worrying you, just say it."

"Why were you rowing with Zinnia von Eschenbach? It seems out of character for you."

Could Inga be jealous? Or was it merely her pride talking? Since they'd presented themselves as a married couple to the outside world, perhaps she didn't wish to be seen as a woman whose husband was stepping out on her.

"Zinnia went to London to check up on detained German civilians and was reporting back to me."

"In the middle of Lake Tegel?"

Inga was *definitely* jealous, and for some absurd reason that pleased him. "Yes, in the middle of the lake. Spies, you know. Zinnia is betrothed to a colonel, who is serving on the Western Front. Our only interest in each other is in facilitating prisoner exchanges."

"Ah," she replied, still tracing the edge of his encyclopedia. The silence lengthened, becoming uncomfortable.

"So the encyclopedias helped?" he asked.

A slow smile curved her lips, the gleam of it reaching all the way to her pretty blue eyes that sparkled with guilty amusement. "Not really," she said, moving to perch more firmly on the desktop. "But I learned a lot about Abelard and Heloise. Why do you like them so much?"

He quirked a brow. "How do you know that I do?"

"You wrote more notes about the entry on Abelard and Heloise than anywhere else in the book."

She must have spent a lot of time flipping through that volume because, yes, she was correct. And she looked extraordinarily fetching the way she perched on the desk. Her knee brushed against his arm, but he didn't back away.

"I've always found the forbidden nature of their relationship intriguing."

"You wrote things in the entry on Bavaria too."

That was a little more awkward. He couldn't precisely recall everything he'd written, but he knew it was all about Inga. Her look told him she wanted an answer. "Once again the forbidden nature of Miss Inga Klein is intriguing to me."

The gleam in her eye deepened. The scent of apples came from her skin, arousing memories of their embrace in the train station. She seemed to be enjoying this moment as much as he was. What would she do if he . . .

Without breaking eye contact, he rested his hand on her knee. She didn't back away, just kept her gaze locked with his.

"Come closer," he prompted. He wasn't sure what to expect when she twisted off the desk and moved directly onto his lap. Surprise flooded Benedict as he placed his hands around her hips, settling her more comfortably on his lap.

"You've read my thoughts on Abelard and Heloise," he said. "What are yours?"

She laid a hand along the back of his neck, triggering a tingle that ran across his shoulders and down his arms. "I don't like sad love stories, you know that," she teased. "I have a theory that elite people like you distrust romance and want to punish lovers. Romeo and Juliet . . . Lancelot and Guinevere."

He battled a smile because, yes, there were dozens of tragic love stories to choose from. "Tristan and Isolde. Anna Karenina. Madame Bovary."

"Yes, yes, and yes," Inga said, jabbing him with her finger with each word. "I think all those high-flown authors are afraid of feelings and give everyone a sad ending."

He ran his hands to the small of her back, amazed she was allowing such intimacy. "You may be right, Miss Klein, but Abelard and Heloise were real people, and they had a sad ending too. It's why I am glad they were at least buried together."

"I never thought of you as someone with a romantic soul," she said.

It was impossible to look away from her deep blue gaze. "Now you know my secret, Miss Klein."

Rather than pulling away, she looped her arms around his shoulders, then tilted her head and leaned down to him. Her kiss barely brushed his mouth, but he cupped the back of her head and drew her more firmly down.

She met him kiss for kiss, returning everything he gave and more. This was no clumsy, impulsive kiss. He'd been thinking about a long, leisurely kiss with Inga for months. He cupped her face in his hands, nibbled and drank her in, growing breathless in the process.

At last she lifted her head, and she beamed down at him. "That was nice," she said, looking every bit as ecstatic and breathless as he felt. He settled his hands back on her hips. Everything about having her here was oddly thrilling and natural at the same time.

Yet they shouldn't be doing this, not if they were going to get an annulment. He and Inga were as different as sweet and sour, and yet they had learned to rub along okay.

More than okay. He'd been thinking that ever since he saw her in the train station this afternoon, holding her citizenship certificate out as if it were a gold medal. It wasn't so much the way she looked as how she made him feel, as if the world brimmed with love and hope and accomplishment. It was becoming impossible not to smile when she was near. She had the unique ability to remain joyful even during the darkest hours.

"Inga, have you ever considered keeping things between us permanent?" He slid his hands further around her hips, and he held his breath.

"You mean, stay married?" she asked.

"Yes."

She glanced away, and a little light dimmed in her eyes as an array of expressions flashed across her face. "Sometimes," she said. "It seems rather daunting, though. I'm already homesick for New York, and you'd probably want to live all over the world. Right?"

That was the life of a diplomat. It was what he was trained to be, and he was good at it. As war threatened to drag civilization into chaos, the world needed diplomats more than another cannon or battleship.

And yet he wanted this marriage. He wanted *Inga* and intended to fight for her.

"Stand up," he said impulsively, and she hopped off his lap. Then he stood and scooped her up, carrying her draped in his arms as he took her to the window overlooking the front yard. She'd instinctively looped her arms around his shoulders, and he tilted her to look outside. Lampposts illuminated the tree-lined avenue where diplomatic staff from all over the world made their homes.

"Look out there," he said. "The Argentinian staff lives across the street, and almost all those men have their wives here with them. Children too. Next door are the Bulgarians, and they brought their families. It's a normal street where people live and make love and raise their children. It can be a good life."

Having her in his arms felt amazing. He wanted to hold her, support her, linger long into the night wrapped around her.

"Benedict, this is all too new," she said. "What if we tried it out first?"

He practically dropped her in shock. "Share a bedroom?" There'd be no chance of an annulment in such a case.

"No," Inga said, twisting a little bit, a sign she wanted to get down. Her heels clicked on the floor, and she turned to face him. "What if we just toy around with the idea of it? We hold hands, flirt, pretend to like each other."

It was a battle, but he stopped himself from laughing. "You want me to pretend that I like you?"

"Yes," she said, a little excitement coming back into her eyes. "I know it may be challenging for you, Cold Oats, but let's try. Can we?"

It would be flirting with danger. Cracking open the veneer of reserve and letting Inga in was tempting fate, and yet he was willing to risk it.

"Excellent idea, Miss Klein. We shall begin tomorrow."

29

Inga snapped awake early the following morning, barely able to believe her audacity the previous night. Had she really suggested that she and Benedict should start testing the waters of a real marriage? What had she been thinking?

There were only two possible outcomes. Something magnificent was about to happen, or she was embarking on a mortifying and painful mistake.

She'd been intimidated by Benedict before they even met. The way the Gerards described him ensured that, yet it wasn't until Inga saw Benedict in person that she felt dwarfed by his lofty education and stern good looks. She made up silly nicknames for him like Doom & Gloom or Cold Oats because it helped keep a distance between them.

And now she'd suggested they strip away the pretense and see if they could actually function as normal people. Man and wife. Lovers.

Don't think that way! They weren't going to hop into bed together; all she'd suggested was to see if they could get along, maybe share a kiss or two. Even so, she took extra care as she smoothed her hair up into a chignon and pulled a few tendrils down to frame her face. And earrings. She chose her dangly blue earrings because they played up the color of her eyes.

Downstairs, breakfast was already under way. The warm kitchen smelled of vanilla and maple syrup as everyone except Benedict indulged in waffles. He, of course, nursed a bowl of cold oats as he read a magazine. He didn't even look up as she joined the others at the table.

Everything seemed perfectly normal as she took a seat between Larry and Andrew. She drizzled syrup over her waffle, stealing surreptitious looks at Benedict on the far side of the table. He was engrossed in the financial magazine balanced on his knee, one hand holding the magazine, the other rubbing his jaw. It was oddly appealing. Inga couldn't even read two paragraphs of that dreary magazine without losing interest, but Benedict was different. *Nothing* bored him. He lounged in the hardback chair with his magazine, tall and slim and effortlessly cultured.

It was disconcerting, and she picked at her waffle, too nervous to eat. Benedict had quit rubbing his jaw and now mindlessly traced the rim of his coffee cup as he continued reading, and somehow she found *that* weirdly arousing too. Where had this roaring attraction to Benedict come from? Was it knowing he'd returned her interest that suddenly made her so aware of him?

The breakfast table, crammed with everyone from Alton House, wasn't the place to start testing a new courtship with Benedict. If they decided to go through with an annulment, they needed to maintain the pretense of a platonic relationship before the others.

Suddenly, the walls of the house felt suffocating. "Benedict, how about a walk?"

He snapped the magazine closed and shot to his feet. "Let's go."

Larry looked a little taken aback as he watched them abruptly leave. She hid a grin and reached for her wrap from the coat tree.

Outside, the chill of autumn was in the air, so she tugged on her fancy new kidskin gloves. She should have brought a scarf too.

226

The chilly air snaked around her collar, raising goose bumps on her neck. She pulled it a little higher.

"Hand, please," Benedict said.

Oh yes, they were supposed to start holding hands as part of their new agreement. Would it have killed him to have used a complete sentence? She was about to make a snippy comment, then stopped herself. The terse request was typically Benedict, and she shouldn't castigate him for it any more than she'd appreciate it if he told her to quit smiling so much.

Offering him her hand, they headed up the street toward the plaza. Withered leaves scraped along the cobblestones, and acorn caps crunched underfoot. She scrambled for something to talk about that would be appealing to someone as educated as Benedict. His first wife grew up on a college campus and probably had no trouble keeping up with all of Benedict's worldly interests.

"What were you reading this morning with such fascination?" she asked.

"Problems with the foreign treasury notes," he replied. "The war is delaying the payments of dividends, and that's causing liquidity concerns."

He kept talking, and each sentence made her feel more ignorant. She never pretended to be an expert on economic policy and wouldn't start now. She kept her voice deliberately conversational as she interrupted him. "Did you know that if you keep talking about dividends and liquidity, I am almost certain to keel over from boredom?"

"Shhh," Benedict said in an oddly affectionate tone. "We're supposed to pretend to like each other."

"I actually do like you, Benedict, but when you say 'liquidity,' I think about this fountain," she said as they approached the circular fountain with a splendid statue in the center. It would probably be drained for the winter soon. The statue was of an ancient warrior king, holding a sword in one hand and a scepter in the other. The inscription on its pedestal read, *Athaulf, King of the Visigoths.*

"Are the Visigoths the same as the Goths?" she asked Benedict. "And what about the Ostrogoths. Who were they?" When she first arrived in Berlin, she'd tried to learn about the barbarian groups whose statues were everywhere, but they all blended together in her mind.

Benedict leaned down to whisper in her ear, "I get them confused too."

A giggle bubbled up, and Benedict laughed as well. Maybe all this ancient history wasn't so terribly important after all.

She gazed up at the statue of the warrior king. "Once, that man was famous and feared, yet nobody remembers him now. Not like the carpenter's son. Nobody needs a statue of Jesus to remember him."

"We carry his messages carved on our hearts," Benedict said. "'Blessed are the peacemakers . . .'"

"'For they shall be called the children of God,'" she finished.

Benedict nodded. He looked pale and tired as he sat on the rim of the fountain. She joined him, taking his hand and wondering what had put the hollow expression on his face.

"Oh, Inga, I've always wanted to be a peacemaker. Every day I feel like America is getting pulled closer to the war. I fear it is becoming inevitable."

She cradled his hand. "It's been more than two years and we've stayed out of it," she said. "You helped make that happen."

The breeze kicked up, sending a swirl of dried leaves skittering across the pavement. Suddenly the mood seemed as gray and bleak as the October morning. She pulled her wrap a little tighter. Even with the worsening weather, she didn't want this moment to end because for once it seemed as though Benedict actually needed her. It made her feel worthy, as if she were more than just a pretty ornament.

They huddled on the cold stone of the fountain's edge, shivering in the chilly autumn wind and sharing an hour of comfort and comradery unlike anything Inga had ever known. Only when pinpricks of sleet started pelting them did they reluctantly head back inside.

Perhaps she and Benedict had a future together after all.

30

Woodrow Wilson was reelected to the presidency on November 7, 1916.

Benedict and everyone else at Alton House rejoiced because the nation had reelected the man who'd vowed to keep America out of the war. Larry opened a bottle of champagne, and they all shared a toast together.

Then Benedict sneaked out to the garden with Inga to celebrate on their own. In the three weeks since she'd returned from America, they'd maintained their professionalism at the embassy, let down their guard a smidge at Alton House, and threw caution to the wind after dark in the quiet of the garden. They probably weren't fooling anyone at Alton House, but they never shared a bed or got too intimate because Inga insisted on keeping her options open.

The morning after Wilson's reelection, Ambassador Gerard summoned Benedict and Colonel Reyes to his office for a highly confidential meeting to discuss the consequences of the election. The doors were closed, the secretaries dismissed, and guards had been posted outside the door and windows to ensure no eavesdroppers could overhear.

Nevertheless, Ambassador Gerard couldn't resist shouting as he paced around the office. "The president has gone insane! He wants us to kowtow to the kaiser."

"Give me a specific example," Benedict asked, striving to keep his voice calm. President Wilson was no longer beholden to popular opinion, which meant big changes could be looming.

"The president wants to force England, France, and Germany to the negotiating table. He wants 'peace without victory.' He's afraid of making the Germans feel bad about the violence they've unleashed on the world, so he wants me to beg the kaiser to play nice. Who does he think he is?"

"He is our commander in chief, who has given us our negotiating instructions," Benedict said, struggling not to sound like he was delivering a reprimand. If President Wilson wanted the United States to take the lead in negotiating a peace treaty, the embassy had their marching orders and needed to carry them out.

The ambassador settled back in his desk chair, motioning them both closer. The anger in his expression drained into one of concern, and he lowered his voice. "The president's spies believe the Germans intend to resume unrestricted submarine warfare again."

Benedict stiffened. "They promised they wouldn't after they sank the *Lusitania*."

"Proof that the word of a kraut is no good," the ambassador growled, but Colonel Reyes sounded more analytical.

"German submarines are the best in the world. They've been fighting with one arm tied behind their back ever since they made that promise. We should have expected this."

True, but it would be a dangerous move to unleash that particular weapon if it killed more Americans. The United States escaped getting dragged into the war after the *Lusitania* only through the grace of God and President Wilson's firm resolve.

"I advise keeping our communications with the Germans open and friendly," Benedict stressed. "Referring to them as 'krauts,' even in the privacy of our own discussions, can taint our attitude toward them. The president wants us to persuade the warring parties to the peace table, and we are obligated to do so."

"We'll be doing it with a new foreign minister," the ambassador said. "Von Jagow has been fired, and Arthur Zimmermann promoted in his place."

Benedict stifled a curse. Von Jagow was a decent man with whom he'd had cordial relations for years. Arthur Zimmermann was crafty, aggressive, and inscrutable. "No matter who is at the table, we will give it our best shot."

Ambassador Gerard rolled his eyes. "*You* give it your best shot," he said. "Zimmermann invited me to share his box at the opera this evening. My wife is exhausted and suffering a bout of pleurisy. Benedict, you'll have to go in my place."

He instantly agreed. Mingling with high-ranking diplomats at social events was a golden opportunity to start building a productive relationship with Germany's new foreign minister.

He sought out Inga on the second floor of the embassy, where she was taking supply inventory with Larry.

"Inga. A word, please."

The pleasure that lit her face at his arrival never failed to make his heart kick up a notch. Ever since they quietly began exploring the possibility of turning their marriage of convenience into a romantic lifetime together, Inga brought warmth and vitality into his world that made each day a little brighter.

She followed him to his office, where he closed the door and stole a loving but all too short embrace. He never pressed Inga for greater intimacy than she was willing to share, but stolen kisses were a guilty pleasure they both enjoyed. He stepped away and straightened his tie, for they had business to discuss.

"I am expected to attend the opera tonight to represent the embassy. The kaiser and half the court will be there."

Her eyes sparkled. "How exciting! Which opera will be playing?"

He had no idea. Tonight wasn't about enjoying an opera; it was a chance for him to reinforce America's neutral position and ease the tension between their two nations.

"I'm not sure," he admitted. "Probably something by Mozart, since the kaiser is partial to Mozart. I was hoping you would accompany me. I don't expect you've ever seen anything quite as grand as the Staatsoper Unter den Linden. It will be a chance for you to experience a bit of what it's like to be a diplomat's wife." And he desperately hoped she would soon be ready to accept that role and all that it entailed.

She blinked in surprise. "I'm not ready for something like that. What would I wear? And what on earth would I talk about? Benedict, I'm not smart like you—"

"Shhh." He cut her off. "Inga, you will do fine. You are fresh and funny and could charm a doorpost. I think . . . I *hope* you will enjoy the evening. It's the sort of thing I've been doing for years, and I believe you will enjoy yourself."

Inga was smart enough to understand exactly what he was saying. If she wanted to be the wife of a diplomat, this was part of the duties. Anxiety warred with excitement on Inga's face as she mulled over the invitation. By now he could tell exactly what she was thinking. Inside, she worried that she was an uneducated shoemaker's daughter who didn't belong. But after a moment, she straightened her shoulders and met his gaze. "If you need me to be there, I shall do it. Yes, of course I can."

His heart turned over. Sweet Inga, always so desperate to please. "Excellent," he said with relief. Inga had only one evening gown, and it wasn't formal enough for a royal event at the opera. Luckily, the high-end dress shops of Berlin continued to serve customers as though there were no war only a few hundred miles away. "You'll need a formal gown, so we should leave immediately."

Twenty minutes later, they arrived at the Palast aus Seide on Leipziger Strasse in the heart of Berlin. The ultra-feminine shop smelled of lavender and looked like a jewel box inside. Brilliantly colored gowns of silk, satin, and beadwork glimmered beneath a sparkling chandelier. A stern-looking woman wearing a black gown and hard expression descended on Inga like a crow. She frowned at Inga's ordinary white blouse and navy skirt.

Benedict intervened before the woman could try to throw Inga out of the shop. He took Inga's hand. "My wife needs a ready-made gown suitable for the Royal Opera House," he said in his loftiest voice. The saleslady's disdain eased a touch, but Benedict wasn't going to leave Inga alone with this viper. "We need it for tonight. I am happy to pay for immediate alterations."

There weren't many ready-made gowns to choose from at the Palast aus Seide. Some were matronly, some for mourning, and the two white gowns were for debutantes. He homed in on a gown of amethyst silk with a fitted bodice, a softly draped skirt, and a small train. It was the right gown for Inga. It was fresh yet sophisticated, and Inga would look dazzling in it.

Even the stern crow gave a stiff nod of agreement. "Ja. This is the gown for her."

31

Inga felt like an imposter as Benedict escorted her up the grand staircase leading into the Staatsoper Unter den Linden. The three-foot train of amethyst silk trailing after her was a constant distraction as she tried to avoid tripping over it. Benedict wore a formal black coat with tails and an elaborate white tie. The only men not wearing formal attire were the generals and members of the German high command, whose daunting uniforms glittered with sashes, swords, and medals.

How different this was from New York, where the vaudeville opera theaters were *fun*, not stuffy. If this was a foretaste of what it would mean to be Benedict's wife for real, she wasn't sure she was up for the job. The imposing lobby featured white walls that soared upward to a beautifully painted ceiling. The floor gleamed with white, gold, and black mosaic tiles. Dozens of columns surrounded the hall, topped with elaborate gold acanthus leaves. All she had to do was survive the next five hours without embarrassing Benedict; then she could flee back to the wonderfully shabby comfort of Alton House.

Benedict filled her head with instructions during the carriage ride over. Don't eat while wearing opera gloves, but she could drink. Don't initiate a conversation with any members of the royal family or officers of the military. She might encounter ladies she was friendly with from the other neutral embassies, but she must address them by their formal titles instead of their first names.

"There's Fräulein Zinnia von Eschenbach," Benedict said, nodding toward the pretty young woman with the spray of freckles across her nose. "I shall introduce you to her and a few other ladies before joining the men."

She gave a terse nod. Of course, Benedict couldn't babysit her. He needed to use the time before the opera to mingle with the German ministers, leaving Inga on her own. She could make conversation with these people. *She could.* The weather was always a safe topic, wasn't it? And at intermission she could talk about the performance.

So many people! She lay her hand atop Benedict's wrist as he led her toward Zinnia. "Fräulein, may I introduce my wife, Mrs. Inga Kincaid."

"How wonderful," the woman replied, and it looked as though she actually meant it. "Mrs. Kincaid, we should have tea at the Kurfürstendamm. And perhaps a little shopping afterward?"

Another notch of anxiety fell away. "I would like that."

Then, miracle of miracles, Inga recognized Mrs. Jeppesen from the Danish Embassy. Mrs. Jeppesen joined them and had polite comments about the yacht race the Gerards hosted last spring.

By the time Benedict excused himself, Inga was starting to feel more at ease. This was fine. *She* was fine. She actually didn't need to say much, as the other women carried the conversation while she smiled and nodded.

Across the gallery, Benedict joined a group of important-looking gentlemen, one of whom sent a chill through her. She'd recognize that ruthlessly groomed mustache anywhere. The last time she had seen him was right after the *Lusitania* went down, when he made crafty allusions to her German citizenship. Since then, Arthur Zimmermann had been promoted and was now the foreign minister of Germany. He intimidated her down to the marrow of her bones, but Benedict had protected her then, just as he continued to protect her today. There was nothing Zimmermann could do to hurt her now. She was an American citizen. She had a husband who protected her and, amazingly, seemed to genuinely care for her.

"Father, come meet Mr. Kincaid's wife," Fräulein Zinnia said, beckoning a tall man with the same cheerful freckles as his daughter.

"Dear Mrs. Kincaid," the baron murmured, pressing a kiss to the back of her gloved hand. "I shall be eternally grateful for your husband's efforts to attain my release. No man can truly appreciate freedom until it has been taken away."

The sentiment appeared to be sincere, though his accent was as clipped and cultured as a British aristocrat.

"You speak English beautifully," Inga said.

He tipped his head in acknowledgment. "I grew up in England," he said. "I've spent more than half my life over there. I can't wait for the war to be over so I can go to the races at Ascot again."

"Father, look, there's Prince Oskar," Fräulein Zinnia said in an awed whisper. Inga followed her gaze and spotted a young man in uniform standing beside Benedict, chatting with the chancellor. Prince Oskar was slim, intense-looking, and wore a colonel's uniform with plenty of medals, including two iron crosses.

"Isn't he handsome?" Fräulein Zinnia whispered.

"Brave too," the baron said. "The kaiser has six sons, but the empress has managed to keep most of them far behind the battle lines. People were beginning to talk. Prince Oskar took himself into actual battles and has surely caused his mother many sleepless nights."

Inga took a sip of the fine German wine, watching as Benedict conferred with the tight cluster of men. Usually, Benedict mostly listened, but this evening he was speaking rapidly, the other men leaning in to hear him.

How proud she was of him! Some of the highest-ranking men

in Germany were hanging on his every word. Everything was going exactly as she'd hoped.

Footmen wearing white wigs and stockings opened the doors to the theater. A few people began funneling in, although most continued their conversations. Inga intended to follow their lead, grateful she'd survived this long without a gaffe.

Benedict soon joined her, smiling as he folded his hand around hers. "Good news, darling. Minister Zimmermann has invited us to join him and his wife in their box."

It didn't sound like good news to Inga. The man scared the willies out of her, but if Benedict stayed beside her, she would be fine.

She stepped away to set her empty wineglass on a receiving tray. A few matronly women glanced her way, speaking behind their fans. The only words she caught were "shoemaker's daughter." Given the sour expressions, they did not mean it as a compliment.

She kept her chin high as she returned to Benedict. Everyone in this gilded hall wore shoes that had been made by some hardworking craftsman, and she wasn't ashamed of being the daughter of such a man.

The theater was as grand as the gallery, with crimson velvet seats, a painted ceiling, and three tiers of private boxes. Only about half the seats were filled, mostly by women. It was a sad reminder of the brothers, sons, and husbands serving in the war.

Benedict led her to Foreign Minister Zimmermann's private box and introduced her to the other wives. Mercifully, there was no need for further conversation, as the lights were lowered.

Once seated, Benedict leaned toward her, his nose tickling the hair swept up behind her ear. "How are you doing?" he asked quietly.

"Fine," Inga whispered. "You?"

He squeezed her hand and kissed her cheek. "Fine."

He retreated back into his chair, but tingles flared from the spot where he'd kissed her. Never could she have imagined she would be at an event like this. Now that the opera was starting, she could relax.

The ruby-red curtains rose on ropes of gold braid, revealing an enchanted kingdom. A towering forest lit by moonlight filtering through the trees illuminated a thicket of grass and a mountainside with *real water* trickling down like a waterfall. A handsome prince entered the stage, chased by a monstrous dragon. Who cared if there were actors' feet visible beneath the massive scaly costume of the dragon? She'd never seen anything like it and was spellbound as the opera unfolded with fairies and enchanted creatures.

But not so spellbound that she didn't peer around at people in the neighboring boxes. Baron von Eschenbach chatted amiably with half a dozen people, who moved in and out of his box. The fact that the baron was here and not languishing in a prisoner camp was Benedict's doing, and she lifted her chin a little higher.

When the lights came up for the first intermission, Benedict led her back into the gallery. "Will you be all right on your own?" he asked, and she sent him a nod before he headed off toward another group of diplomatic dignitaries.

Inga couldn't continue to monopolize the goodwill of the Eschenbachs. She twitched her fan before her face, glancing about the gallery for someone she might know. There were at least five hundred people there tonight, yet she was still a stranger among those belonging to German high society.

At last she spotted Mrs. Torres from the Argentinian Embassy. Though Inga rarely mingled with the ambassadors' wives, she and Mrs. Torres once played croquet together.

She approached Mrs. Torres, cautiously meeting the older woman's gaze. With a tiara atop her upswept black hair, Mrs. Torres looked regal and imposing. There was no sign of recognition, and no one to introduce her. She managed a timid smile and asked, "Do you remember me? We played croquet together at the Danish Embassy."

Recognition dawned, and the woman nodded. "Yes, you're the secretary who married Benedict Kincaid."

"That's right," she said, relief battling with embarrassment over having her lowly profession announced so bluntly around the other ladies.

Mercifully, Mrs. Torres provided introductions to an Austrian baroness and a German countess, whose husband served in the Imperial Marine.

"You must be very proud," Inga said, and the countess gave a stiff nod but said nothing else. Neither did Mrs. Torres, and an awkward silence stretched.

Conversing with the Eschenbachs had been so easy, yet intruding on this group of ladies had been a blunder. What sort of secretary did that? Inga's rustic Bavarian accent probably didn't help matters. None of the women appeared willing to speak, and she scrambled for something to say.

"Have you seen Baron von Eschenbach?" she asked the group. "He seems to be fully recovered after his time in England."

The German countess gave a polite nod. "Praise to the kaiser for making it happen."

Actually, praise to Benedict and American diplomacy, but she wouldn't push it. "I gather more prisoners might be exchanged soon," she said. "Both sides have so many civilians trapped in internment camps, and I know the baron is trying to work with other neutral parties to release more men. Wouldn't that be marvelous?"

Mrs. Torres grabbed Inga's arm just above her elbow. "Come along, Mrs. Kincaid, let us find some refreshments." The older woman propelled Inga away from the group, squeezing her arm as though Inga were a disobedient child. Had she done something wrong? Inga tried not to cringe as they reached a private area behind a row of columns.

"*Never* gossip about embassy business with outsiders," Mrs. Torres hissed into her ear. "Your husband should have instructed you about confidentiality, and yet you babble about it with highly placed women from the German side? Shame on you. I only hope Baron von Eschenbach's efforts do not falter because of this."

Mrs. Torres whirled away, leaving Inga alone behind the column, trying to control her panicked breathing as every scrap of confidence collapsed like a tower of ash. All those men in Ruhleben, suffering at this moment in horse stalls, and she just put their release further into jeopardy. The backs of her eyes prickled, and it was getting harder to control her breathing.

She had to get out of here before she started bawling like an infant. It meant cutting through a crush of people to get through the front doors. She kept her chin down, avoiding curious glances as she angled her way toward the doors.

"Pardon," she mumbled when she stepped on a woman's train, then bumped into a gentleman, causing the wine in his glass to slosh. She kept muttering apologies as she veered around people to get out. If she lifted her gaze, she might make eye contact with someone and start crying.

At last she reached the front doors, where a footman looked at her curiously.

"Please," she whispered. "Outside."

He opened the door for her, and she escaped onto the well-lit portico. A freezing December cold penetrated her gown instantly, triggering a round of shivers. Her cloak was somewhere inside, but she'd eat nails before going back to retrieve it.

She hugged herself as she paced the wide, vacant portico. Stupid, stupid, *stupid*! Never had she felt so small. Beside her, monumental statues of great Prussian generals stood in the alcoves, the only ornamentation outside the opera house.

There were four of them, all looking grim and scary. Who were they? The writing on the pedestals was in some ancient language she couldn't read. Benedict would probably know who they were. He knew everything.

Another shiver raced through her. Was it from the cold or the fear of walking back inside that awful place? She gazed down the wide avenue that ran toward the heart of Berlin on one end, and back toward Alton House on the other. It was tempting to walk home, but she wasn't close enough, and Benedict would be expecting her back in that private box soon. The only way she could make this evening worse would be to flee and leave him to try to explain her absence. It was time to go back inside, join Benedict, and quit feeling sorry for herself.

Inside, the gallery was almost empty because the second act had already begun. The glare of white marble made her blink after the soothing darkness outside. Benedict was pacing about, and the look of relief when he spotted her was humbling. She glanced away.

"Where were you?" he asked, hurrying to her side. "I was beginning to fear you'd run away."

"Not quite," she said but still couldn't meet his gaze. He needed to know what she'd done, even though confessing her stupidity would bring another round of humiliation. "I'm afraid I misspoke in front of some ladies. Mrs. Torres from the Argentinian Embassy let me know how atrocious it was."

Benedict frowned. "Let's head outside, and you can tell me what happened."

"Are you sure? The second act has begun."

"It doesn't matter. I need to know what you said."

Once again, she was back on the portico with the towering German statues frowning down at her. As was Benedict. He had that stern look that always intimidated her, but he needed to know exactly what happened in case there was something he could do to salvage the situation.

"I so enjoyed meeting Baron von Eschenbach that I got carried away with his story," she began, then told him everything, including the way Mrs. Torres looked white with anger. "I'm sorry," she concluded, braving a look at Benedict for the first time since she began speaking. It was impossible to read his expression in the weak illumination from the gaslights.

"Mrs. Torres is right," Benedict said. "There needs to be a bright, inflexible line surrounding every scrap of embassy business. I'm sorry I didn't do a better job explaining that."

It wasn't Benedict's fault she was such an idiot. "Is this going to hurt your odds of getting others released from Ruhleben?"

Benedict's sigh sounded as dry and hopeless as the withered leaves scuttling along the pavement. "Probably not. Everyone knows we're working to free the prisoners, but Mrs. Torres was right to nip it in the bud. It's important to keep your cards close to your chest whenever we're in public."

It was a gentle reprimand, but she recognized it for what it was. Uncontrollable shivers raced through her, and he wrapped an arm around her shoulders.

"You're cold. Let's head back inside."

Her lower lip started to wobble. Mrs. Torres had been in a neighboring box, and the prospect of seeing her again made Inga's stomach plummet. Benedict must have noticed.

"Unless you'd rather not," he added. "I can summon a carriage and take you home."

She blinked. "I thought you had important business to carry out. Wouldn't it be terribly rude to leave in the middle of the opera?"

Benedict's smile warmed as he shook his head. "Nobody comes to the opera just for the performance. I've already met with everyone I needed to speak to. We can head home now if you like."

It was the answer to a prayer. "Yes. Thank you."

Her teeth started chattering, and all she wanted was to get home. No more pretending. No more making a fool of herself. Tension unknotted from her neck as Benedict gave instructions to a footman to summon a cab, and then he returned inside to make their excuses to the Zimmermanns.

An uncomfortable silence stretched between them during the carriage ride home. If nothing else, this evening proved how supremely ill-equipped she was to become a diplomat's wife.

Benedict didn't like seeing Inga cowed, but yes, she'd made a bad blunder tonight. Nobody knew how urgently Baron von Eschenbach was working behind the scenes to free the British civilians, and it wouldn't reflect well on him if news of it leaked. Many people in Germany already mistrusted the baron because of his unabashed love of England.

Inga remained silent on the ride back to Alton House. He gave her a reassuring smile as he helped her alight from the carriage. She tried to apologize again as soon as the carriage rolled away.

"Benedict, I'm sorry—"

He put a thumb on her lower lip. "Shhh. It's okay, Inga."

Her eyes turned a little watery before she nodded and headed inside. He needed to write up his impressions of the evening and retreated to the library to do so. It was nearing midnight before he finalized the report and was surprised to hear voices in the kitchen. One of them sounded like Inga.

He moved silently down the hallway, cocking his ear to listen. Yes, it was definitely Inga speaking, describing the events of the night. To his dismay, Inga's humiliation was rooted in a lot more than her slip of the tongue.

"I'm afraid everyone could see right through me," she was saying. "They knew I didn't belong. It was as plain as day every time I opened my mouth."

"People in Germany are elitists." It was Larry, his voice unusually empathetic. "You need to ignore it and carry on."

"I just feel so stupid everywhere I go," she replied, her tone sounding vanquished with exhaustion. "This gown cost Benedict a fortune, but I'm still a peasant from Bavaria with no more than an eighth-grade education. I don't belong here."

Larry murmured more words of comfort, although given her noncommittal snorts in reply, none of it seemed to penetrate her wall of misery.

The sorrow in her voice tormented Benedict. Everything Inga had done since she arrived in Berlin had been selfless. She came here because Ambassador Gerard took advantage of her good nature. She helped Nellie clean the kitchen every evening. She used her free time doing relief work for the prisoners in Ruhleben.

It was high time somebody did something nice for Inga. As her husband, and the man who hoped to make their temporary alliance permanent, it was up to Benedict to solve this.

32

Inga did her best to forget what happened at the opera house as she threw herself back into work at the embassy. Larry timidly approached her desk the next morning.

"Have you recovered from the horrors of last night?"

"It wasn't that bad," she admitted. She'd spent the morning typing reports about soldiers suffering from trench foot, dysentery, and shell shock. It forced her to put her piddly troubles in perspective.

In the days that followed, she tackled crates of letters that flooded the embassy. Some were from American businesses having difficulty collecting payment for goods shipped to Berlin. Some requested help locating Americans believed to be traveling in Germany. One was from the mother of a Red Cross volunteer who'd died in an automobile accident, and his body needed to be transported home.

Her hands were chapped after opening hundreds of letters and they hurt from paper cuts, so Inga kept a jar of rose-scented cream at her desk to soothe them. And yet how could she complain about a little paper cut in the middle of a war?

She'd just finished rubbing the cream into the skin of her abused hands when Benedict approached and set a postcard on her desk. It featured a colorized photograph of a quaint village nestled in a steeply sloped mountainside. The spires of pine trees were so deeply green they almost looked black against the shockingly blue sky. She looked up in question to Benedict.

"The Bavarian Alps," he explained. "The town is Rosendorff."

"Rosendorff! That's where I was born. My cousins still live there."

"I know."

She looked at the postcard with renewed interest as fond memories bloomed. She barely remembered what the town looked like, only how it made her feel. She'd been happy there, but her parents found it hard to make a living in the small town of shoemakers nestled in the woods. Her biggest regret during her time in Germany was that she'd been trapped in Berlin and hadn't been able to visit her hometown.

Benedict loitered at her desk. He was usually so direct, and the way he watched her seemed odd, like he was expecting something of her.

She held up the postcard. "Can I keep this?"

"I bought it for you," he said with a nod, then started fidgeting again, clearing his throat before speaking. "It occurred to me that we never had a honeymoon, and you may enjoy a trip to Rosendorff. I would be happy to accompany you."

"We can't leave the embassy with all this work piling up, can we?"

"I can clear my calendar for a short visit," he said. "The week after Christmas is always a slow time, and Mr. Gerard agreed that Larry can cover your duties."

It sounded like everything had already been arranged. Inga glanced at the postcard again, its beautiful mountain landscape summoning nostalgia, and she had to blink a little faster. "This might be the nicest thing anyone has ever done for me."

He brightened. "You'll come, then?"

She shot to her feet and flung her arms around his neck. "Thank you, Benedict. Yes, yes, I'll come!"

Inga exchanged telegrams with her uncle Albrecht in Rosen-dorff to arrange the visit. There were no hotels in the tiny village of only two hundred people, so they'd be staying with her uncle. She barely remembered her father's younger brother, except that he was gruff and scary.

Albrecht closed his final telegram with three terse words: *Bring ration coupons.*

Did he mean to sound so curt? Perhaps he was merely thrifty and economized on words since telegrams charged by the letter. Americans weren't issued ration coupons, and she couldn't ask her family to stretch their meager food allowances. Milk was now strictly rationed, and meat was almost impossible to get. Inga filled a large crate with luxuries hard for ordinary Germans to find, such as chocolate, coffee, sugar, and strawberry jam. Most precious were the fifteen cans of condensed milk. Hopefully, the bounty would help soften Uncle Albrecht.

She and Benedict set off on the fifteen-hour train ride to Rosen-dorff the day after Christmas. Benedict tried to get them a private compartment, but such luxuries were a casualty of the war. Lack of fuel limited civilian train service, and cars with private compart-ments had been eliminated throughout Germany.

All kinds of people got in and out of the train during their trip—schoolchildren, soldiers, a pair of elderly sisters. A woman with a cage of smelly chickens sat opposite them for over an hour. Benedict offered to lift the cage to the overhead rack, but the woman clutched the cage, refusing to let it out of her sight. Fortunately, the lady with the chickens got off the train at Leipzig. Her place was immediately filled by a soldier with a hollow expres-sion who never stopped twitching. When Inga tried to welcome him, he averted his eyes and refused to speak.

It was difficult to make conversation with so many people crowd-ing the train, so she simply gazed out the window at the countryside speeding by. They passed a dairy farm, where a one-legged soldier sat in a tree stand, a rifle propped on his shoulder as he guarded the cows.

Was hunger so bad in the countryside that they needed to guard the livestock? She glanced at Benedict, and he nodded, answering her unspoken question. She'd heard rumors about how things were worse outside of Berlin, and here was proof of it.

She'd never seen so many mountains and fields and rivers, all of them reaching as far as the eye could see. They passed small towns where the spires of country churches were the only things to reach above the trees. Other times the train chugged through grand cities like Leipzig and Nuremberg. The farther they traveled from Berlin, the sparser the crowd on the train. Soon they were approaching the outskirts of Munich, which meant they were getting closer to Rosendorff.

In Munich the trembling soldier disembarked until at last they were alone and could speak freely.

"There's a prisoner camp not far from Rosendorff in a town called Puchheim," Benedict said. "If possible, I'd like to visit the camp and check its conditions. It's only about five miles from where your family lives. Would you mind if I excused myself for a few hours to do so?"

"Visiting prisoner camps and bunking in with my scary uncle," she said. "This honeymoon gets better and better."

He winced a little, and she squeezed his hand. "Benedict, I'm teasing. The fact that you're taking me all this way, in the middle of a war . . . it means the world to me."

He leaned down and kissed her. She shifted to fit closer against him, never breaking contact with their kiss. Benedict wasn't the sort of man she ever imagined for herself. Maybe he was a stuffed shirt with a chilly demeanor, but beneath that starchy veneer, he smoldered.

It was after ten o'clock at night when the train pulled into the station at Puchheim. Inga clenched her suitcase while Benedict went to ensure their crate of food was safely off-loaded from the baggage car. She hadn't feared for its safety when they boarded the train this morning, but that was before she witnessed the deprivation throughout the interior of the country.

How cold it was here in the mountains! Only a single lantern glowed at the redbrick train station, casting its small pool of light. Throughout Germany, lanterns were kept dark because of fuel shortages. The people gathered on the platform loomed like dark silhouettes. How was she to recognize Uncle Albrecht?

A tall, blocky man approached. "Did you bring your ration coupons?"

So much for a warm welcome. Uncle Albrecht's gruff, surly voice was exactly as she remembered.

Benedict spared her from replying. "We aren't entitled to ration books because we aren't German citizens. Instead, we brought plenty of food and supplies for everyone. We will not be a burden."

As Uncle Albrecht grunted his reply, a younger man came forward. "Inga?" he said. She nodded, and his smile revealed white teeth in the dim light. "I am Gerhard Mueller, your cousin Gita's husband. Welcome home!"

She impulsively hugged him, relieved to be greeted by at least one smiling face. His name pricked an old memory, and she pulled back to squint at him in the darkness. "Gerhard Mueller . . . didn't you once hide a dead fish in my lunch pail?"

Gerhard howled as if in pain. "Argh! I was hoping you would not remember! Gita and I had a bet about that, and now I have lost."

His good humor was contagious, and she laughed as she introduced Benedict. Only Uncle Albrecht did not smile as he hurried them toward an old farm wagon hitched up to an aging nag. Benedict carried both their suitcases, while Gerhard insisted on hefting the crate.

The crate landed with a heavy thump in the back of the wagon. "It feels like there is a ton of bricks in here."

"Canned milk," she said, and Gerhard whirled to gape at her.

"Milk?" he exclaimed, his voice brimming with hope.

"Yes, condensed milk," she affirmed. "We brought fifteen cans of it."

"Gita will be so glad," Gerhard said. "We have a ten-month-old boy, but Gita has had so little decent food that her milk dried up, and there is none to be had in the shops anywhere. Thank you, Inga!"

"Come along, the night grows darker," Albrecht growled as he slid onto the driver's bench of the buckboard wagon. He insisted that Inga sit beside him, and Benedict and Gerhard would walk alongside the wagon to spare the old horse.

It was two miles to Rosendorff. Little did she know when she agreed to this trip just how rustic it would be. Soon they were beyond the light of the train station and traveling on a one-lane road into the dark forest. Gerhard halted the horse to light a lantern that hung from the wagon.

"There was no point in wasting fuel while the light of the station could still be used," he said as he hefted himself back onto the bench.

"I hope we are not inconveniencing you," Benedict said.

"No imposition," replied Uncle Albrecht. "You shall have the master bedroom while you are here. It is the best room in the house."

Inga winced. "We couldn't ask that of you." She glanced at Benedict, pleading for him to back her up. He needed no urging.

"Herr Klein, we could not impose in such a fashion. We are grateful simply for a roof—"

Uncle Albrecht held up his hand, cutting off the conversation. "I won't have it be said that we are unwelcoming to guests. My wife has already prepared the room, and that's the end of it."

All that could be heard was the clop of hooves and the slow, steady creak of wheels as the wagon thumped along the dirt road. An awkward silence stretched, and Inga strained to peer into the darkness, trying to make out the shapes of the trees, but beyond the pale circle of lamplight, all was black except a few patches of snow.

The night air felt wet and icy, causing her to burrow deeper into her coat. At least Benedict and Gerhard were getting along okay. It turned out that Gerhard was a cook at the prisoner camp in Puchheim. He said he could probably arrange for Benedict to tour the facilities. She tilted her ear to listen in on their conversation. Apparently, half the prisoners were Russian, and the rest French.

"They hate each other," Gerhard said. "I get called out of the kitchen to break up fights all the time. The Frenchies think I favor the Russkies because I serve so much borscht, but that's all I can get these days."

They rounded a bend, and a few lights flickered in the distance. "This is Rosendorff," said Uncle Albrecht. "I expect most of the village is asleep, though my wife and the girls are probably still up."

"The girls" were her cousins Johanna and Gita. They were the only people Inga clearly remembered from Rosendorff. The three of them used to play hide-and-seek behind the chicken coop. Would they even recognize each other anymore?

Uncle Albrecht turned the wagon down a narrow lane toward a half-timbered house. A steeply pitched roof overhung the ground floor that had small, deep-set windows. Inga's feet had no sooner touched the ground than the front door flung open, and Aunt Frieda raced out to greet her.

"Inga!" she shrieked. Then came Johanna and Gita, both laughing and squealing. There were other people too, strangers she didn't know but whose smiles were wide and welcoming. Aunt Frieda hustled them inside, where the warmth of the fire in the large front room was like a balm. The kitchen and a huge brick fireplace took up most of the front room. Woodsmoke and the musty scent of old plaster stirred a rush of childhood memories.

Benedict lugged the crate inside and set it on the scuffed kitchen table.

"Let's see what you brought," Uncle Albrecht said, and Benedict began lifting out the bounty. Aunt Frieda's eyes widened in astonishment at the sight of the large smoked ham.

"Look, Gita . . . milk!" Gerhard said, holding one of the cans aloft as though he'd just found manna from heaven.

"Bless you!" Gita said, and she hugged Inga.

Benedict continued lifting food out of the crate, eliciting gasps as each new item emerged. Soon the table was filled with cans of milk and sacks of sugar and coffee. Uncle Albrecht watched with a frown, his arms crossed as he scanned the offerings.

"Plenty of jam," Benedict said as he brought out the selection of jars Inga pilfered from the Alton House pantry late last night.

One of the jars prompted Uncle Albrecht to pick it up and hold it to the lantern. "Brandied cherries," he said in a wistful tone. He met Inga's gaze across the table, and for the first time his craggy features softened. "I remember the cake your mother made the year your sister died."

Inga caught her breath. She hadn't expected him to remember. Marie's death had knocked her sideways. Her parents' insistence on celebrating Christmas with their traditional Black Forest cake had been bittersweet. A pall settled over the family. Marie's death was part of the reason her parents decided to leave Rosendorff for America.

"I thought perhaps we could make a cake to remember Marie," Inga said, trying to contain the emotion welling up inside her.

Uncle Albrecht set down the jar of cherries. "I think that would be a fine idea," he said, his voice breaking as he turned away.

In the past, Uncle Albrecht always seemed so gruff, and yet there was a tender side buried beneath his scary exterior. This wasn't the first time Inga misjudged someone based on superficial impressions. They were all living through a terrible time, but tonight she would give thanks to God for the chance to see her family again and celebrate the blessings they'd been given.

33

Benedict tried a final time to decline the master bedroom, but the Kleins were adamant that he and Inga have the only decent bedroom in the house. Most of them slept on pallets in the front room. Gita and Gerhard shared the single upstairs room, along with their three children and baby boy.

That left him with Inga in the bedroom with the large four-poster bed and no other seating. The bed was a family heirloom with elaborate hand-carved posts, railings, and hanging fabric panels for warmth. Aunt Frieda teased that the Klein babies had been conceived on this very bed for generations, which caused a good bit of ribbing from the men and a mortified blush from Inga.

The enormous bed left little room for the modest dresser next to it. There was a fireplace, although it had been swept clean. Wartime shortages of everything, including firewood, meant it hadn't been lit in a long time. As a result, the room was so cold he could see his breath. Nevertheless, Benedict was determined to get some sleep tonight and refrain from pouncing on Inga—an urge he'd been feeling ever since they started playing the dangerous game of testing a genuine marriage.

He left Inga alone in the bedroom to change into her nightgown, explaining his behavior to her family that he needed to use the facilities. The house had no plumbing, so he had to bundle up to visit the freezing outhouse behind the stables. It wasn't the first time he'd used an outhouse, but it was so dark he had to leave the door cracked open to let in a little moonlight.

By the time he got back, Inga was covered up like a nun, clutching her plain white gown and robe all the way to her chin. But no matter how frumpy her gown, she couldn't disguise the fact that she was still *Inga*, with piles of blond hair spilling over her shoulders, and wide eyes that looked at him with admiration. And he was a normal, healthy man who'd been attracted to Inga from the first day he saw her.

"You should take the bed," Inga offered as soon as they were alone in the room. "I can sleep on the floor."

"Absolutely not. If anyone sleeps on the floor, it will be me."

"This is my family," she protested. "I'm in your debt for bringing me here. The least I can do is let you have the bed."

He hunched down to let his hand hover over the floorboards. The house was built on a raised foundation, and chilly air leaked up between the weathered old boards. Sleeping on it would be a misery. Everything about this ancient, crowded house with scant heat, scantier food, and no plumbing was uncomfortable, but at least they had a decent bed—if he could bring himself to share it without taking advantage of Inga like a man who'd been starved of a woman's embrace for years.

Outside, a gust of wind howled and came straight up through the floorboards. Inga shivered and blew in her cupped hands.

This was ridiculous. He reached across the bed to flip the blanket and sheets down. "Hop in," he ordered, and mercifully she conceded and jumped in. He flipped the covers over her the second she landed on the mattress.

"Better?" he asked.

"Yes, thank you. This bed is plenty big enough to share. And I know you won't . . . I mean, I hope that you won't—"

"I won't," he assured her. But maybe it was time to press the arrangement. He braced a hand on the railing above the bed, leaning down to see her better. "Have you thought any more about making our arrangement permanent?"

She blushed and looked away. "I think about it all the time. I still don't know what to do. The only thing I know for sure is that I don't want to lose my virginity with Uncle Albrecht on the other side of that door."

He smothered his laughter with a cough. "Agreed," he said simply. One thing he learned about Inga long ago was that when she got nervous, she got chatty, and she had a lot to say as she held the blanket up to her chin.

"I have a feeling you know a lot more about this side of marriage than I do."

The side of his mouth twitched. "Almost certainly."

"I've had a lot of boyfriends over the years," she said, "so I know what it is to kiss and cuddle. Of course, we had the world's strictest chaperone at my apartment building back home, meaning there was never any real . . . well, never anything *more*, if you know what I mean."

He kept his eyes locked with hers. "No. Tell me what you mean."

She grabbed a pillow and threw it at him, and he caught it with a laugh. She sank back down into the mattress and hid a guilty smile.

"One of my friends had a book called *The Young Wife*," she said in a conspiratorial voice. "It explained all about 'conjugal duties.' I'd never heard that word and had to look it up in a dictionary."

"Did that clear it up?"

"Absolutely. In Germany we call it *hüpfen im heu*. 'Jumping in the hay.' Or maybe that's because I grew up in the countryside, and people have fancier terms for it in the cities."

Not really, but he didn't want to stop Inga from talking because she was flushed and pretty, and he wanted nothing so much as to hop in bed with her, but he was still fully dressed.

He tugged the cotton panel across the railing so she couldn't see as he shucked off his coat, fumbled with the buttons on his shirt, and peeled off his trousers. He grabbed a sleeping shirt from his suitcase and tugged it over his head, shivering from the chilly fabric.

"I'm coming in," he warned a moment before tugging the panel aside to leap beneath the covers. Straw crackled, ropes creaked, and a dusty scent rose up from the mattress, but it must have been recently stuffed because it provided a decent amount of padding. Jumping in the hay, indeed!

The problem with a rope bed was that unless the ropes were constantly tightened, it tended to sag, leaving the ones lying on the mattress rolling toward the middle. While Inga tried to scoot back to her side, she would inevitably roll toward the middle the instant she relaxed.

"Come here," he murmured, extending his arm toward her. She hesitated only for a moment, then surrendered and settled against his side. He tucked the blanket around her back and shoulders. Then he wrapped her in his arms and buried his nose in her hair, breathing in the soft, lemony fragrance.

"Thank you again," she whispered, her breath warm against his neck.

"Shhh." He didn't want her gratitude; he merely wanted her. Cradling her like this was a uniquely marvelous torture. She kissed the side of his neck, and he stroked her hair. At some point she tilted her face up to his, and they indulged in long, lazy kisses.

After a moment, he had to turn away. This wasn't the time to make their marriage permanent, though he wanted to. With every fiber of his being he wanted Inga to be his forever.

It wasn't the first time Inga shared a bedroom with Benedict, though it was the first time they'd wrapped up in each other's arms all night. The rope bed made sure of that. He hadn't tried any greater intimacy beyond a little kissing and nuzzling, and nothing had ever felt quite so nice.

Now Benedict was up and dressed while she was still too lazy to leave the warmth of the bed. Her breath left little white puffs in the air, and she savored the coziness of huddling beneath the covers to watch Benedict shave.

It was a disturbingly agreeable sight. He'd lathered a bar of soap to cover the lower part of his face, then carefully dragged a straight razor along his jaw. The mirror on the dresser had been tilted so he could watch as he angled his head this way and that, dunking the blade in the washbowl.

"Do you do this every morning?" she asked.

"Every morning," he confirmed. The twinkle in his eye indicated he found her question amusing, but he couldn't smile as he swiped the razor alongside his mouth.

She wiggled deeper into the pillows as she continued enjoying the intimacy of watching the mundane act of shaving. If they stayed married, she could do this every morning. Strange how Benedict's formality used to intimidate her. Now his straitlaced decorum was rather appealing to her.

"I wonder why it seems so much colder here than in Berlin."

"It's the altitude. We're up in the mountains here."

"But I thought hot air rises?"

Benedict swiped the last of the soap from his face. "It does, but the air gets thinner the higher you get. It can't hold on to the heat like it does when you're near sea level."

He continued to explain about molecules and atmospheric pressure. She wasn't paying much attention. It was more interesting to watch him fasten the buttons on his shirt cuffs. Then he went about carefully folding his nightshirt and putting everything away instead of leaving it draped over the bedstead like she would have done.

He finally ended his explanation about atmospheric pressure and looked at her. "Does that make sense?"

"Not really," she admitted. "If we stay married, I'm afraid

you're going to find me terribly stupid. I'm not smart like Mrs. Torres or Mary Gerard."

He braced his hand along the top of the bedpost like he'd done last night and frowned down at her. "Why do you keep insisting you're stupid? I wish you'd quit doing that."

She shrugged. "Because you read the *Encyclopedia Britannica*, while I like the gossip columns. That's never going to change."

And he needed to know that about her. She couldn't pretend to be someone she wasn't, and she probably wouldn't be a good wife for a diplomat.

Benedict sighed as he sat on the edge of the mattress, his weight causing everything to shift and prompting her to roll onto her side next to him. She angled her elbow to prop up her chin, facing him without shame or embarrassment. She was who God made her to be and wouldn't pretend to be anyone else.

"You're not stupid," he insisted. "You don't have much of an education, but you're bright and clever, and you have a heart of pure gold. That's worth more than all twenty-six volumes of my encyclopedia."

He pressed a quick kiss on her forehead, then gave an affectionate swat on her rear end. She could barely feel it beneath the mound of blankets, but she rather liked the impulsive familiarity.

"I hear people moving about in the front room," he said. "I'll join them and leave you to get dressed."

She watched him leave, feeling her heart pound and wishing the sight of Benedict Kincaid shaving hadn't been the sexiest thing she'd ever seen in her life.

Warmth enveloped Benedict as he joined the rest of the family where an ancient cast-iron stove warmed the front room. The entire Klein family was already gathered around the long dining table, where hot coffee scented the air and silverware clattered as children gobbled oatmeal.

"Benedict, come have breakfast," Aunt Frieda urged, spooning oatmeal into a bowl. A can of condensed milk had been opened and diluted. All the children had a glass of milk before them, and Frieda reached for a stoneware jug, about to pour some into his bowl when he stopped her.

"Just oats please, no milk."

Frieda looked at him curiously, the pitcher suspended above his bowl. "Are you sure?"

"Yes. I like simple plain oats," he said. Actually, cold oats with cold milk was his favorite, but he wouldn't deprive this family of a single drop of milk. Albrecht shot a hasty look at his wife, telling her not to argue, and Freida set the bowl of plain oats on the table for him.

The house looked even more humble by morning's light. The pallets had been stacked in the corner, and Albrecht's table where he cut leather for shoes was beneath the window where the best light was to be had. Baskets of wooden shoe molds sat beside the worktable, along with pliers, awls, and cutting shears arrayed on the windowsill. This was the sort of humble workshop Inga's father had fled decades earlier, and Benedict could understand why.

Gita sat across the table with her ten-month-old boy on her lap, who happily sucked on a bottle of milk. "When are you and Inga going to have a little one?" Gita asked.

"Hopefully in good time," he said, and it was true. He'd always wanted children, and Inga would be a fine mother. All he had to do was convince her to stay married to him.

Inga soon emerged from the bedroom. Like him, she accepted a bowl of oatmeal but declined the milk. Was it his imagination or did the day brighten the moment she joined them? The lilt in her voice and her cheerful demeanor always had that effect on him, but it seemed even Albrecht softened a little as Inga shared about life in New York.

The table had room for a dozen people, and soon both benches were full as neighbors began congregating at the house to meet the long-lost daughter of Rosendorff. Inga didn't know or remember most of the visitors, yet she still eagerly greeted them all.

Benedict silently watched. He didn't have Inga's natural buoyancy, and nobody was here to see him anyway. It was more than enough to enjoy watching Inga's delight as she mingled with family and new friends.

Mostly. One visitor, an apprentice shoemaker named Siegfried, seemed especially impressed with Inga, hanging on every word she spoke. Was Siegfried really that eager to hear about the shoemaking business in New York, or did he merely like leaning in close to her?

Inga hiked up her skirt a bit to model the factory-made boots she'd bought in America. Siegfried dropped to his knees to admire them while Inga gushed about the stores in New York with their ready-made shoes in dozens of sizes and colors. She didn't mind at all when Siegfried poked and prodded at the fit of the boots, even laying a hand on the side of her heel and testing the leather.

It would be nice if Benedict could stop pondering what Inga said last night about all the boyfriends she'd had over the years. She attracted men effortlessly, even though last night she hadn't seemed to care a fig about them. She'd seemed entranced with *him*, and he returned the sentiment with full force.

How long could Inga return his affection? She liked him now, but would it last? Somebody as bright and flirtatious as Inga might grow bored with him quickly. Claudia certainly had.

He rose from the table to help carry dishes to the rinse tub. Inga wasn't anything like Claudia, and he should be ashamed to think of them in the same sentence.

Gerhard joined him. "I am leaving for the camp at Puchheim soon," he said. "I cook lunch and dinner each day, so I will not return until late tonight, but you are welcome to join me."

"I'd like that," Benedict said. It was easier to sink into diplomatic work rather than make conversation with people with whom he had so little in common.

He asked Inga if she would mind him leaving, and she sent him a blinding smile of agreement before turning back to Siegfried and a few other men from the town who were curious about New York.

She seemed so happy that it was a joy to simply watch her. Benedict could take credit for bringing her here, but could he make her happy in the long run? Or would she tire of him as Claudia had done?

He strolled over to press a goodbye kiss to Inga's forehead. Inga was nothing like Claudia, and he would fight to keep this marriage.

34

Although Inga enjoyed meeting the townspeople, she was more excited to get reacquainted with her aunt and cousins again. Gita let her hold the baby and give him a bottle of milk at lunch, which made Inga long for a baby of her own someday. The other children were amazingly well-behaved. When the three-year-old approached a basket of her uncle's shoemaking tools, all it took was a single glower from Albrecht to turn the boy away.

Once again, it seemed everyone wanted to know when she and Benedict expected to have babies of their own. It didn't feel right to evade the questions, so she simply replied that it would happen if God willed it.

Which was true. While she and Benedict still didn't have a real marriage, someday they might. Benedict had been so extraordinarily decent to her lately, and she looked forward to their stolen hours together. He was handsome, educated, and honorable. She was proud of him. Even now, on one of his rare days away from work, he spent it touring a prisoner camp, trying to make the world a better place.

She spent the day soaking up old memories and new insights. Aunt Frieda taught her to make the family's traditional recipe for a cold vegetable salad she hadn't had since her mother died. They sliced mounds of pickled beets, radishes, and two types of cabbage. The only challenging part was mixing a dressing with the proper amounts of horseradish, salt, and vinegar. Her first taste of the salad was like stepping back in time. Her father had complained this salad was "peasant food." Maybe so, but she loved it and wrote out the recipe so she could make it once she got home.

By six o'clock the sun had set, and they ate supper by the light of a few flames in the fireplace. Aunt Frieda apologized for how dim the room was.

"We've always been frugal with the kerosene, but ever since the war . . ."

"I understand," said Inga. A row of kerosene lanterns sat unused on the top shelf in the kitchen. All types of fuel had been severely rationed throughout Germany. At least the Kleins were able to gather wood from the forest surrounding them to keep the fireplace burning.

The children stretched out on their pallets after dinner while Inga sat with the women at the table, talking softly long into the night. Johanna was twenty-four and would have married two years ago except that her fiancé was serving on the Eastern Front. The only reason Gerhard hadn't been drafted was because he worked at the prisoner camp.

She wanted to stay up to welcome Benedict home, but the others were fighting back yawns. Inga gave an immense yawn of her own and asked to be excused, which the women instantly accepted.

It was pitch-dark and freezing in the master bedroom, although not so bad once she burrowed beneath the mound of blankets. Gita told her to expect Gerhard and Benedict back around nine o'clock, but Inga soon dozed off.

She snapped awake when the door quietly opened. Benedict's

tall silhouette was lit from behind by the flickering fire in the front room. It was impossible to see his expression or his mood.

"Are you awake?" he whispered.

"Yes," she whispered back.

He closed the door. "Good. I'm freezing! Don't get out of bed. I'm joining you in sixty seconds."

The chill came off him in waves as he shucked his overcoat, jacket, and began unbuttoning his shirt. She ignored his command to stay in bed and hopped out to fumble through his suitcase, searching for his nightshirt.

"How was the camp?" she asked as she tossed him the shirt.

"Freezing as well," he said as he pulled the nightshirt over his head. It was hard to tell if he was laughing or angry. He shivered as he removed his shoes and trousers and threw it all in an ungainly heap atop the suitcase, which was very unlike Benedict!

They raced to their respective sides of the bed and dove beneath the covers, laughing as she cradled his icy hands between hers, blowing on them.

"Oh, that feels good," he said with a delicious sigh. They both giggled as another round of shivers overtook him. "Come over here," he growled.

Not that she could help it, as the saggy bed naturally rolled them together. She rubbed his hands, his arms, and his back. At last he stopped shivering and relaxed against her.

"Tell me about the camp," she prompted.

"It's quite different from the civilian camps I've seen," he said, sounding thoughtful and not the least bit sleepy. "It's a mishmash of nationalities. Mostly Russian and French, but I came across a few Serbians and some British too. Oh, and a guy from Canada. It wasn't as bad as I feared. I got a good look at the kitchen because Gerhard let me in. There's not a lot of food to be had. The men are thin, although no one is starving."

"How many prisoners are there?"

"Twelve thousand."

She gasped.

"My biggest fear is what will happen if the war drags on much longer. The Red Cross is sending food, but it takes tons of it to feed that many men."

He went on to describe the hastily erected long buildings that served as barracks. The men were put to work digging drainage ditches, so that in the spring the swamp outside the town could be drained to create more farmland.

"The work keeps them busy, and the men who participate get an extra ration of food. Most don't mind the work since it's not in a munitions factory making weapons that will be turned against their brothers. Enough of that, though. Tell me about what you did today."

She snuggled deeper against him as she recounted playing with Gita's baby and cooking old family recipes. Benedict asked questions and traced patterns along her back.

Was this what it would be like to be married to him? Cuddling together and talking about their day? She liked it, but living among her rustic family was stark proof of her humble roots. She didn't really belong here anymore, and yet being a diplomat's wife didn't seem to fit her either.

Benedict adored her. She could tell from every furtive look, every time he protected or defended her. Even his teasing was a form of affection. It was obvious he wanted to keep this marriage, and her indecision was unfair to him.

It was time to decide if she had what it took to be a diplomat's wife.

On Sunday morning, Inga walked alongside Benedict and the rest of their family to the tiny village church. This was where Inga attended as a child, and she wanted to share it with Benedict. The interior was plain, the walls whitewashed, and the altar no more than a bare table at the front. The only charm was the shape of the windows, which were ordinary clear glass but with a pointed arch at their tops.

"When I was little, this was what I thought all churches looked like," she whispered to Benedict as they sank onto a pew. What a shock it was when they arrived in New York and sought shelter in the colossal church that glittered with stained-glass windows and gilded statues. Inga had now seen cathedrals in both New York and Berlin, yet this simple and intimate church had always been more meaningful to her. No grand art, no grand organ music, but just a gathering of believers who took an hour each week to center themselves on God and his eternal kingdom.

"Can we stay for a few minutes?" she asked Benedict after the service was over.

"Of course."

Inga knelt down to pray, unexpectedly moved by a feeling of gratitude mingling with grief. The last time she'd been in this church, she was sitting between her parents. They were long gone, but suddenly they felt very close, as if the veil between this world and the next had become paper-thin.

"Oh, Mama," she whispered as an ache bloomed inside, painful and joyous at the same time. She bowed her head and prayed for her parents, whose life in America hadn't been easy. She prayed for the soldiers at Puchheim and for the millions of men on the front and in the trenches. She prayed for Johanna's fiancé and for Benedict in his quest to keep America out of the war.

Benedict knelt beside her. What sort of things did he pray for? They had grown so close these past few months, and yet she didn't know what went on deep in his soul.

"Ready?" he asked as she settled back into the pew.

She nodded. "Would you mind if we visit the graveyard now?" It was where Marie was buried. Her mother's only reluctance over moving to America was leaving Marie behind, all alone in an untended grave.

Benedict held her hand as they walked to the burial grounds. There were a few grand headstones from centuries ago when Rosendorff had well-to-do families. Most of the weathered markers were modest headstones, but one was brand-new for a soldier killed at Verdun.

"I don't know if I can find Marie," she said. Patches of snow lingered in shady areas, and Marie never had a headstone, only a small rock with her initials and a simple cross.

Luckily, the heat on the stones melted the snow quickly, and she soon found the rock marker near the edge of the graveyard. Time had tilted it to a crooked angle, and Benedict helped her lift it from the ground to position the marker evenly. He used his handkerchief to clean the grime from the markings her father had chiseled so long ago.

A lump swelled in her throat. Poor Marie. She was only six when she died, and she never had a chance to see America or fall in love. Few people even remembered her.

Inga drew a ragged breath. "It doesn't seem fair," she said. "Why would God take such an innocent child, who never had a chance to become anything?"

"She's in heaven now," Benedict said, "where one day you and Marie will be together again. We'll never know why she was taken while so young, but it was her death that prompted your parents to leave for America."

Inga nodded.

"Could that be why God sent her?" Benedict asked. "Was her life and death part of a larger plan we can't yet see or understand? You only met the Gerards because you were in that church the day after you arrived in America. Maybe God led you there for a reason."

She didn't know whether to be comforted or terrified at the thought. "You make it sound like we're chess pieces."

"Maybe," Benedict said with a wry smile. "Would that be so bad? If God was using you and Marie so that you might somehow come into contact with Ambassador Gerard, then there was a reason. You have a purpose. *We* have a purpose. We'll never know, but I would like to think we are doing God's will. We can't give up. Don't despair."

She impulsively reached up to hug him, feeling the pounding of his heart against her own. He was a pillar of strength, and she savored the safety and protection of his embrace. When it was time to leave, she pressed her hand over Marie's stone to say farewell, knowing they'd meet again when all the heartache and despair of this fallen world was but a memory.

Rather than return to her uncle's house, she took Benedict up the street so he could see the house where she once lived. Rosendorff had only one major street, and it seemed so much smaller than she remembered. In New York she lived in a building with five hundred women; the entire village of Rosendorff had less than half that many people.

Their steps slowed outside one of the larger houses. The spacious building of three stories with steep gables and dormer windows had once belonged to a wealthy landowner. Now it was shared by several families.

She pointed to a window on the second floor. "That's where I was born," she said. "I remember being so proud that I lived in the biggest house on the street. It didn't matter that we shared it with four other families."

Even so, the house seemed shabbier than in her memories. She never knew they were poor when she was little, but it was easy to see now.

"Would you like to go inside?" Benedict asked. "I would be happy to knock and inquire."

She opened her mouth to say yes, then paused to sort through a few hazy memories of the house. There had been a little cuckoo clock in the front hall, and lavender sachets her mother used to cover the musty scent. The steady clink of her father's hammer as he tacked heels onto shoes, and her mother singing her to sleep at night. The bed she shared with Marie.

"No," she finally said. "My memories of this house are all good ones. I don't want to taint them with what it has become."

Seeing Rosendorff again had been marvelous, but she didn't belong here anymore, and it was time to go.

35

February 1917

I nga's first day back at the embassy felt as though it would never end. The journey back from Bavaria had left her exhausted, and Mr. Gerard was unusually caustic. He barked out orders and hosted a nonstop series of meetings with representatives from the other neutral embassies. Inga sat in the corner of his office, taking notes and trying to calm her growing alarm over America's rapidly deteriorating relations with Germany.

Benedict attended most of the meetings. Despite their closeness while in Rosendorff, he slipped back into diplomatic austerity like a puzzle piece snapping into place. Once she'd been frustrated and intimidated by that demeanor, but now it represented stability as Mr. Gerard's temper careened between anger and aggression. The situation worsened throughout the month as German losses at sea made them eager to resume unrestricted submarine warfare. It was only President Wilson's resolute stance on freedom of the seas that prevented the Germans from unleashing their most powerful weapon.

The staff usually left the embassy around dinnertime—except for Benedict, who often remained locked in meetings with the ambassador long into the night. On such occasions, Inga stayed because she and Benedict were a team now and therefore she wouldn't leave without him. Besides, the quiet of the embassy in the late hours gave her time to transcribe her notes from the marathon of meetings earlier in the day.

One evening in the middle of February, Mr. Gerard tapped on her office door around eight o'clock.

"I know it's been a long day for you, but please go upstairs to check on my wife," he said. "She's still down with a chest cold and could use some company. Benedict and I need to finish the report for the president tonight. Can you sit with her until we are finished?"

"Of course," she answered and headed up to the Gerards' apartment on the third floor. The tapestries and crystal chandeliers were reminders of the German princess who once lived in this opulent suite of rooms. Inga's footfalls echoed on the hard marble and high ceilings as she headed for Mary's open bedroom door.

"James?" Mary's voice sounded weak but hopeful.

"It's just me," Inga said. The bedroom featured hand-painted murals and elaborate crown molding. Silk hangings from a cornice suspended over the bed made Mary look tiny in the queenly bed.

"It's freezing in here," Mary said. "Can you stoke the fire?"

Inga obliged. It *was* cold in the room, and the fireplace at the far side of the room wouldn't help much. Why did aristocrats build their palaces with such tall ceilings? She added wood to the fire, then returned to Mary to arrange the comforter tighter around her shoulders.

"How is poor James doing?" Mary asked.

"He and Benedict are working on a report for President Wilson," she replied as she drew up a spindly gilt chair. "How are *you* holding up?"

Mary sagged against the pillows. "I want to go home. I didn't know it was going to be this hard."

Had any of them? Yes, they lived in the lap of luxury, but the weight of the war was on everyone's shoulders. Reading about dead and wounded men was demoralizing regardless of which side they fought for.

"I can't wait to leave," Mary said. "Mrs. Torres called on me to bring me a nice silver cup as a farewell gift. She's going home next week, along with all the other wives from the Argentinian Embassy. I envy them."

Inga caught her breath. "Have you thought of going home?"

"Every day," Mary said. "I don't want to leave James, but I'm beginning to hate it here. As soon as I've shaken this terrible cold, I'll probably sail home. And, Inga . . ." Mary wiggled to sit higher among the pillows, her expression urgent. "No one will take it amiss if you want to come with me. So many of the wives are returning home, so it won't hurt Benedict's reputation if you leave."

Temptation clawed at the surprising suggestion. Serving the American Embassy had been both the hardest and best thing she'd ever done, but she longed for home. Could she really leave with Mary? Just thinking about it lifted an invisible weight.

The telephone clanged, sounding unnaturally loud in the quiet of the night and making Inga jump from her chair. "I'll get it," she said to Mary and hurried toward the telephone anchored to the wall near the kitchen.

"Inga, get down here," Mr. Gerard barked the instant she lifted the receiver.

"What's wrong?"

"The telegraph machine is spitting out a message. It's been thumping out an endless stream of code ever since you left. It's coming from London. Something important must be going on, and I need you down here at once."

"I'm on my way." She hung up the telephone receiver and rushed back to the bedroom. "That was Mr. Gerard," she told Mary. "Will you be all right if I pop down to decode a message?"

"Heavens, yes. Your work never stops, does it, poor dear?"

Inga's footsteps clattered in the stairwell, and she was breathless by the time she arrived at Mr. Gerard's office. He and Benedict stood in the center of the office as the telegraph machine continued shooting out the strip of paper. Yards of it piled onto the floor, filled with dots and dashes.

Benedict handed her the beginning of the message. "I'm afraid this is going to take a while," he said, looking almost apologetic as he cleared a space for her at the secretarial table. Inga reached for a notepad while Benedict shifted the mound of paper toward the table.

She began decoding as quickly as she could, her stomach plummeting with each word she transcribed onto the notepad. The cable had come from the American ambassador in London, reporting that the British government had intercepted a dangerous message between Germany and Mexico.

It was unbelievable. Her hand started to shake, a chill racing through her, but she kept writing out each terrible word. Mr. Gerard had gone back to conferring with Benedict as she worked. The peppery scent of cigar smoke filled the office as she wrote out line after line of the horrifying message.

At the end she simply stared at the transcribed words in disbelief.

"Well?" Benedict asked from across the room.

Inga tried to speak in a calm voice. "Britain's Secret Service Bureau intercepted a communication from the German foreign minister to the ambassador from Mexico."

She handed the notepad to Mr. Gerard. Benedict stood over his shoulder, and she watched as both men read the information she'd written on the notepad. Benedict's face went white while Mr. Gerard's darkened with rage.

Germany had confided in the Mexican government their plan to resume unrestricted submarine warfare. They acknowledged that this was likely to provoke the U.S. into declaring war on Germany. In such an event, Foreign Minister Zimmermann wanted Mexico to attack Texas to distract Americans from a European war. In return, Germany would help Mexico reclaim their lost territory in Texas, New Mexico, and Arizona.

Mr. Gerard threw down the notepad and let out a string of curses as he began pacing the office. Inga looked at Benedict, whose expression was coldly furious.

"Is this as bad as I think it is?" she asked.

He nodded. "There's no way we can stay out of the war now."

"It's time to break diplomatic relations," said Mr. Gerard.

Inga swallowed hard. Breaking diplomatic relations was viewed as an insult by the host country, and their trying to back away from that precipice would be almost impossible. It was the final step before going to war.

Benedict shook his head. "We can't break diplomatic relations without the president's authorization. We need to verify the truth of what the British have told us."

"You think the British would lie?" Mr. Gerard demanded.

"No," Benedict answered, "but we can't gamble a million American lives on it. It may take a while before our intelligence agency can confirm the authenticity of this information."

"How could the British have intercepted this message from Germany?" Mr. Gerard asked. "If the Germans sent a communication to Mexico, it had to have been sent by way of an undersea cable owned by the United States."

"The British intelligence agency has been tapping the wires of all the neutral countries," Benedict said.

Inga gasped. "The British are spying on *us*?" Inga could scarcely believe it, but Benedict didn't seem surprised.

"I'd be disappointed if they were not," he said. "Britain's cryptographers are the best in the business."

Mr. Gerard collected the notepad he'd flung across the room. Inga watched as his eyes traveled over the message line by line. He seemed to have calmed down by the time he returned to sit behind his desk.

"We can't do anything until Washington sends us orders," the ambassador said. "I hate sitting here helpless while Germany is getting their ducks in a row by conspiring with Mexico to attack Texas."

The thump of Inga's heart felt so strong she feared the whole room could hear it. "What are we going to do?" she asked Benedict.

"We prepare to evacuate," he said, his voice so clinically cold and detached it sent a chill clear to her bones.

Inga was grateful for the huge range of tasks Mr. Gerard asked of her the following morning in preparation for leaving Germany. The ambassador chartered a train to take them to Switzerland, but Inga needed to pick up the paperwork. He wanted her to visit a jeweler to commission personalized engravings on platinum cigarette cases to be used as farewell gifts. He wanted a two-month supply of the medicinal drops Mary used, which seemed excessive to Inga. Surely it wouldn't take them two months to get home, would it? And yet Inga had to visit three separate pharmacies to find enough.

It wasn't unusual for there to be a shortage of drugs in the pharmacies. What was odd was the lack of American newspapers. Mr. Gerard wanted Inga to buy a copy of every German and American newspaper she could find for them to monitor the worsening sentiments between the two nations. Inga had no difficulty finding the German-language newspapers, but there were no American newspapers anywhere, not even at the finest newsstand in Berlin.

The war meant shops were understaffed, and only a single worker manned the cash register. She waited in line to speak with the overworked clerk. "Have any American newspapers come in?" she asked when she finally got to the front of the line.

"We canceled our order," the clerk replied. "Nobody wants to read one-sided propaganda."

"Could I place a special order for the *New York Times*? I am willing to pay an extra fee."

Her request triggered hostile comments from others in line. "The Americans have been siding with the British all along," a woman wearing widow's weeds said behind her. "We should never have trusted them."

The clerk agreed with the widow. "We shot ourselves in the foot by bowing to Wilson. Our submarines are the best in the world, and we'd have total command of the seas if we hadn't been hobbled by that stupid agreement with the Americans."

"My husband drowned because of President Wilson," the widow said, and the teenaged boy beside her seemed just as hostile.

"Go back home if you want to read American newspapers."

Inga felt their angry eyes boring into her back as she hurried from the shop. The encounter bothered her during the entire walk back to the embassy, where she delivered Mary's medicine before heading to Alton House. She'd missed dinner but didn't have much of an appetite after the dispiriting encounter at the newsstand.

She looked with fondness at the stately, honeyed stones of Alton House as she meandered up the front path. How much longer would she be here? She'd always felt safe on this street filled with embassy staff and wonderful old linden trees. She would miss this place if they had to leave.

As she reached the front door, banging from inside ratcheted her already tense nerves even higher. It sounded like hammering, and she rushed inside to see what was going on.

The noise came from the study, where Benedict was sitting on the sofa, his face bleak as he hammered a lid onto a crate.

"Your encyclopedias?" she asked.

Benedict didn't look up as he continued hammering. "Yes. We've got time to prepare, so a shipping crate for the whole set seems the best option to get them home."

His words smothered what little hope she had left. "There's no chance for a peaceful solution?"

He lowered the hammer and drew a heavy sigh. "I doubt it," he said. "Everything is pointing to war. I've failed."

She sat on the crate and put a comforting hand on his knee. It was odd to see Benedict so despondent. He was the one who always had an idea for the next tactic or a solution to whatever crisis was at hand. Now he was packing up to retreat.

"You did the best you could, and under very difficult circumstances," she said. "You helped keep the peace for more than two years. And it's not over yet, is it? A miracle could still happen."

He sighed again. "It's over, Inga," he said, then began tracing a pattern on the back of her hand. "It will be hard on you, going to war against your native land."

She looked away. He was already speaking as if it were a foregone conclusion, and she refused to believe it. President Wilson had kept them out of war before; he could do it again.

"I can't believe it's going to happen," she said, and if anything, Benedict's face looked even sadder as he laid a gentle hand on her cheek, regarding her with a look of pained sympathy. How could she have ever thought him cold? He might be the most tender man in the world.

A man she might have to leave soon. If war broke out between the United States and Germany, she would have to return to New York, and he'd be off to some other diplomatic post.

She pressed a kiss to his palm, desperate to escape his searching gaze. Then the slamming of the front door startled her, and she rose. Benedict did as well.

Colonel Reyes strode into the study, his expression grim. "Germany has just announced the resumption of unrestricted submarine warfare," he said. "President Wilson has ordered that we break diplomatic relations, close the embassy, and return home."

The downward spiral into war had begun.

36

Benedict and Ambassador Gerard both wore ordinary civilian clothes to the Reich Chancellery, where they would sever diplomatic relations with Germany. The time for negotiation and diplomacy was over. It would be a straightforward meeting and the biggest failure of Benedict's life.

Officers of the Kaiserliche Garde met them at the front doors of the chancellery. The palace was the administrative hub, where hundreds of government bureaucrats worked in offices to keep the empire running.

But not today. It was a Saturday, and the building appeared vacant except for the expressionless imperial guards.

"Chancellor von Bethmann-Hollweg is expecting us," Ambassador Gerard announced, and the guards snapped into formation, their leader barking out orders as all six guards flanked them during the long walk to the cabinet assembly hall.

The cascade of their footsteps echoed down the empty marble corridors of the chilly building. Why heat an empty palace on the weekend? Nevertheless, Benedict's palms were sweating as they approached the meeting room, where another set of guards opened the doors to the assembly hall.

Inside, a dozen German officers sat at a long table. A crackling fire warmed the room, which was framed by monumental tapestries and heroic paintings. The men at the table stood as the Americans entered, their faces grim. Chancellor von Bethmann-Hollweg and Minister Zimmermann were the only Germans wearing ordinary civilian clothes. Everyone else around the table wore military uniforms covered in ribbons and medals.

Two empty chairs awaited them, but after the Germans returned to their seat, Ambassador Gerard remained standing, which meant Benedict did as well.

"We have come to inform you of our decision to cease diplomatic relations and leave Germany," Ambassador Gerard began. "We do not seek war, but we cannot tolerate Germany's attacks against American shipping, nor your attempt to incite Mexico into attacking our southern border. Zimmerman's telegram to Mexico reflects a complete disregard for international law and basic human decency. Kaiser Wilhelm is a dangerous megalomaniac, and his cabinet is made up of warlords."

Minister Zimmermann shot to his feet and looked directly at Benedict. "We have no argument with the Americans," he said. "Come, Mr. Kincaid. Like President Wilson, you are a man of reason. Surely you do not echo Ambassador Gerard's gross attack on our legitimate efforts to protect ourselves."

There was a time when Benedict would have agreed with Zimmermann's sentiment. Ambassador Gerard had been consistently blunt, rude, and impulsive. And yet the careful diplomacy of President Wilson had not worked.

"Ambassador Gerard has my full support," he stated. "We have been ordered home by President Wilson and will leave immediately."

"Not so fast," von Bethmann-Hollweg said, his voice silky. "I've received word that the German ambassador in Washington is being shamefully treated. Ambassador Bernstorff reports that German ships in America are being seized, and he has had his privileges curtailed. We will not allow you to leave Germany if our ambassador is being mistreated in America."

Gerard stepped forward. "You won't *allow*?" he huffed. "We have diplomatic privileges and will leave whenever we see fit."

"Not if our own ambassador is being mistreated."

Ambassador Gerard clenched his fists. "This is an outrage!"

Benedict agreed. There would be no more pretending, no more diplomatic niceties. He stepped forward and locked eyes with the chancellor. "If you do not allow us to leave Germany, it will be considered an act of war."

"As you like," von Bethmann-Hollweg said with a tense nod. "We have already begun the process of ensuring your continued presence in Berlin until we have our own ambassadorial staff released from Washington."

It had to be a bluff. President Wilson wouldn't condone the mistreatment of the German ambassador, but they had no way of proving it.

"We're leaving," Gerard said, turning on his heel and striding from the room. Benedict remained looking at Zimmermann, a diplomat he once respected but who was now orchestrating a plot to provoke a war with Mexico.

"Farewell, Arthur. I don't think we will see each other again." He managed to sound calm despite the despair growing in his chest as he turned to follow Ambassador Gerard out of the chancellery.

Benedict raced back to Alton House. The chauffeur dropped him off at the end of the street, then continued speeding toward the embassy with the ambassador. Perhaps he should have gone on to the embassy, but he had obligations to the staff at Alton House too. Inga was *his wife*.

He jogged down the street, his breath leaving white puffs in the freezing air. Two German guards were posted at the end of the path leading to Alton House.

"Nobody is allowed in or out of that house," the sergeant said.

"I live here," Benedict bit out.

The sergeant shifted uneasily. "Oh. I suppose then it would be all right if you went in."

Tension simmered and threatened to boil over. "I want you out of here," Benedict told the soldiers. "This house is part of the American Embassy, which means you are standing on American soil. You have no authority here."

He wasn't entirely sure that was correct. The American Embassy where Gerard lived was entitled to full diplomatic immunity, but he wasn't sure if that extended to Alton House. It didn't matter. He stood nose to nose with the sergeant, who quickly backed down.

"We'll be across the street until we get further instructions," he conceded.

Benedict strode angrily up the path and through the front doors. "Inga?" he bellowed.

"Back here!" she called from the kitchen, a note of panic in her voice.

To his horror, two German soldiers were ransacking the kitchen, where cabinets and drawers hung open. Inga and Mrs. Barnes huddled in the corner, their faces white.

"What are you doing?" he demanded of the nearest soldier.

"They say they're looking for contraband," Inga said in English. "I told them they don't have any right to be here, but they won't listen."

Canisters of sugar, flour, and other goods had been dumped into pots and pans, which lay everywhere. The soldiers weren't looking for contraband; they were stealing!

Benedict grabbed a canister of tea and some chocolate bars that had been set beside the soldier's kit. "Did they take anything else?" he asked Inga. Almost everything of a sensitive diplomatic nature was kept at the embassy, but he didn't want these soldiers leaving with so much as a matchstick.

"Boxes of stationery and your diplomatic stamp from the study," she replied, her voice still shaking.

He jerked the soldier's rucksack open, and sure enough, his official document stamp was inside. It had no value other than as a trophy of war. He pocketed the seal, then put an arm around Inga's shoulder, hating that she was trembling. Never could he have imagined when he left for the chancellery that the Germans would begin retaliating so quickly. They obviously anticipated every move the Americans made that morning.

"You are on American soil, and I'm ordering you out of this house," he said. "Your commanding officer is outside. Go join him."

Once again, he relied on bravado to convince the two soldiers to clear out and leave. He watched them walk down the front path to join the others across the street.

Mrs. Barnes was badly rattled as she started putting the kitchen back together. "What's going to happen to us?"

Benedict didn't know how to answer her. This was uncharted territory for them all. "For today, I want you all to stay inside the house while I go to the embassy to see if the ambassador needs us. Inga, please call the Marine barracks and ask them to send guards to Alton House."

Inga lifted the telephone receiver on the hall table and cranked the dial. Then cranked it again. She met his gaze, her eyes wide and frightened. "The line is dead."

Benedict strode outside, stomping through the snow to get to the side of the house. Sure enough, the telephone line had been cut. So was the line that supplied electricity to the house. They hadn't noticed since it was the middle of the day and there had been no need for the light, but he sent an annoyed glance at the soldiers congregating across the street. At least the sergeant had the decency to send him an embarrassed shrug in acknowledgment.

Benedict approached the soldiers. He was tempted to demand

they reconnect the telephone line, except they couldn't be trusted to do it without figuring out how to tap it.

"I'll be having a team of engineers out to reconnect those lines," he said. "Should you try to interfere, I will notify President Wilson so that he may determine how the German Embassy staff in Washington are to be treated."

The officer clicked his heels. "Sir."

The vague reply meant nothing, so it was anyone's guess if the engineers would be allowed to repair the lines, but only time would tell.

Inga huddled with Benedict and the rest of the staff in the Alton House parlor as night closed in. Only light from the fireplace illuminated the room. They had no power, no telephone, and only the fire for heat. She hadn't been this frightened since Mr. Gerard found her in that church on her first night in America. Now here she was, twenty years later and once again freezing in the dark, wondering what daylight would bring.

It wasn't so much fear for her own safety as fear for America heading into war. They would soon be joining the exodus of Americans trying to get to safety beyond the borders of Germany.

Benedict was calm and in command as he explained their duties for the following day. "We must delegate our embassy responsibilities to the other neutral embassies," he said. "Just as we've been trying to help the British and French manage affairs in Germany, we will need to find someone to do the same for us."

An image of Percy Dutton, the gentle English artist still trapped in a horse stable, rose in her mind. "What's going to happen to the prisoners held at Ruhleben?" she asked.

Benedict's eyes darkened. "There's no longer anything we can do for them. I'll ask the Swiss or the Spanish if they can intervene, but I doubt they'll succeed in getting them traded."

"What will happen to *us*?" Mrs. Barnes asked.

Benedict outlined the coming days. "We'll be evacuating to Switzerland, then make our way to Spain to sail home. We will travel as a group. Once we get to Washington, D.C., those who wish to remain serving the U.S. diplomatic corps will be reposted to other embassies around the world. War means most of them will be getting even more staff, so nobody should fear the lack of a job."

Inga had no intention of seeking more work overseas. Once she was back in New York, she would never leave her home again.

A knock at the front door startled everyone. Inga reached for Benedict's hand. The loud, abrupt knock was exactly how the intrusion of the soldiers began this morning, and maybe they were back to cause more trouble.

The chauffeur stood. "I'll get it," McFee said. Benedict and Colonel Reyes stood as well, proof her fears weren't paranoid. But soon the warm laughter coming from the foyer set everyone at ease.

"We've got a hot dinner coming our way, folks," McFee said. A squat man with a narrow mustache, carrying a large covered pot, waddled in after the chauffeur.

"Compliments of the Swiss Embassy," he said. "We heard you had no power, and I had enough extra pork to make you some meatballs and cabbage rolls."

A cook from the Norwegian Embassy brought pickled herring, and a bald man with laughing eyes brought bottles of wine.

Inga's eyes prickled with tears. She'd often seen the cheerful bald man from the Bulgarian house next door but hadn't formally met him because the Bulgarians had sided with the Germans. How kind of them to extend such hospitality despite their political differences.

"Shhh!" the Bulgarian said as he passed her the wine. "Don't tell anyone I was here."

She bowed respectfully. "It shall be our secret. Thank you, sir."

"Will you join us?" Benedict asked. There were half a dozen people who carried the food over, and all declined the offer.

Despite the war and all their worries, the world was still a good place, and tonight was proof of it. After their neighbors left, they joined hands and prayed, giving thanks to God for this brief respite.

Their real challenges would begin tomorrow.

37

rief hovered over Benedict as he carried out his final
duties before leaving. For more than two years, the
American Embassy had been acting as an intermediary
for the British and the French. Now that work would need to be
turned over to other neutral embassies. He rode his horse to the
Dutch Embassy to ask them to accept the duties for Great Britain.

Ambassador Jeppesen readily agreed. "I'm sorry it's come to
this," he said. "Any word when the official declaration of war
will occur?"

Benedict shook his head. "President Wilson is addressing Congress tomorrow. That's probably when it will be announced. Most
of the British affairs have been settled, but I'm worried about
the civilians still incarcerated at Ruhleben. There are about four
thousand of them, and the Germans have lost interest in trades.
Perhaps you'll have better luck than I."

Benedict's next visit was to the Spanish Embassy, and it was far
more complicated, for Spain would be handling American affairs
after their embassy closed. He turned over the telegraph codes to
communicate with offices in Washington. Once American soldiers

started showing up at German prison camps, the Spanish would be their intermediary.

"I'm glad to assist however I can," Ramon said.

Benedict shook Ramon's hand, thankful for Spain's cooperation. He had another request, however, and it was a painful one. "Ramon, I have a horse that has served me well. Her name is Sterling. She's a gentle horse, even-tempered and well-trained. She's got a good heart, and I don't want—"

"You don't want the Germans to get her," Ramon said.

"They'll make her a war-horse, and I can't bear for that to happen."

Being a fine horseman, Ramon understood. He rested a hand on Benedict's shoulder. "We've got extra stalls in our stables. We'll take good care of her, I promise."

He bid Ramon farewell, yet it was harder saying goodbye to Sterling. He would leave her with the Spanish starting today. Once the official declaration of war occurred, there wouldn't be time to bring her here.

Sterling shifted and stamped a hoof as he approached, probably preparing for a ride home. He walked her to the stables and found a grooming brush. She always loved to have her coat brushed, and he carried out the task one final time.

"You were a good friend, Sterling," he said, continuing to stroke the brush along the strong column of her neck. "We won't be seeing each other again, but I wish you the best."

He hoped Spain didn't get sucked into the war and this gentle horse get shuffled off to the German cavalry. He replaced the grooming brush and gave Sterling a quick kiss on her forelock before walking back to Alton House.

The power and telephone lines had been restored by the time Benedict reached Alton House. Inga was in a good mood as she relayed the news.

"The German ambassador in Washington wired the chancellor to say he was being well-treated, so the Germans let our engineers hook everything back up. And look! The cigarette cases Mr. Gerard ordered were delivered this morning. Aren't they darling?"

Typical Ambassador Gerard. The platinum cigarette cases were lavishly engraved with a likeness of his signature and lined with red velvet. They would be handed out as farewell gifts.

Heavy thudding of footsteps on the front stoop sounded as Colonel Reyes arrived back from the embassy. He looked tired and despondent. "The train Ambassador Gerard has chartered for us has arrived. We need to leave immediately."

Inga set the cigarette case down, her blue eyes wide with disillusionment. "A part of me still hoped everything could somehow be fixed."

He couldn't help it. He drew her into his arms, holding her tight. Eternal optimists like Inga were bound to have their spirit crushed over and over, but he never liked seeing it happen. He stroked her back, gently rocking her from side to side and not caring a fig that they were in full view of Colonel Reyes. He could tell by her shaky breath she wanted to cry. Didn't they all?

At last he released Inga. "I'll help you carry your trunk out."

Colonel Reyes had already called for a couple of wagons to deliver them to the train station, and soon everyone from Alton House was hoisting their bags into the wagons.

Inga raced to his side. "Benedict, there's no room for your encyclopedias."

"I know." He had hoped to arrange for the postal service to pick up the crate that held them, but there was no more time.

Inga twisted her hands. "But we can't leave it. We can't!"

The wagons didn't have enough room for everyone's belongings as it was. Inga had to leave all her hatboxes, and Larry was hastily repacking his three bags into a single one. There wasn't room in the lumbering wagons for Benedict's crate of books.

"It doesn't matter," he assured Inga, and it didn't. A million

American men were about to be drafted into a war Benedict had failed to prevent. The fate of a few books was trivial at this point.

"Benedict!" a familiar voice called from an automobile that just pulled up to the curb. Baron Werner von Eschenbach unfolded his tall frame from the front seat. Several other officers in German uniforms followed. "We've been sent by the foreign office to ensure you don't have any difficulty on your departure."

Relief made Benedict's shoulders sag, and he returned the baron's hearty handshake. "Thank you, my friend."

"It is the least I can do," he said. "Without you, I would still be incarcerated in England."

"I only wish I could have gotten more men released. On both sides."

A hint of sorrow darkened the baron's expression. "I fear there will be a great many more decent men who will find themselves trapped behind enemy lines before this is all over."

No doubt he was correct. As their convoy of automobiles and wagons departed for the train station, Benedict glanced over his shoulder at Alton House. He'd probably never see it or his encyclopedias ever again. It was surely the first of many losses he would face in the coming years.

Inga gawked at the crush of people at the train station, desperate to board the railway car Mr. Gerard had reserved for evacuating Americans. Why hadn't these people left before today? Many of them were American journalists or staff from other American consulates scattered throughout Germany. In all, more than a hundred people would be sharing their train to Switzerland.

The Gerards were already here, and Inga pressed through the crowd to deliver the box of cigarette cases.

"Can I give one to Baron von Eschenbach?" she asked. "He's been so kind to us."

"Of course!" Mr. Gerard said, taking the box. "Take several.

We have many friends here who have come to see us off. Make sure they all get one."

A closer look at the crowd proved him correct. Staff from the Swiss and Dutch Embassies were here. So were the Greeks, the Spanish, and the Norwegians. Even the Bulgarian cook who had brought over the wine was here to see them off.

She approached him and extended a cigarette case. "I'm sorry we never got to know each other. Now we're on opposite sides of this terrible war."

The stocky man's eyes widened in surprise at the elegant gift. "Perhaps we shall meet again someday, in happier times."

She nodded, blinking back tears as she wove through the crowd, handing out cigarette cases and hugs and farewell wishes to all the wonderful people who'd come to see them off. She would likely never see any of them again. As soon as she was safely back in New York, her foreign adventures would be over. Even so, she would never forget these twilight days in Berlin when the world teetered on the edge between hope and disaster.

She boarded a passenger car, where Mr. Gerard had laid in cigars and champagne. Many of the Americans traveling with them marveled at the bounty and eagerly partook, while Inga stared out the window at the people on the platform as the train pulled away. Staff from the other embassies waved little American flags to see them off. She touched the window, trying to engrave the image in her mind forever.

Tears filled her eyes as the station faded into the distance. Benedict joined her on the bench, folding her hand between his own.

"Are you okay?" he asked.

"I don't know. Are we safe yet?"

"Not until we cross the border into Switzerland. This entire train was chartered for Americans leaving the country, and there's always the possibility of sabotage of the tracks or some other interference."

The Swiss border was five hundred miles away. They'd need

to travel south through the Black Forest, coming close to the tiny village of Rosendorff. She'd probably never see her cousins again either.

Soon the moon rose high in the night sky, and the air grew colder in the railway car. A chill ran through her, and Benedict went in search of a lap blanket from one of the overhead compartments. He spread it over them, then went back to holding her hand.

The chugging of engines mingled with soft chatter from others in the car, but all she thought of was Benedict.

"What's going to happen to us?" she asked as the train barreled through the night.

There was a long pause. "Once we get to Washington, I will be assigned to another embassy," he finally said. "You can go on to New York or come with me to my next post. The decision is entirely yours, but I hope you'll come with me." His hand tightened around hers beneath the blanket. She already knew what he wanted and couldn't look at him. It was too painful.

She and Benedict had gotten along quite well, all things considered. She'd come to like his fusty ways, and he enjoyed her humor. Even so, she'd been an embarrassment to him time and again. She didn't know how to be a diplomat's wife, and if he was posted to somewhere like Japan or Russia where she didn't speak the language, things would be even worse.

With the exception of a brief trip home to take her citizenship test, she'd spent two and a half years in Germany. During that time there hadn't been a single day she hadn't felt homesick for New York.

If they were to get an annulment, others from Alton House would need to testify that she and Benedict had not been intimate. Although they'd gotten a little careless about showing affection, they never shared a bedroom while at Alton House, and they never consummated their marriage. There mustn't be any doubt about that, so they'd need to sleep in separate cabins on the voyage home.

Which meant this could be their last night together. She shivered again and slid closer to Benedict, laying her head against his shoulder. This was another moment she wanted to remember forever. No matter how long she lived, there would never be another Benedict Kincaid, and she would miss him.

She must have dozed at some point because she awoke with a crick in her neck from leaning on Benedict's shoulder. The first hint of dawn lit the horizon behind them.

"Where are we?" she asked him.

"We just crossed into Switzerland," he answered. "We made it. We're safe now."

38

Dawn was still breaking over the tiny Swiss village of Winterthur as their train slowed and pulled into the station. Benedict had been holding Inga in his arms ever since she awoke ten minutes ago, and they would be disembarking soon. Winterthur was only the first of many stops before they reached a port in northern Spain to board a ship home. But this village was the most monumental, for *they were free.*

"It looks like they've sent a welcoming party," he told Inga with a nod toward the window. A squad of Swiss Army soldiers in their formal blue-and-red dress uniforms stood at attention. They wore ceremonial swords instead of carrying rifles.

As was customary, the Gerards left the train first. As soon as Ambassador Gerard set his foot on Swiss land, the soldiers drew their swords in unison, then raised them in a salute as their commanding colonel handed Mrs. Gerard a bouquet of roses. It was an unexpectedly kind welcome after their harried flight from Berlin.

Benedict guided Inga onto the train station platform. The air was crisp and cold, with snowcapped mountains in the distance. He didn't care that every muscle ached after eighteen hours cooped up on a hard bench. They had safely made it out of Germany. He reached for Inga's hand and squeezed it.

Once everyone had disembarked, they assembled on the platform, where the Swiss colonel offered another formal greeting to them all.

"Ambassador and Mrs. Gerard," he called out, his voice echoing across the platform. "Ladies and gentlemen, it shall be our privilege to escort you to your next train, but first we have prepared a light repast before your departure."

Thank heavens! There was no dining car on their trip from Berlin, nor had they dared stop along the way. The colonel led them down the platform toward a charming station house with a steeply pitched roof, wooden siding, and a cozy overhang. A hot buffet awaited them inside, where long tables were already set with service for the travelers. The aromas of scrambled eggs, fresh bread, and fried potatoes made him even hungrier. His stomach growled as he and Inga filled their plates, then carried them to the tables.

"Look, chocolate!" Inga said as she settled onto the bench beside him. Bars of Swiss chocolate had been left at each place setting by their host.

Benedict smiled, thankful to have her close by his side. He raised his glass of water as though it were a flute of the finest French champagne. "To freedom," he said.

Inga clinked her glass to his. "To freedom!" she echoed. They both took a long, healthy swallow.

While they dined, Swiss porters were busy transferring their luggage to a different train that would carry them across Switzerland and into Italy. Their route would then pass through portions of France where the war had yet to reach, wending onward to the neutral country of Spain and finally a port, where the *Infanta Isabella* would take them to Cuba. It would be too dangerous to sail directly to New York, a route heavily patrolled by German U-boats. Instead, they'd follow the longer but safer route from Spain to Cuba. As soon as the next train was loaded, it would be time to leave.

"Pick a carriage, everyone," Ambassador Gerard crowed. "There's plenty of room to spread out and be comfortable."

Benedict led Inga to the front car. "The view will be better from the front," he said. "We'll be moving through the Italian Alps, so the fewer cars ahead, the better."

They boarded the first car, where he settled his hands on her hips to guide her down the center aisle. God bless the Swiss! This train was much nicer than the one they had just left. Plush, private compartments lined each side of the aisle. Each compartment's benches were upholstered with royal-blue velvet. A dinette table took up the center. Each one seated four people and had a door for privacy. With luck, he and Inga wouldn't have to share, and they could spend the next few days of travel flirting and exchanging covert kisses and a caress or two.

"Inga!" Nellie cried from the interior of the compartment they had just passed; the door was still open. Nellie and Mrs. Barnes had already claimed one of the benches. "Inga, come join us! We can play dominoes."

"Okay," Inga readily agreed. Benedict's hands fell to his sides as she slipped away from him, angling to slide onto the bench opposite the women. She fluttered a little goodbye with her fingers as he stood in the aisle.

Benedict sent her a terse nod and continued down to the next empty compartment on the opposite side of the aisle. Maybe she was just being polite. Inga could be like that. Besides, now that they were out of Germany, the train would be making regular stops along the route, where they could stretch their legs and change seating arrangements. Hopefully, he could get her back later in the day.

Larry slipped onto the bench opposite him, looking tired and miserable. "I think there's something in this upholstery that is triggering my allergies," he said after a tremendous sneeze.

It was going to be a long ride to Zurich.

Benedict tried to concentrate on the passing countryside as the train chugged its way along mountain passes while moving deeper into Switzerland. They went through Zurich and Interlachen, where additional passenger cars were appended to the train. After each break, Inga steadfastly returned to the game of dominoes, which covered the table in her compartment.

"You don't mind, do you?" she asked on the platform outside the Interlachen stop.

How could he object when her smile was so cheerful? He claimed not to mind and returned to the compartment with Larry. It was nightfall by the time they crossed the Italian border and stopped at Turin so that everyone would have time to select sleeping berths. The Gerards had a sleeping car entirely to themselves, while the rest of them would spend the night in either the men's or the ladies' sleeper cars. The berths weren't so bad; soldiers in the trenches had it much worse. They were stacked three high along the sides of the sleepers, with a curtain that could be drawn for privacy.

Benedict climbed the stepladder to an upper berth, which was a little wider and longer than a coffin. It had a narrow mattress and a cubby at the foot of the bed for toiletries. After he pulled the curtain closed, moonlight from a narrow window was the only illumination, leaving him plenty of time to gaze at the night sky and think. The vibration of the train soon lulled him to sleep.

When morning arrived, he hoped to escape Larry, but it was not to be. People naturally returned to the same compartments as the day before, leaving him with a view of Inga, who chatted happily with Nellie and Mrs. Barnes across the aisle. She never once spared him a glance all morning.

They crossed into France by lunchtime, and things got worse. Nellie and Mrs. Barnes went to another carriage, where they'd been invited to join a game of pinochle. Before Benedict could slip inside Inga's compartment, Lieutenant Carter and two engineers from the corps grabbed all three empty places. They supplied chocolate mints they'd bought in Zurich and a deck of cards, seeking a fourth player for a round of bridge.

All three of those men had wives back home, so Benedict needn't fear they were moving in on Inga, but the amount of merriment pouring out of their compartment annoyed him. Instead of concentrating on the card game, Lieutenant Carter taught Inga how to balance a mint on her nose and then tip her head to pop it up and into her mouth.

Larry must have noticed his glare. "I think everyone is still feeling the aftereffects of getting safely out of Germany," he said quietly.

Maybe so. It was embarrassing that Larry could have arrived at such an empathetic conclusion while Benedict simmered in a toxic vat of jealousy.

Outside, the fields of France looked remarkably serene for a nation at war. Their route pushed through the southern part of the country to avoid the battle lines. It would be a few more months before the stubbly land would be plowed and planted with their traditional fields of lavender. Or perhaps the war had taken its toll on luxury crops like lavender, and they'd plant wheat or oats. Ancient stone walls marked out fields, and picturesque churches dotted the countryside. An olive grove, with its silvery bark and twisted limbs, sped past the window. Everything was so different from what they had in America. Was Inga even watching? She would probably never pass this way again, but a glance through her compartment window showed her still working on balancing that mint on her nose.

The medieval city of Avignon was straight ahead, where the old walls and the imposing fortress dominated its skyline. The fortress once housed the popes during the years Rome became too politically dangerous to serve as the capital for the papacy. The medieval ramparts that protected the pope still commanded the skyline, an impressive sight even five hundred years after that turbulent century.

If Inga had been beside him, he would have told her about the Avignon Papacy, one of the countless stories that had captivated him as he plowed through the *Encyclopedia Britannica*. Inga always liked it when he told her these old stories. Or maybe she just pretended interest to be polite. At the moment she certainly seemed more interested in demonstrating her newfound talent of balancing candy on her nose rather than learning about medieval popes.

They had another night on the train, then by morning they would be in Spain. They would arrive at the northern port of La Coruña to board a ship to take them to Cuba.

Maybe things would be different aboard the ship, where everyone would need to pair up for the five-day Atlantic crossing. Mrs. Barnes and Nellie had become like mother and daughter and would surely want to share a cabin. That would leave Inga looking for a roommate, and they were still married.

Benedict's time to persuade Inga to remain married was dwindling fast, and sharing a cabin could be the perfect opportunity to solidify their marriage for good.

Benedict managed to snag Inga the next afternoon after arriving in the Spanish port city of La Coruña. Even though it was February, the sun and balmy temperatures made it comfortable to stroll around without a coat. The crowd of Americans waiting to board the steamship mingled on the esplanade, enjoying the sunshine and salty tang in the air. Inga browsed the outdoor market stalls, her arms already filled with packages.

He hurried to her side. "Let me carry those," he offered, and she turned the bulky packages over without complaint.

"Thank you! I have more shopping to do, and it's best done with both hands." The table before her brimmed with scarves, shawls, and colorful Spanish fans. She stated her intention to buy a souvenir for everyone who lived on her floor at the Martha Washington, which meant a little something for fifty women. She'd already bought a dozen Spanish fans and ten hand-painted platters, each carefully wrapped in newspaper.

Inga perused a wire rack covered with castanets, the little wooden disks used by flamenco dancers to tap out rhythmic clicks. The old woman selling them showed Inga how to loop the leather cords around her thumb, then tap her pinky finger to strike the top castanet. The motion was awkward, and Inga giggled as she tried them out. Finally, the vendor slipped a pair of castanets on each of her age-spotted hands and unleashed a spectacular cascade of trills and clacks, drawing a crowd.

"I *must* have a set," Inga gushed when the vendor came to the end, and he choked back a laugh. What was she going to do with castanets in the real world? But the other tourists were egging Inga on, and trying to dissuade her would be pointless.

He waited patiently as she sampled several different sets against the size of her hand, finally settling on a pair of glossy black disks made of polished chestnut wood. Then she bought five additional sets because they'd make good gifts for her friends at the Martha Washington.

A tiny barb stung each time she mentioned the Martha Washington. Had she already determined to make her life in Manhattan? Time was growing short for them to decide if they intended to stay married or go their separate ways.

He feared the conversation, but it was overdue. They moved on to a vendor's stall with more Spanish scarves, and soon they were out of earshot of other shoppers.

"Ambassador Gerard will be distributing cabin keys at four o'clock," he said.

"Yes, I know," she replied. "Mrs. Barnes has already said she would pick up the keys for me and Nellie."

He swiveled to look at her. "But the cabins only have two beds per room."

"I don't mind sleeping on the floor," she said, running her

hand along the fringe of a scarf. "It's not like I haven't done it before."

"There's no need to," he said. "I've already got a cabin for myself, and you're more than welcome to share it with me."

She glanced at him in surprise. "But we can't. If we did, people from Alton House couldn't testify in an annulment proceeding."

This was it, the moment he needed to make his intentions clear and risk losing the friendship and the intimacy they'd shared for the past several months. "I'd hoped there wouldn't be an annulment," he said, feeling his face begin to heat. "Inga, I want to stay married. It will take five days to get to Cuba. It would be a good opportunity for you and me to have a honeymoon." He cleared his throat because her eyes widened. It was impossible to tell if she was intrigued or appalled, but he feared it was the latter. "We don't need to consummate anything if you aren't ready. It could be like in Rosendorff."

Inga picked up a fan from the table and snapped it open, waving it briskly before her. "Oh dear," she said. "Benedict, I know I've been avoiding you ever since we left Germany. That was cowardly of me. It's just that I don't know what I want."

That meant a glimmer of hope remained. He'd rather have her indecision than an outright rejection. He cleared his throat and strove to sound calm.

"We've been married almost two years," he said, and she looked up at him curiously.

"Has it been that long?"

"May twenty-fifth, 1915," he said.

Inga stared into the distance, her expression wistful. "That day seems like another lifetime. So much has happened since then, and yet . . ." She folded the fan closed and carefully set it back on the vendor's table. She touched the American flag pinned to his lapel, outlining it with the tip of her finger, but she didn't meet his eyes. "I will always be grateful for what you did. If we share a cabin, there can't be an annulment."

He had to fight for her. If she wouldn't share a cabin on the ship, he could at least persuade her to remain in Washington, D.C. A gem like Inga needed to be courted and won, and Washington would be a good place to do it.

"Would you be willing to stay in Washington after we get home? I'll book us into separate rooms in a hotel. It will give you more time to decide about our future, and we could court like a normal couple in a way we never could in Berlin. I'll take you to the Smithsonian or sailing on the Potomac. I'll take you to the ballroom at the Willard Hotel, and we can waltz until dawn."

"We're so different . . ."

"We're different on the outside, but inside we share the same values. The same mission. We're stronger together than when we're apart. Inga, we're walking on the same path in life, and we've been good together."

Her shoulders curled inward. "But my path is in New York, and yours will be all over the world."

He couldn't deny it, nor could he dismiss Inga's longing for her home. In all the time she'd been in Berlin, she never stopped yearning for New York.

He looked away, forcing his expression to remain impassive as the foolish, lost dream of stepping out into the world with Inga as his wife began to fade. They never had a real marriage, but they had something great. An alliance? A partnership? Those were pale, puny words for the joy she had given him over the years.

The mound of Spanish scarves was a convenient excuse to turn his attention from the aching regret on Inga's face. One of the scarves was the exact shade of Inga's eyes, a pale blue with flecks of silver. He set her packages down to pick up the scarf, then looped it around the back of her neck and arranged it just so. The colors perfectly highlighted the silvery-blue depth of her gaze.

"Let me buy this for you," he said, but she pulled it off.

"Please don't," she said, looking ill as she returned the scarf

301

atop the stack. She reached for her parcels without meeting his eyes. "I need to go check in at the ship."

An ache of loneliness grew as he watched her walk away from him and probably out of his life.

He bought the scarf anyway.

39

Inga quickly learned that the *Infanta Isabella* had two classes of passengers: first class like the Gerards, and everyone else who would be staying in steerage.

Her inside cabin had no window and only a few feet of floor space between the bunkbed and the wall, but it wasn't too terrible. A cabin steward provided a pallet for Inga to unroll on the floor of their snug cabin. A tiny electric night-light anchored to the wall made it feel cozy as she stayed up late talking to the other women.

Unfortunately, the conversation soon turned to her relationship with Benedict. Inga hadn't seen him since their conversation in the marketplace, and she was still heartsick about it.

"I thought you and Benedict might have made a go of it," Nellie said from her position on the top bunk.

"We all thought so," Mrs. Barnes added. "Opposites attract, isn't that what they always say? My husband and I were like chalk and cheese, God rest his soul. That didn't stop us from having sixteen good years together. I think you and Benedict would make a fine match."

Deep in her heart, it was exactly what Inga wanted, but it was also terrifying. They eventually got along smashingly well together and supported each other in the twilight world of Berlin. That time was over, and they were heading back into the real world.

She angled up on her elbow to see the others. "Benedict's career is going to take him all over the globe. What if he gets sent to someplace like Peru or Japan? I couldn't even find those places on a map. The only reason I didn't humiliate myself in Berlin was because I could speak the German language and understood the culture. I would be an embarrassment to Benedict anywhere else. I care for him too much to burden him with a wife who'd rather read the gossip pages than diplomatic briefings."

"Couldn't you stay in New York while he was posted overseas?" Nellie asked. "A lot of diplomats leave their wives at home."

It wasn't the kind of marriage she wanted. Over the past few months her affection for Benedict had grown into something far deeper and lasting. He made every day more interesting, and she was a better person when she was with him. She had grown to love him, but there would be no point in a marriage if they couldn't live together and share their lives.

"No," she finally said as sadness settled over her. "I want a real marriage where I can wake up in my husband's arms every morning." Like she had with him in Rosendorff.

Nellie perked up. "Why don't you wait and see where he gets posted next? Maybe it won't be so bad. Maybe it'll be Canada or England."

Perhaps, but there was no telling where he'd be sent in the years ahead. If they were to marry for real, she would have to follow wherever he went. His career would be her career. His home would be her home. If she was to join her life with Benedict's, she would need to support him fully, and do so gladly.

And she feared she couldn't do it.

———

Benedict spent his first morning on the *Infanta Isabella* locked in a breakfast meeting with Ambassador Gerard and the staff of the American consulates who had been posted in Frankfurt, Leipzig, and Munich. They gathered in a private dining room to compile a report on their impressions of Germany during the final few months before things had gone awry. The men at the far-flung consulates had starkly different experiences than what he'd known in Berlin. War shortages and public discontent were far worse away from the capital, so it was a sobering discussion.

By eleven o'clock the outline of their report had been drafted. They planned to reconvene after lunch to complete the job. While the other men headed to the smoking room to relax and enjoy a cigar, Benedict went on the hunt for Inga.

He checked both dining rooms, the bowling alley, and walked the promenade deck. He even peeked into the ladies' tearoom, but she wasn't to be found in any of these places. He finally spotted Mrs. Barnes sunning herself on a lounge chair on the aft deck and inquired after Inga's whereabouts.

"That nice Officer Romero offered to show her the wireless room," Mrs. Barnes answered. "That was hours ago, so I don't know if she's still there."

It shouldn't be a surprise that Inga had managed to get a special tour. He asked a crew member to show him to the wireless room. The area was off-limits to the passengers, so it took a bit of haggling before he was granted an escort to the wireless room, which was tucked behind the bridge.

Most of what he'd seen of the *Infanta Isabella* had been pure luxury, yet there was nothing grand about the steel hallway with low ceilings and dim lighting leading to the wireless room. Cables tacked along the top of the hallway passage connected the wireless to the ship's antenna.

He grinned at his first sight of Inga in the wireless room. She wore a pair of headphones and sat behind a long counter loaded with communications equipment. Radio gear, switches, coils, and sounding equipment were packed into the windowless room.

Inga noticed his arrival and tugged off her headphones. "Mr.

Perez is teaching me how to locate alternate frequencies at sea. I've never done this before!"

It was so like Inga to take delight in everything around her. "I'd like to watch," Benedict said, and Perez nodded before instructing Inga to put on her headphones and dial in a new frequency. The instructions were incomprehensible to Benedict, but Inga carried on a perfectly lucid conversation with the technician in the chair next to her.

How could Inga ever consider herself stupid? She tapped a message without even looking at the telegraph sounder. Infinitesimal movements on her fingers tapped out a stream of dots and dashes, communicating with a ship miles away.

"Can I send a message to a friend in New York?" she asked once she finished her message.

"Not directly," Mr. Perez said. "This equipment has a range of only about a hundred miles. We'd have to send the message through a daisy-chain of ships to reach New York."

"I figured as much," Inga said, her shoulders sagging a little. "It seems like the closer I get to New York, the more homesick I become. Isn't that strange?"

"We can do it," the technician rushed to say. "Tell me what you want, and we can send it together."

Inga shook her head. "I couldn't ask that of you. The world is at war, and I don't want to clog up the frequency with chit-chat. Thank you, though." She briefly touched the technician's knee before turning her attention back to the transmitter. The technician leaned in so close to Inga it looked like he might fall off his chair.

Benedict tamped down the surge of jealousy. Inga was more interested in the equipment than the technician sitting just inches away, so he had no cause for jealousy. But with each passing hour, he felt her slipping a little further away.

The technician twisted a dial and started listening to whatever was coming through his headset. "Hey, I think this message is in German," he said, and Inga perked up, her face intent as she listened.

"Yes, it's German," she confirmed. "I'll translate." She reached for a pad of paper and began writing the message out, letter by letter. The fact that Inga could understand the message meant it wasn't confidential information because those were sent in secret code, and yet Inga's expression darkened as she continued transcribing.

"Is it anything important?" the technician asked.

Inga nodded slowly. "It's from a German reporter stationed in Washington," she said, still transcribing. "He's sending a message to the *Berliner Tageblatt*."

It was the most influential newspaper in Berlin. With so many German immigrants now living in the United States, the *Berliner Tageblatt* always carried plenty of news from America.

Finally, Inga set her pencil down and turned to face Benedict. "The reporter says that the wife of the German ambassador in Washington had rotten fruit thrown at her when she attended a luncheon. The president apologized, but Ambassador Bernstorff is incensed at how his wife was disrespected."

"They threw fruit at her just because she's German?" Perez asked, and Benedict shook his head.

"Countess Bernstorff is an American," he said. "She was born in New York, not too far from where the Gerards once lived. She is good friends with Mary Gerard."

"I'm not sure if it makes it better or worse that the ambassador's wife is an American," said Inga. "What an awful thing to happen to anyone."

Benedict remained silent. Inga was leery of making their marriage permanent, and if they did, they'd face similar problems. Ambassador Bernstorff had always been looked at askance while in Germany because of his American wife, but it was one of the reasons he got the top job in Washington. It was hoped that his wife's legendary charm might buy goodwill with her fellow

Americans. It had been working until the *Lusitania* went down. Now the couple were regarded with suspicion by people in both countries.

"Inga, can I persuade you to accompany me on a stroll?"

It was time for them to decide their future, no matter how potentially painful the conversation might be.

Questions swirled as Inga accompanied Benedict onto the main deck. How could people be so horrible to a fellow American simply because she was married to the German ambassador? There were many reasons Inga feared she'd be an inadequate wife for Benedict, and now she needed to add her German heritage to the list. She settled her hands on the ship's railing and gazed at the towering white clouds billowing on the horizon. At the moment they looked harmless, but things could change so quickly.

"Once we're in Washington, do you know how long it will take to get your next assignment?"

"It will probably come within a few weeks," he replied.

"Do you have any say as to where they send you?"

"Very little," he said, looking out at the same bank of clouds. "The irony is that the higher you go, the less freedom you have. I'm ready to be promoted to an ambassadorship, and that means I need to accept a position wherever one opens up."

It was as she'd feared. "It sounds as though you have no freedom at all."

The salty breeze ruffled his hair as he stared out to sea. "The soldiers in the trenches don't have freedom. My job is easy in comparison."

A chilly wind from the north sent a shiver through her, and Benedict stepped behind her, opening his coat to draw her against him. She savored their closeness, his arms wrapped around her middle. They probably shouldn't be seen embracing this way, but nobody was around on this part of the deck, and they had such little time left together. She reached back to cup his jaw, and he pressed a kiss to her palm.

"Thank you for everything you've done for me," she said.

He leaned down and kissed her neck. "You've done a great deal for me as well. Inga . . ."

There was a long pause, and all her senses went on alert. Benedict was rarely at a loss for words, and she sensed he was about to say something very important. If she weren't such a coward, she would turn around to face him, but it was easier to keep staring at the sea and the white clouds in the distance.

"Inga, we'll be home soon," Benedict began, his breath warm against the shell of her ear. "I don't want an annulment. I love you, and I want us to be together always."

He gently nudged her to face him, but she couldn't. She clasped his arms, holding them tight so he couldn't turn her around. The clouds on the horizon blurred, and she had to blink back the sting of tears. Their wonderful friendship was in its final hours, and its loss would linger with her forever.

"Benedict, I would be a terrible diplomatic wife. Look what happened the one time you took me to the opera."

"You were still new," he said. "And it's a mistake I know won't happen again."

She swiveled in his arms to meet him face-to-face. "Yes, but I hated the night even before everything went downhill. I didn't know how to make conversation with grand ladies. You can dress me up in fancy clothes, but I'll always be a peasant in their eyes. I'm not like Mrs. Torres or even Mrs. Gerard. They love mingling with upper-crust people, but that's not me. I would be an embarrassment to you."

His expression was sorrowful as he caressed the side of her face. "Never," he said. "I'm proud of you, and I love you."

This might be the most beautiful, painful moment of her life. She loved him too, although confessing it would only make this conversation more difficult for them both. "I don't think I could ever be the kind of wife you need. I'm sorry—"

"Shhh," he said soothingly. "Don't keep telling yourself something that isn't true. I love you, and we're a good team, Inga. I have faith in you. We still have time to make this decision. Let's wait until we're in Washington before you decide."

She drew a ragged breath. Dear, sweet Benedict. Still holding out hope that she would change her mind, but that wasn't going to happen. She loved him too much to saddle him with a wife who would forever hinder his dreams.

And yet they could still savor this perfect hour, out at sea on a lovely afternoon, cradled in each other's arms as their wonderfully unique love story entered its final hours.

40

The *Infanta Isabella*'s arrival in Cuba was met with tremendous fanfare. A flotilla of boats escorted the ship their final mile into the American naval base. Dozens of American flags snapped in the brisk harbor winds as the naval band played patriotic songs. Benedict stood beside Colonel Reyes on deck as the Gerards walked down the gangplank to be greeted with applause, photographers' flashbulbs, and an armful of roses for Mrs. Gerard. It was a hero's welcome as reporters shouted questions and civilians pushed forward, seeking the ambassador's autograph.

It was to be the pattern for the next several days. The following evening, they arrived in Key West to be greeted by more reporters and more roses for Mrs. Gerard. Then they boarded a train to take them to Washington, stopping every few hours for another ceremony at another city. It was a triumphal procession as they made their way back to the capital. At each stop the Gerards disembarked to allow the ambassador a chance to make a brief speech to the assembled reporters, government officials, and soldiers.

Men in uniform filled the crowds, eyes eager as they listened to the ambassador recount their ominous months in Germany. They stopped in Jacksonville, Savannah, and Charleston. In

311

Richmond, Benedict stood beside Inga on the platform as the governor greeted the ambassador and Mrs. Gerard with another splendid bouquet.

"Will she ever get tired of roses?" Benedict whispered to Inga, who smothered a laugh.

"I wouldn't know," she said. "Nobody has ever given me roses."

Benedict silently kicked himself. Why had he never given this woman roses? If there was time, he'd dash off the train to buy a bouquet. Yet the stationmaster was already securing the train for departure for the final leg of their journey to Washington, D.C., where he would remain while Inga continued on to New York City. She hadn't changed her mind about that, and it was increasingly unlikely that she would.

He shared a bench with Inga in the crowded passenger car, and to his surprise, Mr. Gerard came down the aisle toward them.

"I've just had a telegram from the White House," he said. "Benedict, you and I will meet with President Wilson for a private dinner tonight. Inga, I need you to accompany my wife on a visit to the German Embassy."

Benedict stood, for this was highly unusual. "What's happening?"

"The German ambassador's wife is close to having a nervous breakdown. She continues to be brutalized by the press, and we need to smooth her feathers before she returns to Germany. Jeanne Luckemeyer has been a good friend to Mary. Of course, she's Countess Bernstorff now. It hasn't been easy for either her or the count. They're mistrusted in Germany and mistrusted here. Inga, you're always a jolly good sport. Perhaps you can help Mary cheer up Countess Bernstorff?"

Inga agreed. Of course she agreed—she had a heart of pure gold. She was probably disappointed not to be heading on to New York immediately, but Benedict silently rejoiced. Inga's delay in Washington gave him that much longer to win her over.

Inga tried not to gape like a tourist as the carriage took them past the Washington Monument and the U.S. Capitol. The iconic buildings triggered a lump in her throat. How proud she was to be an American, and what an irony that her greatest service to her adopted country had been carried out in Berlin.

Her last act of service on behalf of the Gerards would be to help calm the German ambassador's wife, the former Jeanne Luckemeyer, now Countess Bernstorff. The carriage turned onto Massachusetts Avenue, which was dense with embassies from all around the world. The German Embassy was in a surprisingly modest three-story brick building with a turret and a mansard roof.

The ambassador's apartments were on the second floor, which was sumptuously decorated, though the countess's bedroom was a disaster. Wardrobes hung open, and clothing was draped everywhere. The countess was a pretty woman with a heart-shaped face and masses of dark hair mounded atop her head. She burst into tears the moment she saw Mrs. Gerard.

"Oh, Mary," she wept, clinging to her old friend. "Could you ever have imagined back in our school days that we would find ourselves in such a pickle?"

Mary returned the weeping woman's embrace. "There, there," she soothed. "Surely it hasn't been that bad?"

"They hate me in Germany, and I dread going back, but we can't stay here anymore. Everywhere I go, people hate me."

"But you're a countess," Inga said, to which the other woman stifled a bitter laugh.

"They think I'm a jumped-up Yankee who isn't worthy to be married to a man like Johann. I've followed him all over the world, hosted his dinners, raised his children, all while living like a nomad. I've survived Russian ice storms and nearly died of heatstroke in Egypt, but I'll never be good enough for those awful snobs in Berlin."

"Do you know where Johann will be posted next?" Mary asked.

The countess took a fortifying breath as her eyes darkened. "We're off to the Ottoman Empire, in a junior role, and it's going to be terribly lonely there. Where are you going next?"

Mary shook her head. "I'm not as brave as you. We're finished and are going back to New York. James will write his memoirs and then return to his law practice. The life of a diplomat's wife was not for me."

The countess blotted her tears. "I envy you," she whispered.

It was time for Inga to do what she'd been sent here for. Cheer the countess up so she wouldn't return to Germany with a sour impression of Americans. She scrambled for something to say that wasn't a lie, but it was clear this woman loathed her husband's career.

"I admire you," she said. The countess looked to Inga in surprise as if noticing her presence for the first time.

"I've been working as a secretary for the Gerards for the past two years," Inga continued. "I've seen how difficult your duties are. The wives have no power to direct the course of the war or create alliances. All they can do is watch from the outside and try to support the men who make the decisions. It's a special kind of stress most people don't appreciate, but a good wife is worth more than rubies. Isn't that what is said in the book of Proverbs?"

Mary gave the countess a playful nudge. "Get Johann to buy you a nice ruby necklace," she said, and the countess managed a watery laugh.

Inga scanned the room of this highly educated, worldly woman who loathed her fate as a diplomat's wife. Even Mary was coming to loathe it. As much as she might wish it otherwise, Inga already knew down to the marrow of her bones that this was not the right course for her either.

It was time to give Benedict a definitive answer. The longer she remained in Washington, the crueler it would be to put it off. Each time they locked gazes she could sense his anticipation, the hope he could barely conceal. They both wanted this strange marriage to work, but Inga was the only one who understood it was impossible.

Inga's chance to speak with Benedict came at breakfast the morning after their arrival in Washington. The hotel's dining room had an Egyptian flair, with pillars, palm trees, and stylized hieroglyphics painted on the walls. He was eating alone at a corner table as she approached.

He gestured to the other chair, but she shook her head because this wouldn't take long. Then she got a look at his breakfast and couldn't resist a smile.

"Did they make you cold oats?"

His eyes twinkled. "I tipped them outrageously."

They shared a laugh, but then she sobered quickly, setting his mother's wedding ring on the tablecloth beside his plate.

Benedict froze. After a moment he took a long sip of coffee. His face remained expressionless even after he carefully set the cup back onto its saucer without making a sound. "Your decision is final?"

"It is. I'm leaving on a train for New York tonight."

Once again he gestured for her to sit, and it would be impolite to refuse. There were legalities to finalize. She took a seat, keeping her hands beneath the table lest he see how they trembled.

"I will ask the ambassador to begin the annulment proceedings," he said, his voice kind. "Do you have a place to stay in New York?"

She nodded. "My friend Delia has a large apartment at the Martha Washington. She'll let me stay with her until I can find a place of my own. Benedict, I'm so sorry."

He slipped his mother's ring into a jacket pocket and smiled weakly. "It's okay. I never should have expected more, and I respect your decision."

She still couldn't look at him, but the tenor of his voice was as warm and comforting as a cashmere blanket. She stared at his bowl of cold oats and abruptly stood. She had to leave before she started to bawl and embarrass them both.

Benedict escorted Inga to the train station to see her safely on her way to New York. An early March storm was brewing, the cold air buffeting them with tiny specks of falling sleet. The distant clang heralded the arrival of the train and the end of his marriage to Inga.

He tipped a porter to wheel her trunk to the baggage car. "Thank you, sir," the porter said before pushing the cart across the wooden boardwalk. Benedict was about to put his wallet away when a sudden thought occurred to him.

"Do you have enough American money?" he asked Inga. They'd only been in the States two days, and she might not have changed her currency.

"Yes, Mr. Gerard provided me with an advance on my paycheck."

She might run short once she got to New York. A woman with her skills could probably secure employment quickly, but nothing was certain. He took a few large bills from his wallet and extended them to her.

"Benedict, keep your money. I'm fine."

He folded the bills and tucked them into her coat pocket with a gentle smile. "No arguing, Miss Klein. Take this as well."

She studied the small card with a series of addresses and a Morse code call sign. "What's this?"

"My next diplomatic assignment," he said, barely able to contain his smile. "My orders came through this afternoon. I'm going to be the next ambassador to Japan."

Inga's eyes lit up. "Oh, Benedict, congratulations!" She leapt into his arms, and he hugged her back, both of them laughing. This was probably the last hug they would ever share, and he made the most of it.

"I'm so proud of you," she said against his shoulder.

"I leave in three weeks," he said, still holding her tight.

The appointment to Japan was a huge promotion. An ambassadorship was the pinnacle of any diplomat's career, and Japan was a more prominent country than he had any right to expect. He finally disentangled himself to look down at Inga.

"Should you ever change your mind about us, you can send a message to the embassy in Tokyo."

She winced. "I'm not ever going to—"

He put a finger on her lips. "I know your feelings, but I want you to have that code. If you ever need anything, anything at all, don't hesitate to contact me."

"Okay," she whispered.

The train rolled into the station, gears clanking and steam hissing as it settled on the tracks. Given that they'd be handling the annulment from his overseas post, this was probably the last time they would see each other. He cupped her face between his palms and gazed down at her, trying to memorize every facet of her beautiful face.

"Good luck, Inga."

Her eyes got bluer when filled with tears, but she tried to smile. "You too, Benedict."

He waited on the pavilion as her train pulled away. There had been a time when she annoyed him to no end. Now he suspected he would go through the rest of his life wishing he could recapture every hour of those halcyon days.

41

MARCH 1917

An odd, dreamlike sensation haunted Inga during her first day back in New York. After months of being constantly on edge, everything was so strangely *normal*. Shelves at the pharmacy were fully stocked with medicines, and the butcher's windows displayed a bounty of ham, pork, and beef.

Once at the Martha Washington, she hugged old friends, who laughed and gossiped and invited her to a new theater that just opened on Broadway. It took almost an hour to escape the crush of people and head to Delia's eighth-floor apartment. Even there, several friends crowded into the apartment, gushing over Inga's wardrobe as she unpacked.

"Look at this adorable blazer!" Delia marveled.

Blanche scooped up Inga's green walking suit, the one she wore for her wedding. "Please tell me I can borrow this sometime. Pretty please?"

Inga and Blanche used to swap clothes all the time, but no, her wedding outfit was off-limits to others. Nobody in New York knew of her marriage, and she intended to keep it that way, which meant she had to scramble for an excuse.

"It's very itchy. You'll like this one better," she said, handing Blanche the violet gown with a portrait collar. She tucked the green suit deep into the wardrobe and closed the door.

Each gown that came out of the trunk was laden with memories. The lavender gown that got drenched the day she wheeled the piano out into the garden. The red wool jacket she wore in Rosendorff. All the while, chatter continued around her.

"Did you see any fighting over there?" Margaret asked.

Inga shook her head. "No, we were far away from the front lines."

"All the fighting has been in France and Russia," Delia pointed out. "Germany is completely unscathed."

Not exactly, but Inga said nothing as she lifted another gown from her trunk.

"Thank heavens you were spared having to see any suffering," Margaret said.

"Yes. I was very lucky." Inga reached into the bottom of her trunk to lift out the sketchbook Percy gave her on her final visit to the Ruhleben camp. She must write to him soon. He was so lonely, and with all the chaos of escaping Berlin, she hadn't had a chance to say goodbye to him.

A knock on the door interrupted her thoughts.

"Come in!" Delia shouted. Instead of another friend, a wall of red roses was all Inga could see.

"A delivery for you," the downstairs clerk said as she carefully angled the enormous bouquet into the room. "Where shall I set it?"

Inga cleared space on the top of her closed trunk. Bouquets of roses would probably always remind her of how Mrs. Gerard had been bombarded with them at every whistle-stop on the East Coast.

"Who are they from?" Delia asked.

"The kaiser," someone joked.

Inga opened the card and read:

Miss Klein,
*   You reported the sorry fact that you had never received*
roses. That sad oversight is now a thing of the past.

*   Welcome home,*
*   Benedict*

"Well? Who are they from?" Blanche pestered, then snatched the card. "Who is Benedict?"

Inga drew a calming breath as a lump grew in her throat. "A man I cared for in Berlin. It's over."

"Inga the heartbreaker strikes again," Blanche teased.

Inga slipped the card into her pocket. It *was* over with Benedict. She nearly burst with pride over his promotion to be an ambassador. He deserved it, and yet his being posted to Japan confirmed that she'd made the right decision. She would be a disaster in Tokyo.

"The dining room closes soon," Margaret said. "Shall we head down for dinner?"

Most of the ladies took their meals in the first-floor restaurant, but Blanche rolled her eyes. "Don't get your hopes up about the quality of food," she said. "The manager has been in a dispute with the dairy company, so we've been stuck with nothing but condensed milk for the past two weeks. Can you imagine? I can barely choke it down."

Inga's lips began to tremble. Did Gita and Gerhard have enough milk for their baby? Shortages were bound to get worse with the Americans entering the war.

"I think I'll stay and finish unpacking," she said, unable to meet anyone's eyes. Hopefully, a few minutes alone would beat back this weepiness.

"What are these?" Margaret asked as she lifted one of the

smooth, wooden castanets from the trunk. Inga managed to smile. She'd had plenty of time to practice with them during the voyage home, and she slipped the leather cord around her wrist to demonstrate.

It was enough for her to shake off the gloom as she dug deeper into the trunk to begin passing out some of the Spanish fans. Suddenly the room was filled with laughter again as the women fluttered the fans and played the castanets.

Then memories of that breezy, balmy afternoon with Benedict in Spain swamped her. Had there ever been a sky so blue? Had he ever looked more handsome as the wind tousled his hair, and he gazed at her with such pained admiration?

Leaving him had been the right choice, but at the moment everything felt so wrong. So oddly frivolous. Nobody in this room understood what she'd been through, and she didn't have the heart to explain.

Midge would understand. Midge had served during the Civil War and might understand Inga's strange feeling of disconnect.

"Please excuse me," Inga whispered. She dropped the fan and ran like a coward away from the people she'd always considered friends.

Fortunately, Midge hadn't left for her overnight shift at the hospital yet. The old woman already wore her white nurse's uniform, but she invited Inga to curl up on the corner chair in her apartment and unload her burdens.

Inga confided everything to Midge, including her marriage to Benedict and wanting to smack Blanche for turning up her nose at canned milk.

"Don't hold it against Blanche," the old nurse gently said. "I remember feeling the same as you when I returned home after the war. Nobody in Idaho had experienced what I saw throughout those terrible years. I assumed my life would go back to normal, but I was a different person. I didn't belong in Boise anymore and ended up moving back to New York to work in a veterans' hospital. Don't resent Blanche because she doesn't understand. Thank heavens she doesn't! What a wonderful world it would be if nobody knew what war can do to a soul."

Inga's attention strayed outside the window, where the skyline of Manhattan was as familiar as the back of her hand. How she loved it here, but half her heart was elsewhere. It was in Ruhleben. It was with her cousins in Rosendorff and the staff from Alton House who had scattered to various outposts around the world.

It was with Benedict.

"You're thinking about *him*?" Midge asked, and Inga nodded helplessly. Half the reason she didn't want to return to Delia's apartment was having to see the roses.

"I'm going to miss him for a long time," she confessed, her lip starting to wobble.

Midge seemed unusually thoughtful as she stood before a mirror to pin the folded nurse's cap atop her head. "I fell in love once," she said. "He was killed in the Battle of Chancellorsville. I mourned him for years and thought I'd never get over him. It was work that saved me. Carrying out the mission I believe God wants of me has given me joy and purpose. People sometimes worry about me. They wonder why I'm still working when I'm seventy-six years old, but I'm the happiest person I know! In the quiet of the night, when the rest of the world is asleep, people are still in pain, and I can be there to lend a hand. It has always given me great satisfaction to follow this mission in life."

What was Inga's mission now that the embassy had closed? She didn't want to be a legal crusader like Delia or tend the sick like Midge. What had given her the greatest satisfaction of her life?

Working alongside Benedict.

She pushed the unwelcome thought away. She ought to aspire to something higher, but when she was side by side with Benedict, rowing toward the same goal, it felt like she was fulfilling a calling.

And frankly, Benedict needed her help. He was cold and prickly when she wasn't there to warm him up. Between the two of them, they had accomplished a great deal, and she loved every minute of it.

Even so, that night as she said a prayer for his success in Tokyo, she knew she'd made the right decision to stay in New York.

42

Summer came to New York, and with it a whole new list of challenges for Inga as the city geared up for wartime production. Thousands of young men flocked to the recruitment centers scattered throughout the city. Factories were retooled to support the manufacture of weapons, ammunition, and uniforms. War rallies and fundraisers continually clogged the streets.

Inga landed a job as a telegrapher for the American Red Cross, but finding a place to live proved more challenging. The influx of workers to the city had made securing an apartment almost impossible, and she couldn't bunk in with Delia forever.

In the end, she moved in with her old friends Katherine and Jonathan Birch. Katherine was a dentist who once lived across the hall from Inga at the Martha Washington. She and her husband had recently bought a town house and had a room to rent, and it was walking distance to her new job. Soon everything was magically falling into place.

Except for the lingering issue of Benedict. The Gerards knew and understood all aspects of her complicated marriage of convenience to Benedict, and she visited them often.

"Benedict sent me a telegram, pestering me about the annulment,"

Inga said one afternoon when she joined Mary for tea in the Gerards' plush suite of rooms overlooking Park Avenue. Mr. Gerard wasn't there, which was a blessing because it was easier to seek Mary's advice without Mr. Gerard's blustery presence.

Inga handed the telegram to Mary. It was typical Benedict: short, cold, and inscrutable.

Miss Klein,
   Please sign annulment document and submit to court.

—B.

"Why haven't you done so?" Mary asked. After all, Mr. Gerard had prepared the paperwork shortly after they arrived in Washington, and Benedict signed it before sailing for Japan.

"I don't know," she confessed. "I liked being married to Benedict, and I think about him all the time. I even went to the public library to read about the American Embassy in Tokyo. Did you know some of the most beautiful gardens in Tokyo are on the grounds of the embassy?"

Mary stared at Inga for so long it became uncomfortable. The last thing Inga wanted to confess was that she'd been going to the library to learn everything possible about Japan and Tokyo and what Benedict's life there was like . . . and if she might be able to join him there after all. That was the real reason she hadn't signed the annulment papers, though she would never admit it. The prospect of moving to Japan to assume embassy duties was dreadful, yet she dreaded ending her marriage to Benedict just as much.

Mary finally spoke. "If Benedict lived in New York, would you want to stay married to him?"

"Absolutely," she said. "I love him. I'm a better person when he is near. I think I made him happy too."

Memory of their time in Rosendorff flashed before her. Cuddling in bed and recounting their day to each other. Watching him shave in the mornings. Leaning on him for support when old memories threatened. They'd both been happy.

Mary pursed her lips as she poured more tea. "The two of you are such opposites," she said. "He doesn't seem at all like the kind of person I envisaged for you."

A smile hovered as Inga summoned memories of watching Benedict in action at the embassy. "He's a *man*," she said. "I don't want a boy who is flirtatious and fun. I want a man who can stand up for what is right whether that's bullies on the street or diplomats at the German chancellery. I never realized how attractive that was to me until I met Benedict."

Mary replaced the teapot with a loud clink. "That's all fine, but I've never been happier than after James promised me his career as a diplomat was over. We're home where we both belong, and I never intend to leave it again. My dear, as much as you care for Benedict, and as hard as you might try to become a good wife to a diplomat, you can only force a square peg into a round hole for so long before one of them breaks."

The words haunted Inga on her walk home. Benedict was born into a diplomatic life, which came naturally to him. It never would for her. The prospect of sailing to Japan or any other foreign land to assume a role where she'd never belong made her sick at heart.

She signed the annulment papers and filed them in court the next afternoon.

The heat of August finally released its grip on New York as a cool September breeze swept through the city streets. Inga expected her heart to have mended by now, but still she obsessed about Benedict. When she bought the latest issue of *The Perils of Pauline*, all she could think about was wishing he were there to tease her about it. Had she made the right decision in refusing to go to Japan?

"I know he'd take me back if I asked," Inga said one evening as she sat with Katherine and Jonathan at the small dining table in their new town house. Although they didn't know about her marriage, she'd confessed how she and Benedict had carried on a whirlwind romance while in Berlin.

"Wouldn't that mean you'd have to move to Japan?" Jonathan asked as he set a plate of warm apple cake on the table. Though he was a police officer, Jonathan was also the world's best baker. Perhaps God had a sense of humor in having a dentist marry a man with a wicked sweet tooth.

"I've been wondering if I could adjust to life in Japan," she went on. New York was home, even though she hadn't been overflowing with joy since her return. It felt as if she'd lopped off a piece of her heart after shedding Benedict from her life.

"Maybe you could visit and see what it would be like," Katherine suggested. "You could sail there, spend a week in Japan, and be back within a month."

Inga sighed. "I've only been at my new job since April," she said. "I don't think they'd give me a month off to visit Japan."

"Someone with your qualifications could get a job anywhere in the city," Jonathan said. "I hear they are short-staffed down at the harbor again. Jenkins quit just last week."

"He did?" That was a surprise. Frank Jenkins had a wife and five children to support. He loved the overnight shift and had worked at the harbor for the past twelve years. Something drastic must have happened for him to suddenly quit, and she prayed he wasn't heading off to become a soldier.

The question plagued her so much that she resolved to visit her old workplace to discover what had become of Jenkins.

The sun had just begun to rise when she arrived at New York Harbor the following morning. Signs of the war were everywhere. Being the largest port in America, the city had forever struggled to manage the constant influx of ships and goods. Now things were worse than ever. A haphazard-looking quilt of rail lines and electrical wires crisscrossed between the warehouses. Every berth on the aging piers was in use, forcing ships to remain offshore, sometimes for days, before they could dock. The entire waterfront was a whirlwind of disorganization, the epitome of chaos in motion.

Inga climbed the steps to the communications tower. Had it only been three years since she worked here? It felt like a lifetime. Carson was still at his post, as was her former supervisor, Mr. Guillory, who shot out of his seat the moment he clapped eyes on her.

"Inga! Please tell me you're here in search of a job."

"Sorry," she said. "I came to check up on Jenkins. I heard he no longer works here. Is that right?"

From his place at the desk overlooking the harbor, Carson tugged off his headphones and swiveled to face her. "Jenkins left last week. He got a job at Western Union, lucky devil. The war is making a hash of everything. We have to work more hours, and the new rules are insanely strict. It's why Jenkins left."

So long as he hadn't suited up and gone to war, she could breathe a little easier.

"So, Inga," Mr. Guillory said agreeably, an overly bright grin plastered on his face, "you like the overnight shift, right?"

"Not particularly."

"I'll pay you a nickel more than I pay my dayshift employees. And if you work at night, you won't ever need to see the tyrant who is now in charge of everything, including this office."

She blinked in surprise. "Who's running the office now?" In the past she always reported directly to Mr. Guillory.

"A brand-new entity called the War Board for the Port of New York," Mr. Guillory said. "President Wilson wants the port pulled apart and rebuilt to accommodate the needs of the war. They're tearing down old warehouses, building new ones, and adding more docks. All of it means more work and more hassle. You should see the rules they're cramming down our throats. Two weeks ago, the War Board got a new boss, and he came by to read us the riot act. I tried to explain to him that's not how we do things around here, and the stuffed shirt nearly bit my head off."

"You poor dear," Inga said in genuine sympathy, even though she secretly agreed that changes were overdue. Her time in Germany gave her a better understanding of war and the need for cooperation up and down the lines of authority. She didn't envy any outsider appointed to shake things up in the Port of New York, but it was necessary all the same.

"So many persnickety rules," Mr. Guillory grumbled. "Why can't we file monthly reports like we always did? Now everything must be filed weekly, with copies going to the state, the feds, and the new tyrant."

Carson nodded. "It wouldn't be so bad if the guy didn't look like he relishes the prospect of catching us in an error. He's like a vampire lurking for blood."

She cast her gaze around the communications room. When she worked here, it was a cluttered mess of unfiled paperwork with aging equipment stuffed into the closets because Mr. Guillory was afraid to discard anything. Now everything looked refreshingly tidy.

"You've done marvelous work organizing this place," she said. "Don't be so hard on the new guy. We're about to send a million of our men overseas, and we owe it to them to have this place running like clockwork."

Mr. Guillory rolled his eyes. "That's the exact thing the new guy said. He wants the office to run like clockwork as if we're nothing but machines."

Inga wouldn't waste more time consoling them. Either they could roll up their sleeves and get to work, or they could quit.

"Look at the time," she said as she rose to her feet. "I'm off for breakfast. Would anyone like to join me?"

"Not a chance," Mr. Guillory said. "The new rules say we have to work until ten o'clock each morning. If we want something for breakfast, we have to bring it to work."

Carson sounded equally annoyed. "Maybe if the new guy ate something besides cold oats each morning, he might appreciate the benefits of a hearty breakfast."

The complaining continued, but Inga had quit listening after the words *cold oats*. Her mouth went dry, heart pounding. She had to wait until she could speak with a calm voice.

"What is the new supervisor's name?"

Mr. Guillory snorted. "Benedict Kincaid, but we all call him Benedict Killjoy."

Was she dreaming? If Benedict was in New York, why hadn't he sought her out? None of it made sense, and yet it felt like the sun was rising inside her, filling her with joy. If Benedict was really here in New York, she needed to see him. Immediately.

"Where's his office?" she asked. Benedict had always been an early riser, and he might already be there.

Mr. Guillory provided her directions to the administrative building a few blocks away, and she scooped up her handbag and bolted out the door without even saying goodbye.

Outside, hundreds of people were on their way to work at the various buildings near the port, but there was only one man she was interested in seeing. She ran around piles of construction equipment and bumped into pedestrians in her mad dash down the street. The administration building loomed at the end of the street, and she was breathless by the time she reached it. A flight of stairs led up to the entrance, and she scampered up them two at a time, then pushed through the heavy front door so hard it banged against the wall. Tension zinged as she stared at the directory in the front hall. It listed Benedict Kincaid in the top slot as *Director of the War Board for the Port of New York*.

Her heart thudded as she wended her way down a narrow, tile-lined corridor toward his office. She calmed her breathing, smoothed her hair, then peeked through the window in his office door. He sat at an imposing desk, attired flawlessly in a three-piece suit and tie, a watch chain looping to his vest pocket.

His face was drawn and grim as he surveyed some papers in his hands.

She tapped on the door, and he looked up. A fleeting look of surprised happiness lit his face. Then he quickly schooled his features and stood. He adjusted his suit jacket as he stepped around the desk to open the door.

"Miss Klein," he said. "It's nice to see you again. Come inside."

Couldn't he come up with something a little more personal? But no. She must never forget that this was Benedict.

She remained standing in the open doorway. "Rumor has it there's a new man in charge of the port."

"So I hear," he said with a nod.

"He's not very popular."

Benedict's expression remained stoic except for tiny laugh lines crinkling the corners of his eyes. "Some things never change."

The new War Board agency Mr. Guillory described had a challenging mission. Being in charge of it would take a spine of steel and an unlimited supply of diplomacy. Benedict would be a good choice for it.

"I thought you were in Tokyo," she said, sounding a little wounded.

"I turned it down."

Her jaw dropped, and she could barely draw a breath. "Why?"

He locked gazes with her. "Can't you guess?"

It couldn't be because of her. If he turned down a plum assignment on her behalf, wouldn't he have sought her out? She was easy to find since everyone at the Martha Washington knew where she lived.

"If you came here for me, why didn't you contact me?" Frustration mingled with elation as she scanned his face, still finding it hard to believe he was here.

"Inga . . ." He cleared his throat and tried again. "Pardon me, *Miss Klein*," he corrected. "The whole world is at war, and the largest port in America is a chaotic mess of corruption and inefficiencies. I thought it best to get the port in order before turning my attention to . . . personal issues."

"Is that what I am? Nothing more than a personal issue?"

He stepped around her to glance down both sides of the hallway, as people were beginning to arrive. Then he tugged her inside the office and closed the door.

"I can't call you 'my wife' since you finally got around to signing the annulment papers. Very slipshod of you, Miss Klein."

How she'd missed his teasing. He looked stern and sexy and unbelievably attractive as the undercurrent of attraction hummed between them. "Did you follow me here?"

A flush heated his cheeks. "I was on my way to Japan when I got a telegram from Mary Gerard, telling me you may be willing to keep the marriage if I left the diplomatic corps. When the ship docked in Hawaii to refuel, I changed ships and set off for home. Of course, by the time I got back to the mainland you'd already signed the annulment papers, so coming here to win you back was a gamble. I've been screwing up the courage to address the issue."

She sagged, bracing her hand against the wall. She never dreamed of asking Benedict to make such a sacrifice, and yet he had done so anyway. "You always wanted the top job. To be an ambassador."

"I want you more," he said, his tone gruff with affection. "I thought of you every day and wished you were by my side. I want a family, Inga. We had something like a family at Alton House, but I want the real thing, and I want it with you. I don't want a marriage of convenience. I want a real marriage."

"So do I."

He reached behind her, pulling down the shade to cover the window in the door. The expression in his eyes was enough to set the room ablaze as he cupped her face between his hands and leaned down to kiss her. She twined her arms around his neck, letting him deepen the kiss.

Even after the world's most amazing kiss came to an end, they clung to each other. Benedict's voice was warm as he whispered in her ear, "Are you ready to do a marriage properly this time?"

She pulled back to look into his eyes. "Was that a marriage proposal? It had a touch of reprimand in it, Benedict."

Humor lit his face as he sank down to one knee. He looked overjoyed as he cradled her suddenly chilly hand between his warm ones. "Inga, will you do me the honor . . . ? Oh, drat, I don't have a ring."

"Ask me anyway," she prodded.

He sprang to his feet and swept her into a hug, laughter shaking his whole body. "Oh, Inga, I love you. Will you marry me so I can tell you that every day for the rest of my life?"

Inga was barely able to speak because her smile was so wide. "I love you too. Let's find a priest and get married for real this time."

In a world churning with turmoil, a piece of Inga's life was settling into perfect harmony.

43

OCTOBER 1917

Benedict stood alongside Mr. Gerard in the foyer of the church, waiting for Inga. Their first wedding had been a hasty civil ceremony in Ambassador Gerard's office, but this time they would have a real wedding in a church before God, friends, and family.

"If she doesn't hurry up, we're going to lose our slot," Mr. Gerard grumbled.

Benedict cast a worried glance toward the front of the church. Six weddings were scheduled to take place this afternoon, each slated for only an hour. In light of the war, thousands of couples were hurrying to marry before the men shipped off for England and France. He and Inga were up next, but they were already ten minutes late because Inga and Katherine, her matron of honor, were still primping somewhere behind the scenes.

Inga's friends from the Martha Washington filled the front row. Mr. Gerard, the man who'd been like a father to Inga since she was ten years old, would give the bride away, which meant James Gerard was about to become his father-in-law.

Had there ever been a more drastic change of sentiment than between him and James Gerard? A relationship that began in mutual animosity had transformed into genuine respect and friendship over the past three years. James Gerard had been ill-equipped and inexperienced when he became ambassador to Germany during those twilight months before the world began sinking into darkness, but in the end he had been the right man for the job.

A patter of footsteps behind him made Benedict turn. Inga peeked around the corner, a white veil falling over her shoulders as she peeked toward the front of the church.

She looked breathtaking, her face radiant behind the veil. It was hard to believe that the magnificent and thoroughly delightful Inga Klein was about to become his wife for real. She was his partner, his equal, and the love of his life . . . but if she didn't hurry up, they were going to lose their slot to the next couple waiting in the wings to be married.

And yet Inga appeared to be in no hurry as she hid behind a column, scanning the guests at the front of the church.

He tamped down his frustration. "Inga, snap to it, or we're going to lose our slot."

She blanched. "Sorry! I'm not quite ready yet."

"You look marvelous," Mr. Gerard assured her. "Never has there been a more lovely bride. All right, no more primping. We're late."

The words made no dent on Inga. Katherine stood beside her, and they both looked with dismay toward the front of the church. The organist was ready, the priest stood to the side of the altar, and they were late.

Inga shook her head. "Sorry, we'll be back soon!" she said, then disappeared back into the vestibule.

"Women," Mr. Gerard muttered. "Inga would look lovely in a potato sack. Why must she keep fiddling with perfection?"

It was a good question, but Benedict had gotten used to conceding to Inga's quirks. Half the time she was right anyway. Like agreeing to stay in New York instead of letting his ambition take him to a lonely life in Japan. Marriage was going to be a never-ending kaleidoscope of compromises, but they would be stronger and happier for it in the long run.

A commotion at the front door caused Benedict to turn as a man in an army officer's uniform pushed through the cluster of wedding guests waiting for the next slot. He looked familiar, but before Benedict could place him, Katherine came barreling through the crowd to fling herself into the officer's arms. It was Jonathan Birch, Katherine's husband.

"Sorry I'm late," Jonathan said, a grin breaking through. "I had to twist the captain's arm for permission to disembark. I've got three hours of official leave before the ship sails."

The reason for Inga's stalling suddenly became clear. Jonathan was a newly commissioned officer who would soon be serving as a combat engineer, charged with dismantling bombs and land mines in France. It ranked among the most dangerous assignments any soldier could have, and these final three hours before shipping off might be the last Jonathan would ever have with his wife.

Suddenly, the wedding's ten-minute delay no longer mattered. Jonathan and Katherine hurried down the aisle to join the others at the front of the church. Inga then emerged, her smile relaxed and radiant as she took Mr. Gerard's arm.

Benedict ought to have headed to the altar to await his bride, but he couldn't help himself. He lifted Inga's veil and kissed her with everything he had in him.

"Kissing the bride before the vows breaks all rules of convention and decorum," Mr. Gerard teased.

Benedict clasped Inga's hands, gazing down into her eyes. "Inga and I haven't done anything the conventional way," he said. He tugged her veil back into place, gave her hands a final squeeze, then jogged to the front of the church, where the priest was waiting.

Women from the Martha Washington now filled the first few rows, along with a few telegraph operators from the harbor where

Inga used to work. The port telegraphers disliked him intensely, and they surely wondered how a stick-in-the-mud had won a prize like Inga. Maybe he could win them over like he'd done with the staff at Alton House, or maybe not. It didn't matter. He intended to get the port functioning like clockwork. The fighting men at the front deserved nothing less.

His chest expanded with pride as the music began and Inga walked toward him down the aisle.

Soon he and Inga were kneeling before the altar, her hands in his as they bowed their heads to receive God's blessing. They were entering one of the darkest times in human history, but even so, God had provided flashes of joy to light the gloom, and this was one of them. No matter what lay ahead, he and Inga would face the future side by side, with love and faith, until the sun rose over their world once again.

Author's Note

I was inspired to write this novel after reading the memoirs of Ambassador James W. Gerard (1867–1951). Prior to his diplomatic career, James Gerard was a successful attorney and judge in New York, but was mostly known as an avid sportsman with a lively social life. His marriage to Mary Townsend, heiress to a huge copper fortune, made the couple one of the wealthiest in America. They had no children, but she is lovingly mentioned throughout Ambassador Gerard's memoirs.

Shortly after returning from Berlin, Gerard published *My Four Years in Germany*, which documented his service when in Berlin. It stands as an insightful firsthand account of the decaying relations between Germany and the United States in the early years of the war. Ambassador Gerard's initial blunders in German high society were widely recounted by his contemporaries, yet his blunt style of communication succeeded in pressuring Germany to concede to American demands, keeping the U.S. out of the war longer than what otherwise may have happened.

The ambassador received a hero's welcome upon his return to America. He resumed his legal career and remained active, writing about German American political interests for the rest of his life. Inga, Benedict, and the others at Alton House are entirely fictional.

The Englishmen at the Ruhleben Internment Camp remained imprisoned for the duration of the war. The camp held a diverse group of people, including businessmen, students, artists, and musicians who had been trapped in Germany after the outbreak of war. The camp became known for organizing their own activities such as sports teams and theater groups, and they produced a weekly newspaper called the *Ruhleben Camp News*. The experience of the men at Ruhleben is an example of the human capacity for resilience and creativity even during the harshest of times.

Reading Group Discussion Guide

1. "Opposites Attract" is a common trope in romantic novels and movies. While it works great in fiction, can such a romantic pairing work in real life?

2. Benedict and Ambassador Gerard disliked and disrespected each other at the beginning of the novel, but this changes by the end. What happened to change how they perceive each other?

3. Inga considered herself "stupid" because she lacked a formal education and because of her preference for lowbrow entertainment. How did her poor view of her intelligence impact her choices in the novel? Do you think she still believes herself to be stupid by the end of the story?

4. The sinking of the *Lusitania* remains a controversial topic to this day. In all likelihood, it was indeed carrying munitions to England, although the Germans could not have known that when they fired on the civilian passenger ship. What are some of the ethical dilemmas Germany was faced with when deploying their submarines in the battle for control of the Atlantic?

5. When Inga sees Eduardo again after she'd spent two years in Germany, she realizes they are no longer suitable for

each other. If she hadn't taken the assignment in Germany, do you think Inga would have outgrown Eduardo of her own accord? Does living through challenging times cause us to become different people?

6. Midge Lightner, the elderly nurse who lives at the Martha Washington, tells Inga, "The best opportunities in life are usually the scariest." What are your thoughts on this idea?

7. Inga believes she lacks the skills necessary to be a good ambassador's wife. Do you think she could have been effective in this role in Japan? Will she and Benedict be happier in New York?

8. As a German American, what sort of divided loyalties do you think Inga suffered during the war? Were any of your ancestors on opposite sides of either World War I or World War II? What family stories were passed down to you about their divided loyalties?

9. Inga and Benedict enter into marriage fully expecting it to end with a quick annulment. Was this ethical? Does it matter that the marriage was a civil arrangement handled by a judge vs. in a church with a priest presiding over the ceremony?

Read on
for a *sneak peek* at
the next book of the

Women of Midtown series

by Elizabeth Camden

Available in the spring of 2026

As America is drawn into World War I, Delia Byrne stands firm in her crusade for peace. As a committed pacifist, she's been ostracized by her friends and her community and now risks losing her job. Through it all she remains steadfast—that is, until a man from her past reenters her life.

Lieutenant Finn Delaney is a wounded pilot who has returned home from France as America's first official war hero, and he's been tasked with raising funds for the war effort. This mission will bring him face-to-face with Delia, the only woman he's ever loved and once hoped to marry.

As the war in Europe takes a perilous turn, Delia and Finn must join forces to help rescue millions of civilians who are at risk of starvation. Battling against steep odds, they confront not only the horrors of war but the painful wounds that tore them apart years earlier.

OCCUPIED BELGIUM • AUGUST 1917

Finn dragged himself another yard through the mud, the pain from his mangled leg nearly blinding him. He needed to find shelter quickly because the pilot who shot him down had probably already landed at the German airfield less than a mile away, and they would be sending out a search party to capture him. Finn's airplane had burst into flames moments after he crashed, and now it billowed sooty clouds of smoke into the air, signaling the enemy. And Germans sometimes shot downed pilots rather than taking them prisoner.

345

There was a village close by, though Finn's chances of getting there with a broken leg weren't good. He clenched his teeth and elbowed his way another few feet through the sludge, trying to keep his head up enough to breathe and not drown in the mud.

He couldn't die now. Delia hadn't forgiven him yet. She was the best, purest part of him, the shining inspiration that fueled his dreams ever since he was a young boy. He *had* to survive, if only to get home and win Delia's forgiveness. He elbowed farther with renewed determination.

"*Monsieur, laissez-moi vous aider.*"

The urgent whisper startled him, and he lifted his eyes to see a woman hunkered beside him. Frizzy copper hair surrounded a face filled with fear. The Germans would shoot her too if they caught her helping him.

She repeated herself, and his pain-addled brain finally made sense of the French words. She was offering to help him. A boy in his teens stood behind her, barely old enough to shave.

"Run!" Finn gasped. "They'll be here soon. *Run!*"

The woman ignored Finn's command and crouched down to reach beneath his shoulder. "*Pieter, aidez-moi.*"

Pieter rushed to Finn's side to grab his other arm, and together they began dragging him. He nearly screamed but managed to get his other leg pumping. His right leg dragged uselessly behind him.

The rumble of an automobile sounded in the distance. It was the Germans. Only Germans had gasoline rations.

Waves of agony rolled through him as he focused on the timber-framed cottage straight ahead. A little girl held the door of the house open. The woman started issuing orders to other children in the front room of the house.

"*Vite, remonte les planches.*"

Quick, pull up the floorboards, she ordered. Finn understood the words, but he couldn't make his brain work well enough to reply in French.

"Don't risk your life for me," he said in English. She had children. They'd be orphaned if the Germans found him.

The floorboards had been pulled up, revealing bundled newspapers and tins of beef. In short order, the mother emptied the space, and Finn rolled himself into the shallow hideaway. His spine slammed against the foundation stone, shooting another wave of pain down his leg.

He got a glimpse at her panicked face as she prepared to cover him with the boards.

"Madam, thank you. I owe you my life."

Darkness descended as she replaced the floorboards and dragged heavy furniture over them.

As he lay there in total darkness, he started praying. The Germans were coming. His odds of surviving the next few hours weren't good, but if by God's grace Finn managed to get home, he would somehow find a way to thank this good woman and then seek Delia's forgiveness.

Elizabeth Camden is best known for her historical novels set in Gilded Age America, featuring clever heroines and richly layered story lines. Before she was a writer, she was an academic librarian at some of the largest and smallest libraries in America, but her favorite is the continually growing library in her own home. Her novels have won the RITA and Christy Awards and have appeared on the CBA bestsellers list. She lives in Citrus County, Florida, with her husband, who graciously tolerates her intimidating stockpile of books. Learn more online at ElizabethCamden.com.

Sign Up for Elizabeth's Newsletter

Keep up to date with Elizabeth's latest news on book releases and events by signing up for her email list at the website below.

ElizabethCamden.com

FOLLOW ELIZABETH ON SOCIAL MEDIA

Author Elizabeth Camden   @AuthorElizabethCamden

More from Elizabeth Camden

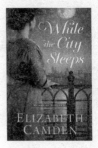

Dentist Katherine Schneider has always admired police lieutenant Jonathan Birch from afar, but they are brought together when Katherine is the only person who can identify the mastermind behind a string of deadly bombings. With lives on the line, Katherine and Jonathan must hold on to hope—and each other—if they want to survive.

While the City Sleeps
WOMEN OF MIDTOWN

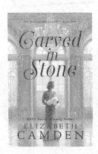  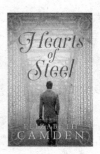

Set against the backdrop of twentieth century New York City, THE BLACKSTONE LEGACY series weaves together the tumultuous and tender love stories of three couples thrust into the heart of danger. From forbidden romances to alliances forged in the face of corrupt elites, each pair navigates their own trials of trust, betrayal, and redemption that will test all they know about love and sacrifice.

THE BLACKSTONE LEGACY: *Carved in Stone, Written on the Wind, Hearts of Steel*

BETHANYHOUSE

 Bethany House Fiction

 @BethanyHouseFiction

 @Bethany_House

 @BethanyHouseFiction

 Free exclusive resources for your book group at BethanyHouseOpenBook.com

 Sign up for our fiction newsletter today at BethanyHouse.com